ANCIENT ENEMY

A Howard Moon Deer Novel

Robert Westbrook

A SIGNET BOOK

SIGNET
Published by New American Library, a division of
Penguin Putnam Inc., 375 Hudson Street,
New York, New York 10014, U.S.A.
Penguin Books Ltd, 27 Wrights Lane,
London W8 5TZ, England
Penguin Books Australia Ltd, Ringwood,
Victoria, Australia
Penguin Books Canada Ltd, 10 Alcorn Avenue,
Toronto, Ontario, Canada M4V 3B2
Penguin Books (N.Z.) Ltd, 182–190 Wairau Road,
Auckland 10, New Zealand

Penguin Books Ltd, Registered Offices:
Harmondsworth, Middlesex, England

First published by Signet, an imprint of New American Library,
a division of Penguin Putnam Inc.

First Printing, December 2001
10 9 8 7 6 5 4 3 2 1

PUBLISHER'S NOTE
This is a work of fiction. Names, characters, places, and incidents either are the product
of the author's imagination or are used fictitiously, and any resemblance to actual
persons, living or dead, business establishments, events, or locales is entirely
coincidental.

For
MARLON TORO HOPE
my grandson, with love

ACKNOWLEDGMENTS

My sincere thanks to Bill Hubbard, investigator for the Taos County District Attorney's Office, who shared his vast forensic knowledge, and kept me abreast of New Mexico matters via e-mail to Alexandria, Egypt, where this book was written. Thanks also to my wife, Gail Westbrook; my agent, Ted Chichak; and Dan Slater, my editor, who read various drafts of this work and offered many wise suggestions. My gratitude also to the good people at The Boot Doctor of Taos Ski Valley, who have kept my life on a downhill course. I would like to stress that the town of San Geronimo, the Indian Pueblo I have created, and all its citizens are entirely imaginary. In real life, New Mexico towns are peaceful, honest, and sober; it's an enchanted land where the diverse ethnic groups are fabulous friends and no one has ever been known to eat another person for dinner.

PROLOGUE

Ancient Terror

An unspeakable dread seized Sky Watcher, the old priest, as he stood alone on the high mountain ledge outside the cave. It was fear such as he had never known, like a cold hand clutching at his belly and balls, stealing the very breath from his body.

He peered beyond the steep valley to where Father Sun was setting in the west. An icy wind blew among the rocks, shrieking like a thousand angry spirits. The longest night of the year was fast approaching and the sky was unforgiving, hard and dry as stone. There had been no rain in the summer, nor snow in the winter, year after year. In the lands below, there was bloodshed and evil. It was a time when all the world was out of balance, and decent people huddled close to their fires, avoiding strangers who were not of their clan.

Sky Watcher heard a footstep on the rock behind him. He spun around, ashen, ready to defend himself. But it was only Clan Mother. She smiled with bemused irony to see the fright that was so clearly visible in his eyes.

"Well, is this truly the night?" she asked scornfully.

"Yes, Mother," he answered. He took a deep breath to calm his mind.

"Frightened old men make mistakes. Are you certain?"

Sky Watcher nodded. He had been measuring the lengthening angle of the sun with increasing concern for many days now. At noon today, he had taken a final measurement and had known without question from the mark the sun had reached inside the cave that this was indeed the night of the Winter Solstice.

"Look at Father Sun," he said, pointing his long bony finger toward the red ball of light sinking quickly beneath the horizon.

Clan Mother squinted in the direction he was pointing, pretending to see. She was the ruler of his extended family, even older than himself, nearly forty—vastly old by the reckoning of their people, toothless and gray.

"Do you see the column of rock on the horizon? It is called Night Pillar. That is the ancient mark," he said. "When Father Sun descends directly upon Night Pillar, he will sleep in his Winter Home."

"You know I can't see that far!" Clan Mother admitted testily. It was a mark of intimacy that she allowed such honesty. "My eyes are misty with age. But I believe you, Sky Watcher, if you say it is true. Cast off your gloom, my old friend. Tomorrow Father Sun will shine again with more light than yesterday, and the day after that there will be more light still. Soon it will be the Time of Planting Corn, and you will be standing here telling me that Father Sun is going to his Summer Home, and I will pretend to see where you are pointing."

Sky Watcher only sighed.

"Isn't what I tell you true?" Clan Mother did not like to be contradicted and her tone was sharp.

"Yes," he obliged. "The days will get longer from this time onward. That is the way it has always been before."

"Then be of good cheer," she repeated obstinately. "It is not seemly for Sky Watcher to live with gloomy thoughts. The others see this and take note. And when they worry, they cause me many problems."

"I am already more cheerful, Mother." The old man forced a smile.

They stood together, Sky Watcher and Clan Mother, watching the red sun sink down upon Night Pillar, a needle of rock on the western horizon. The sun seemed to flatten until it was like the thin piki bread the women made in the hearth. At the last moment the dying light caught a wisp of distant clouds, setting the sky on fire. Clan Mother saw this only indistinctly, but she knew well enough when it was night.

"Well, another year passes and we're still alive," she announced. "A new year begins. Remember, you stood here last year almost as gloomy as you are tonight, telling me the end was near. It is in your soul, Sky Watcher, to live among dark shadows. I remember your father. He was a more cheerful man."

"My father lived in more cheerful times."

She turned and studied him with her faded eyes.

"Come to my mat tonight," she said softly. "We'll pretend to be young together for a little while, you and I. There are things for a man and woman to do on the longest night of the year."

"I will come," he promised.

She turned and left him on the rocky ledge, returning inside the cave to the others of the clan. Alone, Sky Watcher studied the heavens in order to find Evening Star, but a bank of black clouds had crept in from the north and Evening Star could not be seen. It was one more bad omen.

"Clan Mother is right—I must be cheerful," he reminded himself. "Nothing good can come of gloom." Yet as he watched the night overcome the living warmth of day, the fear continued to grow inside him that he would never again see the comforting rays of morning.

It is proper for a man to sing sacred songs when he is fearful. Sky Watcher was about to begin a powerful hymn against evil when he heard a sound in the darkness near where he stood, a scraping of rock. The song died in his heart, unsung. He stood very still, listening intently. A foul carrion smell drifted into his nostrils. But he heard nothing more.

What could it be? The high mountain cave was impregnable against all enemies except thirst, hunger, despair, and the will of the gods; the two ladders took care of the rest. Sky Watcher looked near his feet to make certain West Ladder had been raised as it should be. His breath caught sharply. The ladder was down!

Sky Watcher was dizzy with fear and adrenalin. Who could have been so careless? He knelt and with shaking hands he quickly pulled up the length of woven hemp that dangled far

*down the rock precipice. He was rising to his feet and turning
to check East Ladder when he found a darkness standing before him, blocking his way. The darkness had the face of a
man: a long nose, war paint on his cheeks and forehead, evil
eyes.*

*"What do you want here?" Sky Watcher asked contemptu-
ously.*

The unclean being smiled cruelly. "You know what I want!"

*Yes, the old priest knew. He raised his bare hands to defend
himself, but it was no use, for he was unarmed and unprepared. He watched helplessly as a stone club rose into the air
and came down in a violent arc toward his forehead. His final
thought was of Clan Mother, and that he would not climb to
her sleeping mat tonight as he had done so many times over
the years. He would never again hold her warm body close.*

*At the last moment, the man who was about to die screamed
with all the horror of his great loss: warmth and daylight,
memory and longing, swallowed forever by monstrous night.*

His scream echoed in the high mountain air.

Dr. Rutherford Hughes stopped writing, holding his ballpoint pen poised near the spiral notebook. His kerosene
lantern lit the page with a dim yellow glow. A cold shiver of
dread crept up his spine. He thought he had just heard a sound
come from the nearby trees. Footsteps? A human sigh? He
wasn't sure.

It was a ghostly night, an uneasy breeze disturbing the trees.
He listened intently, but now there was only the usual rustling
of branches and the occasional sharp crackle of sap exploding
in his campfire. A small animal cried out in the far distance: a
death struggle, from the sound of it, some hungry beast eating
another unfortunate creature lower down on the food chain.

Closer to camp, his black horse stirred and snorted in her
corral, gently pawing the earth. This was a restful sound, the
movements of a horse at night, ancient and comforting.
Rutherford Hughes felt his body relax. Surely it was his horse
that he had half heard, absorbed in his writing. He was almost

certain of it. He was getting edgy living in solitude in this wild place, that was all.

He returned his attention to what he had written in his notebook. Dr. Hughes had been working on this particular scene, the massacre of a small clan of prehistoric Indians, for nearly two weeks now, a few hours every night. It was a way to kill time, he supposed. And kill off a bunch of ancient people as well, he acknowledged wryly.

Well, the book wasn't going to be a bestseller; it was simply an exercise, after all. A way to piece together gathered evidence into some semblance of imagined life, laying the groundwork for the more serious academic volume he would complete on his return to England. This was the glory of archeology: to reconstruct the past from fragments and clues and sudden hunches. To discern what had happened eight hundred years ago in a mountain cave in an obscure corner of northern New Mexico that contained the butchered remains of thirteen human beings.

Despite his literary fantasy, the prehistoric people whose deaths he was investigating were a profound mystery. Even their identity was unknown. The modern Hopi called them *Hisatsinom*. The Zuni had a different name, *Enote*, and the Navajo a different word still, *Anasazi* which meant, simply, "ancient enemy." Dr. Rutherford Hughes shivered; whatever name they went by, he could imagine too well the terror of an ancient killing ground. He put down his pen and notebook, poured a shot of brandy from the bottle on the ground into an aluminum cup, and stared moodily into the flames of his campfire. It was late August, but his mountain camp stood at nearly 11,000 feet, just below the tree line, and nights were bitterly cold at this altitude. The moon was directly overhead, almost full, hanging like a phosphorous ball in the high-altitude sky, so clear and sharp he could see the craters and shadows of lunar mountains.

Dr. Hughes feared he had been living on this mountain of the dead far too long. His hands were nicked and weathered by digging in the ground and moving rocks. His clothes were filthy, his long blond hair matted and greasy. He had taken to wearing a shark's-tooth earring that dangled from the lobe of his left ear, knowing very well that this made him look more like a pirate than a former professor from Cambridge University. The tooth was a memento of an underwater adventure off the Great Barrier Reef nearly a decade earlier that he had barely survived. He wore the tooth now as a reminder of his will to live. The tooth also impressed the local Indians, which was sometimes necessary.

Dr. Hughes squatted close to his campfire and turned over the two potatoes that were roasting on the coals. "No, we don't want you to burn, my darlings," he told them fondly. He was running low on supplies, so this would be his dinner tonight. Tomorrow or the day after he would bow to the inevitable and make a shopping run into town. Meanwhile, barbecued potatoes were a treat for a hungry archeologist. He basted the potatoes with a mixture of salt, pepper, virgin olive oil, and wild thyme. When this was done, he stood up, stretched, took another sip of brandy, and gazed at the moon overhead.

Dr. Hughes was thinking about the work he planned to do in the cave tomorrow when his horse whinnied from the corral nearby. Her cry was strangely human and the archeologist once again felt a tingle of fear.

"What is it, girl?" he asked anxiously.

She neighed again, restless and alarmed. Dr. Hughes reached for the flashlight near his flat cooking rock and shone the beam into the woods toward the corral he had constructed about thirty feet from the fire. The corral was hexagonal, enclosed by saplings that he had cut with an ax and lashed with rope to a group of skinny trees near a fast-moving mountain stream. The horse was a beautiful creature but easily spooked: coal black, nearly sixteen hands high, a white star on her nose. The flashlight beam showed the whites of her eyes.

"Well, Sazi? What's the matter? You hear *chindi*?"

Chindi was an old Navajo word for ghosts. The horse's name was Anasazi, but over the course of time, living intimately together like two hermits in the forest, the name had become shortened to Sazi, Saze, and many other names as well—sometimes the names of women he had known long ago. It would have been better to have a more workaday horse up in these mountains, for the mare was too high-strung to make a good trail pony. But Dr. Hughes had a weakness for fine horses.

Moving slowly, feigning unconcern, Dr. Hughes reached into the backpack on the ground and drew out a huge, long-barrelled Colt .45 revolver, an old cowboy gun. Like the horse, the gun was not entirely practical—it was, in fact, an antique, an indulgence, a romantic artifact left over from a British schoolboy's imagination. He cocked the hammer and turned with the gun in hand toward the surrounding circle of trees. He rotated slowly, ready to fire at any enemy who appeared. But there was nothing. Nearly ten minutes passed before Dr. Hughes lowered the gun to his side. This was not good, imagining danger at every sound in the night. He needed to calm himself. Paranoia was dangerous to a man in his situation.

"My dear, I believe we are hellishly overdue for a return to civilization," he said to the black mare. "What do you say, Sazi? Shall we go to London for Christmas? Oh, yes, you'd like that! A pint of bitter at the pub, a stroll through Harrods Boxing Day! We'll take a bath and go see the queen!"

Dr. Rutherford Hughes turned back to the campfire and set his gun on the ground close to his cooking rock, leaving the hammer cocked in case his paranoia turned out to be not so silly after all. He put another log onto the back of the fire and basted the potatoes one last time. They were sizzling and soft, very close to being ready now.

Abruptly, he heard the crunch of a footstep directly behind him. Dr. Hughes stood quickly and turned to the human shape that had appeared in the darkness. The face reflected an angry glow of firelight.

"What do you want here?" he demanded.

His visitor smiled cruelly. "You know what I want!"

Dr. Hughes did his best to put on a show of icy disdain, but his breath was shallow and his voice was not entirely steady. He considered reaching for his gun on the ground close to the cooking rock, but it was too far away.

"Well, I'm just about to have some dinner," he said. "There isn't much, but you are welcome to join me."

Rutherford turned his back and squatted near the fire. He was still pondering the revolver, so close yet far away. The gun was cocked, ready to fire. But could he reach it in time?

"I'm going to kill you," the visitor said, almost humorously. "How about that? Hell of a way to end an evening, don't you think?"

The archeologist shook his head and chuckled sadly. "Don't be daft. There's some brandy left. We'll have a drink and talk this over."

He pretended to reach for the brandy, but it was the revolver he was after. Very quickly now, he grabbed the gun, spun around, and tried to fire. But he never had a chance. The big gun was knocked violently from his hand by a raging force that didn't seem human. There was an explosion and the dark shape of the killer was upon him. The British archeologist felt a shock of pain. It seized him entirely, body and soul . . .

The black horse, maddened with the sudden smell of blood, whinnied and reared and slashed at the corral with her front hooves, trying to escape. Rutherford Hughes heard her struggle in some distant part of his mind. His thoughts were strangely clear, as though he were a camera in the sky watching all this from a distance. He appreciated the irony, how the past and present intertwined, a universe in which all things repeated endlessly . . .

At the last moment, the man who was about to die screamed with all the horror of his great loss: warmth and daylight, memory and longing, swallowed forever by monstrous night.

His scream echoed in the high mountain air.

Bellowing with rage and triumph, the killer severed the head from the body with a slash of a knife, and held the gory prize by its hair high in the air. The black mare, Anasazi, could stand no more. Crazed with fear, she burst free of her corral, jumping the last hurdle, and galloped away into the ancient forest.

PART ONE

<hr>

COPYCAT

1

A cat crossed the alley, moving in a slow, predatory crawl toward the Dumpster at the rear of the Shanghai Café. Howard Moon Deer raised his infrared binoculars to get a better look. It was a fat cat, a long-haired Siamese, clearly someone's pet. The binoculars gave the cat, the Dumpster, and the back door of the Chinese restaurant a red-orange psychedelic glow, as though they were radioactive. The color was sickening, reminding Howie of the sweet-and-sour mystery meat he had eaten here a month ago: pork, according to the menu, but now he wondered.

"They're eating pussy at the Shanghai Café," was how his boss, Jack Wilder, had put it, chuckling at his own joke. Jack had a truly awful sense of humor. "Your assignment, Howie—should you accept it—is to catch them in the act of putting puss in the pot!"

Howie lowered the binoculars and the night returned to its usual color, a harsh blue-white from the streetlamp shining down on the alley. He was parked at the rear of a strip mall on the north end of town. As strip malls went, this was low-rent even for New Mexico. Along with the Chinese restaurant, there was Suzie's Sewing Shop, Anita's Wash-O-Matic, a small pet store with one lonely parakeet in the window, and an accountant's office—Timmy's Tax Returns. It was said in town that Timmy was the sort of accountant to see if you wanted to keep two sets of books for your business, official and unofficial. The only halfway upscale business in the entire complex was the San Geronimo Pharmacy, which in the past few years had been waging a heroic but losing battle to compete with Wal-Mart.

It was still August, but the night air was chilly. Howie was
bundled up in a black turtleneck sweater with a thermos of hot
coffee propped up on the passenger seat alongside him. The
coffee was a special blend of organic Kona beans, for Howie
had upwardly mobile tastes when it came to caffeine—a fact
that Jack teased him about mercilessly. Jack always insisted
that coffee from 7-Eleven was an essential part of the Holy
Trinity of the detective experience: angst, indigestion, and
boredom. Last night Howie had come on the stakeout in the
Wilder & Associate pickup truck, but tonight he was using his
own car, a battered old MGB with a convertible top held together with silver duct tape. The idea was that if someone
spotted him, they wouldn't see the same car in the same alley
two nights in a row. He logged a note in his journal:

11:14 P.M. *Plump long-haired Siamese visits Dumpster.
Color probably white. . . .* He debated adding a small twist to
the old joke that all cats were gray in the dark—except when
you looked at them through infrared binoculars, then they
were orange. But Jack was an ex-cop and took paperwork seriously. So Howie finished his entry with a simple, *Can't determine if animal is wearing a collar.*

He raised the binoculars once again and watched the cat on
the Dumpster. After a few minutes, something frightened the
animal and it dashed off down the alley, out of sight. Lucky
puss, so plump and juicy. Add a little MSG and some gloppy
bright orange-red sauce . . . Howie gagged at the memory of
the dinner he had eaten at the Shanghai Café earlier in the
summer. He had been on a date with a self-serious young
woman who kept asking him all sorts of anthropological questions about the Lakota Sioux, his faraway people. Between the
questions and the lousy food, it was no wonder that romance
had never gotten off the ground.

This was Howie's sixth night on the stakeout: he put in
three nights last week, took Saturday off for good behavior,
then Sunday, Monday, and now Tuesday night back on the job.
Six nights of the Great Pussycat Caper and he was nearly *cata-
tonic* with boredom. (He giggled at his own joke, showing just
how bored he was.) Last week hadn't been so bad. He had

been fresh then. He had maintained a positive attitude. But this week was hell. A person got a little wonky in the head sitting hour after hour in a parked car in an alley. Sunday night he had spent reviewing his life, like a drowning man—Part One, from his childhood on a desperately poor South Dakota reservation to his fancy scholarship education at Dartmouth and Princeton. Monday night he relived Part Two, a year in Paris, some romance and heartbreak, and the various reasons he had put his PhD dissertation on hold. Tonight he had been pondering Part Three, wondering what in the world had ever possessed him to move to the small New Mexico town of San Geronimo and take a job as a seeing-eye assistant to a blind ex-police commander from California.

As cases went, keeping watch on the rear door of the Shanghai Cafe was bottom of the barrel, even for Wilder & Associate. Still, they had an actual paying client, always a miracle. An elderly lady who lived near the strip mall, Mrs. Eudora Harrington, had lost three of her seven cats during the past month and was convinced that the Chinese restaurant was responsible, abducting her dear pussies for nefarious culinary purposes. Mrs. Harrington was a nasty old lady who wanted Jack and Howie to "nail the perp bastards"—she obviously watched a good deal of television—and hinted furthermore that if there happened to be a shoot-out and the entire management and staff got blasted off the face of the planet, she wouldn't be a bit displeased.

Howie found it all very discouraging. "Remember, there are no small cases, only small detectives," Jack liked to say. Still, after six nights, Howie was pondering a career change; even academia hadn't been quite as boring as this.

He was in a double-entendre mode, *cat*aloging past girlfriends—grading them from one to ten for their sense of humor, now that he was thirty-one years old and past the mere allure of flesh—when the rear door of the restaurant opened. It was Yang Li in food-splattered kitchen whites putting out the garbage for the night. Howie raised the night-vision binoculars to his eyes, thrilled to have some action at last, hoping that this might prove to be a crucial moment of cat-nabbing. Yang Li had recently arrived from Beijing, a cousin of the Wei family who owned the Shanghai Café. He was a short, stocky man in his late thirties, a hint of Mongolia in his wide cheekbones. He could almost pass as Indian, Howie decided, focusing the lens more sharply.

"*Meeoww!*" cried a pussycat. Howie was so excited he accidentally unfocused the binoculars to a blur and couldn't see a thing. He refocused, calming himself, but it still took a minute of scanning the alley to find the source of the meow. It was the fat Siamese he had spotted earlier on the Dumpster, now sitting prissily balanced on a wooden fence on the far side of the alley, watching the Chinese cook with fascinated feline eyes.

"Go for it, Yang!" Howie whispered, encouragingly. "Mmm, sweet and sour puss . . . puss with dumplings and plum sauce . . . puss with snow peas and cashews!"

All Yang Li had to do was make a grab for the animal, or lure it cagily into the back door with the promise of warm milk, and Howie could take a photo of the event with the Nikon he had handy near the thermos on the passenger seat. One good picture with the telephoto lens and super-fast film of the Siamese getting shanghaied into the restaurant for tomorrow's All-You-Can-Eat Buffet and Howie could give up this foolishness. He could go home and get some sleep. But Yang Li ignored the cat. For the next ten minutes, Howie watched as the man pulled out first a number of large black plastic garbage bags, then a small flotilla of cardboard boxes from inside the back door, crushing them flat with brutal resolve and carrying them to the Dumpster. As a spectator event, it was not fascinating. Fortunately, the cousin from Beijing didn't bother to glance down the alley to where Howie was lurking in his car a hundred feet away. He was probably too tired to notice much of anything.

"You should recycle that cardboard, Yang, my friend," Howie thought with a discouraged sigh. With the exception of this lapse in environmental correctness, he had witnessed no crime. Eventually, Yang Li returned inside and shut the back door securely behind him. A few minutes later, all the lights inside the restaurant went off.

It was nearly 12:30 in the morning, another long day over. Now the entire family began to file wearily out the rear door of the restaurant. Besides Yang Li, there were Connie and Cherry, the two teenage daughters, both very pretty and Americanized. Then came Rose, the shrewish mother. Albert Wei was the last to leave, carefully locking the door behind him with two separate keys. He was a small, exhausted-looking man. The group walked in silence toward the south end of the alley, in the opposite direction from where Howie was parked, to the family's ten-year-old Dodge van. After a fourteen-hour day, their steps were heavy; they would get only a short rest before rising to begin once again the endless cycle of lunch and dinner. Howie was impressed and strangely moved; it seemed to him vaguely heroic, working so hard in the service of such truly awful Chinese food.

"Good night, Shanghai Café!" Howie said aloud, shaking his head at the folly of it all. He turned on a flashlight, since secrecy was no longer required, and did his best to chronicle the past hours of nothingness he had just witnessed in a way that might conceivably justify the salary he was receiving from Jack for this particular assignment—twenty-five dollars per hour, a small fortune in New Mexico.

Howie was still writing when he heard a vehicle suddenly rev its engine and roar into the alley, tires squealing, from the direction of the San Geronimo Pharmacy at the far end of the strip mall. He looked up and saw a single headlight heading his way. At first he thought it was a motorcycle, but something about it was wrong, off-kilter. As he looked more closely, he realized it was either a car or a pickup truck with one headlight out. Howie felt his whole body tense. The engine was too loud and the vehicle was coming too fast down the alley, weaving erratically.

"Slow down!" Howie muttered. As if the driver heard, there was a crunch of brakes and the one-eyed monster came to an abrupt stop alongside the trash Dumpster behind the restaurant. With the headlight shining directly in his eyes, Howie had to squint; he was just able to make out a figure stepping from the vehicle and carrying something to the Dumpster.

Most likely a drunk driver getting rid of his empty bottles in case the cops stopped him. If so, this was a particularly tidy drunk; usually the late-night rowdies of San Geronimo just threw their dead soldiers out the car window onto the road. The figure got back into the vehicle and pushed down on the gas hard, revving the engine and making the tires spin before they grabbed hold of the asphalt. The pickup—it *was* a truck, Howie decided—lurched forward, gathering speed.

My God! It was coming right at him, bearing down directly on where he was parked! The drunken fool was going to run him down!

Howie managed to start his own engine, but there was no time to get out of the way. The white glare of the single head-light seemed to explode in his face. The noise was sickening, a screech of metal against metal. The front of the oncoming pickup smashed against his rear fender, spinning him around violently. Howie felt as though he had been seized by a cy-clone until he jerked to a stop against a telephone pole at the rear entrance to Anita's Wash-O-Matic. He sat for a moment catching his breath, making certain all his body parts were still attached.

"*Asshole!*" he shouted belatedly, full of impotent rage. He stepped from his car in time to see a pair of glowing red tail-lights disappear onto the four-lane road that led toward the center of town. Howie was okay, just shaken up, but the left rear fender of his MG looked as if it had been hit by a freight train. The metal was crumpled against the tire and Howie saw that he wasn't going to be doing any more driving tonight.

"Dysfunctional idiot!" he cried. He let loose every four-letter word he could think of, and some five-, six-, and seven-letter words as well. They helped a little, but not much. As it happened, Howie was particularly fond of his old MG con-vertible, which he believed made him a very cool Sioux, highly desirable to the opposite sex. He raged and ranted, but it was useless. There was nothing to do but sigh, shake his head, and walk around to the pay phone at the front of the laundry to call 911 and AAA. The way things worked in San Geronimo, he expected it would be at least fifteen minutes until the cops arrived and probably an hour before AAA deigned to send him a tow truck.

With time to kill, Howie walked down the alley, curious to see what kind of empties this mother of all maniacs had left behind in the Dumpster. Tequila, he imagined, probably a liter bottle, for the collision had been too violent and senseless to be inspired by a mere twelve-pack of beer. He opened the green metal top of the trash container and froze in shock and disbelief.

There was a terrible smell. Some messy organic thing the size of a large cantaloupe lay on top of the flattened cardboard boxes. Only it was blackened and smashed in, totally disgusting. And it wasn't really a melon after all, it was ... *it was* ...

What the hell *was* it? An animal head?

A dog, maybe?

Except there was an ear that looked horribly like the sort of ear he had himself, not as blackened as the rest of the pulpy mess. And from the ear dangled an earring. It was an odd earring, a tooth of some kind that was attached to a gold loop that pierced the dead ear lobe ... in these days of fashionable piercings, it was hard to say for certain, but Howie sensed it was a rare day in hell when dogs wore earrings.

There was no way around it. Dear God in heaven. *It was a ... human ... head!*

The heavy metal lid of the Dumpster slipped from his fingers with a crash that scared him half to death. Howie stumbled backward. Then something brushed against his leg and he screamed. It was the same plump Siamese he had seen on and off all night long. The cat had something in its mouth, a late-night snack.

Howie bent over and vomited on the animal's magnificently furry back. The Siamese let loose an outraged yowl. Then gathering its dignity, it pranced off into the night, clearly not impressed by the graceless ways of man.

2

At four o'clock in the morning, the streets of San Geronimo were quiet as a tomb. Even the traffic lights seemed to be dreaming, flashing their orange warning at empty intersections.

Howie caught a ride with Officer Rick Sanchez across town to Jack Wilder's house on Calle Santa Margarita. Officer Sanchez was a young cop, younger than Howie, and he didn't seem pleased that the ranking officer at the crime scene had ordered him into chauffeur duty. To show his displeasure, he drove dangerously fast down the middle of the road, tires singing along the pavement, no siren, the rack lights overhead broadcasting kaleidoscope patterns of red and blue against the passing buildings. Everything about Officer Sanchez said, *Look out, here I come!* He was a studly guy, very spiffy and pleased with himself, probably a heartthrob to the opposite sex with his tight blue uniform and bulging gun.

Howie was exhausted and numb, still in shock. He had seen death before, but never death like this: a severed head rotten and stinking in the garbage. Officer Sanchez had turned on the heat in the squad car. Howie rolled down his window, feeling sick.

"Hey, man, put the goddamn window up. I'm cold."

"I think I'm going to throw up again," Howie told him.

"Don't you puke in here! . . . Goddamn it, lean out the window."

Howie had his head out the window as they rushed through the historical district of town, a few quaint blocks of adobe buildings, cute little stores, and overpriced restaurants that had been designed to satisfy tourist yearnings for an entirely fictitious Southwest. Several blocks later, the real San Geronimo reappeared, ungentrified and unrepentant: more shabby strip malls and fast-food franchises, all of it architecturally ugly as sin. It was a good thing the surrounding land was magnificent, the desert and mountains of northern New Mexico, or all the arty newcomers would have returned in a hurry to California and New York in their brand-new SUVs.

Officer Sanchez was obviously irritated at the need to slow down on Calle Santa Margarita, a narrow road that twisted through an old residential neighborhood, past darkened houses and thick adobe walls. "You'd think they'd widen these streets!" he muttered. To the east, the moon was just rising above San Geronimo Peak, the brooding mountain that guarded the town. Howie told Officer Sanchez to let him off at the foot of Jack's driveway. It was a joy to step out of the cruiser and breathe cool, clear air.

"Don't let me see you again too soon," the studly young cop said before he drove away.

Howie managed a weak smile. "Yes, sir. You betcha." As a kid growing up on a reservation, he had learned it was necessary to be nice to cops whether you liked them or not, because these people had a huge and undue amount of power over your life. But he hated cops, he truly did. Most of all, he hated his own fear of them. It never ceased to amaze him that he had ended up working for one.

Howie stood beneath the shadows of a huge old cottonwood tree watching the taillights of the police cruiser disappear down the lane. He felt discouraged and weary in every bone of his body. From some distant corner of his mind, he remembered the Lakota word for cottonwoods: *waga chun*, which meant "rustling leaves." Like many Sioux children of his generation, Howie had grown up speaking English and his knowledge of Lakota was spotty. He wished now that he had paid more attention to his great-uncle Horace Two Arrows, who had tried to teach him the traditional ways. Maybe then he wouldn't be feeling so rootless and dispossessed, not to mention dog-tired and sick to his stomach with the horror of violent death.

At the end of the driveway, the Wilder house stood in the velvety darkness. It was an old two-story adobe farmhouse on several acres of land that Jack and Emma had fixed up in the usual ways that people from California fixed up houses here— enlarging the windows, tearing down walls to make larger rooms, adding modern plumbing and solar panels, spending more money than the local Spanish and Pueblo Indians would probably see in several lifetimes. Howie had phoned Jack on his cell phone around two A.M. to tell him what had happened and that he was coming over, but there were no lights on so he imagined that Jack had most likely gone back to sleep. Howie was just as glad; frankly, he wasn't much in a mood for conversation. He had the key to the Wilder & Associate red Toyota pickup that was parked near the house, and there was nothing he had to tell Jack that couldn't wait until morning.

Without warning, a large dog leapt at him from the shadows, nearly giving Howie a heart attack. The dog jumped up with her front paws on his chest, knocking him off balance. Howie staggered off the path into a bed of Emma's petunias. It was only Katya, Jack's German shepherd guide dog, saying hello in her usual overenthusiastic manner. Katya was a $25,000 animal, but Jack had allowed her expensive training to go to seed.

"*Yah!*" he swore at her softly as she gave him a big, wet doggy kiss with her tongue directly on his mouth. Katya adored Howie. They danced a brief tango before he managed to disentangle her paws from his chest and push her back to the ground. He was surprised to find her outside this time of night.

"You took your time getting here," came a low voice from the shadows near the house.

Katya's appearance had startled him, but the suddenness of human speech nearly made Howie jump out of his skin.

"Man, you scared the holy shit out of me!" he cried.

Jack chuckled. It took Howie a second to locate him in the darkness. He was sitting on the swing beneath the overhanging shadows of the front porch. Jack could have spoken earlier without giving Howie such a scare, but as usual he was having his little joke at Howie's expense. As Howie approached, he saw that Jack was dressed in a bulky down parka over his pajamas and had a wine glass in his right hand. He was a big, gruff bear of a man, six feet tall, midfifties, overweight, curly gray hair and a well-trimmed gray beard. As always, his wraparound dark glasses were perched on his nose. Sometimes Howie wondered if Jack wore his dark glasses in bed, but it wasn't a question he felt entitled to ask.

"You know, Jack, I have to be honest with you—you make sort of an eccentric figure sitting out here at this hour of the morning drinking by yourself."

Jack smiled thinly. "I haven't been sleeping much. But that's okay. It gives me more time to remember things. I hope you're seizing every moment, Howie, because youth doesn't last nearly as long as you probably assume it will."

"Hey, I'm seizing moments like crazy," Howie assured him. "*Carpe diem*, that's my motto. Particularly on a night like this, Jack—it reaffirms my wild and crazy joy just to be here on Planet Earth."

Jack was about to say something witty, but he changed his mind, hearing Howie's tone. "Go ahead and pour yourself a glass of wine," he suggested.

"I'm ready, believe me. What are we drinking?"

"Some Bordeaux that Emma bought in Santa Fe—I don't know what it is." He added merrily, "Frankly, I couldn't see the goddamn label!"

Howie studied Jack more closely. It was hard to read a blind man; the blind were closed in upon themselves in some way that Howie didn't entirely understand. As far as he could tell, Jack wasn't drunk—Jack didn't really *get* drunk, only more oblique than usual. But there was something wrong, even beyond the wrongness of Howie's two A.M. phone call about a severed head.

"You okay?"

"Sure. Just visiting with some ghosts. Hell, it doesn't

matter." He stood up from the porch swing to fetch the bottle from inside the house.

"No, I'll get it," Howie offered.

"Don't be ridiculous. You'll need to turn on the lights and stomp around like some bull in a china shop, and then Emma will wake up."

"I *don't* stomp around like a bull," Howie objected indignantly. "We Indians move with a certain natural grace, thank you."

Jack laughed. He was a ponderous man, courtly and old-fashioned. But he could be unexpectedly silly as well, boyishly full of humor, and Howie was never certain which Jack Wilder he was going to encounter at any given moment.

"Fabulous. *You* get the bottle, then," Jack said, settling down again on the porch swing. "We'll have a drink, and then you can tell me all about your head."

Howie felt better after sharing the gory details with Jack. It was like the New Agers said—and there were plenty of New Agers in San Geronimo—it was good to unburden yourself, communicate your intimate traumatic moments in order to avoid psychic damage and not bum out your family and friends.

The eastern sky was gray with false dawn by the time he finished talking. The true sunrise came late to San Geronimo, for the town sat in a high desert valley surrounded by an abrupt ring of mountains, a branch of the Southern Rockies that shot up to heights of 13,000 feet and more. Altitude was a big part of the dysfunctional magic of northern New Mexico. But it was a hard land, not for the faint of heart.

"Good thing I only had a small dinner last night," Howie admitted. "I threw up all over the place. Out the window as we were driving here, even onto a cat."

"Decapitation bothers you, apparently?"

"It makes a person wonder about a whole lot of issues, Jack. I mean, think about it. On one hand we have poetry, philosophy, love, all our fine illusions. And then, my God, suddenly, it's like there's nothing but garbage and rot and . . ."

"Howie, Howie, Howie!" Jack interrupted. "Dead's dead. We all turn to compost in the end. Does it matter if a banana is separated from its peel, or a person from his head?"

"It matters," Howie insisted solemnly.

Jack shrugged. "Personally, I'm more concerned with who did this. Dismemberment generally indicates an angry sort of killer. Someone for whom simple murder isn't enough—he must mutilate the corpse, continuing with his rage even after the victim is dead. Of course, it can also indicate a killer who is simply very practical."

"Why practical?"

"In disposing of the corpse. If you cut it up, you can get rid of the body more easily. I remember a serial killer we had in San Francisco, in the Haight. He liked to cut up young women and fit them very neatly into a suitcase. Then he'd leave the suitcase in a storage locker at the bus station downtown. Finally, of course, the smell would get so bad . . . what's the matter, Howie?"

Howie had gagged. "Please, my stomach's still a little queasy."

Jack grinned mischievously. "Did I ever tell you about the perp who liked to cut off the left hands of his victims? Only the *left* hand, mind you. He had quite a collection of human hands in a drawer in his bedroom and sometimes he'd bring them out and masturbate with 'em."

"*Jack!* For chrissake!"

"My apologies. Go home, Howie. Get some sleep. That old MG of yours is insured and I'm sure they'll be able to fix the fender just like new. Meanwhile, you've got the office truck to use so there's nothing to worry about. In the afternoon, you can visit our client and tell her what fabulous progress we're making on her case. Who knows? Maybe tonight will be the night you catch the cat-nabber in action."

"You're kidding, I hope? I'm *not* going back to that alley."

"Why not?" Jack raised a questioning eyebrow over the black plastic rim of his dark glasses. "We've got a client, remember? We've taken the lady's money, and we've got to deliver the goods. *Comprendez*?"

"*Je comprends* perfectly well. Nevertheless, I'm through with cats. What I'm going to do is find that asshole maniac who bashed my car and left that head in the garbage—"

"Screw the head!" Jack interrupted. "You can't get sidetracked by every body part you happen to find in the garbage."

"I'm definitely *not* going to screw the head," Howie replied haughtily.

"Then at least leave it to OMI," Jack told him, meaning the Office of the Medical Investigator in Albuquerque. "Look, Howie, a case like this is going to be solved in a pathology lab, not by two private detectives. So what you need to do, my friend, is to concentrate on who's eating pussy, not who's getting head."

Howie groaned, appalled at Jack's humor. "My God, do *all* cops make bad jokes?"

"Yes, Howie, we do," Jack assured him. "It comes with the boredom, the bad food, the bad hours, and the bad pay. Now go home."

They argued until they heard Emma in the upstairs shower getting ready for work. Howie insisted he wasn't going back to that alley, no way. Jack said he'd better, at least if he wanted to keep on collecting twenty-five bucks an hour for the easiest gig Wilder & Associate had ever been lucky enough to score.

At last they came to a compromise. Howie did not need to resume the stakeout in the alley. Instead he could continue the investigation for Mrs. Eudora Harrington by canvasing the neighborhood, going door to door, street to street, asking if anyone had seen Floozie, Miao-Miao, and Mr. Stud—the missing felines in question.

"And, hell, if *that* doesn't get results, I tell you what—just go to the damn Chinese restaurant and pick up some take-out. We'll send the cartons to the FBI lab and have them analyzed. Okay, Howie?"

"Sure, Jack."

"Don't get so bent out of shape next time." Jack smiled wisely. "Fortunately, there is always more than one way to skin a cat."

3

Howie woke up slowly, confused by the afternoon light. He felt all wrong, even with his eyes closed.

The first thing he thought about was the severed head. He played the scene again in his inner movie theater, from the moment the one-eyed truck had appeared in the alley to finding the gory mess in the Dumpster. The memory filled him with stress and nausea. Frankly, he wasn't certain he was cut out for this line of work. From the beginning, Jack had assured him that being a detective was mostly a matter of research. Almost like being back at dear old Princeton, Jack had promised. No guns, no violence. Indeed, Jack said, a good detective was a kind of intellectual, only more serious because he took his skills out into the real world.

Sure, Jack, you manipulative bastard! Back at Princeton, I have to tell you, we did not find decapitated heads in the goddamn garbage!

Unfortunately, Howie was unable to distance himself with black humor and atrocious puns the way Jack could after twenty years of being a big-city-cop—several homicides a week, Jack had told him once, not to mention the suicides, accidents, and bodies of old people half eaten by rats in cheap hotel rooms. Howie feared the memory of what he had seen last night was going to haunt him for many years.

After a while Howie dared to crack open an eyelid and inspect the digital clock by his bed. It was 1:47. Outside his window, the sun was hot and the air was dusty, a full-blown summer day—but a day that was already more than halfway gone.

Howie surveyed his one-room cabin from the vantage point of his pillow. It wasn't much, a small guest house on a dirt road in the open desert north of town, on a remote corner of a forty-acre estate. He had a double bed that took up most of the room, a tiny kitchen alcove, a table, a rocking chair, a few plants, a minuscule bathroom, and windows looking out toward the sagebrush and nearby mountains. Every surface was piled high with books and CDs. A number of women had come and gone from Howie's life in this small cabin. He spent some time puzzling over this fact as he tried to summon the energy to rise and make coffee. He was thirty-one years old and nothing had really jelled for him, domestically speaking. Oh, he was still good friends with all his women. Good old Howie, encouraging them to follow their dreams! But their dreams had led them away from this bed: One was now a doctor in a clinic in Africa, another had become a classical musician in a string quartet in Chicago. They all sent him Christmas cards and E-mail, saying how much they missed him.

Howie sat up decisively in bed, telling himself it was a new day, and that on new days, new things happened. And that's when he saw her: the beautiful young woman standing on the flagstone terrace just outside the sliding glass door at the rear of his cabin. She was peering in through the glass, her hands cupped around her face. She was looking the wrong way, toward the tiny kitchen alcove rather than the bed, and hadn't seen him yet.

Howie couldn't imagine what good fortune had caused a lovely woman to appear at his cabin. She was lanky and elegant as a fashion model, early twenties, long-limbed, dressed in tight, faded jeans and an oversized T-shirt that had SAN GERONIMO POWWOW 2000 written across the front. Howie sensed he had seen her someplace before, but he couldn't immediately remember where. In a magazine? A dream? Then he placed her. Her name was Donna Theresa, D.T. for short. They had met once before, but they had exchanged only a few words, and she looked different today, more casually dressed. He was astonished to see her.

From what he remembered, D.T. was half Italian, half Pueblo Indian, an intriguing mix. Physically, she combined the best of both worlds: olive-brown skin, high cheekbones, and huge eyes. Her long black hair was lustrous with sunlight, parted in the middle, hanging in a very simple way down her shoulders. She wore no makeup. Everything about her seemed as natural as a summer day.

Howie was soaking up her loveliness when she turned and caught him staring at her from the bed.

"Oh!" she cried, stumbling back from the glass. "I'm sorry. I . . . I didn't think you'd still be in b-b-bed."

She had a slight stutter, which was one more endearing thing about her.

"I had a late night. Come on in," he said.

She hesitated, ill at ease. "No, I'll w-w-wait out here. I didn't want . . . I was wondering if we could talk . . ."

"Of course." Howie smiled reassuringly. Unfortunately, he was experiencing a problem: in bed, naked, with a certain condition common to males when they first rise and before they have a chance to pee. He didn't want to alarm her unduly so early in their relationship. Finally he was forced to say, "I'll just, you know, pop into some clothes . . ."

D.T. turned her back, making a show of studying a flower box on his terrace where he was growing basil, his favorite cooking herb. Howie seized the moment to wrap the blanket from his bed around his waist and make a dash to the bathroom. His jeans and a flannel shirt were waiting for him on the bathroom floor. He relieved himself, dressed quickly, and gave his teeth a three-second brush. He tried out a seductive smile on the bathroom mirror, but the mirror wasn't seduced. It reflected a round moonlike face with the flattish nose of his ancestors and long black hair in a sloppy ponytail. It was a pleasant face, he supposed, but he wasn't exactly a native Robert Redford, not by a long shot. There were times he believed he possessed redeeming features of intelligence and humor and resolve, but not today. Today he looked old and tired and ashen, like a man who had just woken from a nightmare.

He took a swig of mouthwash before leaving the bathroom, hoping minty-fresh breath would make up for a host of other failings.

Howie had met D.T. just a few days before, on his Saturday night off from the endlessly boring stakeout of the Shanghai Café. An old Cheyenne friend, Lester Wounds Eagle, had called him from Santa Fe that morning to say he was passing through San Geronimo "scouting locations" with a group of movie people and Howie should join them for dinner. "Scouting locations," apparently, was a new sort of native skill, different from the old kind of scouting for which Indians had once been famous.

Lester and Howie had been roommates their sophomore year at Dartmouth, where they had both been enrolled in the NAD, the Native American Department. But after Dartmouth, their lives had gone in different directions: Howie continued in academia while Lester moved to New York to write a novel about his childhood in Oklahoma that eventually became a minor classic. A few years later, Lester managed to turn his book into a low-budget movie that he produced and directed himself. The movie was a hit at the Sundance Film Festival, picked up by a major Hollywood studio for distribution, and Lester was in the clover. It probably couldn't have happened to a nicer guy.

Howie joined Lester and his group that Saturday night at the Anasazi Grill, San Geronimo's most expensive restaurant, but no longer what it once had been in terms of quality. Howie found Lester with a crowd of seven or eight people at a long, noisy table—he never did get all their names straight, but they were mostly Anglo men with ponytails and hip young women. Everyone was extremely witty and seemed to know a lot of famous people by their first names.

D.T. had been sitting halfway down the table in a skimpy black cocktail dress that hugged her body. She caught Howie's eye immediately for several reasons. The first was that she was beautiful and stylish and looked intelligent as well, which wasn't a bad combination of attributes. The second was that

Howie ID'd her immediately as someone who had grown up on the rez, even though she looked more Hollywood than anyone there. She was definitely a new breed of native, not your grandfather's aborigine; yet the aura of the rez lingered about her in a tangible way that Howie recognized. The final reason D.T. caught his eye (as if the first two reasons weren't enough), was that she hardly said a word. She just sat at the table smoking cigarettes and looking alternately bored and disgusted by the scene. It took Howie a good part of the evening to realize that she was not actually as cool and untouchable as she appeared: she was merely shy. Later still, he decided that passive was a better word to describe her, maybe even passive aggressive. She did not look happy.

It was a noisy, freewheeling sort of dinner party with a lot of hopping from chair to chair. Somewhere between salad and the main course, Howie found himself sitting next to a ponytailed screenwriter who looked about sixteen years old, and who told him a bit more about the mysterious Donna Theresa. In a low voice, he confided that her mother was from the San Geronimo Pueblo, but her father was an Italian communist poet, somewhat well known, who had come to New Mexico for several months in the mid-1970s, eager to experience the huge vistas of the American West. It had probably been quite the romantic fling for a trendy European intellectual to seduce a Native American girl, then return home blithely to Rome, careless of what he had left behind. Luckily for D.T., Indians were tolerant about half-breeds and kids born out of wedlock; it didn't matter much if you had blond hair or black—if you grew up on a reservation, you were an Indian.

"She's an actress, I suppose?" Howie asked the screenwriter.

"Lester would like to *make* her one, believe me—it's his current mission in life. But, actually, she's not—she's an archeologist at UNM."

"Really?" The information caused Howie to study D.T. with new curiosity. In truth, he wasn't wild about actresses, at least the ones he had met, who all seemed very full of themselves.

But an archeologist was another matter. He could dig an archeologist.

"So how does Lester know her?"

"They met in Albuquerque, at the university. He was giving
a talk or accepting an award, I forget which—you know
Lester. He's been trying to cast her in his new film, says she's
perfect. But D.T. just laughs and tells him he's a jerk. So naturally Lester thinks he's in love. It's the novelty, you know. He
hasn't been rejected for years."

Howie found it a depressing dinner party, except for the
presence of the beautiful, silent Indian woman. He proceeded
to drink too many margaritas and tried to pretend it was great
to hear movie gossip and talk about old times at Dartmouth
with Lester. In general, he liked his life in San Geronimo, yet
it was hard not to feel like a failure in comparison to his old
roommate's success. Lester had gone on to big things. And
what had Howie gone on to? He was thirty-one years old, still
struggling to finish up his PhD dissertation, supporting himself
with a foolishly quixotic part-time job as an assistant to a blind
detective—a job that had once appeared romantic, but was
seeming less so by the second. Sitting at the noisy table,
Howie took stock of himself, imagining how these movie people must see him: Someone who was neither rich nor famous,
and who didn't know a single celebrity by their first name.

He didn't exchange a single word with D.T. until dessert.
He left the table to go to the men's room and when he returned
there had been a shifting of chairs. The only seat available was
next to hers. Howie sat down apologetically, feeling shy. She
was nibbling on a piece of key lime pie. He smiled at her and
she frowned back, not inviting conversation. The waitress
brought him his own small slice of heart-attack heaven, Black
Forest cake, and they ate in silence, side by side. He tried to
think of a way to start up a conversation, but his mind drew a
blank. He debated between "How's the key lime pie?" and
"What's an archeologist like you doing in a place like this?"—
but wisely he decided to keep his mouth shut.

Then, to his surprise, she turned to him.

"Lester says you're a private eye?"

"Well, yes."

"Sounds interesting."

"Not very often," he assured her. Doing his best to make her laugh, he told the entire saga of Mrs. Eudora Harrington, the Shanghai Café, and how he was stuck sitting in a dreary alley night after night in order to determine the fate of Floozie, Miao-Miao, and Mr. Stud. Normally, Howie would not talk so freely about an ongoing case, but she kept staring at him like he was mad, and he found himself with diarrhea of the mouth. He had no idea what she thought of him, and he feared the worst.

"And you . . . I understand you're an archeologist," he managed.

"Mmm," was all she said on this subject as she swallowed a forkful of key lime pie. "Lester says besides being a detective, you're also a . . . c-c-c-cultural anthropologist?"

It was the first time he heard her stutter. Howie regarded her more closely, sensing deeper layers. Her stutter, he soon discovered, was not constant, it came out only at certain unpredictable moments. He wondered what had happened to Donna Theresa that had marked her in such a way, wounding her confidence.

"I'm a culinary psycho-sociologist," he explained.

"What's *that*?" He had finally got a laugh out of her.

"I'm doing my dissertation on how people eat in America, who eats who on the food chain, so to speak. Specifically, I'm trying to show that the heart of the great cultural divide in America is culinary—between people who eat iceberg lettuce and white bread, as opposed to the very different part of the population that must have whole wheat, arugula, and baby greens. If you think about it, it's a more profound difference than Republican or Democrat. Even the language of food is divisive—between, say, people who use the word shrimp, and those who say prawn. You see what I mean?"

"You say pasta, I say noodles—that's what you're talking about?"

"Exactly. We *are* what we eat. And in my theory, if you gobble down enough Jell-O salad with Cool Whip on top, you pretty much *become* a Republican, whether you want to or not."

D.T.'s smile erased her fashionable boredom and made her look years younger, like a mischievous little girl. "But it's education mostly, isn't it?—how people eat. And money, of course."

"Well, partly. But there are plenty of educated Texans with a ton of money, for instance, who are still eating red meat three times a day. So in my opinion it's cultural. Of course, with culinary psycho-sociology, you're always asking yourself what came first, the chicken or the egg."

Howie had been known to bore people into a coma when he got going on "his subject," particularly at dinner parties, but D.T. nodded with seeming interest.

"Culinary psycho-sociology," she said with a smile. "I like it. It sounds like a big field, though."

"Well, yes. In a sense it's everything, the whole banana— food, culture, where different people exist in the pecking order. That's why my dissertation is still dangling, I guess."

"What do you think about c-c-c-c . . . c-c-c-c-c . . ."

Whatever word she was trying to say, she couldn't get it out. Her stutter had just gone ballistic. Howie listened patiently, maintaining a neutral expression, trying not to be embarrassed for her, willing her to finish the word.

"Culture?" he tried. "Cuisine?"

She shook her head, exasperated. "C-c-c-c . . . c-c-c-c . . ." At last, she took a deep breath and got it out: "Cannibalism!"

He stared at her, speechless. The word was unexpected, to say the least.

Cannibalism?

Howie was trying to think of a suitable reply when Lester came over, squatted next to her chair, and began talking about a screen test he wanted her to take next week. All the animation faded from D.T.'s face. She listened scornfully, retreating into herself. Meanwhile, an Anglo lady on Howie's left engaged him in conversation, wanting to know the best place to buy a Navajo blanket in San Geronimo. Howie did his best to explain that the Navajo did not inhabit this particular corner of

New Mexico and directed her to Gallup, several hundred miles away.

He did not have another opportunity to speak with D.T. Half an hour later, the party broke up and everyone wandered together into the parking area in front of the restaurant. It was one of those typically disorganized postdinner scenes, not entirely sober, with lingering good-byes and people getting into several cars. Lester invited Howie to come back with them to the Holiday Inn, where they were all staying, but Howie begged off, claiming he had a lot of work tomorrow. In truth, he thought Lester probably wanted to be alone with D.T. and he didn't want to get in the way.

Howie said his own good-byes and was wandering toward his MGB when a mud splattered, much dented Toyota Land Cruiser pulled off the highway and stopped in front of D.T. and Lester with an angry squeal of brakes. Howie was a dozen feet away, but he turned and watched, sensing trouble. D.T. appeared to know whoever it was who was breaking in on her evening. She walked to the open passenger window and began to speak to the driver in Tiwa, the language of the San Geronimo Pueblo. From where he was standing, Howie couldn't see who was in the Land Cruiser. Her father? Husband? Boyfriend? It was a man, at least, obviously Indian, and from the sound of their voices, D.T. was not pleased to see him.

"Look, I've got to go," D.T. called over her shoulder to Lester.

"Everything okay?" Lester asked nervously. He seemed to be worried that he could get himself beat up by D.T.'s father/husband/boyfriend.

She didn't answer. With an angry motion, she slipped into the passenger seat and slammed the door.

"Call me!" Lester shouted after her, as the Land Cruiser jerked out of the parking lot.

When they were gone, Lester walked across the parking lot toward Howie. There was a rueful, lovesick expression on his face. "Man, I don't believe this! Could you understand what they were saying?"

"I don't know Tiwa," Howie confessed. "Sounds like some guy has a claim on her. Is she involved with someone?"

"I don't know. That girl is driving me crazy. But I just can't get anywhere with her!"

Lester Wounds Eagle sighed, forlorn with romantic disappointment. Then he looked at Howie and laughed, and Howie laughed, too. As roommates in college they had been through plenty of moments like this before: love lost, and—worse still—love never gained. It was good to laugh together like in the old days, the first close moment they had shared all night.

"Hey, Wounded Ego, I guess you're not doing so good in the girlfriend department!" Howie taunted, using an old nickname.

"Yeah? And what about you, Moony Deer? At least I almost got laid, my brother . . . come on, forget about working tomorrow. Let's find some beer!"

And that's what they did, escaping Lester's new Hollywood friends, making their way to Pinky's, the sleaziest bar in San Geronimo, a place where no one ever thought of calling celebrities by their first name. Howie assumed he'd never see D.T. again, certainly not at his remote cabin retreat, wanting to talk.

4

Howie walked through his sliding glass door into the bright afternoon light on the flagstone terrace. D.T. was standing near a green patio rocking chair that Jack and Emma had bought Howie for his birthday. Behind her, the desert stretched out in a soft carpet of tan and sagebrush to the foot of the mountains a mile away. It would have made a nice photograph, an ultimate Southwest scene with a Pueblo woman in foreground, except for the fact that the Pueblo woman in question seemed tense and unhappy. There was a tangible sense of melancholy surrounding Donna Theresa, and Howie found himself once again wondering what it was that had happened to make her this way. Meanwhile, she was doing her best to be unreadable. She had put on a pair of sleek designer sunglasses to shield her eyes from the midday glare.

"Would you like a cup of coffee?" he offered.

But she had begun to speak at the same time. "How much do you charge?"

"Charge?" Howie was momentarily at sea without a paddle. "The coffee's free, honest."

"Not coffee. On Saturday you told me you were a private d-d-detec . . . detective."

"Oh, well, yeah. Though actually it's my boss, Jack Wilder, who has the license. I'm his assistant."

"Then how much does *he* charge?"

"It depends on the case, of course. But our usual rate is forty dollars an hour, plus expenses."

Her mouth fell open. "*Forty* dollars an hour! You've got to be kidding!"

"Well, it is a lot," Howie admitted. "But it's what you pay for a car mechanic, after all. A plumber, even. So if you look at it that way, it's not so much. Particularly"—he added with what he hoped was dashing nonchalance—"when we sometimes risk our lives."

"On Saturday you said the job wasn't that interesting."

Howie shrugged. "Well, I was trying not to upset your digestion with tales of blood and gore. Are you looking for a private investigator?"

"Not me. It's for s-s-someone I know," she said, turning away. "I knew it would be expensive, but I guess I didn't realize how much."

"Let me make a suggestion. Why don't you have a seat, get comfortable, I'll put on some coffee and you can tell me about your friend's problem. The first consultation's always free, and if your friend wants to go ahead, we can work something out about the money. If you don't want to go ahead, that's okay, too. Everything you tell me will remain confidential."

It was a nice pitch, but she didn't take a seat, and she didn't make herself comfortable; she stood on the flagstone terrace in a way that reminded Howie of a deer caught in car headlights.

"Jack Wilder's the *real* detective your, uh, friend would be hiring," Howie continued. "And Jack's good, honestly. He's an ex-commander from the San Francisco Police Department, something of a genius. A lot of people in California thought he'd make police chief eventually, maybe even go higher. But he lost his eyesight in an accident and ended up moving here to San Geronimo."

Howie was trying to strike a balance between courtesy, professionalism, and general nice-guyism, but D.T. did not appear to be listening. She stood with her back to him staring moodily at the mountains.

"You have a nice view from here," she remarked vaguely.

"I love it. Lucky you, growing up here."

"You think I'm lucky?" she asked with a snort of laughter.

"Aren't you?"

She didn't answer. They stood for a while without talking. D.T. studied the mountains, while Howie studied the back of

D.T.'s right shoulder, trying to figure her out. They could have been in an old Ingmar Bergman movie, one with long silences where everybody commits suicide at the end.

"So how's archeology?" he asked, mostly to break the icy Swedish mood that had settled upon them.

D.T. answered without turning around. "Hard work. The PhD program at UNM is demanding."

"You got your master's there?"

She nodded.

"It's not so easy to grow up on a reservation and get yourself through college and graduate school," he said.

She shrugged. "You did it, didn't you?"

"Well, I got scholarships up the wazoo. It wasn't so hard. Guilt money, you know. Those fancy East Coast schools need an Indian or two so they can pretend that they're not really elitist breeding grounds for the future white masters of the universe."

"I hate them," she said in a flat voice, without passion.

"Hate who?

"The w-w-w . . ." She had to stop and start again. "What you just said. The w-white masters of the universe. I hate how they've squeezed and exploited every last square inch of earth for every penny they can get. There's nothing left, nothing they haven't ruined."

It was true, probably, except for the fact that there happened to be hundreds of square miles of unspoiled, unexploited land visible at the moment beyond D.T.'s shoulder. Howie wasn't sure precisely what she was so angry about.

"Don't you sometimes wish you lived on a different planet?" she asked moodily, shaking her lovely head.

"I'm not too sure other planets are necessarily an improvement. From what I hear, they don't have hot tubs or margaritas, or any of the other amenities."

"Pluto's perfect," she assured him. "I've been there often. . . . I heard you found a body last night."

Howie had begun to smile, but his smile froze with the non sequitur.

"Where did you hear that?"

"It was on the radio, this morning. KSGR," she said, naming San Geronimo's local FM station. "Is it true?"

"Well, it's partly true."

She turned to face him. "How can something like that be *partly* true?"

"Because it was only part of a body that I found. A head."

"Who was it? Do you know?"

Howie shook his head. "Don't have a clue."

"The police haven't ID'd it yet?"

"Not as of four o'clock this morning. And to be honest, I'd be surprised if they ID'd it anytime soon. It was not in good shape, as heads go."

She paused to consider this. She wet her lips slightly with the tip of her tongue, meditatively. Her stutter had disappeared for several minutes, but now it returned with a vengeance: "Wh-wh-what do you-m-m-m-mean, not in g-g-g-g . . ."

"Good shape?" he finished, finding it almost unbearable to listen to her struggle.

"Don't make f-f-fun of me!"

"I'm not," he told her. "Honestly, I'm not."

"Then t-t-tell me."

"Are you sure you want to hear this?"

She nodded.

"Well, it was blackened all over. I don't know exactly how, if it was burned or if it was just decayed. And the front of the skull was crushed in."

She took a deep breath. "On the radio they said there was some kind of jewelry on the head. An earring."

"They said that on the radio?"

"You'd think they'd be able to identify someone from an earring, wouldn't you?"

Howie was surprised that this information had been on the radio. The police sergeant at the crime scene had specifically warned him not to say anything to the media about the animal tooth earring, that they wanted to keep this information secret for the time being in order to facilitate the investigation. Still, he supposed information had a way of leaking to the press.

"Well?" she demanded. "*Was* there an earring?"

"Yes."

"Just a normal everyday sort of earring?"

"What do you mean?"

"Was there something special about it?"

"Special? Maybe you should tell *me*," Howie prodded. "What kind of earring are you looking for exactly?"

She stared at him but did not answer.

"D.T., is this head we're discussing the reason you're considering hiring a private detective? Are you worried about someone who's missing?"

"I told you, Moon Deer, it's my friend who's thinking about a detective. But I . . . I want to know about the earring."

"Why?"

She hesitated. "Okay. Maybe someone I know *is* missing. I'm not sure. I don't want to make a big thing about it, but I'm curious."

Howie decided to take a chance and tell the truth. "All right. It was just a single earring in the left lobe. A tooth of some kind, but I don't know what sort of animal it was from. Does your friend have an earring like that?"

"No," she said immediately. "He doesn't."

She turned her back to him again and made a point of studying San Geronimo Peak. For someone who had grown up in this high desert valley, the local mountains seemed to fascinate her.

"D.T., please. Talk to me. Who do you know who might be missing?"

"I told you, I'm not sure anyone's missing. Anyway, the person I know doesn't wear an earring like that. It's someone else."

"I'm glad to hear it," Howie told her. "I guess that's it, then. Just out of curiosity, what kind of earring does your missing person wear?"

She spun around angrily and for a second, Howie thought she was going to slap him silly. She had come all the way out of passive into truly aggressive. But as he watched her, a veil seemed to descend and she went slack and sullen again, giving nothing away.

"I don't know any missing person. I told you that. Don't you listen?"

"I try, D.T. I tell you what," he suggested, "why don't I get you my business card and you can think it over, whether you or your friend needs a private investigator. You can give me or Jack a call any time if you make a decision, or if you just want to talk some more. Okay?"

She nodded. "Okay. Thank you. I'm sorry, I know I'm being difficult." She paused, then added unexpectedly, "You're a nice guy, Moon Deer."

He smiled modestly at the compliment, but it was discouraging news. *Nice guy!* A number of women had told him this and he was starting to suspect it was the reason he was living alone rather than in the state of connubial bliss to which he aspired. Women, in his experience, appreciated "nice guys" but did not fall in love with them. Nice-Guy Moon Deer walked inside his cabin in order to find a Wilder & Associate business card. But when he returned, the patio was empty. Donna Theresa had fled.

Howie walked quickly around the side of his cabin, card in hand, but he was too late. By the time he reached his driveway, she had started up an old green Ford pickup truck and was pulling away. Her truck was a real clunker, circa 1970. Howie was surprised by her vehicle; being a modern Indian lady and an archeologist, he would have imagined her in something yuppie, like a Volvo, maybe even a Saab.

He stood in his driveway alongside the Wilder & Associate office truck, watching D.T.'s pickup jolt down the bumpy dirt road that led to the highway a few miles away. After a while, he reached into the front seat of the Toyota and pulled out the cell phone that Jack paid for him to have. He dialed the number of KSGR radio and asked for Lyle Stewart, the station manager. Lyle was an old ski buddy of numerous winter after noons, and in the summer they sometimes got together for tennis.

"Well, Moon Deer! I hear you had an adventure last night," Lyle said. He had a rich, deep FM voice, smooth and easy.

"That's what I'm calling about. I'm curious what you had about it on the news."

"It was just a quickie. Howard Moon Deer, local PI, came across a decapitated head in an alley last night and the police are investigating. Anything you'd like to add?"

"Not right now. Was anything said about jewelry of any kind? An earring, to be specific?"

"An earring? Nope. We got all our info from the state police, from Captain Gomez—apparently he's taken over the investigation. But he didn't tell us much. Certainly nothing about an earring."

"Thanks, Lyle. Listen, I gotta run."

"Let's play tennis soon."

"You bet," Howie told him, cutting off the connection. In the distance, he could still see D.T.'s green truck racing toward the highway, a plume of dust rising from her back tires into the vastness of sky and mountains and open land.

He liked her. But he wished she hadn't told him quite so many lies.

5

Later that afternoon, Howard Moon Deer sat in the stuffy, overfurnished living room of Mrs. Eudora Harrington, doing his best to keep his mind on business. Several hours had gone by since he stood and watched D.T.'s dusty pickup become a small speck in the desert, yet his retinas still seemed to retain an impression of her troubled, lovely face.

"Are you listening to me, young man?" demanded the old woman unpleasantly.

"Of course, Mrs. Harrington."

"Well, you don't look it. You look all dreamy-eyed. And now you've made me forget what I was saying!"

"You were describing eating customs in China, Mrs. Harrington."

"Was I? Oh, yes . . ."

Mrs. Harrington's entire house smelled like a huge kitty litter box. There were cats everywhere. A fat ginger-colored puss had settled on Howie's lap for a siesta, digging her claws into his groin from time to time. Three more overweight kitties lurked near his feet.

"Well, you *know* what they say about Chinamen, don't you?" she continued venomously. "They eat *everything* that flies except a B-52. And everything with legs, except the kitchen table! You think I'm kidding you?"

"Not at all, Mrs. Harrington," Howie replied patiently. But he couldn't resist adding, "*Chinese*, Mrs. Harrington—that's what we call the people who live in China. Chinaman is a pejorative."

"I'll call them anything I want to," she snapped. "I've *been* to China, young man—*you* haven't. Have you ever eaten a Thousand-Year-Old Egg? . . . I'm asking you a question!"

"No, I've never tried one," Howie admitted.

"It's an egg that's been soaked in horse urine for over a year. They consider this a delicacy. Sounds good, huh?" she cried in a high-pitched voice. "Just make sure you brush your teeth before you kiss your girlfriend!"

Mrs. Eudora Harrington was eighty-four years old, a retired public schoolteacher from Dallas. Howie had described her to Jack as a bone-thin, beady-eyed, opinionated old lady with whiskers on her chin—but even this was being chivalrous. Without doubt, she was the meanest old hag Howie had ever met in his life. She lowered her voice dramatically:

"I was in Canton in '87—the commies call the city Guangzhou now for some reason. The problem is, you can't tell a pet shop from a restaurant! They eat foxes, cats, dogs, snakes, anything at all. The poor little animals are kept *alive* in cages outside on the street. The big delicacy, of course, is monkey brains. They kill the monkey at your table, you see— they break open the skull and eat the brain while it's still hot and throbbing!"

"Please, Mrs. Harrington," Howie pleaded, "I don't really need to hear this!"

"What's the matter?" she laughed. "You're looking a little pale for a redskin! I'm surprised to find a private eye who's so squeamish!"

Mrs. Harrington smoked cigarettes and drank cheap brandy; it was hard to imagine by what odd stroke of fortune she had managed to live so long. Still, she was a client, as Jack had reminded him last night. An actual paying client, and in a small town like San Geronimo, a blind detective with an Indian assistant couldn't afford to be choosey. Howie tried to concentrate on the possible culinary end of Floozie, Miao-Miao, and Mr. Stud. He had stopped by today to report his progress (which wasn't much) and pick up some mugshots of the three missing felines. Fortunately, all of Mrs. Harrington's pussies had been well photographed.

At last she shut up, gave him an envelope with three photographs, and told him she wanted the pictures back when he was through. As she handed him the envelope, Howie had a vivid image of the old woman falling dead one day out of her rocking chair onto the floor. She had to die eventually, and with no friends or relations to check on her, only a dozen hungry, housebound cats, it wasn't difficult to picture what might happen.

Howie was so happy to escape Mrs. Harrington's claustrophobic living room that he burst into an old Lakota hunting song on his way out the door. But the image stayed with him: the corpse on the floor, the lonely decomposition of death, sharp teeth nibbling on fingers and toes and bloated organs. Cats, in his experience, were particularly fond of liver and kidneys. With an effort, he shut down his imagination. It was a dog-eat-dog world, he supposed. You just had to accept it. Even when sometimes the dogs were cats.

Howie spent the rest of the afternoon taking the three mug shots of Floozie, Miao-Miao, and Mr. Stud door to door in a five-block area around Mrs. Harrington's house. The residential area in which the old woman lived was not one of the prettiest parts of San Geronimo. There were cheap tract houses on quarter-acre lots, double-wide trailers, and small adobe homes that often had junk cars and old engine parts spread out in their front yards. The people who lived here were mostly poor Hispanic families and longtime Anglo residents—not the posh newcomer Anglos of a more recent migration, who tended to have plenty of money and had come here looking for peace and quiet and the meaning of life, the latest installment of the illusive American Dream.

Howie walked up and down Chamisa Road, Lobo Lane, and Mesa Vista. He rang doorbells and called politely through screen doors, dutifully bringing out the photos of the missing cats for housewives and husbands who looked at him like he was deranged. Several individuals slammed doors in his face and told him to go away or they would call the cops. A unshaven man with sad eyes and an Oklahoma accent gave him a copy of the New Testament. Of those who were willing to speak to an Indian on foot asking weird questions, a few claimed to have seen similar-looking cats in the neighborhood from time to time, but it was hard to say for certain. A blowzy blond woman with a can of Budweiser in her hand made it clear that, no, she had not seen these particular cats, but if pussy was on his mind, he might step inside to her bedroom. Fortunately, a private eye learned to be impervious to threats, insults, ridicule, and minor seductions.

At the end of Mesa Vista Road he came out unexpectedly onto the south end of the alley behind the strip mall where he had been the night before. There were two entrances to the alley from San Geronimo Boulevard, one at the north and one at the south end of the strip of buildings. Howie had always assumed that the pickup truck from hell had entered the alley from the main road, but he saw now that there was another possibility: It could have come down Mesa Vista from the residential neighborhood where he had been walking.

Howie crossed to the north end of the alley, passing the rear door of the Shanghai Café and the Dumpster where he had found the head. There was some torn yellow crime-scene tape near the Dumpster, but the police had apparently finished their investigation and there was no sign of the county vehicles that had converged on the severed head after Howie's 911 phone call. The alley seemed even more shabby and dispirited in the daylight than at night. There was a greasy smell of wok oil wafting from the Chinese restaurant, mixed with a sudsy aroma and the hot smell of the dryers from Anita's Wash-O-Matic. A car radio played in the distance, the bass turned up loud.

Howie stood at the precise spot where he had been parked last night on his stakeout and a shiver of fear floated up his spine. He realized he had had a close call. The killer in the pickup could have done a lot worse than smash up his car; Howie was very lucky to have survived the night with his head still attached to his shoulders. His MGB had been towed off to Fred's Foreign Auto Shop and earlier today he had received an estimate of $2,200 for the repairs. He had spoken twice to his insurance company and they were offering to give him only

$1,000, which they claimed was the full value of his car. It was all extremely annoying. Howie tried to imagine what sort of lunatic could have been driving a pickup truck with a missing headlight and a severed head lying next to him on the front seat. The guy certainly had to be drunk, careening around town with evidence of his homicide. Much of the violence in this part of the world was due to alcohol and drugs, but this homicide felt different. Nightmarish. Illogical even by the standards of weird alcoholic happenings. Howie just couldn't get a grip on it.

He stared down the alley and tried to remember the crash exactly as it had happened. The question boiled down to whether the lone headlight had appeared from the right or the left of the alley. It was hard to say exactly, but he decided that the truck had entered the alley from Mesa Vista Road, the residential area, and not from San Geronimo Boulevard, the main drag. He was almost certain of it.

The afternoon faded into a languid late-summer evening as Howie continued to canvas the neighborhood. Children played games in the streets on their bicycles. Dads in cutoff jeans stood in their driveways washing their cars; the air was scented with barbecue smoke. A summer evening like this always filled Howie with a vague nostalgia for something he had never personally known: family happiness. Maybe he would find it in his future, since it certainly hadn't existed in his past.

As Howie continued door to door, he added a new question to his list, as he was putting away his mug shots of Floozy, Miao-Miao, and Mr. Stud. He tried to make it casual:

"Hey, by the way, did you notice a pickup truck with one headlight about 12:30 last night? The guy was speeding, probably drunk as a skunk?"

Everybody shook their heads in disgust at what a problem drunk driving had become. These days in San Geronimo, everybody agreed, drunk as a skunk was mild. For some people in town, comatose as a crocodile was more the norm. New Mexico had the highest DWI rate in the nation, and it was getting worse all the time, what with methamphetamine and heroin, and every road in the county littered with cases of empty Tecate cans. But no one recalled a particular pickup truck from hell careening through the neighborhood last night. Until, at 158 Mesa Vista, Howie got a nibble.

The house was pretty much the same as the other houses on the street, an inexpensive FHA box with a built-in carport on one corner, the kind of home low-income people in New Mexico were able to finance with government loans. Still, it looked as if someone had gone to the effort to plant several apple trees in the front yard, hang colorful curtains in the windows, and make it as pretty as a little box could get. A tall redheaded woman answered the door with a pleasantly goofy smile. She was in her thirties and she looked familiar to Howie, though he couldn't imagine from where.

They stood in her front doorway while he showed her the photographs and went through his well-rehearsed spiel. She studied the pictures for a long time, really trying to be helpful. But finally she shook her head.

"No, I'm sorry, I haven't seen them. I sure wish I could help you. Cats are my favorite people—I'm nuts about them."

"Well, thanks anyway," he told her. "You know, I have this weird feeling I've met you somewhere, but I can't remember where."

She laughed. "You probably saw me at the Anasazi. I'm a waitress there. I've got the night off, thank God."

Howie remembered her now. "Right! I was there on Saturday. You were our waitress! I didn't recognize you out of context."

"Yeah, you were with that big party. I thought you looked familiar. You were the venison enchiladas, right?"

"No, I was the salmon with mango salsa," he told her. They spent a few minutes revisiting Howie's meal and comparing different restaurants in town. They bemoaned the fact that a sushi bar had just opened up in San Geronimo—by the time you had a sushi bar in a small New Mexico town, it really wasn't much of a small New Mexico town anymore. Howie liked her. She was a big, raw-boned woman with pale, milky skin and freckles. He sensed she was gay, but he had always gotten along well with gay women. It was relaxing, really, not even to have to think about flirting. It was so pleasant to have a conversation that had nothing to do with cats that Howie almost forgot to ask his final question. He had said good-bye and was walking down her path, when he remembered and turned around.

"One more thing. You didn't see a pickup truck, did you, late last night? One headlight was out, the guy who was driving was wrecked as a racoon . . ."

"About twelve-thirty? Yeah, he was loose, all right."

"You *saw* him?"

"Yeah. I was just getting home from work, unlocking my front door. He drove by like a bat out of hell. He must have been going fifty."

Howie was stunned. Everybody had been saying no to him all afternoon; he could hardly believe he was finally getting a yes. He walked back to where she was standing at the door. He needed to make sure they were talking about the same truck.

"Which direction was he going?"

"Down to where Mesa Vista comes out just behind that strip mall—it's a shortcut to San Geronimo Boulevard. I didn't see him come back this way so I guess that's where he went."

"Did you notice what sort of truck it was?"

"Sure did. It was a white '98 GMC. One of the big kind."

"You're certain of the year?"

"Yeah, I recognized it. It belongs to the restaurant. The dishwasher smashed out the left headlight a couple of nights ago playing softball out back with one of the bartenders. The boss was pissed as hell."

"Did you see who was driving?"

"No. It went by pretty fast. There are about three or four different people who use the truck, but the driver's window was closed so I couldn't tell."

"But you're positive it was the truck from the restaurant? I imagine a lot of white GMCs look pretty much the same."

"Well, I *thought* so at the time. Mostly because of the single headlight, I guess."

"Is there any sort of logo on the side that actually says 'Anasazi Grill'?"

"No. It's just a white truck. There's no writing on it."

She invited Howie inside and he spent some time going over her account. In fact, the truck had sped by very quickly and the more Howie questioned her about it, the more she acknowledged that maybe it wasn't the Anasazi Grill pickup after all. She had assumed it was, in an impressionistic way— it was certainly a *similar* truck and the missing headlight had caused her to make the leap. But there were more than a few one-eyed cars and trucks in San Geronimo County, and as she thought it over, she realized that perhaps she was mistaken.

But then again, maybe not.

The waitress's name was Sharon Pfeiffer. Howie wrote it down in his notebook, along with the names of the manager, the chef, the dishwasher, and the janitor who cleaned the restaurant each night—the four people she knew who generally had access to the vehicle.

It was 8:30 and almost completely dark when Howie left Sharon's house. He was tired. His feet hurt and his face ached from the earnest expression he tended to fix on his face while knocking on strange doors. But he was on a roll now, in no mood to quit for the night.

From Sharon's house, he drove to the Shanghai Café, entering by the front door like an actual person rather than a sneaky private eye who had to lurk around the back. It felt good to emerge from deep cover. The dining area was only a small rectangular room with twelve tables that had red oilcloth covers and white paper placemats. A few colored lanterns hung overhead in an attempt to provide some semblance of the exotic East, along with a poster showing the old palace complex, the Forbidden City in Beijing. At the far end of the room, there was a line of steam tables containing trays of food, all protected with a clear plastic sneeze-guard, the $6.99 All-You-Can-Eat dinner buffet. There were only two customers in the restaurant and they looked like out-of-towners.

One of the teenage daughters, Cherry, was sitting behind the cash register watching a quiz show on a tiny portable black-and-white TV. Howie had to clear his throat a few times to get her attention.

"Can I place a takeout order?" he said. The Chinese girl continued to watch TV blankly while Howie studied the menu, wondering what they would like to analyze at the FBI lab in Washington, D.C.

"Let's see," he meditated. "How about one sweet-and-sour chicken. One Gongbao Jiding chicken. One cashew chicken. One sweet-and-sour pork. One shredded garlic pork. The stir-fry pork with bamboo shoots. The beef with broccoli and special Mongolian sauce. An order of chicken chow mein. And maybe one of each of all the appetizers."

Cherry wrote all this down, dutifully.

"Rice?" she asked.

Howie didn't need rice, but thought he'd better order some anyway. He didn't want to look suspicious. He asked for ten orders of plain white rice, along with extra fortune cookies for his ten Sioux friends who were waiting in a van outside.

"We're on our way to a powwow in Oklahoma," he explained. "And I gotta tell you, the Sioux are nuts about Chinese food. Probably it comes from some ancestral memory, back before we migrated across the Bering Sea from Asia."

The girl smiled reluctantly, sensing that he was making a joke. Howie paid for the take-out with his Wilder & Associate credit card, a whopping $123.94. He had to wait twenty minutes until everything was ready, then he drove away with the cartons of food piled up precariously on the passenger seat of the Toyota. With so much food at hand, he felt a little silly stopping off at Bongo's Burrito Wagon on the north side of town for his own quickie dinner. However, there was no way he was going to dine on mystery meat from the Shanghai Café ever again.

He gobbled two chicken burritos in record time and figured he had done his duty to Jack, Mrs. Eudora Harrington, Floozie, Miao-Miao, and Mr. Stud, wherever they might be. He was on his own time now. Belching salsa and beans, Howard Moon Deer continued driving north to the Anasazi Grill.

6

The Anasazi Grill had a trendy Southwestern name, but whether or not San Geronimo had any actual connection to the Anasazi was a controversial matter. The local Pueblo Indians proudly claimed the great pre-Columbian civilization of Chaco Canyon as their direct ancestors, but mainstream archaeologists were often more skeptical.

The restaurant was located north of town in a converted adobe house. It was a nice rural location with a view of the mountains, but the remoteness was probably one of the reasons the restaurant had enjoyed only a brief popularity. Another reason, Howie imagined, was the pretentiously expensive *nouvelle* menu where you often ended up with one miniature enchilada in the center of a huge empty plate; the currently hip places in town tended to be looser, cheaper, and a lot more fun. Howie pulled off the highway into the parking lot at close to nine o'clock. This time of year, the summer tourist season, the place should have been jumping, but there were only three cars out front.

Howie parked near the spot where Donna Theresa had been plucked away so unceremoniously by a mysterious Tiwa-speaking stranger on Saturday night. Beautiful women like D.T. had men lurking in every spare corner of their lives, he supposed. They came with baggage. Howie imagined a youthful marriage to a local boy from the Indian Pueblo; maybe now she had different aspirations, to get her doctorate in archeology and hobnob with fancy Hollywood natives like Lester Wounds Eagle. But Mr. Youthful Mistake wasn't willing to be written off so easily, so she required a heroic PI to rescue her. Was that her problem? Howie didn't think so. He sensed it was a lot more complicated than that.

"*C-c-c-c-cannibalism!*" she had stuttered inside the restaurant, so unexpectedly. It summed her up, really. Everything about Donna Theresa was odd and unpredictable.

Howie was thinking hard about D.T., knowing he was going to need to tell Jack about her, when he noticed an elderly man and woman walking from the restaurant over the crunchy gravel toward a Cadillac DeVille with Colorado license plates.

"Oh, look, *there's* an Indian," the woman whispered loudly, pointing at Howie. "Let's ask *him*."

"Debbie, I *know* I'm right," the man told her, exasperated. He was a big red-faced man shaped like a bowling pin, over six feet tall with a size forty-four belly. She was a little woman, gray haired and petite.

"Well, *I'm* going to ask him," the woman insisted. She called over to Howie, "Excuse me—do you know what time the Pueblo opens in the morning?"

Howie walked over to their Cadillac with a helpful smile.

"About eight, I guess," he told them in a singsongy drawl he sometimes put on for tourists who wanted to meet a real Indian. He thought he had the right time, at least. The Colorado couple obviously believed he was a local and Howie didn't want to disappoint them by letting on that he was a Lakota Sioux with about as much in common with Pueblo Indians as the French had with Hungarians.

"Eight o'clock—you see, Bill, I was right. *He* said they didn't open until nine," she confided to Howie, giving her husband a sharp look. "And how much is the admission charge?"

"Five bucks," he told them. "But if you only have five does, that would probably be okay, too."

Bill laughed reluctantly. Probably he would not have caught on that Howie was joking except for the fact that the joke was about money. Bill looked like he was pretty sharp when it came to money.

"It must be wonderful to be an Indian!" the woman told Howie ardently. "I just love it how you're all so close to nature and everything!"

Howie kept grinning his slow country grin. He could tell what Bill was thinking, that it was whole lot better to be a white man with a fat gut and a big car and leave nature alone.

"Debbie, come on, we'd better let this young man be on his way." Bill pressed a remote control on his key chain and the doors of the Cadillac clicked open.

"May the Great Spirit watch over you," Howie called wisely as they climbed into their car. "And may your Cadillac never run out of gas."

The tumblers of the door locks clicked shut, like a bank vault closing, and the hermetically sealed car with the tourists from Colorado drifted off into the night.

"Hoka, hey!" Howie muttered to their taillights.

The adobe walls of the restaurant were lit up with amber spotlights and there was still an afterglow of sunset in the far western sky. Howie walked around the side of the building toward the back. He was starting to feel like he could write a book on the rears of restaurants. There were profound things one could say. Restaurant fronts entailed a certain amount of illusion, lifting the animal realities of hunger, eating, and defecation to a level of civilized chic. But at the back door, all illusions ceased. The front was the mouth, so to speak, all smiles; but the rear was the rectum, and often a bit smelly, at that.

At the rear of the Anasazi, Howie found the usual trash Dumpster, several old cars, and three pickup trucks. This was clearly where the employees parked. Someone was playing Pink Floyd from inside a brightly lit screen door that led to the kitchen. There was a whiff of marijuana smoke mixing in with the aromas from the kitchen and the ripe smell of garbage in the Dumpster. Restaurants in tourist towns like San Geronimo were generally staffed by young people who liked to party.

Howie avoided the screen door and spent some time examining the three trucks in the employee parking area. There was one GMC, but it was a dark red color and much older than 1998. The two other trucks were Japanese, a Datsun and a Mitsubishi, both much too small to have been the truck from hell he had seen in the alley. He gave the red GMC a closer inspection, since it was the only possible suspect among the three. As far as he could tell, both headlights were intact and it certainly didn't match the waitress's description. So either Howie had reached a dead end, detectively speaking, or the Anasazi Grill truck was off somewhere on an errand, perhaps delivering more body parts to various alleys in town.

He was about to call it quits when the screen door from the kitchen burst open and three men tumbled outside in a blur of motion, grunting with effort and pain. One of them fell hard onto the ground near the front fender of an old Volvo, while the other two began kicking and pounding at him with their fists. All three were in their twenties and looked like Indians. It was an unequal fight, two against one, which bothered Howie. The guy on the ground was definitely having a hard time of it. He was trying to curl up in a ball and protect his head with his arms, but the other two were doing their best to uncurl him so they could get at him better. They were all shouting at one another in Tiwa, which left Howie out of the communication loop. No one had noticed him in the shadows near the GMC truck.

Howie looked around helplessly for a weapon with which to intervene, spotting a fifty-gallon plastic garbage drum that was half full of aluminum for recycling. Maybe he could hoist the garbage can above his head and bring it down not so lightly on Indians #1 and #2 so that Indian #3 could escape. He sensed this might result in complications for his own person, but he had to try something because he couldn't stand to see two against one.

The garbage drum was heavier than it looked. Howie had just managed to raise the thing above his head when a fourth man appeared in the back doorway, throwing open the screen.

"Hey, what the hell's going on here?" he bellowed.

He was a very large white man dressed in a kitchen uniform and wielding a huge knife in his right hand. His head was shaved, his bare arms were covered with tatoos, and his voice had the ring of authority. Howie sensed he was the chef.

"Goddamn Indians!" he roared. "If you gotta fight, do it on

your own time. Now get back in here—I need some frying pans washed and a tub of salsa for the bar."

Indians #1 and #2 moved away from the figure on the ground, smiling apologetically, smoothing out the food-splattered kitchen aprons. Indian #3 got to his feet more slowly, breathing hard, his face bleeding in several places. He wore a waterproof black plastic apron and Howie imagined he must be the dishwasher. This would make him Charlie, according to the list from Sharon the waitress of people who sometimes drove the restaurant truck.

"So what the hell's this all about?" the skinhead chef demanded, forgetting momentarily his need for frying pans and salsa.

"Charlie was trying to steal some beer, man. A case of Bud. I caught him at it," said Indian #1. He was a big, mean-looking mother, close to three hundred pounds.

"Yeah, he was carrying it out the back door," said Indian #2, who was lean and ratty-looking. "This sort of thing reflects bad on us, you know. So we was teaching him a lesson."

"Were you?" The skinhead chef shook his head disgustedly. "So that's where the goddamn beer's been going! Well, what you got to say for yourself, Charlie?"

Charlie managed to unbend himself and stand fully upright. He had a stubby body; in a few years, he would probably be seriously fat, but now he was merely plump. His face was round and pleasant. A humorous face, Howie thought, even scrunched up in pain. He reminded Howie of an overweight kid he had known in the sixth grade, a joker who was always throwing spitballs at people.

"So?" the chef insisted.

Charlie managed a weak smile. "Ain't true, man," he said, wiping his bloody nose with the back of his hand.

"You're saying they're lying?"

"I'm saying if I was going to steal beer, I'd go for the Guinness, *not* the Bud."

Howie was impressed by the answer; in times of adversity, it was vital to stand on firm gourmet principles. But the chef with the knife wasn't buying it.

"You're fired. Frankly, I don't give a shit who's telling the truth, and who isn't—you're the slowest goddamn dishwasher I've ever seen and I'm sick of your smirking face. You can wait here while I get your pay, and then get the hell out."

Indians #1 and #2 were looking ready to stomp Charlie again, now that the boss had rallied to their side. But the chef wasn't having it. "Come on, you two," he said. "You're both washing dishes tonight! So get back inside."

The chef and Indians #1 and #2 filed back inside the screen door. When they were alone, Charlie turned toward where Howie was standing in the shadows.

"Thanks for thinking about helping me," Charlie said, nodding his head at the garbage can that Howie had lowered back to the ground.

"Well, I didn't do much."

"No, you didn't."

"So what's this all about?" Howie asked.

"What does it look like? I saw a case of long-neck Bud and I went crazy with lust for the white man's firewater. You know how it is. Anything for a high."

Howie walked closer and smelled the pungent aroma of marijuana clinging to Charlie's clothes and hair. His eyes were red and his grin wasn't entirely natural, under the circumstances. Howie wasn't sure if being stoned made getting beat up better or worse.

"Are you hurt?"

"Man, that was some tumble! But I'm okay. Hey, didn't I see you here the other night with my cousin?"

"I don't think so."

"Sure I did. D.T. The beautiful Donna Theresa. You were at a table with her."

"She's your cousin?"

Charlie's nose was still bleeding. He leaned his head back and wiped again with the back of his hand. "Whew!" he said. "What a trip, man!"

"Tell me about D.T."

"Hey, we're all related on the Pueblo, bro. One big happy family. Do you play drums?"

"No, I don't play drums."

"You should come join the drum circle some night. There's always room for a Lakota brother from the icy north."

Howie studied Charlie more closely. "Who told you I'm Lakota?"

Charlie's grin got wider. "What? You think you can keep a secret in a small town?"

"Tell me something. Do you drive the restaurant truck?"

"Hey, sure. You bet. I used to, anyway, before I got my ass fired."

"A white GMC? One headlight out?"

"Them's the wheels, bro. I haven't seen them around in a few days, though. Sometimes the manager takes the truck when he's cruising for pussy. A white guy named Brad."

"What do you mean exactly, cruising for pussy?" Howie asked suspiciously.

Charlie laughed. "Jesus, don't you Lakota brothers know about the birds and the bees?"

Howie sighed. "So you don't know who was using the truck last night?"

"I was off last night, man. Sometimes I do other things besides wash dishes, y'know. Hey, look, if you know anybody who wants to buy ounces, I'm selling lids for two hundred bucks. It's last year's crop, but real nice buds. I can give you a sample if you'd like."

It was a big change of subject. Howie was about to tell Charlie, no, he had left marijuana back in his distant undergraduate past, when the skinhead chef reappeared, bursting out angrily from the screen door.

"Here's your goddamn money," he said, handing Charlie an envelope. "Now take a hike."

"Gladly." Charlie flashed Howie a final ironic smile. "Well, I guess I'm going to have to tear myself away from all this fun. See you around, Moon Deer."

Howie watched Charlie stroll over to one of the clunky old cars parked at the rear of the restaurant, a Corolla that had seen better days, start up the engine, and drive away. He wondered how Charlie knew his name. While he was wondering, the chef turned his way.

"All right. Now who are *you*? Seems we got ourselves a regular powwow here. Maybe you were helping Charlie lift the beer, huh?"

"Hey, not me!" Howie assured him, taking a step back. "I was just walking around back here, and all of a sudden there's a brawl in my way. I didn't like the odds."

"You just *happened* to be walking back here?" the white man repeated with sarcasm.

"I heard there was a truck for sale. A white GMC," Howie tried. "I thought I'd check it out. Sharon told me about it."

"*Waitress* Sharon?"

"Yeah. She told me she worked here. We were talking about trucks, you know. She had the idea that the white GMC here, the restaurant truck, was for sale and said I should have a look."

The skinhead chef seemed puzzled. "She told you that?"

"Well, maybe I got it a little wrong. The Jimmy isn't for sale, huh?"

"No, the Jimmy ain't for sale," he said fiercely, "because the Jimmy's been *stolen*—you dig?"

"Stolen? No kidding. Did you report it to the cops?"

"You bet I reported it to the cops." The chef was staring at Howie in an increasingly suspicious manner. "And maybe *you* had something to do with stealing it? Is that what you're doing here, giving me this bullshit story?"

Howie backed away from the screen door because the monstrous chef was advancing on him.

"Wait a minute, why would I steal a truck and then come back here? Listen, I think we have a misunderstanding."

"You bet we have a misunderstanding!" the chef growled. But he didn't come any closer. "What a goddamn job *this* shithole has turned out to be! Man, I should have stayed at the Holiday Inn!"

Howie saw an opening. "So who owns this place, anyway?" But the chef wasn't biting.

"Get lost," he told Howie without much energy. He shook

his head and disappeared back inside the kitchen, slamming the screen door behind him.

Howie stood in indecision for several moments before walking back to the Toyota pickup. It bothered him that the dishwasher had known his name and that he was D.T's cousin. Everything about the Anasazi Grill felt wrong. As far as Howie could tell, life was not such a merry fiesta on this particular link of the food chain.

7

Howie pulled off the highway onto a shoulder and called Jack on his cell phone. Rural New Mexico roads are lonely places at night, lost in a great dark nowhere, and Howie felt a tug of melancholy.

Jack's wife, Emma, answered the phone. Howie waited while she went to get Jack in the living room where he was playing a slow blues riff on the piano. Jack wasn't exactly Ray Charles, but he wasn't bad for a blind player. As Howie listened, the music stopped and a moment later Jack came on the line.

"I got the Chinese takeout," Howie told him. "I think I'll just drive it up to Denver tonight instead of UPSing it to Kevin in the morning. To tell you the truth, I'm all turned around sleepwise and I'd just as soon be driving as tossing in bed."

"That head's still bothering you, huh?"

"It's hard to shake the image of it, Jack. Not to mention the smell."

"Well, I'll give Kevin a call so he'll be expecting you."

Special Agent Kevin Neiymer of the Denver office of the FBI was an old friend of Jack's and had agreed to forward the cartons of food to Washington for analysis. Denver was only a five-hour drive from San Geronimo, over the La Veta Pass, then up I-25 along the eastern edge of the Front Range, and Howie was in the mood for restless, late-night motion.

He spent some time telling Jack about his progress today: the meeting with Mrs. Harrington and Sharon the waitress, the white GMC truck with one headlight, and the violence behind the Anasazi Grill. He was expecting Jack to be angry over the fact that he had been investigating the Case of the Severed Head alongside the Great Pussycat Caper, but Jack was too much of a cop not to appreciate a good lead when he heard one. He said he would call in the information to Captain Ed Gomez of the state police. Meanwhile, Jack would phone Mrs. Harrington to tell her they were suspending her case until they received the lab results on the Chinese food.

"So be happy," Jack told him. "Stop searching for the meaning of life. Do something fun for yourself. Spend a few days in Colorado if you like."

"Yeah, sure," Howie told him. "Look, there's one more thing. I met a girl today."

"Really? That's good news!"

"I highly doubt it. She was asking some strange questions about Shanghai Man—whether the head had any jewelry on it."

"What's the girl's name?"

"Donna Theresa. I don't know her last name, or anything much about her."

"Well, tell me what you know."

Howie gave Jack an abbreviated account of the mysterious Donna Theresa, leaving out how he had met her last Saturday night in a social setting. He would come to that eventually, he supposed, if it proved to be necessary, but meanwhile he wanted to keep his description of her as impersonal as possible. Frankly, he was reluctant to speak of her at all. He wasn't entirely sure why. Maybe it was her stutter, the sense he had that she was very vulnerable under her mask of fashionable indifference.

"Anyway, I'm not even sure why she came to see me," Howie admitted. "She might know someone missing who wears an earring, but maybe not."

"I'll pass it on to Captain Gomez. Meanwhile, when you get back, try to find out more about her. She's beautiful, I suppose?"

"Come on, Jack! How the hell can you infer something like that?"

"I hear it in your voice. The way you say her name. Donna Theresa. Like she's an opera in three acts."

With a sigh, Howie disconnected and drove from the shoulder back onto the open highway, heading north. His headlights ate up the empty miles of asphalt between New Mexico and Colorado. After a while, he turned on the radio and listened to distant stations playing late-night music of love and loss.

Driving into Walsenburg, Colorado, a memory tried to surface in Howie's mind. It sputtered and gurgled and finally worked its way fully into his consciousness as he was speeding through Colorado Springs on the interstate. It was a very bad memory from early childhood: watching helplessly as two men held his father while a third man beat him unconscious with a stick. It was probably the reason he had been so upset at the sight of the kitchen workers beating up on Charlie, two against one.

As far as Howie could reconstruct it, his memory came from about 1974, which would have made him five years old at the time. There had been big trouble among the Sioux tribes of South Dakota in those days. Two FBI agents had been killed at Pine Ridge, but worse than that, as far as the Indians were concerned, was the strife among themselves: between those who had called themselves "traditionalists," supporting the American Indian Movement (AIM), and the others, the "progressives," who had backed the corrupt tribal president, Dick Wilson, and his goons. The whole matter was extremely acrimonious and complex, and it had resulted in a good deal of violence and death among the Sioux. Bad feelings lingered even to this day.

At the age of five, Howie had not grasped much of what was happening among his people, except for the fact that there was a shadow of fear over everyone, and the adults always seemed to be speaking in angry voices. He knew now that his father had been a progressive, one of the goons, so the men who had beaten him must have been AIM guys. As an adult, talking with people and reading through the old accounts, Howie's own sympathies lay more with the anti–Dick Wilson

contingent and AIM, which made the whole thing even more
complicated in his mind. There was no beginning or end to
such poison: son against father, brother versus brother, a tribe
divided in hatred. You would think Indians had enough problems without turning on themselves. But this was the way it
always was among the poor and disenfranchised.

Howie replayed old scenes from childhood all the way to
Denver. He woke SA Kevin Neimeyer at his suburban home at
four in the morning, dropped off the Chinese food, refused
breakfast when Kevin finally yawned himself awake, then
sped back south before the morning commuter traffic could
block his escape. On the journey home, his inner movie theater changed from violence to sex. He thought about Donna
Theresa, how beautiful she was, and how complex: her passive, sullen, I-don't-give-a-shit exterior that revealed only an
occasionally glimpse of the fireworks inside.

He was intrigued by the fact that she was an archeologist,
about to start work on her PhD, obviously no dumb bunny. It
gave them something in common, an intellectual bond. This
was very alluring for Howie, a mental aphrodisiac. And there
was another matter, too: For a number of months now, Howie
had been thinking that it would be good for him to be involved
with a Native American woman at this time of his life.
Frankly, he got away with a certain amount of bullshit with the
left-leaning, arty Anglo types with whom he was generally involved—bright women, certainly, but they were always just a
little too thrilled with the romantic notion of being involved
with an Indian, and probably cut him too much slack. Naturally, he would not be able to get away with such things with
Donna Theresa. He would be forced into a greater honesty . . .
yet thinking about honesty (whizzing through Pueblo, Colorado) reminded him that she had lied, and that he would be a
fool to lose his head over her.

"Maybe I only want to go to bed with the lady!" Howie said
to himself, trying his best to get down to true motives. It
seemed a little shallow, looking at it that way. But my God,
she was sexy, he was single, and biology had a certain insis-
tence that was hard to ignore. It wasn't just the way she

looked, but the energy she sent out. That smoldering passive vulnerability that made a horny guy want to kiss her silly. He wondered what she looked like naked. In fact, he could imagine her body very well ...

Stop it, Moon Deer! You need a cold bath, a good long run, and something else to think about!

Dawn came while Howie was in the mountains, recrossing La Veta Pass. The dawn was so pure and clean and philosophical that Howie felt suddenly almost monastic. He soaked in the rays of a new, unsullied day and decided he didn't need a woman, after all; he would live a simple life without sex or emotional attachments. He would be complete in himself, as the New Agers liked to say.

It sounded fine. And best of all, when he was unneedful of sex, complete in himself—one hell of a strong, independent, guy, almost a guru—then all the women were obviously going to melt into puddles at the very sight of him and he wouldn't have to be so boringly complete in himself after all.

Howie arrived back in San Geronimo late Thursday morning to a hot summer day and roads that were clogged with RVs with out of-state license plates and bicycles, canoes, and lawn chairs tied to their roofs. He stopped at the Texaco station at the northern end of town, filled up the tank of the Toyota, then bought a large coffee, a semistale Danish pastry, and a quart of orange juice, then sat in the shade of a cottonwood at a picnic table outside the minimart with the local newspaper.

The San Geronimo Post came out once a week on Thursdays, complete with classified ads, the latest municipal scandals, and other juicy tidbits of local life. The headline this week was larger than usual: HUMAN HEAD FOUND IN ALLEY. Howie's own name was mentioned prominently in the story. It was strange to read about himself, a kind of dislocation, but the story didn't tell him anything he did not already know. After nearly two days, the owner of the head had still not been identified. Nor had the rest of the body been found. Nor did there appear to have been any progress at all on the case. As Howie had learned yesterday from his friend at KSGR, the

San Geronimo Police Department had wisely turned the case over to the New Mexico State Police, who had more resources to handle a major homicide investigation. Captain Ed Gomez, the officer in charge of the San Geronimo State Police substation, was quoted as saying, "We are pursuing several leads, but at the moment we have not yet been able to identify the victim of this brutal crime."

The *Post* mentioned in passing that this was the fourth homicide of the year in San Geronimo, and not one of the subsequent investigations had resulted in an arrest. It was an artistic little town, but it was a violent town as well, and killers tended to vanish without a trace. Meanwhile, as Jack had predicted, the human remains had been sent to OMI in Albuquerque. Notably, the article said nothing about the unusual earring or even the fact that the head had been found in a trash Dumpster; these were the sort of withheld details that gave the police a better hand to play when it came to separating false confessions from true.

Howie gurgled down the last of the orange juice, then plucked the cell phone from his pocket to check in with Jack.

"Where *are* you?" Jack answered briskly.

"I'm just outside of town, at the Texaco station."

"Good, you're back. Come over right away, please. Gomez has stopped by and he wants to talk to you about your head."

"*My* head?"

"You know what head I mean. Now stop screwing around. We've got a problem on our hands."

"I'll head right over, Jack," Howie said, disconnecting before Jack could groan.

Howie parked alongside Captain Ed Gomez's shiny black state police cruiser in Jack's driveway. He found Jack and Ed in the kitchen, a snug, old-fashioned room with lots of wood and multipaned windows that opened out onto the green shade of the garden. It was a farmhouse kitchen as visualized by expat Californians who wouldn't know a real American farmhouse if it hit them over the head. Just about everything in the room looked as if it had been bought at Macy's—from their

Southwest Collection, no doubt. There were expensive pots
and graphite pans hanging from the viga beams overhead, a
thick round oak table crowded with potted herbs, two rocking
chairs, and every cooking gadget known to man.

Jack was standing at the stove stirring a pot with a wooden
spoon. He was wearing an apron that had KING OF THE RANGE
written on the front at the exact place where his stomach made
a pregnant bump. Under the apron, he was dressed in baggy
blue sweatpants, food-splattered sneakers, an inside-out T-
shirt, and his usual wraparound dark glasses perched on his
nose. Captain Gomez, dressed more conservatively in a crisp
black New Mexico State Police uniform, was seated at the oak
table in one of the rocking chairs, shelling peas. There was a
rich aroma in the air, something simmering in wine sauce.

"What's cooking?" Howie asked.

"Chicken *cacciatore,*" Jack answered from the stove. "With
a few improvements on the recipe, naturally." Jack was the
cook in the Wilder family and he generally made up large
batches of food in advance, often taking a morning off to make
certain he and Emma would not go hungry at night. He was a
fabulous cook with a multi-ethnic repertoire, but his cuisine
was not exactly low-fat. Howie watched as Jack dumped a pint
of sour cream into the pot. If you weren't careful, you could
gain five pounds just breathing the air here.

Howie turned his attention back to Ed.

"How's the dating game going, Ed?"

"Not so good," Ed Gomez admitted. "Though I almost got
lucky Sunday night."

Ed's wife had left him a few years back after twenty-three
years of marriage; he was fifty-six years old and trying to
learn how to date again. Howie and Ed often shared their tales
of romantic woe, though from different sides of the genera-
tional divide.

"So what happened?" Howie urged.

"Well, I met a lady Sunday afternoon on Highway 72.
Florida plates, a late-model BMW, powder blue. Nice machine."

"Yeah, Ed—but what was the lady like?"

"Well, she was fast. That's what she was like. She was doing over seventy in a fifty-five zone, so I pulled her over to give her a ticket. Normally I don't do traffic citations, but I guess I had a feeling about her right from the start. She was brunette, early forties, very attractive. Nice, somehow, too. She had kind eyes. Know what I mean?"

"And you slapped her with a speeding ticket!" Howie laughed. "I gotta tell you, that's not an especially romantic way to make a seduction."

"Don't be a smart-ass, Howie. She was a tourist, she didn't know the roads, so I ended up giving her a verbal warning. No ticket. I was chivalrous."

"You flirted, I hope. Made goo-goo eyes. Stroked your gun in a suggestive manner . . ."

"Are you telling this story, or am I? She asked me about local hotels and restaurants and we talked for a while, that's all. But somehow it was very nice leaning in her car window, talking together at the side of the road. It just felt comfortable. Finally she said that the reason she was in New Mexico was her husband in Orlando had just run off with some young bimbo who worked at Disney World. I told her that was real goofy of him—"

"Come on, you didn't say that! *Goofy?*"

"Well, yeah. I did. Then I mentioned how my own marriage had crashed recently, too. Well, we kept on talking for maybe another ten minutes and then I said, 'Hey, why don't you have dinner with me tonight?' She said that sounded like a very sweet offer. So we made a date to meet at seven o'clock at the Blue Mesa. I told her where the restaurant was, even drew her a little map. Then I sort of floated back to the station and looked forward to it all day."

"And how did it go at the Blue Mesa?"

Ed shook his head. "Well, she didn't come. I waited for her until eight-thirty, had a few margaritas, then I drove home."

Howie didn't know whether to laugh or cry. Captain Ed Gomez had lived in San Geronimo all his life. He was a dry man, generally understated, gaunt and wiry; dry in wit and from a lifetime in the New Mexico sun. He was quite a dapper gentleman, almost handsome with sliver hair and a thin well-trimmed mustache. But he seemed to be shrinking inside his uniform from year to year, and his neck was so leathery he reminded Howie of a turtle poking out from its shell.

"How was Denver?" Ed asked finally, glad to change the subject.

"Denver was dandy. Kevin says hello to everybody."

"Does he?" Ed turned from Howie to Jack. "You know, sometimes I wish I'd joined the FBI instead of the damn state police. Maybe I would have had the pleasure of solving a crime occasionally."

"Well, the Fee-Bees just have a whole lot more money to throw around," Jack told him consolingly. "And good training. And of course, the best crime lab in the world. That's the only difference between you and them, Ed. They've got everything and you've got nothing. Howie, bring me a string of garlic from the pantry. You'll find a jar of cumin back there, too—you'd better get that as well."

Katya had positioned herself on the kitchen floor near Jack's legs, wagging her tail hopefully, her long snout alert for any food that might fall her way. As a blind cook, Jack was astonishing, mincing and mixing and knowing exactly where everything was in his kitchen; nevertheless, a lot of food generally ended up on the floor. Howie fetched the garlic and cumin from the back pantry, then sat at the kitchen table and helped Ed with the peas.

"By the way, thanks for the lead about the white truck from the Anasazi Grill," Ed said. "I spoke to that waitress, Sharon, this morning and had her give a statement."

"Have you found the truck yet?"

"No. The manager at the Anasazi is a guy named Brad Mallory and he *did* report it stolen—but get this, not until Wednesday morning, *after* your encounter in the alley. He said it had been missing for several days. Monday night is the last time anyone at the restaurant saw it for certain."

"That seems kind of vague."

"You bet it's vague. And I pressed him on it. Mallory said that several people use the truck, they all have their own keys, and for a couple of days everybody thought that someone *else* had it. That's his story, anyway. Then they got together and realized that none of them had it, so it must have been stolen. I have one of my officers questioning the staff right now, trying to get all their stories straight. I sense they party hearty over there and coherence isn't anyone's strong point."

"Speaking of the point, Ed . . ." Jack put in from the stove.

"Yes, yes, I'm *getting* to the point, Jack, in my own goddamn way, thank you very much . . . now where was I? Your head is causing us a bit of a problem," he mentioned, turning back to Howie.

"I wish everybody would stop calling it *my* head. Frankly, Ed, I'm glad to give up any proprietary claims on the thing—let's make it *your* head, okay?"

"Did you read the *Post* this morning?"

Howie nodded.

"Well, the *Post* got it right for a change. We still haven't ID'd the damn thing. So far, OMI has told us it's *probably* male, an average-sized man aged somewhere between thirty to sixty, and most likely he's been dead anywhere from twenty-four hours to three weeks. The head was in such bad shape that these are only approximations—sex, age, time of death, we really can't say very much for certain. At the moment, the only really definite thing we have to go on is the earring."

"I assumed a single earring in the left lobe meant it must be a guy," Howie said.

"There may have been a second earring that got lost," Jack warned from the stove. "What do I always tell you, Howie?"

"Don't assume anything," Howie repeated dutifully. "Did you find out what kind of animal tooth it was?"

"Well, this is interesting. Take a guess," Ed told him.

"It looked like a predator of some kind. A bear? A coyote, maybe?"

"A shark. Some kind of reef shark, according to the people in Albuquerque. Which means this probably isn't a local person. The chances are the victim was a tourist, or at least a newcomer."

"A local person might have bought the earring from some-one at a flea market. Or stolen it," Jack suggested.

"Possibly," Ed agreed, "I've never seen anyone around here with a shark's tooth earring, but who knows? Some of our local Rainbow People get fairly elaborate in their personal adornment. In any case, we don't have a single missing person report of anyone who even comes close to matching the vic-tim. We've checked with all the surrounding states as well, of course. Texas, Oklahoma, Colorado, Arizona—there are plenty of missing persons, but nothing that would really figure with your head."

"*Your* head," Howie reminded.

"Just out of curiosity, did you get a good look at the thing. Did you really *see* it?"

"Only for a second," Howie admitted. "Once I realized what it was, I got sort of grossed out and turned away."

"For chrissake, *tell* him, Ed!" Jack said impatiently.

"Tell me what?"

"Okay, but this is something we're keeping totally to our-selves. This absolutely cannot get out. You understand, Howie?"

"Of course. Now what's the big secret?"

"There's a forensic anthropologist coming in from Arizona tomorrow to look at the thing, and the people at OMI are plan-ning to run a lot more tests next week. So this is only tentative. But what they believe so far, Howie—at the moment, at least—is that what you found was the remains of someone's dinner."

After such a big build-up, Howie wasn't certain he was un-derstanding correctly what Ed was saying. "Dinner? An ani-mal had been eating on it?"

"Yup. The sort of animal who could roast a human head on a bed of coals, then break open the front of the skull with a heavy instrument, then season the insides with salt, pepper, and a few dabs of extra-virgin olive oil. Are you starting to get the picture?"

Howie was starting to get the picture. "The head was . . . cooked?"

"Howie, the head was not only cooked, it was partially eaten. OMI found utensil marks on the inside of the skull where it looks like someone scraped away part of the brain with a spoon. Interesting that it was found behind a restaurant. Makes you think, doesn't it?"

"In fact, *two* restaurants are involved," Jack mentioned. "The Anasazi Grill and the Shanghai Café. Personally, I'm not planning to eat out in this town again any time soon."

Howie had stopped listening. He felt nauseous and his head was hot. He didn't even groan aloud when Jack made an atrociously sick joke about how places like the Anasazi Grill were fine, except they cost you an arm and a leg.

"C-c-c-cannibalism . . ." Howie said thoughtfully.

"What?" Jack asked turning his dark glasses on Howie like twin barrels of a shotgun.

Howie shook his head sadly. "Nothing. I was just wishing I lived on a different planet, that's all. Someone once told me Pluto's perfect this time of year . . ."

Jack and Ed continued to discuss the grim forensic details, not noticing how quiet Howie had become. It seemed to excite their law-enforcement brains that there was a cannibal on the loose in the arty little town of San Geronimo.

8

Secrets seldom stay secret long in small New Mexico towns. Howie had discovered the mysterious head on Tuesday night—early Wednesday morning, to be exact. Captain Gomez visited Jack's kitchen on Thursday, and by Friday, the news that there was a cannibal in town was everywhere. How the news had leaked out, no one could precisely say. Howie only knew that he had not been the one to blab.

On Friday morning, Howie woke after nearly ten hours of sleep and drove to his favorite downtown haunt, the New Wave Café, for his favorite power breakfast: a double cappuccino and bear claw. The New Wave was a center of town gossip and Howie listened with astonishment to the wild stories that were being told at every table.

Some said a baby had been eaten, others that it was a young woman—no one got it entirely right. Jimbo the jeweler assured his friends that the whole thing was the work of a Satanic cult. Shasta, a New Age real estate agent who had made a fortune selling ecologically correct solar homes, believed aliens from outer space were involved. Someone else said that the Los Alamos Lab sixty miles away was obviously to blame—they were conducting weird experiments on human beings. Biff Crane, a big shot in the local Green Party, announced that this was the sort of thing you had to expect in a nation dominated unfairly by a corrupt two-party system. In San Geronimo, Green politics had spawned several small-town demagogues like Biff, contractors and chiropractors in real life who had visions of personal grandeur and quarreled among themselves rancorously as to the proper road to power, thereby creating several opposing factions: Green, Greener-Than-Thou, and Greenest Still.

Howie listened to all the talk in mute despair. A number of people had seen his name in the paper and pestered him for the inside scoop. But he only smiled and said, *"Please*, not while I'm eating breakfast!" Nevertheless, thoughts of cannibalism nibbled away at his peace of mind. He wasn't certain why he had not spoken more fully about Donna Theresa to Jack and Ed, for she certainly knew something: It was too much of a co-incidence that she had mentioned cannibalism last Saturday night, and that yesterday she had known details of the murder that had not been released to the public. Howie had been partially honest, he supposed: He had told Jack about D.T.'s visit to his cabin, though in such a way that he had deliberately minimized its importance, implying that the gossip grapevine in San Geronimo was such that she might have heard about the earring in an innocent manner—from a cop friend, say, or a blabbermouth county official. In fact, Howie did not believe this. She needed to be questioned, but meanwhile her stutter filled him with a vague sense of chivalry and gave him pause. Yes, she had lied, but she seemed so troubled and alone that he could not quite find it in himself to be angry. She confused him in a slightly delicious way, and he wasn't sure whether to give into his romantic inclinations or his suspicions. It would be easier, he thought grimly, if she weren't so damn lovely.

As for the crime itself, it was horrendous. From a culinary psycho-sociological perspective, cannibalism was the ultimate food taboo. For Howie, it was the idea of the extra-virgin olive oil, for some reason, that made the idea of eating a human brain particularly hideous. He kept thinking about it. What sort of ghoul would baste his dinner in olive oil? A gourmet, perhaps—which in this instance was terrifying.

He had been surprised that a forensic lab could come up with such detailed information—extra-virgin olive oil, no less, not just regular olive oil—but Ed Gomez assured him that this was routine. The old-fashioned method of chemical analysis (Ed had lectured) was carried out by a piece of equipment known as a spectrophotometer. The unknown substance was placed into a solution, which was then subjected to various light sources; its reactions were recorded by computer, then compared to the known reactions of various substances in a database. Both Ed and Jack could talk about things like this for hours, the nifty machinery of modern criminology, and their faces always lit up with a kind of boyish enthusiasm— like ski fanatics debating the new technology of shaped skis, or computer geeks discussing gigabytes.

Unfortunately for crime nerds, spectrophotometers weren't quite as nifty as they sounded, and plenty of mistakes had been made in the past. So a new technology had been invented and the leading edge of forensic analysis was now done by a process known as Scanning Electron Microscopy, or SEM. The machines cost over $100,000 apiece, so not everybody had one, but there did happen to be an SEM device in Albuquerque at the Office of the Medical Investigator, a lab run by the University of New Mexico. It was this technology that had identified traces of extra-virgin olive oil, which Howie suspected he would never be able to use happily on a salad again.

After breakfast, he drove to Calle Santa Margarita, picked up Jack and Katya and ferried them back downtown to the Wilder & Associate office, which was located on the second floor of an old adobe building just off a small courtyard in the historical district. There was no interesting mail waiting for them at the office. No news from the FBI lab in Washington regarding the Chinese takeout. Nothing but bills, an Eddie Bauer catalog, and some personal mail for Jack.

Howie helped Jack get installed behind his desk with his mail and his new Kurzweil reading machine for the blind, another nifty device—like a photocopy machine, only it was able to turn printed words into robotlike human speech when you put a page against the glass. Once Jack was taken care of, Howie led Katya back downstairs to the truck, to take her for her yearly appointment with the vet. He was very fond of Katya, but it was starting to seem like he was always getting relegated to animal duty of one kind or another. Halfway to the vet, a thunderstorm broke unexpectedly, a deluge from heaven. "My God, now it's even raining cats and dogs!" he muttered to Katya.

Dr. Greyson, the vet, worked out of his ranch house ten miles north of town, and like everybody else in San Geronimo, he seemed to know more about the local case of cannibalism than Howie. He assured Howie that the whole thing was the work of Christian Fundamentalists who were disappointed the world hadn't ended on January 1, 2000 and were busy getting revenge, eating all the people who had laughed at their erroneous predictions. This made as much sense as anything else Howie had heard.

On the return ride to town, both Howie and Katya were subdued—Katya, because she hated getting shots, and Howie because he was wondering if the world was really as crazy as it seemed. The rain had settled into a dreary drizzle and Howie had the windshield wipers slapping back and forth at their lowest speed, like a metronome ticking out a sad, slow waltz. Coming into town, the road wound past several miles of open range to the east, an expanse of high desert that climbed into the piñon-covered foothills. This was Indian land, part of the 90,000-acre reservation that belonged to the San Geronimo Pueblo.

Howie was just leaving Pueblo land when he saw a figure walking on the side of the highway. It was an old Indian man with long silver hair pleated in two braids down his back. He was dressed in a straw cowboy hat, a checkered shirt, jeans, and pointed cowboy boots. Howie slowed down to offer him a lift, for it was a custom that Indians always offered other Indians a ride.

"Hey, grandfather, want a ride?" Howie cried, reaching over Katya to lower the passenger side window.

The old man turned and smiled. "You bet, Moon Deer!" he greeted.

Howie was so surprised, he was momentarily speechless. "Raymond!" he managed. "What the hell are you doing out here in the rain?"

"Oh, I'm going to town. I woke up this morning saying to

myself, 'Hey, old man, it's time to see what all those crazy palefaces are doing with themselves!'"

Howie pulled on the emergency brake and hurried out of the cab to put Katya in the back and give the old man a hand. This wasn't any old Indian, it was Raymond Concha, the *cacique*, the spiritual elder of the San Geronimo Pueblo. The old man had a face that was as weathered and craggy as a granite mountain. His eyes were a faded brown, hard and predatory, like a hawk. God only knew how old he was.

"For chrissake, why didn't you get someone to drive you, Raymond? You're not such a young guy anymore."

Raymond slipped into the passenger seat with a sigh of pleasure to get off his feet. "Well, I was waiting for you, Moon Deer," he said cheerfully.

"For *me?*"

"Of course, for you. You stopped, didn't you? So why should I have someone else drive me and waste a whole bunch of gas?"

Howie grinned at this piece of irrefutable logic.

"Come on, Moon Deer. Don't stand there like a donkey. Let's go see your white man."

"*My* white man?"

"Sure. That white cop fella you work for."

"Jack? But Raymond, he's a private detective. What in the world do you need to see a private detective about?"

"I'd be glad to explain it to you, little brother, except for the fact that we're in a hurry. My granddaughter just called on my cell phone"—he proudly tapped the small plastic device in the pocket of his cowboy shirt—"and said your Jack Wilder is expecting us in twenty minutes. So we'd better not dawdle."

Howie closed Raymond's door and walked around the truck to the driver's side, wondering what all this could mean. He drove nearly a mile down the highway before certain bells and lights started going off in his mind.

"Your granddaughter?" he questioned. "She's tall, beautiful, shiny black hair down to her waist, about twenty-three years old?"

Raymond nodded happily. "That's Donna Theresa. All the

young bucks go into a kind of swoon when they see her. But personally, I wouldn't get fuzzy-headed about her, if I were you. A girl like that, she'd eat up a guy like you for a midday snack and hardly even have indigestion. Are you hearing me, Moon Deer, or should I write this down on a piece of paper?"

Howie heard the *cacique*'s advice as if from a great distance.

Donna Theresa Concha! The name flowed like running water. She was the *cacique*'s granddaughter. The information completed her somehow, put her into focus. Just as they were approaching the downtown plaza, the rain stopped and the sun came out from behind a thundercloud, illuminating the little red Toyota pickup truck in a blazing swath of light.

9

"Well, well! I've certainly heard a great deal about you, Mr. Concha," Jack Wilder was saying, on his best behavior. "When your granddaughter phoned, she told me you don't get to town much these days. I imagine you've seen a lot of changes in San Geronimo over your lifetime."

"Oh, you betcha," said the old *cacique*. "People just keep moving here. When I was a young man, I didn't know there were so many people in the whole damn world. Tourists. Skiers. And holy shit—now we have a big-shot cop from California!"

Raymond pronounced the state, "Califor-nai-yea"—which was laying it on a little thick, Howie thought. Jack smiled, unperturbed.

"It must feel like an invasion, all of us outsiders," Jack sympathized.

Raymond laughed, a mirthless *tee-hee*. "Well, heck—us Indians, we're used to invasions!" He turned his hawklike eyes momentarily on Howie. "We've had plenty of practice in *that* department—ain't that right, Moon Deer?" He turned back to Jack and smiled serenely. "But you will all go away eventually, and then things will pretty much return to normal."

Jack raised an eyebrow at this last piece of news. He was sitting behind his big wooden desk, rocking slowly in his large rocking chair, bathed in a beam of sunlight that flooded through the window behind his left shoulder. Jack was dressed in a blue blazer, a dark pink shirt with French cuffs that was open at the throat, jeans, and Gucci loafers. Howie liked to tell Jack that he looked like a Beverly Hills pimp in this outfit, particularly with the wraparound shades, but at least it was an improvement over his usual food-splattered kitchen attire. Raymond Concha sat facing Jack on the far side of the desk, also in a rocking chair, though a smaller one than Jack's. Howie sat next to Raymond taking notes, ensconced in the smallest rocker of all, a fiendishly uncomfortable piece of early Americana. It was one of Jack's design eccentricities that every chair must rock—from the padded platform rocker by the fireplace, to several squeaky folding rockettes that Howie sometimes brought out to seat larger groups. He insisted that repetitive motion was helpful for deductive thought and that the regular pushing off of a big toe against the floor was all the aerobic exercise any adult person actually required.

The office was a pleasant room. There were cool, thick adobe walls, an oval-shaped kiva fireplace, and a floor of polished wood that was dark with age and covered with several strategically placed Navajo rugs. Katya was stretched out on her favorite rug, snoring occasionally, and doing her best to keep her long bushy tail from getting caught beneath the sea of moving wood.

"Would you like some coffee, Mr. Concha?" Jack asked. "A cup of tea? A soda? Howie could probably even rustle up a little brunch if you'd like."

Raymond folded his wrinkled old hands in his lap. "Well, maybe I'll have a Perrier."

Howie put down his notebook—there wasn't much to write about so far, anyway—and went to the small refrigerator at the far end of the room.

"I'm afraid we're all out of Perrier," he told Raymond, making an effort to keep any hint of amusement from his voice. "Will a San Pellegrino be okay?"

"Shit, I don't know, Moon Deer. Does San Pellegrino have big bubbles or small bubbles?"

"Well, Raymond, as far as I can recall, they're sort of *medium* bubbles."

Raymond seemed delighted. "Hey! I love medium bubbles!"

Howie poured the medium bubbly water into a glass and

brought it over, wondering again just how old Raymond really was. He had seen a photograph recently of Raymond in 1972 in Washington, D.C., standing next to President Richard Nixon, and in the photograph the old *cacique* looked almost exactly as he did today: ageless, more like a marvel of nature than a human being. Raymond had gone to Washington to get back 20,000 acres of Pueblo land from the U.S. government; the land had been taken from the tribe by Teddy Roosevelt at the start of the last century as part of his new national park system, and the Indians had worked tirelessly for the next seventy years to have it returned. In the photograph—a very famous photograph in San Geronimo—Raymond Concha looked a great deal more presidential than Richard Nixon, and six months after his visit, the federal government had indeed returned the stolen acreage, along with Spirit Lake, whose sacred waters fed the stream that flowed through the Pueblo village.

"Tell me something, blind brother—how was it that you lost your eyesight?" Raymond asked unexpectedly.

Howie was startled. Nobody asked Jack this question. Even Howie didn't know the complete story. But Jack nodded, and to Howie's astonishment, he answered.

"Well, to tell you the truth, Raymond, I screwed up. It's really that simple. I was a commander with the San Francisco police in those days. 'Commander' may sound very high and mighty, but in fact, it's an appointed rank, which creates problems. Like most commanders in a big-city police department, the last rank I actually *earned* was captain. What happened is that a new chief came in and he chose me for the job—basically a commander is the assistant chief of police, but you serve at the chief's pleasure so you can be busted to your original rank at the drop of a hat if you do something the chief doesn't like, or if he happens to need a scapegoat. So the position is very political, you understand. For me, there was a lot of paperwork involved—I drew up the budget every year for the entire department, and attended a whole lot of meetings. I was a big shot, of course, that was on the plus side—I had prestige, money, my own unmarked car and driver. But after a few years of being the chief's personal boy, I began to miss actual police work. I started to miss it a lot.

"So a case came along, a very big case involving a major drug lord we'd been trying to nail for years. We received word from an informant that a huge shipment of cocaine was going to be delivered by sea a few miles up the coast in Tomales Bay, just north of Point Reyes, about twenty million dollars' worth . . . but I'm probably boring you with this old story?"

"Oh, no," Raymond said quickly. "This is like one of those movies—what's his name? 'Make-My-Day'?"

"I know the character you mean. Anyway, to make a long story short, I decided to personally take charge of the bust, just because I was bored and wanted something more exciting to do than drawing up budgets and sitting in meetings. What I didn't take into account was that I was older, fatter, and slower than I used to be. It was a huge operation. We had the coast guard in on it, three different police departments in two separate counties, a SWAT team, the works. What I decided to do, you see, was allow the boat to unload in Tomales Bay, then follow the truck to a big mansion in Kentfield and nab the drug lord just as he was taking possession of his goods—Kentfield's a fancy suburb in Marin. But I forgot one thing."

"What was that?" Raymond asked, politely, for Jack had paused.

"I forgot about the private security outfit that patrols the residential streets of Kentfield—I didn't tell them about our operation. As a result, these hotshot wannabe cops came by just at the wrong moment and found a bunch of *my* people in dark clothes in the bushes around the mansion. It was three in the morning, you understand, and the private security people believed there was a burglary in progress. So they drew their weapons, rushed out of their patrol car, and things went downhill fast. Before I knew it, everybody was shooting at everybody else. It was crazy—cops shooting at private security, the security wannabes firing back, and the gangsters up in the house blasting away at everybody in the yard below. As for me, I happened to be standing in the driveway just as the main man tried to get away from the garage in his Mercedes. I got a few shots off, killed the driver and the drug lord, too, but the Mercedes ran me down. That was the last thing I ever saw, that Mercedes coming at me. I don't remember much, but I'm told I tried to do a kind of handstand over the hood. I went face-first through the windshield—I would have been killed, except for the fact that I had already shot that windshield to hell."

Raymond made a kind of sympathetic clicking sound with his tongue. "Well, well—that's a lot more exciting than things generally get around here!"

"Unfortunately, seven people died that night who shouldn't have." Jack's voice had turned flat and weary. "Three of my cops were killed, one private security man, and three of the drug dealers. I should have left the whole damn operation to my people and stayed the hell behind my desk where I belonged."

Raymond nodded. "Knowledge is never cheap. So you retired to San Geronimo?"

"My wife inherited a house here years ago. We had always planned to retire to New Mexico. It just came a few years earlier than expected."

"And then you got bored again, huh? So you started a detective agency?"

Jack smiled. "You got it, my life in a nutshell. Actually, I was a pretty good detective at one time, back before I got so ambitious, so it seemed sort of a shame to let all those skills go to waste. Fortunately, I found Howie here to help me—I lied a bit to get him interested, told him what an intellectual challenge it would be, and that he'd have women falling all over him. So here we are. Now, what exactly can I do for you, Raymond?"

It appeared that the preliminaries were finally over. Howie uncapped his ballpoint pen and began taking notes.

"First, you must promise to keep secret what I am going to tell you." Raymond's voice had gone hard, Howie noted, not so folksy as before.

"We always observe client confidentiality," Jack assured him.

"Good. Swear it, then. Give me your oath that you'll never reveal to anyone my business with you today."

Jack raised his right hand. "I swear," he said simply.

"And you, Moon Deer? Be careful, because if you break your pledge to me, your balls will shrivel, your life will become a burden to you, and no woman will ever come into your bed—certainly not my granddaughter."

"I swear!" Howie agreed quickly.

Raymond turned back to Jack. "Something has been found on our land. Some old stones of our ancestors. Frankly, it would have been better if these things had remained undisturbed."

"Old stones?" Jack repeated. "You're talking about some sort of archeological find?"

"I am talking about the ruins of a kiva and several small buildings where people lived many years ago. They have been found high in the mountains in a sacred place, in a cave at nearly twelve thousand feet. My granddaughter, Donna Theresa, is getting her PhD in archeology at the University of New Mexico," Raymond said with a small nod to Howie, just a little proudly. "She tells me the site is over eight hundred years old. It was built by the Old Ones, the people the Navajo call the Ancient Enemy."

"Anasazi, Jack," Howie supplied, since Jack seemed momentarily lost. "'Anasazi' means 'ancient enemy' in Dinè, the Navajo language."

"Really? How coincidental—Howie and I have recently been discussing Anasazi things, haven't we, Howie?" Jack said, agreeably. "I imagine all the scholars will be very interested."

Raymond smiled thinly. "We have kept this discovery to ourselves, so far."

"Why's that?"

"Because human bones have been found that we will need to rebury. I'm sure you can understand how sensitive this is for my people. The cave overlooks our sacred lake, and we don't want a lot of outsiders going there and disturbing our way of life. So for the time being, we have kept the news of the discovery secret—not even many of our own people know about it. Only my granddaughter and me, and of course the tribal council. And now the two of you."

"When was the cave discovered?"

"My granddaughter found it by accident a number of years ago. She has only recently informed me of this, I'm afraid. She is a curious girl, always roaming the land, looking at things. What is that old saying?"

"Curiosity killed the cat?" Howie suggested.

"Yes, exactly. Generally it's a damn good idea to think twice before you poke your head someplace you shouldn't. Donna Theresa is a modern young woman, of course—at least she thinks she is. She doesn't always have the proper respect for tradition. As a result, she did some initial work in the cave without asking permission of me or the tribal authorities. This was back when she was still getting her master's degree. Then a little over a year ago, she decided she wanted to apply for the doctorate program and do her PhD dissertation on the cave she had found. This would have been a big operation, I gather, hard to keep secret, so she finally went to the council to ask for permission. Unfortunately for her, the council turned her down. A man named Lewis Lucero was our governor then—he's War Chief now—and he was angry that she had not asked permission earlier."

"She must have been disappointed."

"Well, she was. It caused her to stay away for an entire year, never coming home to visit. She was bitter, but she got into the PhD program anyway, and she didn't give up—just to spite us, I think. She's been digging around some ruins outside Chaco Canyon. Then, two weeks ago, the tribal council phoned her in Albuquerque and asked her to come home. They've changed their minds, it seems. Now they *want* her to investigate the cave she found and make a thorough inventory of what's there."

"Why the change of heart?"

"To begin with, there's a new governor, Don Lucero—he's Lewis's older brother, and not such a fool. I guess you could say our tribal politics are sort of a family affair, but that's hard to avoid in a small place where nearly everyone is related. The reason Don called her is that he just found out there's been some British fella, an archeologist, who has been sneaking up to the cave over the past few months—this is a big embarrassment and people are pretty upset. Meanwhile, the British fella hasn't been seen for a while, which is good, but now that the cat is out of the bag, the governor wants Donna Theresa to take a good look to see what's there, and if perhaps anything's been stolen. It's a case of locking the barn door after the horse has run away, but better late than never. The reason the governor has asked my granddaughter for help is that she is clearly the only person from the Pueblo who's qualified. Don wants to keep the whole thing among ourselves, naturally."

Jack had begun to rock more energetically in his big wooden chair. "I'm seeing a problem here, Raymond. You've said the cave was at twelve thousand feet, so I gather it must be located in a remote part of the reservation. Realistically, it seems damn unlikely that some British archeologist could find that site on his own, then sneak up there on a regular basis for several months without someone catching on."

"Yeah, that's the problem, all right," Raymond agreed cheerfully. "Some Indian must have been helping him. Showed him where to go and how to stay out of sight."

"Do you have anyone in mind?"

"Not really. This is a serious matter, and I won't make accusations."

"Okay, but how did the council find out about the Englishman? Did someone finally spot him up there?"

Raymond hesitated. "The governor received an anonymous letter."

"Did he? Do you have the letter?"

"No, it was destroyed. This is very distasteful, a person who does not have the courage to sign what he has written. After the governor received the letter, he sent Carl Lucero, the head of the tribal police, up on the mountain to investigate. Carl couldn't find the Englishman, but one of his officers questioned an old man named Roberto Fast Horses who's been grazing cattle up on those high meadows during the summer for the past fifty years. Roberto admitted he had seen the white man plenty of times. Even spoken to him. He hadn't told anyone because the Englishman gave him cartons of cigarettes, and he liked that."

"Could Roberto have been the person who wrote the anonymous letter?"

Raymond laughed. "Oh, not likely! The letter was printed out by a computer, as I understand it, and old Roberto is unable even to write his name with a pencil! Meanwhile, everything is not as it should be at the Pueblo—letters that people are ashamed to sign, white men sneaking up onto sacred land, and maybe some Indians not telling everything they know. Donna Theresa is on her horse at this very moment, riding up to the cave to make her investigation, and I'm afraid she's going to find herself in quite a hornet's nest. There are some tricky tribal politics involved, I'm sorry to say, which complicates matters. To be honest, I am worried about my granddaughter's safety. Which is the reason I am here. The War Chief is riding up to the cave tomorrow and I want Moon Deer to accompany him, to keep an eye on my granddaughter and help with her investigation. Moon Deer would be perfect for this job for several reasons."

"And what reasons are these?" Jack inquired.

Howie was curious as well. He was no longer taking notes, only listening.

"First, because Moon Deer is someone from outside the tribe who isn't part of any of the different factions at the Pueblo. Yet at the same time, he's an Indian, and that's also essential—we would never willingly allow a non-Indian in this particular sacred spot around Spirit Lake. Finally, my granddaughter tells me he's an anthropologist. To be frank, I don't have a clue what the hell's the difference between an archeologist and an anthropologist—I'm just an old man and all these *-ists* sound the same to me. But I imagine he'll be able to make himself handy up there and help her with the work. I would take this as a personal favor. I want her to finish up quickly before there is trouble."

"Yes, but trouble from what, exactly?"

"Well, the mountain is a wild place, after all. There are bears, mountain lions, not to mention some two-legged animals who might be inclined to bother a young woman." Raymond smiled subtly. "And then, of course, there are ghosts. Do you believe in ghosts, blind brother?"

If Jack was taken aback by the question, he recovered quickly. "Certainly I believe in ghosts," he replied. "As a detective, I have often seen how the past haunts the present."

"Then you are a wise man," Raymond assured him. "It is our belief that when a burial site is disturbed, the spirits of the dead are unhappy. Their ghosts are set loose upon the living, often causing grave mischief. Moon Deer may be required to battle both seen and unseen dangers."

"How do you feel about that, Howie?" Jack asked, turning the lenses of his dark glasses toward where Howie was sitting.

Howie shrugged. "Hey, unseen dangers are my specialty," he replied, trying to be offhand.

"So that's it?" Jack returned his attention to Raymond. "You want Howie to babysit your granddaughter, give a hand with the archeology, do battle with any ghosts that might appear, and act as a sort of neutral observer due to the fact there are some divisive tribal politics involved?"

"Yes, that's it exactly. You've understood very well." Raymond pulled a huge wad of money out of his pocket, a thick packet of hundred-dollar bills. "So if you tell me how much you charge, I'll just pay you now, if you don't mind."

"Whoa! Hold on just a minute, please," Jack told him. "We would need to know more about this before actually taking the case."

Raymond sat quietly with the cash in his lap. "Well, now, I'll tell you anything I can."

"Will you?" Jack smiled. "You see, that's exactly what worries me, Raymond. Somehow I have the feeling you're leaving out a lot more than you're telling us."

Raymond laughed, not offended. "Well, yes I am at that! Hey, you're pretty sharp for a white man!" he said easily. "You have to understand, secrecy's sort of a habit with us. Do you know we even have a tribal law against teaching our Tiwa language to outsiders, just so they can't find out too much about us? I tell you this so you'll appreciate how difficult it is for me to come to you today and be as forthcoming as you would like. For the past few hundred years, we've had first the Spanish and now you Anglos doing your best to tell us how we ought to live. As a result, we're kind of defensive and closed."

"I can appreciate that," Jack said.

"Then you can understand why I worry that an Anasazi cave full of bones and pots could draw a bunch of archaeologists and some of those other *-ists* we were just talking about. This Shark Tooth fella who's been snooping around is one outsider too many."

"Shark Tooth?" Jack asked. "That's the English archeologist?"

"Yep. That's what Roberto, the old man, calls him, anyway. The white man wears a shark tooth in one of his ears."

Jack raised his eyebrows very slightly, the only sign that this news was interesting to him. "And you say he's been missing for a while—how long?"

Raymond shrugged. "I don't know. A few days, a week. Since the letter came to the council, several people have now gone up there to try to find him, but he has vanished. Perhaps he is only a ghost. All I know myself is that I am uneasy and I would like someone to keep an eye on my granddaughter. Let Moon Deer go to the cave tomorrow and he will discover the truth of what is there and what is not."

Jack didn't answer. He drummed on the desk with the index finger of his left hand.

"Well, you must do as you see fit, blind brother," Raymond told him. "But you might consider Moon Deer's wishes. He's been sitting here not saying a word, but the boy's so eager it's painful. A beautiful young woman may be in need of protection, and of course, he's dying to go, as you would have been at his age, and myself as well. Personally, I think you should give him the opportunity either to make a fool of himself or show my granddaughter what a big hero he is."

Jack nodded, one cagey old man to another. Howie knew there wasn't any doubt at all that Jack was going to take the case: The shark's-tooth earring had settled that. Nevertheless, he stretched in his chair, as though this all had little importance.

"Well, Raymond, I tell you what," he said. "For Howie's sake, sure—since there's a beautiful young woman involved, I guess we'd better give this thing a whirl."

10

Howie walked Raymond Concha to the street and offered to drive him back to the Pueblo.

"To tell the truth, I'm feeling a little frisky," he confided to Howie with a wink. "Think maybe I'll stop off in town and see one of my old gals."

Howie shook hands with the *cacique*, then returned upstairs to the office.

"I swear, they don't make Indians like that anymore!" he said to Jack, coming back into the room. Jack was in the exact spot Howie had left him five minutes before, in the big rocking chair behind the desk, but Howie could tell by a number of signs that there was something wrong. For one, Jack wasn't rocking, he was sitting still as a stone. Second, the telephone was ringing and he was ignoring it, not picking up.

"Wilder and Associate," Howie said, grabbing for the receiver. It was a little girl asking for someone named Carla. Howie told her she had the wrong number, and put down the phone. Jack still hadn't moved.

"You having a stroke, Jack? Or is it just a thunderbolt of inspiration?"

Jack exhaled. "We have to call Ed," he said. "There's no way around it."

"You're kidding?"

"I'm sorry, Howie. I know we promised Raymond, but this is just too important. There's a very good chance this missing British archeologist is missing his head."

"Jack, I don't goddamn believe this! We did more than promise, we swore—we took an oath on it!"

"Yes, but that was before we knew he had important information about a homicide."

"Before or after, it doesn't matter! For chrissake, Jack, I always took you for a person with some integrity."

"Calm down, Howie. Look, I'm sorry about the old man, I really am. But sometimes in life we're faced with a major dilemma. In this case, we have a moral responsibility to tell Ed what we've got—a *legal* responsibility, too, as a matter of fact. If Ed can ID the victim quickly, it's going to make all the difference in the world. The longer this drags on, the better the chance the killer's going to walk."

"Well, that's too bad," Howie said coldly. "But you raised your right hand and swore. I saw you do that and you can't take it back now just because it suits you."

"Howie, a man has been violently murdered and possibly cannibalized! There's some very sick person out there in this small community who's probably going to get hungry and do this terrible thing again if we don't stop him. Now, we've got a hard decision to make, and I agree it's unfortunate. But what are we going to do? Keep a promise to Raymond, or stop some maniac cannibal from killing a second, maybe even a third time?"

Howie nodded slowly. "You know, this reminds me of what we used to call the Great Sioux Reservation."

"Howie, let's stick to the point—"

"I *am* sticking to the point. About a century and a half ago, Congress made an agreement with my people so we'd end our war against the United States. They gave us a big chunk of land that they thought was worthless—it wasn't what we had before, mind you, but it included most of what is now Montana, Wyoming, North Dakota, South Dakota, and Nebraska. We shook hands over it, smoked a few pipes together, and put our marks on a whole bunch of papers. And then the white man found gold in the Black Hills and, holy shit, they realized what they had given away wasn't so worthless after all."

"Howie! My God, I'm well aware that the United States treated the native peoples of this continent in an abysmal manner, but this is not the right time—"

"Oh, yes, it's the right time, Jack. Because unfortunately, we keep coming around in circles to the same thing—how every time it suits you, you white people break your damn promise to Indians. Half an hour ago you swore an oath to Raymond that you'd keep whatever he told you confidential. It was an easy promise to make because you thought what he was going to say would be just the worthless babblings of an old man. But now, hey!—it turns out maybe there's gold in them thar hills, it wasn't so worthless after all! And look at you. Look how quick you are to pick up that damn phone and call Ed Gomez!"

Jack was starting to get angry himself now. "I have *not* phoned Ed. *Yes*, I am tempted. Yes, I think it *may* be the right thing for us to do. But at the moment, we're only talking it over, trying to come to a goddamn responsible decision, one that we're going to be able to live with down the line."

"There's nothing to decide, Jack. Nothing at all."

"You don't think so? What is this? Suddenly you're some born-again Ivy League Indian! I don't know, Howie, but the last time I checked, you knew French a whole lot better than you could speak Sioux."

"Well, maybe so," Howie agreed. "But I tell you something, I'm not going to break my oath to that old man. And if *you* do, I'm out the door and you're never going to see me again."

Jack began to rock furiously in his chair. "Okay, let's work this through. But first, we need to get off this Indian versus-white-man trip, Howie. I'm not Custer and you're not Crazy Horse, and there's no reason for us to fight the Little Big Horn all over again. Let's just discuss this calmly. Okay?"

"I'm calm, Jack. I'm chilled."

"Good. Now let me run this idea by you for your chilled deliberation. How about if I have a *confidential* talk with Ed. He's a friend, he's lived in San Geronimo his whole damn life, he'll understand. I'll clue him in about Shark Tooth but I won't reveal our source. He'll be able to start looking for the Brit from a different angle, and hopefully find out his real name. There's a lot of stuff Ed could do if we just get him started in the right direction. But we've *got* to help him ID the victim, Howie—if he finds out where he lived, who his friends were, his enemies, his routine, we'll be halfway home."

"I'm sorry, but that would still be breaking our promise," Howie insisted. "Ed's a good enough cop that he'll find out pretty quick how this British archeologist was trespassing on Pueblo land to visit some old Anasazi site. Then Ed will call in the FBI, and before you know it, there'll be a whole shitload of white law enforcement going onto sacred land, poking around up there at Spirit Lake trying to find evidence. Now I know this is hard for you to comprehend, but the fact is—as Raymond told you—the San Geronimo Indians don't *want* white people up there, particularly not white FBI agents. It would be a serious invasion of their sovereign rights, and I'm not going to let it happen."

Jack nodded. "Okay, okay," he agreed. "I see your point. I'm sorry, Howie. I was thinking as a cop. It *does* gall me, however, to let our cannibal off the hook. Every day that passes without an arrest means the killer has a better chance to cover his trail. Statistically speaking, either you solve a homicide in the first forty-eight hours, or the chances are you'll never solve it at all."

"Hey, I'm not in favor of the cannibal getting off, either. I *found* that head, remember? I was the one who was saying let's pursue this, when you were telling me to keep looking for lost pussycats. Nevertheless, a promise is a promise."

"Yes, it is," Jack agreed, with a heavy sigh. Howie had gotten through to him, but Jack wasn't happy at finding himself in such a bind. Howie took a seat in one of the rocking chairs and watched Jack struggle with his conscience. *Wasicu*, the Lakota word for the white man, meant literally "He-Who-Takes-The-Fat." From the expression on Jack's face, his *wasicu* mind was going through a maze of possibilities at this very moment, trying to see if there was any fat he could salvage from this particular meal.

How about coming at this from another angle?" Jack suggested. "Let's say we give you a day or two to go up to that cave and talk with people and find out everything you can about the Brit with the earring. Who he was, how he got back and forth onto the reservation—anything at all. Once you flesh him out a little more, we'll have a better sense of how we can pick up his trail in town. He must have stayed in a motel, eaten in restaurants. As soon as we get something solid, we could call up Ed and say, hey, we just heard about a person with a shark's-tooth earring who was staying at the Sleaze Pit Motel, or wherever—maybe you should go check it out. It wouldn't be coming from Raymond, and it wouldn't connect with the Pueblo. Ed would be able to go the motel, look at the registration card, maybe even get a credit card receipt, and he'd be in business."

Howie thought this over. "All right," he decided. "I could live with that. I'd be willing to pass on to Ed any information we discovered independently of what Raymond told us today, so long as it didn't connect with the Anasazi site. If we could place Shark Tooth in a motel in town, that would be fine. But it's going to take me more than a couple of days up on the mountain to get people to open up. The San Geronimo Pueblo is an extremely closed place if you're an outsider. You heard what Raymond was saying earlier—even their language is a kind of state secret. I'm going to need at least a week and a lot of luck to get anywhere at all."

"That's too long, Make it three days, Howie. Time is crucial at this stage of an investigation. Anyway, surely they won't treat *you* like a outsider."

"Listen to me. Pueblo Indians are *very* conservative. They've been living in that adobe village of theirs since the fourteenth century, and even in the old days they believed themselves hugely superior to the gypsy ways of Plains People like the Sioux. They're farmers, Jack, while my people are hunter-gatherers . . . or were, at least, before your ancestors put my ancestors on reservations."

"Look, I'm sorry my ancestors did that to you, I really am," Jack said.

Howie smiled. One thing he liked about the *wasicu* was how guilty they got with just a little pressure; the residue of Christianity, he supposed. "It's okay," he said. "Your ancestors were escaping the Irish potato famine and the British, and had some problems of their own. All I'm trying to say is that I'm as much an outsider here as you are. So give me five days and one way or the other, I'm confident I'll find out enough about Shark Tooth to be able to pick up his trail in town. A guy with an English accent and a tooth dangling from his ear—it shouldn't be so hard to find someone who remembers him. While I'm up on the mountain, you could even start calling around the different motels. I'd feel okay about that."

Jack nodded. "It's a deal, then. But make it four days. Believe me, Howie—if you tried to spend any more time than that in virgin nature, you'd probably drop dead of cappuccino deprivation. And I'd miss you, actually."

Jack and Howie shook hands on it, and Wilder & Associate were back in business.

11

Howie had dinner Friday night with Bob and Nova Davidson, his friends and landlords. They lived ten minutes away in a rambling neo-hippie adobe home built in strange shapes and angles at the far end of the forty-acre estate on which Howie had his cabin. Bob and Nova were "trustfunders," a group that everyone in San Geronimo loved to hate. Nova's family owned a string of department stores in California—unforgivable, but Howie figured he had faults of his own, so he was tolerant.

Dinner was an outdoor barbecue that began at sunset and continued beneath the summer stars. Bob grilled an entire salmon, they drank a number of bottles of good wine, and it would have been a very nice evening except for the fact that Nova couldn't resist playing matchmaker. For several years now she had been telling Howie that he had to stop wooing unattainable women, that his standards were impossibly high, and that it was obvious to any outside meddler such as herself that Howie had a "princess complex." She warned him that if he kept falling for beautiful, smart, talented, sexy, idealistic women, they would only keep leaving him, and Howie's heart would be endlessly, needlessly broken.

"You have to be more realistic, Howie," she was always telling him. "There are *plenty* of women out there for you if you'd only lower your sights a little. It's like that old Stephen Stills song, 'Love the One You Can Get.'"

Howie sensed she had the song title slightly wrong, but he knew what she meant, and because he liked Nova, he always did his best to accommodate her matchmaking efforts.

Tonight's offering—along with the salmon and wine—was an attractive, late-thirties, recently divorced female by the name of Yahdi who was "into body work" and had wounded, worried eyes. It was odd, but every New Age lady of a certain age that Howie had ever met was "into body work" and had wounded, worried eyes. Yahdi was actually very nice and Howie wished he could fall for her; it would certainly have simplified his life. But she didn't give him a zap, not even a low-watt tingle, and Howie ended up feeling vaguely embarrassed in her presence, knowing he was supposed to be performing and not knowing what to say. Yahdi offered to work on his spine sometime and show him some pressure points on the bottoms of his feet. He told her, sure, let's do that. But he avoided setting a date. Maybe three lifetimes from now he'd find an afternoon.

Howie left as soon as he was politely able, pleading a big day tomorrow. Nova walked him to the garden gate, shaking her head with disappointment.

"Howie! What am I going to do with you?"

"I was nice to her, wasn't I?" he asked with concern.

"Yes, you were extremely polite. But why didn't you ask her out?"

Howie could only sigh. "I don't know, Nova. There's something wrong with me, I guess. I just can't get attracted to women I'm not attracted to."

"Now listen to me, Howie, you've got to stop trying to find some impossible goddess or you're going to end up all alone, with *nada*—is that what you want?"

"I'll settle for Nada," he tried. "You have her phone number?"

Nova pushed him out the garden gate, exasperated. He walked slowly along the path across the sagebrush to his cabin. It was a lovely moonless summer night, with a huge canopy of stars overhead. Far away, there was a lightning storm in progress over the mountains to the east, bright flashes that lit up the clouds soundlessly, illuminating the sky for just an instant, like watching a distant war. Howie stopped on the path to gaze up with longing at the Milky Way. The ancient

Egyptians believed that the god Amun had masturbated and
the Milky Way was the result, a flood of cosmic cum. It was a
very human concept. Even gods got lonely, Howie reminded
himself. Even gods had to give themselves, from time to time,
a helping hand.

He lowered his gaze from heaven to earth, to the Indian
land that began at the southeastern edge of Bob and Nova's
property. This was where he would be going tomorrow, to
D.T.'s archeological dig high in the mountains. Unlike Yahdi,
Donna Theresa interested him, worried him greatly, and gave
him a major case of the tingles. But could this tingle be har-
nessed to domestic purposes? It didn't seem likely. Howie
sensed that Nova was right: He was going to end up all alone
if he didn't get his libido to behave in a more responsible fashion.

He was pondering these personal matters when a bright
flash of lightning crackled over the mountains, an intricate
web that lit up the heavy thunder clouds hugging San Geronimo Peak with an eerie glow. In the flare of light, Howie
thought he saw the outline of a horse and rider coming toward
him across the desert from the east. The apparition was brief,
swallowed almost immediately by the returning darkness.
Howie wasn't sure what it was. A moment later, the lightning
flashed again, closer now, followed by a low grumble of thunder. This time Howie was sure. There *was* a horse and rider
outlined momentarily against the sky. It was a white horse and
the rider was slumped in the saddle, leaning at a dangerous
angle. They were a few hundred yards away, drifting silently
in his direction.

Howie felt an unreasonable fear. It didn't seem possible that
anyone would be riding onto Bob and Nova's land this time of
night. The ghostly horse and rider kept coming. Howie was
tempted to run, but his legs had gone heavy and refused to
move. Soon he could hear soft hoofbeats on the earth. This
made him feel better, for surely a ghost would not be making
such a comforting *clip, clop* sound. As the horse drew nearer,
Howie could see that the rider appeared half asleep in the saddle, jerked occasionally awake by the horse's motion.

"Hey!" Howie called when the rider was only a few dozen feet away. He tried to sound casual, as if hallucinatory horsemen were no big deal. But the rider didn't answer. The horse clip-clopped over and stopped next to Howie, lathered and pungent from a hard ride. The man on the horse studied Howie with a mute, ironic smile. His face was round and catlike, pale in the starlight. It was Charlie, whom he had last seen getting beaten up behind the Anasazi Grill.

"Moon Deer!" Charlie whispered. His voice was low and strained.

"How did you know I live here?"

"The cop . . ." Charlie began, but could not finish. His left hand held onto the saddlehorn for support, and in his right hand there was a small white box. He seemed to sway in Howie's direction, leaning from the horse as though he wanted to give the box to Howie. But he leaned too far and he kept falling, sliding off the horse onto the ground. He fell in a soft tangle and lay on his side with the white box a few inches from his outstretched arm.

Howie knelt by Charlie's head, concerned. "You okay?" he asked, knowing it was a dumb question. Charlie was about as far from okay as a person could be. "Do you need help? Did someone hurt you?"

"*Cop!*" Charlie whispered again. The word came out like the hiss of a tire going flat: co-o-op. The air seemed to keep hissing out of Charlie's lungs in a long, sad exhale. And then he was still. As still as the surrounding rocks and sand.

"God*damn!*" Howie cried, jerking to his feet. *Charlie was dead!* This was unbelievable, that some guy should appear at night in the desert, whisper his name, and fall off his horse dead! With the distant lightning, there was a nightmarish quality to the whole episode that made Howie want to pinch himself. But the white horse took a noisy pee at just this moment, and the smell and sound were much too real for any dream. Howie stood in shock, wondering what to do. The white horse, meanwhile, began munching on the stubbly high desert grass, apparently unconcerned with the death of its rider.

Moments ticked by in indecision: the horse munching, Howie standing still as a statue, the body going nowhere on the ground. Finally, Howie bent over to pick up the white box. It was a small cardboard jewelry box, about the size of something you'd put a bracelet into: perhaps two inches square and a half inch thick, very light, closed shut with two rubber bands. It seemed as if Charlie had been trying to hand him this box, but it was hard to say for certain.

Howie left the body where it was and jogged back toward his cabin with the mysterious little box. The path was dark but Howie made good time, knowing every bend and dip. He entered his cabin through the back door, turned on the overhead light, and set the box down on the kitchen table.

He suspected Charlie had not died of natural causes, which meant that the box was evidence in a homicide, and there were decisions Howie needed to make. He knew the proper course of action was to call 911 and wait for the police to arrive, but Charlie's last word was worrisome and gave him pause. *Cop!* Unfortunately, police officers in San Geronimo received a starting salary of $8 an hour, which opened the door to a lot of corruption. He could phone Ed Gomez directly, of course, but then it would be difficult to keep from telling Ed about Raymond's visit to the office and the secret he had sworn to keep. This had become a problem. He stared at the small white box on the table and debated whether to give in to his curiosity.

The hell with it, he decided. He slipped off the criss-crossing rubber bands and lifted the top. A small twig of organic matter rested on top of some crumpled toilet paper. He touched the thing experimentally and found it was hard as stone. Petrified wood? he wondered. A branch from an ancient tree that had somehow become fossilized over time? Howie had never seen anything quite like it.

Howie examined the unknown object for some time, completely mystified. He couldn't imagine a single scenario that would explain Charlie riding up in the night with this very weird object in a box, trying to tell him about some cop, then dropping dead. Howie pulled a bottle of red wine from a kitchen shelf and poured himself a glass.

He knew he should call Jack without delay, but Jack would refuse to conceal a homicide: He would phone Ed with the information, and this could result in some complications Howie did not want. Cops had their own way of looking at things, even ex-cops like Jack. Meanwhile, a dead Indian meant a possible felony had been committed, and felonies committed on Indian land were the jurisdiction of the FBI. Of course, technically speaking, the death had occurred on Bob and Nova's land, but Charlie had been riding from the direction of the Pueblo and whatever it was that had killed him had probably happened there. In short, this situation could easily result in federal agents coming onto the San Geronimo Pueblo, white law enforcement swarming over their sacred land. And if that occurred, Howie sensed he might very well be prevented from riding up to the Anasazi cave tomorrow to help Donna Theresa.

He poured himself another glass of wine.

The question for Howie was complicated: He needed to decide if he was going to act like a white man in this situation or an Indian. A white man, he presumed, would pick up the phone and call Jack Wilder and Ed Gomez. A red man would not. A red man would not under any circumstances willingly do anything to bring the FBI onto reservation land—particularly a Lakota Sioux like Howie, whose earliest childhood memory was of violence between his people and federal agents.

Howie picked up the receiver of his phone, then put it down again undialed. He was mildly surprised to discover that when a choice was needed, Howard Moon Deer, with his fancy education, was an Indian after all.

Howie jogged back along the path to where he had left Charlie. The dead man and his horse were exactly where they had been before, about halfway to Bob and Nova's: the horse grazing contentedly on the high desert grass, and Charlie still lying in a crumpled position on his side, his right arm stretched out toward a box that was no longer there.

Howie set to work. With an effort, he managed to hoist Charlie onto the white horse across the saddle, his legs dangling on one side, his arms on the other. The night was warm and Howie was panting for breath by the time he was finished. He knew very well that what he was doing was unforgivable from a law enforcement point of view; he would never be able to tell Ed about this, or Jack. He hadn't even bothered to investigate the cause of death. There was blood on the back of Charlie's shirt and it seemed probable that he had been shot. But then again, maybe he had been stabbed. Did it really matter? Dead was dead.

Howie had decided to send the corpse back onto reservation land, and allow the San Geronimo Tribal Police to deal with the situation in their own way, according to their laws and customs. They were, after all, a sovereign people—a fact which non-native Americans tended to forget, refusing to understand why anyone might choose not to be a member of their wonderful United States. Meanwhile, he didn't want Charlie to fall off his horse on the ride home, and this took some creative arranging. He loosened the cinch of the saddle, placed one of Charlie's arms beneath the leather strap on one side of the horses's flank, and one leg beneath the strap on the other. When Howie tightened the cinch, it more or less seemed to fasten the corpse in place. The horse did not like this much, but that was okay with Howie. He wanted the horse to be uncomfortable so it would gallop home and not stop for any more midnight grazing.

By the time Howie was finished, his own arms were slick with blood and he knew he was going to have to burn his clothes and take a lengthy shower. Finally, he pointed the horse toward the reservation and gave it a loud, hard slap on the rump.

"Hoka, hey!" he cried. "Go home, horse!"

The white horse took off with a start across the desert.

"Run, run!" he cried. Maybe it was a coward's solution to send the dead rider back to wherever he had come from, let-

ting someone else deal with the problem. But if the horse succeeded in returning to Indian land, the problem would be handled in a native fashion, and not by the traumatic arrival of the
FBI.

Howie stood watching for a long time as the white horse
with its dead rider disappeared the way it had arrived, a
ghostly outline against the lightning that was flashing silently
in the eastern sky.

12

On Saturday morning, Howie's automatic coffee machine began to gurgle and drip at 6:20 A.M. precisely, and ten minutes later his CD player switched on with Bach, Cantata 140, *Sleepers, Awake!* Howie was in no mood to be roused. He had not slept well, being stressed about dead Charlie, and wondering how he was making out in the afterlife—whether he was in heaven, or hell, or nowhere at all.

Howie knew he had committed a serious felony by concealing evidence of a homicide, and that he could end up in jail for what he had done. Somehow he had overlooked this essential fact, debating back and forth last night on the moral responsibilities of the nouveau native. It didn't help that there was the possibility of some corrupt cop involved in Charlie's death, an individual who might make incarceration even more unpleasant than it generally was. Howie rose from bed with a discouraged sigh and punched off the CD player, preferring silence. In the light of day, what he had done seemed totally nuts, tying Charlie to his horse and sending him back toward Indian land. He looked out his back window, fearing he would see a horse with a dead person lurking on the sagebrush. He couldn't see anything, but that didn't mean he was in the clear.

Howie had an appointment at nine to meet Lewis Lucero, the current War Chief of the San Geronimo Pueblo, at which time they would ride together on horseback to the Anasazi cave. First, he needed to locate his camping gear and get his pack together. He spent over an hour packing and repacking his gear, not certain what he was going to need at 12,000 feet, or even how long he would be there. It took some artful arranging to squeeze all the things he figured he'd better have into his backpack: sleeping bag, one-man tent, several pairs of underpants, long underwear, a sweater, canteen, rain jacket, bathroom kit, extra socks, cell phone, flashlight, a box of Godiva chocolate—a precaution against any sudden caloric loss while camping in nature—and a thin volume of Zen poetry, in case he had spare time to ponder the meaning of life.

By eight, he had consumed three cups of coffee, finished packing, and had forced down a single banana. He gathered up his now-heavy pack, locked the cabin, and made his way to the truck. While the engine was warming up, he pondered the fact that something very nasty was afoot in San Geronimo, and for reasons he did not understand, this nastiness was circling close to his personal orbit. He left the engine running, unlocked the front door, and fetched a .38 revolver from a cookie jar he kept on a high shelf in his kitchen. Howie didn't like guns, and rarely carried one, except in exceptional times.

Armed and dangerous, Howie picked up the phone on the kitchen table and punched in Jack's number at home. This wasn't going to be easy, but the sooner he told Jack about his lapse of judgment last night, the better chance he had of avoiding jail. Jack would be angry, but once he calmed down, he would know how to fix things. Emma answered the phone and told him that Jack was walking Katya and wouldn't be back for at least half an hour—they were heading down to Albuquerque later in the morning, and planned to leave Katya shut up in the house. Howie took the coward's way out and asked Emma to give Jack a message, please. Then, to her astonishment, he proceeded to tell her his hellish tale from last night: the horse, the dead man, the small white box, and why Howie had tied the dead man to the horse and hopefully sent him back to the reservation.

"My God, Howie, what a terrible experience that must have been for you!" Emma said. It was a motherly sentiment, and Howie was grateful. In fact, as confessions went, this had worked out very well for him. He had made a clean slate of things, and even got some sympathy in return. Jack would not have been so nice.

"Be careful," Emma warned. "Are you sure you don't want Jack to call you back on your cell phone?"

"I'll be up in the mountains," Howie told her. "A real black hole, I'm afraid, telephonically speaking."

Howie drove into the northern entrance to Pueblo land, crossing a cow guard shortly before nine A.M. It was a perfect New Mexico summer morning, clear and fresh and cool, with the mountains so finely etched against the blue sky that you could almost make out the wildflowers on the high meadows above the tree line.

There was no other traffic. Coming onto Indian land from this direction, the two-lane highway bumped and wound along uneven asphalt, over a minefield of potholes, and through an open expanse of rolling grassy meadowland where a herd of buffalo were grazing. The buffalo looked good here, very native, but in fact they had been adopted from an endangered herd in Yellowstone Park a few years back. A sign by the side of the road announced that the San Geronimo Pueblo was a drug-free and alcohol-free reservation. The sign was shot full of bullet holes and someone had dumped a case of empty Tecate cans nearby.

Howie's uneasiness increased as he approached the Pueblo village, passing gift shops that sold dreamcatchers, turquoise jewelry, T-shirts, and powwow music on CDs and tapes. The road continued into a high valley where the village was nestled at the very foot of the mountain that the Anglos called San Geronimo Peak—the Indians had a different name for it, of course, but they kept that name a well-guarded secret, along with all their other well-guarded secrets, customs, and rituals. This was an ancient place. As Howie had told Jack, the village itself, with its well-photographed multistory adobe condos and ladders going from roof to roof, was over seven hundred years old. Because of this fact, San Geronimo believed itself to be the aristocracy of the native world; they had roots, they had always lived right here, unassimilated, spiritually unconquered. They had been very lucky, of course, that the white man had not been quite so greedy to steal the barren deserts of the

Southwest as he had been to gobble up the greener, mineral-rich lands of Colorado, Montana, and the Dakotas.

The pavement ended and Howie joined a stream of cars with out-of-state plates that was heading into the central plaza, the only part of the Pueblo open to non-Indians. Howie followed the road past a number of low buildings of mud and straw until he came to a barrier where he was stopped by a young Indian man who was collecting a $10-per-car admission.

"Ten bucks!" Howie cried. "It used to be five!"

"This is a very sacred place, man. The United Nations has listed us as a special heritage site," the Indian told him. He wore mirrored aviator sunglasses, tight faded jeans, a headband, and a T-shirt that said TRIBAL SECURITY across the front. "If you want to take photographs, it'll be an extra ten dollars for a still camera, twenty-five if you have a camcorder."

"What about T-shirts? Can I buy a T-shirt saying I've been scalped at the San Geronimo Pueblo?"

The Indian smiled thinly. "Scalping was more your custom, I believe. What are you? Cheyenne?"

"Lakota. And actually, I'm not a tourist today. I'm meeting Lewis Lucero, the War Chief. I was told to ask for him here."

"Well, that's different. Pull out of line and I'll give Lewis a call. What's your name?"

Howie told him, pulled out of the line, and waited while the Indian raised a cell phone to his ear, punched a preset button, and began speaking in Tiwa. Howie watched the tourist cars stream past him, each driver shelling out the $10 admission, and often another ten or twenty-five for the use of a still camera or camcorder. The approved cameras were given small yellow tags so that the tribal police could make certain that no one who hadn't paid was sneaking photos of fry bread or adobe mud.

The security man lowered his cell phone and ambled back to where Howie had parked by an adobe wall. His jeans were so tight, he had trouble walking.

"The War Chief is tied up in a conference," he announced. "So you're going to have to wait a little."

Howie liked that: *tied up in a conference.* Being a War Chief wasn't much like what it used to be in the old days.

"Look, why don't you beep him on your cell phone and ask where he wants us to meet," Howie suggested. "I'll drive there and wait for him."

"Naw, I can't disturb him. Not when he's in an important meeting."

Howie was starting to feel irritated. "So, what? I'm just supposed to sit here?"

The security guy smiled. "What's your hurry? Tell you what—why don't you park your pony and get yourself some coffee. There's a place just inside the plaza. I won't even charge you the ten bucks to get in."

"That's mighty intertribal of you, bro," Howie said. He parked the truck and wandered on foot into a large open plaza that was surrounded with little tourist stores situated in the bottom floors of the old adobe buildings. It wasn't so much a plaza in the Spanish sense as a large unpaved ceremonial space, big enough for foot races, corn dances, even huge bonfires on Christmas Eve. There was a shallow, fast-moving stream that divided the plaza and the Pueblo itself in half, a single wooden bridge passing from one side to the other. This was the Rio Pueblo, whose waters came from the sacred lake high in the mountains, Spirit Lake, the lifeblood of the village.

Howie heard a number of foreign languages around him: Japanese, German, French, Texan. A Japanese couple, their skin pale as paper, pointed a camcorder in his direction, but he glared at them so hard, they had the sense to point their abominable lens at another subject. "Go eat seaweed!" he muttered. He knew he was being churlish. The Pueblo Indians he passed saw very well that Howie was not one of them, and he received a few mildly curious glances.

He was looking for a place to buy coffee when a small Indian boy came up behind him and tugged on his arm.

"Hey, are you Moon Deer?" the boy demanded. He was eight or nine years old with intense brown eyes.

"I was the last time I checked," Howie told him. "Who are you?"

"I'm a messenger," the boy said.

Howie raised an eyebrow. "Well, okay. What's the message?"

"The message is go to Flora's Fry Bread Shop and ask for a Navajo taco with extra beans. She'll tell you the rest of the message when you get there."

Howie gave the boy a loopy smile. "Extra beans, huh? This is somewhat cryptic."

"What does cryptic mean?"

"It means like a secret code. Do you go to school?"

The boy nodded seriously. "Next year I'm going to the public school in San Geronimo."

"Are you? That's going to be a big change. Aren't you scared?"

The boy narrowed his eyes and stared at Howie intently but did not reply.

"Well, where's Flora's Fry Bread Shop?" Howie asked him.

"Across the bridge, where the Winter People live."

"Who are the Winter People?"

"Don't you know?"

"No. I don't live around here."

"Where do you live, then?"

"I'm Lakota. I'm from way up north in South Dakota. But I don't really live there anymore, either."

The boy thought this over. "My grandfather says that a man has no power unless he is walking upon the land of his ancestors."

"Well, I'm sure your grandfather must be right," Howie said. "But maybe there's a different kind of power that comes from exploring new places."

"*I* want to go to new places," the boy said with sudden enthusiasm. "There's nothing to do around here. My older brother's in a gang, but I don't want to do that because it's so boring."

Howie studied the kid more closely. "So where would you go, if you could go anywhere?"

"Disney World," he answered without hesitation. "That's

where I'll start, then I'll keep on going everywhere. Las Vegas, California. Maybe all the way to China."

Howie didn't smile. The boy reminded him too much of himself at the same age, and the memories it sparked were painful. He had longed to leave the rez, and had finally done so. But had it done him any good?

"Well, the world is a good place to see," he agreed. "But you'd better be careful because once you leave your tribe, you can never go home again, not really. I tell you this from my own experience."

"I don't care," the boy said angrily. "I'm going to leave, and no one can stop me."

"Well, good luck on your journey," Howie told him. He gave the kid a dollar and thanked him for the message. He began walking toward the footbridge that crossed the Rio Pueblo, then turned back. It was on his tongue to tell the kid to stay here among his people, because Indians lost themselves when they left their roots behind, and there was nothing worse than a lost Indian. But he looked at the boy more closely, standing barefoot on the earth of the plaza, and changed his mind.

The boy had wanted to know what cryptic meant. And where else would he find the answer to that question but in the far, lonely places of the world?

13

Howie walked through a screen door into Flora's Fry Bread, a tiny room in one of the old buildings that encircled the plaza. The walls were adobe mud and there was an overpowering smell of wood smoke, dust, and cooking oil. An elderly Indian woman stood near a stove behind a small counter. She was broad-faced, deeply wrinkled, and weighted down by a heavy turquoise-and-silver necklace on her breast, bracelets jangling on her arms, and a concha belt draped around her large waist. Howie imagined this must be Flora herself. Along with her lunch counter, she sold dreamcatchers, which were small wooden hoops that were cleverly tied with a spiderweb of string and dangling feathers. The idea of dreamcatchers was that were supposed to catch all that which was good from bad dreams, a fairly sophisticated notion, Howie had always thought. He tried to remember the exact words he was supposed to say.

"Cat got your tongue?" she asked sharply.

This seemed to Howie an odd comment under the circumstances, though perhaps he had become overly sensitive to feline matters as of late. He stared at her suspiciously.

"Well?" she insisted.

"I'd like a Navajo taco."

"How about beans?" she asked pointedly. "You want beans, boy?"

"Oh, yes. Extra beans, please."

Howie watched her wrinkled hands put together the Navajo taco on a paper plate: a piece of flat fry bread piled high with ground meat, beans, cheese, shredded lettuce, tomatoes, salsa, and sour cream. This was serious heart-attack cuisine. As a final touch, Flora topped off her mountain of high-fat heaven with three huge spoonfuls of sliced jalapeños.

"Whoa! Not so heavy on the heat, grandmother!" he objected.

"This ain't for you, boy. Go on, take it upstairs. He's waiting."

"*He*? Upstairs where?"

"Up the ladder. Now go on, or it'll get cold, and he don't like that."

Howie took the paper plate in both hands and struggled up the ladder that rose at a steep angle at the back of the room toward a hole in the ceiling. The plate sagged in the middle and grease ran down Howie's arm. He came up through the hole into a small, austere room with a single narrow bed.

"Out here!" came a voice.

A door from the bedroom led to the flat roof where an old man with a straw cowboy hat was sitting outside on a wooden stool overlooking the dusty plaza below.

"Raymond! What are you doing here?"

"What does it look like? I'm grabbing me a spot of breakfast. Where's my coffee?"

"Nobody told me anything about coffee."

"You think I'm going to eat breakfast without coffee? Now get on the ball, Moon Deer! You shouldn't need to have someone tell you these things."

Howie handed Raymond his monster taco, then climbed back down the ladder to fetch a big mug of black coffee that Flora laced with four heaping spoonfuls of sugar. Raymond was half through the taco by the time Howie returned to the roof.

"No wonder so many Indians have diabetes! This food's going to kill you, Raymond."

"Hey, I'm not planning to live forever," Raymond replied loftily. "So don't give me any shit, please."

Howie sat down cross-legged on the roof, his back against the building. Below them a tourist bus was disgorging a crowd of chubby white people wearing shorts, loud shirts, and sunglasses into the plaza, all of them gazing about eagerly for possible signs of real Indians living in a real Indian village. Meanwhile, Raymond belched with satisfaction and rolled himself a cigarette from a small pouch of Top tobacco.

"Smoke, Moon Deer?"

"No, thanks. What's the matter, diabetes isn't enough for you? You want emphysema, too?"

"Those are white man's diseases, not mine. Now listen to me, because we don't have much time. There was some trouble last night. A horse rode into the Pueblo with a dead man tied to the saddle. It was a spooky sight, from what I've been told—a good thing none of our tourist brothers were here or they'd probably have peed their pants. The man had been shot in the back."

"Who was he?" Howie asked cautiously.

Raymond didn't answer immediately. He exhaled a long stream of smoke and stared across the plaza. When he spoke finally, his voice was weary. "Well, it was my grandson, Charlie. You'll need to break the news of this to Donna Theresa when you see her. They were cousins and she will be upset. They were close as children, though not so much in recent years."

"I'll tell her . . . I'm sorry, Raymond. I really am."

The old *cacique* remained silent, keeping whatever feelings he had to himself.

"Who killed him? Do you know"

Raymond shrugged. "That is a difficult question. I'm afraid the answer is this: My grandson killed himself by behaving stupidly. And that is the worst kind of death. Meaningless. Men should die as warriors, fighting for honor and justice."

"He didn't shoot himself in the back, Raymond. Who pulled the trigger?"

The old man smoked his cigarette moodily, but did not answer. Raymond was making himself fabulously inscrutable, but it was starting to piss Howie off.

"Look, I met Charlie the other night, behind the restaurant where he worked washing dishes. Two Indian guys were beating him up. I tried to help him out a little—I didn't do much, but later he asked if I wanted to buy some of his homegrown weed."

"Stupid!" Raymond muttered. "This is what I mean!"

"Well, a lot of guys around here grow pot in the mountains, not just Indians. The money's very tempting. Sometimes they rip each other off and quarrel over turf . . . what I'm saying is maybe drugs had something to do with his death."

"No," Raymond said simply. "It was not drugs."

"Then what was it? Who killed him?"

"Do you know who the Summer People are?" the *cacique* asked unexpectedly.

"Sure," Howie answered. "Summer People live in Dallas or Los Angeles and they usually show up here around the July Fourth weekend."

Raymond didn't laugh. "You shouldn't act so foolish," he scolded.

"Okay, Summer People—they're the opposite of Winter People? Am I getting warmer?"

Raymond nodded. He pointed to the stream that flowed through the center of the plaza, dividing the Pueblo in half.

"You see that? On the other side of the river, that's where the Summer People live. On this side, where we're sitting now, this is the home of the Winter People. These are the two societies that make up the Pueblo. There's always been a rivalry between the Summer People and the Winter People dating back as long as anyone can remember. Rivalry is natural, of course, and can be a healthy thing, encouraging the people to become better at what they do. But unfortunately in recent times, this rivalry has become a problem. I'm telling you things, Moon Deer, that we don't ordinarily say to outsiders. So listen carefully and try not to be foolish for a little while."

"Moiety" was the term that anthropologists liked to use to describe such clans as Summer People and Winter People. Long ago, according to Raymond, it was more a matter of dividing up the village for foot races and hunting parties, but over time the divisions had hardened into active hostility. Today the two groups rarely intermarried, except for the odd Romeo and Juliet. The Summer People liked to say that the

Winter People buggered sheep and were such great thieves
they'd steal an outhouse if it wasn't nailed down. For their
part, the Winter People insisted that Summer People were all
drunks and child molesters. All told, there were a little more
than a thousand people at the Pueblo and division was not
much to anyone's advantage; yet once a feud like this got
started, it quickly spread like a raging fire, nearly impossible
to stop.

The two opposing groups were further divided into four
separate kivas where the men of the village conducted their religious ceremonies, and each of these kivas also had long
standing rivalries. As Howie listened to Raymond, he thought
of the bitterness among the Sioux between the progressives
and traditionalists—the AIM guys and the goons. But it wasn't
only Indians, of course, who were endlessly divided; non-
natives had their Republicans and Democrats, black and white,
Christians and Jews. As far as Howie could make out, this was
the natural yin and yang tragedy of Planet Earth: Human beings thrived on conflict.

"Pay attention, Moon Deer," Raymond said sharply, for
Howie was drifting off into philosophical speculation. "The
most important family among the Winter People are the Conchas, my family. And the most powerful family among the
Summer People are the Luceros. For the past sixty years or so,
the Luceros have controlled the tribal council, while one of the
Conchas has always been *cacique*, the spiritual leader of the
community. At present, Don Lucero is governor, and the War
Chief, Lewis Lucero, is Don's cousin."

"Damn!" Howie said, standing up. "I forgot all about the
War Chief—he's probably waiting for me!"

"He's been told you're with me. Lewis won't be happy, but
he'll wait. Meanwhile, you need to know more about this old
feud. Two years ago, one of my sons, Frank, was killed walking across the road in front of his house by a drunk driver. The
drunk driver was Anthony Lucero, one of Lewis Lucero's
boys. It was an accident, I suppose, if you can call the foolish
behavior that alcohol causes accidental. But it didn't help relations between the Luceros and Conchas."

"It must have been hard for you to lose a son."

"Well, I have lost sons before," Raymond said stonily. "It is hard to bear, but death is natural and we must learn to bear it. However, to waste your life—that is not natural, that is what I can not bear. Frank had a son—my grandson, Charlie—and Charlie took his father's death very hard. It was at this time that Charlie began to smoke marijuana and drink alcohol. He allowed himself to be overcome by anger and despair. Anthony might just as well have killed Charlie that night, along with Charlie's father."

"When I met Charlie, he seemed more the jokey type," Howie suggested. "Not so angry."

"Beware of people who are funny, Moon Deer. They are in pain. And the funnier they are, the more pain they are in. It is not always easy to see things squarely, yet we must. I loved my grandson, but he was a fool. Along with drugs and alcohol, Charlie began to have the illusion that he was some kind of great detective—yes, just like you and your white man. He was trying to learn certain things, information he might use against the Lucero family, particularly Lewis. He believed there was a great deal of stealing being done by the tribal council, and that if he could discover the truth of these things and tell people, the Winter People would be able to take control away from the Summer People."

"That's interesting, given what happened to him. I wonder what he found out."

"Not much, I imagine. Charlie lacked the insight and discipline to understand things."

"Aren't you being hard on him?"

"Life is hard, Moon Deer, and we must act like men, not children. There's something else I want you to know. Anthony Lucero is missing. This is the boy who ran over Charlie's father and it is said that Anthony sometimes does the War Chief's dirty business. No one has seen him for several days and there is a rumor that his father, Lewis, has sent him away to stay with relatives in Gallup in order that no one may question him. I think it's possible that Anthony isn't in Gallup after all, but hiding closer to home. He and my grandson were serious enemies, naturally, and it is possible that Anthony was the person who shot Charlie. Perhaps the War Chief was involved in this. I want you to understand how complicated this has become. The tribal police department is under the jurisdiction of the War Chief. They are all Lewis's people—some are honest, some are not, so judge each one carefully," Raymond warned.

"I will. But, you know, Raymond, I still don't understand why you're telling me these things."

"I am telling you these things, Moon Deer, because I want the feuding to stop. It *must* stop or we will destroy ourselves as a people—it is that simple. You can help because you're an outsider, as I was saying yesterday in your office; neither a Summer Person or a Winter Person. I want you to find out the truth for me, Moon Deer—who killed Charlie, and why the British archeologist was allowed to work on sacred land, and where Anthony Lucero is hiding, and what he knows. Once the truth is known, I will go to the council and then I will go to the people themselves, and I will make them see clearly the nature of the disease that has overtaken us. This is my job, after all. I am their spiritual teacher. But first I must have all the facts."

Howie shook his head. "You're asking a whole lot, Raymond!"

"Yes, I am. But this is your task, Moon Deer. I have had a dream about this, and my dreams are rarely wrong. Either you will succeed, or you will die. So there is no need to trouble yourself with worry and doubt—if you die, you will be at peace."

Howie laughed. "That is *not* reassuring!"

"Death is nothing." Raymond stubbed out his cigarette on the sole of his left cowboy boot. "Death is a friend that is waiting for us all."

"Yeah, but this friend can wait a little longer, as far as I'm concerned. Tell me something—how does the Anasazi cave fit into all this feuding you've been telling me about?"

Raymond shook his head. "I am not sure about this. Maybe it doesn't fit, and that is the point. I believe in my heart that our ancestors are trying to help us in this difficult time, that they have a message for us from the past. We must listen carefully, Moon Deer, to what the old stones have to say."

As Raymond was talking, the young boy Howie had met in the plaza climbed up the ladder from the shop below and began speaking to Raymond in Tiwa. Raymond nodded and stood up from his stool.

"You must go now," he said to Howie. "The War Chief is looking for you. He is becoming impatient."

"But Raymond, I still have a shitload of questions," Howie objected.

"We all have a shitload of questions—that is the way life is," Raymond pronounced grandly, cutting him off.

"Raymond!"

"Relax, Moon Deer. Friends will appear when you least expect them. As it happens, there is someone who will be watching out for you, ready to offer help if needed. Listen to me carefully: Be prepared to accept help from an unlikely source when least expected."

Howie stared at the old *cacique*. "You're kidding. A secret helper. But who exactly?"

Raymond smiled slyly. "A great detective like yourself—I'm sure you'll figure it out."

"For chrissake, Raymond, this is ridiculous! I don't even speak your language. I can't do all these things you're asking of me."

"You must free yourself from negative energy, from all this doubt and questioning," Raymond told him, doing a pretty good imitation of a New Ager. "Go now, Moon Deer. Climb the sacred mountain! Be a man! And if you're still alive, come back and tell me your adventures."

14

Howie got directions to the War Chief's house from the security guy with the sunglasses and the attitude. He drove along a deeply rutted dirt road that worked its way gradually into the higher reaches of the valley, away from the tourist part of the reservation, passing double-wide trailers and boxlike adobes that had fallen into gentle disrepair. There were vegetable gardens and chicken coops and country clutter. This could be rural New Mexico just about anywhere, nothing really exciting to take photographs of, especially at ten bucks for still shots and twenty-five bucks for camcorders. Every home had a TV antenna on its roof, and occasionally there was a satellite dish in the front yard with a goat or cow grazing nearby. The new American Indian watched sitcoms and David Letterman and *ER*, just like the rest of the country.

Howie drove for nearly a mile until he came to a sprawling ranch house with a two car garage and sundeck that was very upscale in comparison to the other houses nearby. Two tribal cops with tan uniforms and guns on their hips were busy saddling horses in a corral that stood next to an open field on the north side of the house. The sight of the cops gave Howie a jolt of anxiety, given Charlie's final word. A third Indian in jeans and a blue-and-green-checkered cowboy shirt leaned against the rail, smoking a cigarette and watching the progress from outside the corral.

Howie parked, slung his pack onto his back, locked the pickup truck, and walked over. There were four saddle horses and two separate pack horses that were getting loaded with supplies. This was going to be a bigger expedition than he had expected.

"Howdy!" Howie greeted.

The three men stared at him without a glimmer of friendliness as he approached. One of the cops was fat and tall and in his early fifties, a big, morose-looking man, his belly bulging over his belt, graying hair hanging in two long braids down his back in the traditional manner. Howie presumed this must be Carl Lucero, the head of the San Geronimo Tribal Police Department. The second cop was leaner and younger, late twenties, with short black hair and a mean, narrow face.

Howie turned his attention to the man in the cowboy shirt who was leaning against the corral. This had to be Lewis Lucero, the War Chief. He was a small, compact man in his early fifties, with tortoiseshell glasses and hardly any chin. His hair was also touched with gray and he wore it long in the same traditional manner as the older cop, in two braids that pulled back so tightly from his face that it looked painful. The War Chief smiled as Howie approached. His smile was slick and well-practiced.

"Well, I guess you're Moon Deer," said the War Chief. His teeth were small and white and obviously false. "I'm Lewis Lucero. This here's my cousin, Big Carl, and that handsome young fella is Daryl. They'll be riding up with us today. You've kept us waiting, Moon Deer. What did Raymond want with you?"

"He wanted me to give a message to his granddaughter," Howie said.

"What message was that?"

"Nothing special," Howie lied. "Just personal stuff."

"Whatcha got in that backpack, boy?" Carl asked from inside the corral. "Looks like you got the kitchen sink in there!"

Howie smiled. "Just a change of clothes and a sleeping bag."

"You know how to ride a horse, Moon Deer?" Lewis asked.

"Sure. Just show me where the gear shift is."

Lewis and the two cops, Big Carl and Daryl, stared at him without expression.

"That was a joke," Howie assured them. "I grew up with horses."

"I'd better warn you, just in case you're having second thoughts. The trail's narrow and steep, and there's not exactly what you'd call a guardrail up there," Lewis said, enjoying himself. "If you can't control your horse, you're gonna be one dead Lakota brother."

Howie shrugged. What the hell, he thought, it was a good day to die. The three men ignored him for a time, finishing their preparations for the journey. Of the four horses that were saddled, two were gray Appaloosas, the third was a pretty reddish-brown quarter horse, and the fourth a huge black monster with a white star on its nose, a magnificent but nervous animal that must have been nearly sixteen hands tall. The big black horse was snorting and pawing the ground, looking eager to throw anyone foolish enough to try to ride it. Somehow Howie sensed that this horse was reserved for him. He wasn't surprised when Carl brought the black horse over to where Howie was standing and handed him the reins.

"So this is my guy, huh?" Howie asked skeptically. "He looks kinda wild."

"Not too wild for someone who grew up with horses," Carl said with an expanding smile. "One thing I gotta tell you, though. Your guy is a girl."

The three Indians guffawed with laughter. It was funny, certainly, and Howie tried to show he was good-natured by laughing, too. Next time someone handed him the reins of a horse, he would raise its tail and inspect the private areas before venturing any further remarks. He turned his attention to the black mare.

"What's her name?"

"We don't really know," Lewis admitted. "She just showed up here one morning a few days back, wild as hell, dragging a broken halter. I've been calling her Black Mare, but you can call her anything you like. Found her standing outside my corral saying hello to one of my stallions. I've been trying to find out who owns her ever since, but no one's claimed her yet. She's not an Indian horse, anyway, or somebody would have said something by now. Hey, you know, I think she *likes* you!"

Black Mare was studying Howie with huge, dark, nervous eyes, her sensitive ears pointing at Howie like radar screens.

"Well, hello there," Howie tried. He raised his hand to pet her nose, but she shied, jerking her head away in alarm, showing the whites of her eyes.

"Easy, girl," Howie told her. "I wonder where you came from, a beautiful horse like you."

"Well, if we're gonna go, let's get going," Carl said laconically.

"Just a minute," Howie insisted. He wasn't going to be rushed. He set down his pack, reached into a side pocket, and found a piece of Godiva, dark chocolate with a coconut filling. This was a sacrifice, but Moon Deer sensed his ass was on the line. He put the chocolate on his open palm for the horse to sniff. Black Mare moved cautiously closer, wanting the chocolate but not wanting to be the victim of any sly Indian trick. Howie knew the feeling.

"Whatcha doing, for chrissake?" Daryl, the young cop, demanded.

"Mmm, good," Howie told the horse. "Very expensive chocolate. They eat this in New York, San Francisco, all the fancy places . . . you'll be one sophisticated pony, so go for it, girl."

"Do you *believe* this Sioux?" Lewis asked Carl.

But Carl was enjoying himself, watching what would doubtlessly be a good horse story, however it turned out. Meanwhile, Black Mare was no dummy; she knew good chocolate when she saw it. Inch by inch, the horse moved her whiskered nose closer to Howie's palm. Then shyly, with a single delicate bite—very ladylike, really—the chocolate disappeared. Howie reached to stroke the mare's powerful neck while she munched thoughtfully on the gourmet tidbit. She allowed herself to be stroked, which was a good sign.

"First chocolate—next thing you know, he'll be bringing her flowers!" Carl said with a high, *tee-hee* giggle. For a big man, he had a soprano laugh.

"Must be some kind of Lakota courtship thing," Lewis

added drily, not so amused. "Let's get on the trail, Moon Deer."

Howie was able to climb up onto the mare's broad back on the third try, after trotting around the corral a few times with one foot in the stirrup. Black Mare pranced and danced. She was a big, beautiful animal, with a whole lot of RPMs. With some difficulty Howie managed to hold back on the reins.

"So you ready to leave the corral now, Moon Deer?" Lewis asked sarcastically, sitting calmly on a well-behaved Appaloosa.

"Sure," said Moon Deer. He eased up on the reins, and the black mare took off like an arrow shot from a bow out of the corral. Howie heard laughter behind him, the three Indian men enjoying his predicament. Then he heard nothing at all but the wind and thundering hooves.

15

On Saturday morning, Jack and Emma Wilder left home shortly before nine o'clock for the three-hour drive to Albuquerque where Jack had a noon appointment at the Office of the Medical Investigator.

Emma drove while Jack dozed fitfully in the passenger seat of the Subaru, listening to a Haydn symphony on the radio, courtesy of NPR. Emma knew that Jack was not sleeping well at night and she was concerned. On the surface, Jack appeared to be a gruff old bear, but she knew he was prone to serious bouts of depression since losing his eyesight. In a sense they had traded places emotionally: In California, she had been the moody one, dissatisfied with her life, emotionally dependent on her VIP cop husband who was seldom home. Jack had been the strong one then. But in New Mexico, she had blossomed and found personal strength in the difficult transition. She loved the land itself here, and the hugeness of the sky. It suited her spirit, and now, strangely, it was Jack who was dependent on her, though they both did their best to hide this fact. In many ways, Jack's blindness was as difficult for her as it was for him.

The miles drifted by in endless mountains and mesas and sky. Occasionally, she glanced over to Jack, hoping he was all right. He was dressed in a blue Ralph Lauren Polo shirt and khaki pants that she had helped him pick out this morning— she knew Jack had complicated feelings about this visit today to OMI. In fact, he was a little nervous, returning to such places as he had frequented in his old life, wanting to make a good impression and not have anybody feel sorry for him. Unfortunately, she and Jack had had a quarrel after leaving the house this morning and the silence still lingered between them, full of irritations and unspoken things. She had been rushed leaving the house—there had been a last-minute phone call from her assistant at work, then Katya had gotten out the kitchen door, hoping to come along on the drive today, and it had taken Emma nearly ten minutes to get her settled inside once again. With one thing and another, Emma had forgotten to tell Jack about Howie's call until they were nearly half an hour south of town.

"Damn it, Emma! You should have told me this right away! It's insane—tying a body to a horse and sending it God only knows where! What in God's name could Howie have been thinking?"

"He was sending it back to the reservation."

"Incredible!"

"Look, Jack, what Howie did is very understandable. Indians have their own ways of taking care of Indian matters, that's all—and personally, I say more power to them. After what we've done to Native Americans in this country, it's not our place to tell them what to do."

"Emma! What Howie did was a felony. Am I the only person around here who hasn't lost his mind?"

"That must be it," she agreed.

"I mean, my God, it's not like Howie's some kid who's never left the reservation! There's a simple matter of law and procedure here. A person has been murdered. We're talking about justice, Emma, trying to find a killer. And unfortunately, it's not so easy to find a killer when you don't have a goddamn body!"

"Justice!" Emma had thrown back sarcastically. "Gimme a break, Jack! When it comes to Native Americans, face it— we've used the justice system to rob them blind. If you'll pardon the expression."

He smiled cunningly. "Careful. I'm handicapped, remember. If you hurt my feelings, I'll sue."

Jack and Emma had been arguing about social issues for over thirty years: She was the radical of the family, whereas

Jack could be very conservative about certain matters, particularly his white-male perspective of law and order. Usually, their arguments were good-natured, but sometimes they took on an edge. Frankly, it annoyed Emma that Jack couldn't see how stodgy his notions were of crime and punishment, and how unfair they often were to minorities and the underclass.

"You know, you're such a stubborn mule sometimes!" Emma muttered, passing through Española.

"All I'm saying is if everybody started tying dead bodies to horses, we'd all be in a hell of fix."

"You'll help Howie stay out of trouble, won't you?"

Jack sighed. "Oh, sure, what the hell, I'll just aid and abet in hiding a felony. It's against everything I believe in, and I'll lose my PI license if it ever comes out. But don't let that worry you, Emma."

"I'm sorry," she told him.

"Well, I'm sorry, too. But it's not your fault," he replied grudgingly. "Or Howie's, either, for that matter, I guess. Christ, he's just a kid, an amateur. An *intellectual*, God help us! I never should have hired him for this kind of work."

"You know you're very fond of Howie."

"Of *course* I'm fond of Howie. That's why I should fire him. Maybe it would give him the push to get his ass in gear and finish up his doctorate."

"You couldn't run the agency without him, Jack."

"No. But that would be a small loss. Christ, we're ridiculous—a blind detective and an overeducated Indian kid who should be back in school! Sometimes I wonder what in the hell I'm trying to prove."

"Come on, Jack. You're just feeling discouraged. You and Howie have solved some important cases."

"Very occasionally," he admitted.

Emma kept the books for Wilder & Associate, so she had a realistic idea of how Jack and Howie were doing. In fact, the agency operated in the red, despite an occasional windfall month. It was the overhead that was killing them—the rent on the office downtown, combined with the fact that Jack insisted on giving Howie a steady salary even when there was no work, along with medical insurance, which was an almost unheard of benefit in northern New Mexico. Fortunately, the Wilders were okay for money; along with Jack's disability pension, they had sold a house on Potrero Hill in San Francisco that they had bought for $69,000 in 1970 for $850,000 in the early nineties. This made a money-losing detective agency an allowable indulgence, as long as they were careful in other areas. Most of all, Emma was glad it gave Jack something to do that interested him.

"You're not pouting over there, are you?" she asked thirty miles later.

"No, I'm—"

Just then, Emma slammed on the brakes and blasted her horn. The Subaru fishtailed wildly from side to side, and Jack prepared to die: to career through the black void of his blindness to whatever God awaited him. Then Emma regained control of the car and they continued down the freeway without further mishap.

"Sorry," Emma said. "Some asshole changed lanes without looking. What were you saying?"

"I'm . . . fine."

Emma guided the Subaru into a parking spot in front of a nondescript building on Camino de Salud in Albuquerque, just northwest of the university hospital. The Office of the Medical Investigator, a service run by the University of New Mexico, was officially closed on weekends, but pathologists sometimes used the building on Saturdays and Sundays when a special case was in progress. Shark Tooth was about as special as things got. Emma helped Jack into a small reception area that was empty of people, musty, and eerily quiet in a certain way that busy workplaces became on weekends.

"Hello!" Emma called through a double glass door into the innards of the autopsy suite. "Dr. Adams?"

"Be right there!" a voice called back.

Emma gratefully closed the glass door.

"What's that nasty smell? Formaldehyde?"

"Formalin," Jack told her. "No one uses formaldehyde any-more."

"Yuck." Emma didn't like places like this, never had. "There's another smell, too, something really foul . . ."

Jack smiled. He was on more certain ground again, for this was a world that was still familiar to him.

"It's only death, my dear. Don't pay it any mind."

Emma was relieved to deliver Jack to Dr. Derek Adams, a visiting forensic anthropologist from the University of Arizona. She drove off to run some errands, promising to come back in an hour.

Alone with the doctor, Jack found himself shaking a huge, hairy hand. "Thanks for seeing me, Dr. Adams. I can imagine how busy you are." It was a game Jack played, trying to visualize people from their voices and brief body contact. Six foot three, 220 pounds, a burly man with a trim beard and eye-glasses, Jack decided. Probably dressed in jeans and a sports shirt, casually academic.

The doctor's voice was deep, with a Midwestern twang. "You know, I've been hearing stories about you for years, Commander," he said. "We got ourselves some friends in common."

Dr. Adams led Jack through the autopsy suite into an office he had borrowed, gossiping about people they both knew and helping Jack get settled into a hard, modern chair. By the time this was accomplished, they were on a first-name basis. Derek knew several detectives and a medical examiner from California who were ex-colleagues of Jack's, and this was an advantage; it meant Jack didn't have to waste time establishing his credentials.

"I understand you spent the day yesterday examining the head," Jack said when they were settled.

"You mean Shark Tooth," Derek chuckled. "I gotta tell you something you're not going to like. You got yourself a copycat killer."

"Copycat?" The temperature in the autopsy suite was kept deliberately cool to discourage germs and Jack wished he were wearing warmer clothes. He hugged himself to stay warm. "Copycat of what exactly?"

"Well, get ready because this is going to blow your mind. It's pretty wild stuff!"

In Jack's experience, forensic anthropologists were an odd bunch, though maybe not as eccentric as forensic entomologists, the bug experts who had become a big part of certain homicide investigations in recent years. A forensic entomologist could tell you how long a person had been dead based on the number of maggots and other vermin feasting upon the body; people attracted to professions of this sort were not your average joes.

"Tell me, Jack, what do you know about the Anasazi?"

"*Anasazi*?" Jack repeated in surprise. "Well, I went to Chaco Canyon a long time ago with my wife, back when I could see. I read the handouts they give you at places like that, and that's about the extent of my knowledge."

"What did you *think* of Chaco? Did you like it there? I know this question probably seems off the deep end Jack. But believe me, it's leading back to Shark Tooth."

"I can't wait to see how!" Jack muttered. "Well, sure, I liked it. Chaco Canyon's an astonishing place. The ruins are very impressive. Emma and I spent a few days in one of the campgrounds and pretty much walked all over the canyon. It's intriguing to try to imagine the people who lived there hundreds of years before Columbus. I remember there was one big old house we saw that was three or four stories high. The stonework was amazing."

"You're probably thinking of Pueblo Bonito—it's the biggest of what we call the Anasazi Great Houses. Pueblo Bonito had about 650 rooms and it was constructed out of nearly thirty thousand tons of sandstone blocks. It was a *very* advanced society that built something like that."

"What's this all about, Derek? What does a pre-Columbian civilization have to do with a severed head that was found in a Dumpster behind a Chinese restaurant?"

"It's a stretch, isn't it? Well, you'd better settle in and let me tell you about this, Jack, because like I say, it's wild . . ."

"The Chaco Phenomenon," as archaeologists liked to call it, flowered in the San Juan Basin of present-day New Mexico from approximately A.D. 900 until it ended abruptly and without explanation in about A.D. 1150 It was a culture that left behind no written record, so no one could say what these people had called themselves, or indeed very much about them. A few dates were known from the tree-ring dating of roof-beam vigas and radiocarbon-dating methods, but this was all. During their 250-year span, the Anasazi created astonishing things: great public buildings, irrigation systems, temples, and hundreds of miles of roads, built without compasses, radiating out from Chaco in straight lines like spokes on a wheel. Their buildings and roads were oriented in such a way as to show a sophisticated understanding of astronomy.

The ruins were so impressive that many people today regarded the Chaco Phenomenon as a kind of utopia: a perfect society where all citizens were equal, where there were no rich, no poor, no violence, and no war. It is always nice, of course, to imagine a time when life was better than it is today. Archeological books on the subject were apt to be full of words like "incredible," "astonishing" and "mysterious." The Anasazi were revered as great spiritual elders by modern Hopi and Pueblo tribes, who claimed these people as their ancestors. Among the Indians, only the Navajo held a different view. The Navajo often avoided the ancient ruins on their reservation, believing a hideous evil had happened in these places, and claiming the old stones were haunted by *chindi*, or ghosts.

"The great unresolved mystery is what happened to make this civilization suddenly end," Derek told Jack. "Chaco Canyon was simply abandoned around 1150. There are lots of theories, of course—drought, famine, disease, and erosion usually top the list. But *nothing* really explains it adequately. For another hundred years or so, there was a kind of diaspora—the Anasazi spread themselves out almost like they were running from each other, settling in what we now call the Four Corners region. This was the period of the incredible cliff dwellings that you can still see at places like Mesa Verde, Canyon de Chelley, and Navajo National Monument."

"I've been to Mesa Verde," Jack agreed.

"Good. Then you know how inaccessible they are, high up the sides of cliffs. You would have just about had to be an eagle to get to some of those cave dwellings, Jack. Once the Anasazi pulled up their ladders, no one would have been able to reach them at all. What does that suggest to you?"

"That the Anasazi were frightened of something. They were hiding from their enemies."

"Exactly! No one lives up the sheer side of a cliff unless there is a very good reason to be afraid. So we have to ask ourselves, who were the Anasazi afraid of?"

"Another tribe? How about the Navajo?"

"No, the Navajo, the Apaches—these people didn't appear in the Southwest for a long time yet. You see, this is the problem, Jack. Archeologists have been digging around this area for a century or so and no one has found a single sign of any other ethnic group who lived concurrently with the Anasazi *except* the Anasazi themselves. You getting the picture here? There *was* no enemy. Yet even the fortified cliff dwellings were abandoned a hundred years later, around A.D. 1250. And that was the end of the great Anasazi culture. It simply vanished from the face of the earth. Without explanation."

"So the mystery, then," Jack said, "is who was the ancient enemy's enemy?"

"That's correct. And the answer, I'm afraid, is simply put: They were their own enemy. This is a society that quarreled so badly, it literally ate itself up."

"Literally?" Jack repeated. "You're suggesting . . ."

"Yep—cannibalism!" Derek said with a certain ghoulish delight. "This is one theory, at least. It's not a very popular theory, however. Are you starting to see how this ties in with the present, Jack?"

"Not really," Jack admitted. "But, please, go on."

Dr. Adams went on.

Beginning in the 1960s, several mounds containing ancient human bones were discovered near the so-called Great Houses in Chaco Canyon. In the following decades, other burial sites were found as well, in other parts of the Anasazi empire. They were mass graves, in fact, and alarm bells began going off among the small group of anthropologists who had the opportunity to study these sites. The bones were examined with modern forensic techniques, the same techniques that a police department might have used if an unexplained body had turned up on their beat. The first thing to become clear was that these prehistoric people did not die peacefully; they had been massacred. Then, an anthropologist by the name of Christy Turner II came up with an extraordinary theory: that the Anasazi hadn't been such lovely, spiritual, New Age folk after all, and that a great terror had come over the Southwest around the year A.D. 1150, a social disintegration in which roving bands of cannibal thugs caused the population to literally take to the hills, fleeing for their lives, hiding in fortified caves located high up on the sides of cliffs so that no one could sneak up on them unawares and turn them into barbecue.

That was Turner's theory, at least, and it was about as politically incorrect as any theory could be. Mainstream archaeologists could barely bring themselves even to discuss it; they appeared to truly *want* the Anasazi to be the utopian, spiritually advanced society they had previously believed them to be. And the notion of cannibalism was even more loathsome, of course, to the Indian tribes who revered the Anasazi as their ancestors. The Hopis and the Pueblo tribes were particularly outraged; it offended their belief in the sacred origins of their culture. It was like telling a devout Catholic that proof had been found showing Jesus as a child molester.

"But *is* there proof?" Jack asked.

"Well, yes and no," Derek told him. "When it comes to bones, there are five basic signs that most anthropologists agree indicate the possibility of cannibalism—but I imagine you know this?"

"You might refresh my memory," Jack allowed.

The five indications were: 1) Signs that the bones had been broken open to get at the marrow. 2) Utensil marks on the bones from various tools, suggesting butchering. 3) "Anvil abrasions," as Derek called them, on the backs of the skulls;

these were small, parallel scratches made by the slippage when a skull was placed on a rock and smashed open from the front to get at the brain. 4) Charring on the backs of skulls, usually a kind of flaking to indicate where the head had been placed on a bed of coals to roast the brain. And lastly, 5) The vertebrae and spongy bone were generally missing. Cannibals often smashed up these bones to get to the marrow inside, sometimes making pulverized "bone cakes"—an early version of a hamburger, as far as Jack could understand it.

"And the old Anasazi bones that were found—they exhibit these five markings?" Jack asked.

"Some of them do. You bet. But even with all this evidence, cannibalism is hard as hell to prove. Basically, you can show that someone was cooked, but whether they were actually *eaten* is another matter. I could go on like this for hours, by the way, but probably you're getting a little impatient."

Jack smiled. "I think I understand the general background. Now tell me about the head my assistant found in the Dumpster. Was it cannibalized or not?"

"Well, maybe yes. Maybe no. But whether you go along with the cannibal theory or not, when I saw that head yesterday, the first thing that went through my mind was, 'Bingo! Anasazi!' A few years back, I had the chance to examine some of the charnel bones from Chaco. And I gotta tell you, Jack, the skulls I saw from Chaco and the skull I examined yesterday are nearly identical in forensic details. Of course, Shark Tooth is about 800 years more recent than the Chaco bones, but other than that . . . Say you were able to examine an Anasazi burial mound shortly after the prehistoric people were killed. What you'd see—with the skulls, at least—would be pretty much like Shark Tooth. That's why I've been spending the past half hour giving you a history lesson. The past and present are converging in a mighty strange way."

"So with Shark Tooth, did you find your five classic signs?"

"Oh, you bet. The head was smashed open from the front, probably with a large rock. There were anvil abrasions on the back of the skull as well as blackened charring from where it had been roasted on a fire. There were also utensil marks inside the brain pan. So that makes four out of five when it comes to the classic indications. As for the vertebrae, that's not applicable in this case, of course, since we only have the head. Then, along with that, of course, there's also the traces of salt, pepper, and olive oil that the SEM examination revealed."

"Then it *is* cannibalism?"

"Well, personally I'm still saying maybe on both counts, with the Anasazi and your modern-day head as well. There's simply no way to determine it for sure."

"What about the time of death?" Jack asked. "Can you determine that?"

"Not with any accuracy. Roasting a head on a bed of coals totally destroys normal guidelines. My guess, though, is actually a little narrower than what the people here at OMI have been saying. I'd say the head was cooked anywhere from six hours to six days before it was found in the alley. Now when the vic was actually *killed* is another matter. There are so many possible variables that I'd rather not say."

"Any dental work?"

"Seven fillings. Three are amalgam, four are gold. All the work is very standard so it's probably going to be next to impossible to trace."

"And what about the shark's-tooth earring? It *is* a shark, I presume?"

"Yeah. It's from some kind of reef shark, not a really large species. I'm afraid I'm not an expert on fish—the tooth is going to be sent to a Dr. Prokupek at the Academy of Science in San Francisco, where they have the aquarium. Maybe she'll be able to say exactly what kind of shark it was, and where it might have been swimming. The metal part of the earring, by the way, is twenty-four-carat gold, and it tells us something that the gold didn't melt. It had to be a slow fire that cooked the head, nothing too hot—embers probably. But, of course, that's the best way to barbecue."

Jack sat for a moment in silence, allowing all the information he had just heard to ramble through his mind. He couldn't get a handle on this; as murders go, this one was vague and vast and crossed too many centuries.

"Tell me something, Derek. Have you ever heard about a British archeologist who might have been working in the Southwest?" Jack asked. "Someone interested in the Anasazi, particularly this cannibal slant?"

"Not really. Christy Turner, the man who started all this, is American and he doesn't have many followers. Why? You got a lead on someone?"

"No, it's more of a rumor than a real lead. And I've promised someone not to talk about it."

"Well, no Brit comes to mind. But you should ask at UNM—I'll give you the name and home number of the head of the archeology department. Most of the visiting researchers make contact with the university while they're here."

Jack shook his head. "Jesus! I thought I'd seen everything. But a copycat crime from eight hundred years ago, this is something else!"

"Yeah, but remember, Jack—it's just a *theory* of something that happened eight hundred years ago. And a hugely disputed theory, at that. There's one conservative school of thought that says there are *no* proven cases of cannibalism anywhere in history, not a single reliable first-hand account. Another school disputes that there is any mystery at all about the Anasazi— that the people simply spread out in a kind of centerless fashion until they transformed over the centuries into the Pueblo Indian tribes we know today. Personally, I don't find this convincing. Not only is there a real qualitative difference between the Anasazi culture and the Pueblo folk, but there's no convincing explanation as to why a technological marvel like Chaco Canyon would be suddenly abandoned. But who knows? The point I'm making is that everything I've been telling you over the last hour or so is highly theoretical, up for grabs."

Jack nodded slowly. "This is starting to point to someone from academia, wouldn't you say?" he asked after a moment. "You'd have to be a specialist even to know about this."

"Well, it won't be an Indian, at least. Believe me, they'd be the last people to advertise a theory they just want to go away. You know what I think?"

"What?"

Dr. Adams put on a very spooky voice. "It's the Curse of the Anasazi! So you'd better watch your step, Jack . . . there're some hungry chindi out there just hopin' for a chance to eat yo' brains!"

Emma parked next to the Double Rainbow Café, a college hangout on Central Avenue, and went inside to buy sandwiches for a lunch on the run. Jack remained in the car, worrying about Howie. After his talk with Dr. Adams, the Anasazi cave high on Pueblo land was starting to seem more ominous than it had yesterday.

Do you believe in ghosts? Raymond had asked him. Frankly, he wasn't sure what to believe, but meanwhile Howie was riding to the cave with little notion of the danger he was in. The last outsider there, the British archeologist, had apparently ended up cooked and cannibalized, *a lá* Anasazi.

Jack allowed his worry to rise into the red zone, then he took the cell phone from his pocket and punched in Howie's number.

16

When Howie was a child, his great-uncle, Horace Two Arrows, had taught him how to ride a horse. Two Arrows was a minor medicine man, a *pejuta wichasa* as the Sioux called a certain kind of doctor/herbalist. He drank too much beer and he was not a real holy man, a *wichasa wakan* like the famous Black Elk. But still he knew the old ways, and what Howie knew of these matters was entirely due to his great-uncle.

Two Arrows had always predicted that Moon Deer's journey would take him far beyond the Badlands of South Dakota, and for this reason he insisted that Howie know how to handle a horse. It would be important one day to navigate through distant lands where Two Arrows had heard strange tales of horses with humps—sometimes one hump, sometimes two, but if you knew the basics, a person on a journey was prepared for any hump at all. For several years, Howie had a horse of his own. He called his horse Dickens because at about the age of twelve, Howie had gone through a major literary phase, checking some of Charles Dickens's novels out of the local library, and borrowing others from his teacher Miss Farnsworth, who had taken an interest in him as a very promising boy. She had eventually helped start him on the scholarship trail.

Like all Indian kids, Howie rode bareback, but he generally rode with a book propped up on his horse's mane—*David Copperfield, Great Expectations, Bleak House, The Pickwick Papers*—reading his way eventually clear through to *Dombey and Sons*. At this period of his life, in fact, Howie was a lot more knowledgeable about nineteenth century London than Rapid City sixty miles away. It was probably a good thing that

Dickens was nearly as dreamy a horse as Howie was a distracted rider or he might not have survived his childhood. Still, he wasn't entirely unprepared for the huge black horse this morning, for when you ride bareback as a kid, you never completely loose the skill.

After leaving the corral, Moon Deer and Black Mare galloped together for nearly a mile along the dirt road that led up the canyon past the War Chief's ranch home. It was a gallop so smooth and effortless it felt like both he and the horse were disconnected from the earth, flying together through the summer morning.

Howie let Black Mare run until she tired herself out. After a while, the horse began to canter, then finally slowed to a walk. Howie turned her around and by the time he had rejoined the others, he and Black Mare had come to a working relationship, a marriage, of sorts. Like all marriages, there was no guarantee it would be an easy ride. But at least there was no immediate prospect of a separation.

Big Carl led the way with a packhorse following on a lead rope behind him. After Carl came Lewis the War Chief, then Daryl the younger cop, who also had a pack horse in tow. Howie took up the rear on his prancey-dancey mare. They proceeded in single file along a narrow trail into a V-shaped valley that rose gradually in altitude. As the morning deepened, the sun came up hot and full in the sky and Howie shed his flannel shirt, tying it around his waist. For the first hour they stayed mostly in scrubby grassland dotted with clumps of piñon and juniper. Then they began a sharper ascent on a switchback trail that zig-zagged upward into a dense forest of aspen and conifers. Every now and then, Howie tried to get a conversation started, but it was not a talkative bunch.

"How long until we get to the cave?" Howie asked, riding alongside the War Chief at a wide point on the trail.

"Depends," said Lewis.

"Depends on what?"

"On a lot of things."

"Well, how about giving me a sort of expected time of arrival," Howie tried.

"Maybe two, three o'clock. If we don't have any problems."

"What kind of problems?"

"You'll know what kind of problems if we have any."

Half an hour later, they came out of the trees onto a meadow where they stopped to give the horses a drink of water from a fast-moving stream. Howie stood next to Lewis as the horses slurped.

"Tell me if I'm wrong, Lewis, but I get the idea that you're not too happy about taking me up to the site."

Lewis gazed off at the horizon, refusing to look at Howie. "Well, it was Raymond's idea that you should come, not mine. It's nothing personal, Moon Deer. I'm just against any outsiders coming onto our land, that's all."

"I understand that, I really do," Howie tried. "But the thing is, in case you haven't noticed, I'm an Indian, just like you are. And, you know, it seems to me that if only all the tribes had joined together in the old days instead of quarreling among themselves, it would have taken the white man maybe another fifty years or so to steal our land. They would have beaten us in the end, of course, but at least we'd have given them a run for their money."

The War Chief smiled. "The white man stole *your* land, not mine. We're *on* my land, Moon Deer. We've been riding on a trail where my great-great-grandfathers used to ride, and *their* great-great-grandfathers as well. That's the difference between us."

Put that way, Howie felt like a very landless sort of guy. He tried not to let Lewis's standoffish manner get to him, though, because there wasn't a lot he could do about it. He gave Black Mare another Godiva chocolate and they continued in single file upward into the mountains. The trail kept climbing and there were occasional patches of snow now in the shadows of the trees and a cool wind was blowing. Howie had to stop and put on his flannel shirt again. Finally, they came out of the trees onto a high alpine world of rolling green meadows, dotted full of bright, tiny blue and red wildflowers. They looked fragile but in fact had to be very tough in order to survive here. From this altitude, Howie could see the sandy tan of desert far below to the west, and a seemingly endless expanse of mountains to the north, south, and east. All the world was beautiful from this high vantage point and not even the unfriendliness of the War Chief and the two cops dampened Howie's pleasure at being on horseback on a fine day with the sun in his face.

They followed a high ridge up and down the spine of the mountain. After riding for nearly an hour, the trail descended sharply back below the tree line into a hidden valley where there was a cold mountain stream and a small oasis of trees. They were riding in the green shadows of the forest when Howie's cell phone began to ring with "Ode to Joy" from inside a pocket of his backpack. Howie regarded cell phones as a nuisance, a new form of human slavery, about as much fun as having a ringing alarm clock tethered to your neck. He had programmed his phone to beep him with Beethoven, hoping this would make him feel more affectionate toward the thing, but the music was extremely irritating, like some tiny chipmunk orchestra on amphetamines.

"What the hell is *that*?" Carl demanded from farther up the trail, turning around on his horse.

"Sorry. It's just my phone."

Howie struggled to slip his pack off his shoulders, reach for the telephone in the outside pocket, and still hold on to the reins with one hand. At last, Howie managed to hold the device to his ear with his right hand, balance the pack on the saddle horn, and grip the reins in his left hand.

"Yes!" he demanded, taking out his irritation on the caller.

At first there was only static. The mountains of New Mexico were notorious for their black holes, unfriendly to cell phone use. Then he heard Jack, his voice fading in and out.

". . . you there, Howie?"

"*I'm* here. Where are *you*?"

". . . kerky . . . ten . . . fully."

"*Where*? I can't hear a thing, Jack."

"Albuquerque." Jack's voice was suddenly clear, as though he were riding alongside him on the trail. "Listen carefully. I

just came from OMI where I had a long session with a forensic anthropologist. Where exactly are you now, Howie?"

"I'm on a trail at about eleven thousand feet on the back of
a horse, riding up the mountain with the War Chief and two
tribal cops. We're all having a splendid time."

"Okay. You can't talk, so just listen. What I want you to
do . . ."

But suddenly, just as Jack was about to tell him what to do,
Howie's world went ballistic. It happened without warning.
One moment he was listening to his little black telephone,
feeling quite the modern Indian, then a low branch swept him
off Black Mare's back. He hadn't been paying attention. The
cell phone flew from his hand and he landed with a painful
thud, all the breath knocked out of him. He sat up slowly,
painfully.

"Man, you're really something, Moon Deer," Lewis said,
turning his horse around to see what had happened.

Howie had to agree that there should be a warning put on
cell phones against horseback use. He was picking up his pack
from the ground when he noticed bits of black plastic and telephone innards scattered across the trail. His phone had hit a
rock and died: At least there would be no more chipmunk or-
chestras bugging him with Beethoven.

He pulled himself back up onto Black Mare, wondering
what it was that Jack was trying so urgently to tell him.

17

Emma Wilder was enjoying Albuquerque, watching all the college types in the Double Rainbow Café. She couldn't imaging what it must be like to be a student at the start of the twenty-first century—probably not as much fun, she thought, as her own youthful epoch, the 1960s. She walked out of the restaurant with lunch for two in paper bags and found Jack sitting tensely in the passenger seat, cell phone in hand. She saw immediately from his rigid body language that something was wrong.

"I was talking to Howie and he disappeared on me!" he bellowed. "Son of a bitch! I tried to get him back, but his phone didn't even ring. The problem with technology, Emma, is that it . . . doesn't . . . goddamn . . . work!"

Jack was easily frustrated by inanimate objects. He was a passionate man, her husband; he had once thrown a toaster across the kitchen after it had burned four pieces of toast to a blackened crisp on a memorable Sunday brunch from hell.

"Relax, Jack," Emma told him. "You're going to give yourself high blood pressure. You know how it is with the mountains around here—Howie's probably in a black hole."

"Black hole, my ass!"

"That would be a very black hole indeed, my dear," she quipped. "Look, you can try him later—maybe he'll be in a better place to receive a call. Meanwhile, I've got you a chicken sandwich with roasted red peppers, avocado, and sprouts. Hopefully that will soothe my favorite savage beast just a little."

"Rye bread?"

"No, they didn't have rye. It's on their own fresh baked whole wheat."

"Well, that's okay. You got me a Beck's?"

"No, we're *not* going to drive around Albuquerque with an open container. It's illegal, remember. I got you a mango smoothie. Now fasten your seat belt, 'cause here we go."

Emma had a serious shopping agenda planned for the rest of the day. She had taken the day off work from her job as director of the San Geronimo Public Library in order to be Jack's chauffeur—in fact, Saturday was the busiest day of the week at the library, so this was not especially convenient for her. To make the trip tempting, Jack had promised her a fancy dinner at Santacafé, their favorite restaurant in Santa Fe, and the chance to shop until she dropped in Albuquerque, where things were cheaper than San Geronimo and many more choices were available. As a rule, Emma disliked shopping; she often said that the great bonus of being married to a blind man was that she didn't have to worry about her wardrobe. So her hope was to use her one day in the big city to advantage, spend oodles of money, and not even have to *think* about buying anything for at least another year.

After leaving OMI, Emma's mission was to search for a new laptop computer. She left Jack in the car in front of a strip mall on Montgomery Avenue, parked in the shade, and walked inside a huge electronic mega-outlet. Twenty minutes later, Emma was more confused than ever about what she wanted, but at least she had some prices to compare with other stores. She returned to the car to find Jack sitting with the cell phone in his lap.

"Well, my dinosaur, did you manage to solve any crimes in twenty minutes?"

"I spoke to the head of the UNM anthropology department—a Professor Jonathan Lehman. Dr. Adams gave me his home number. Unfortunately, the professor turned out to be a space cadet. I told him I was looking for a British archeologist who was interested in the Anasazi and who might have been working on a site up north. He said, 'Oh, yes! I know exactly who you mean.' Then he proceeded to spend the next ten min-

utes telling me all about his good friend, Professor Kenichi
Yakura. Who it turns out isn't British at all—surprise, surprise,
he's Japanese. And his interest is the modern-day Zuni, not the
Anasazi at all."

"He sounds like some librarians I know."

"It certainly was a challenge, my dear. I was about to hang
up on him when suddenly he says, '*Wait*!'—some memory
cells are starting to stir. He recalled hearing *something* about a
British archeologist a few years back, but it was all very slippery and vague. Two or three years ago a student in one of his
graduate seminars came to him and said that she had a British
friend, an archeologist, a Dr. Whosey-What's-It—she told him
a name, but Lehman's the sort who probably can't remember
his own phone number, much less a name he heard only once
two or three years ago. What she wanted, apparently, was a
color copy of a satellite photograph of the Sangre de Christo
mountains up by San Geronimo to show her British friend.
Apparently, it's occasionally possible to locate buried archeological sites from space, using infrared photography, computer-
enhanced images—that sort of thing."

"And you think this British archeologist is the man you're
looking for?"

"Well, it's a lead, anyway. Naturally, the prof couldn't remember the name of the young woman who came to him
with the request. Fortunately, Professor Lehman remembered
he had a boy student in the graduate seminar who had a crush
on the girl student. And here, thank God, we struck paydirt.
He remembered the young man's name for the simple reason
that it was a literary name, the name of an American author—either John Updike, Philip Roth, or F. Scott Fitzgerald,
he wasn't sure which."

"You're kidding!" Emma laughed. "So all you have to do is
find a graduate student who was studying at UNM two or
three years ago with one of those three names? And then if
you find him, hope he still remembers the girl student he was
in love with back then who once said something about a
British archeologist and a satellite photo?"

"You got it, Ophelia. But no one ever promised that being a detective would be easy."

Ophelia! Jack hadn't called her that in years and it brought back such a flood of memories that Emma drifted through Pier I Imports, her next shopping destination, with a soft smile on her face, lit from within in a peculiar way that caused people to smile at her in return.

Ophelia was a nickname from 1967, when Emma had been in her bohemian phase, going around San Francisco barefoot in long dresses that Jack always said reminded him of nightgowns. At the time, Emma had managed a small bookstore in Northbeach and Jack was a young uniformed policeman who responded one afternoon to her call about a robbery at the store—a street person had grabbed all the money from the till when her back was turned. It was not an especially auspicious start. In those days, Emma had enjoyed her freedom, along with a revolving collection of arty boyfriends—poets, musicians, painters, dancers, even a middle-aged novelist with hair like Albert Einstein, a genius, she was sure. Sometimes it was hard to imagine whatever had possessed her to throw over all these creative types for an intense young cop who liked to take her for long, drug-free hikes in the Marin headlands—a pig, as people in her crowd called the police back then.

Reliving the past, misty with nostalgia, Emma bought a dozen candles and four wineglasses and returned to the car, where Jack was finishing up a phone call.

"Guess what? I found my graduate student!" The grin on his face reminded her more of the young San Francisco cop from 1967 than the gray-bearded old bear with wraparound glasses of today.

"No, I don't believe it," she said, putting the shopping bags in the back. "I mean, that's impossible, Jack!—Philip Roth, John Updike . . . what was the other name?"

"Scott Fitzgerald. The graduate student is actually named Scott Updike, so our spacey Professor Lehman got it just a little jumbled."

"But I was only gone ten minutes. How could you find him so quickly?"

"Easy as pie. I phoned Lehman back and got the name of his secretary. Then I called her and she turned out to be a lovely lady with a grandmotherly voice, and when I mentioned the three authors, she knew immediately who I meant. She even had a home number for Scott Updike, since it turns out he's still in the PhD program. I just spoke with Mr. Updike and I have an appointment to see him in fifteen minutes."

"And how exactly are you going to get to this appointment, Jack?" Emma inquired ruthlessly.

Jack's smile didn't falter. "I'm meeting him at the coffee bar at Page One. It turns out he lives only a block away. You wouldn't mind a little jaunt to Page One, would you, Emma?"

This was fairly cagey of Jack. Page One was a huge independent bookstore, by far the best bookstore in Albuquerque. As a person who cared about books, Emma Wilder always shopped at independent booksellers whenever possible, rather than the big chains. She needed some new reading material and didn't mind a trip to Page One at all.

To tell the truth, and despite her better inclinations, Emma was finding herself just a wee bit interested in Jack's case.

18

Emma shook hands briefly with Scott Updike in the coffee/wine bar at the front of Page One. Scott appeared to be in his late twenties, early thirties—Howie's age, more or less. To Emma, all young people looked so much alike these days that it was difficult for her to judge anyone's age except by using Howie as a kind of yardstick. Scott was blond and willowy with his hair parted on one side in a manner that seemed vaguely retro-1940s. He looked to Emma like an actor on daytime television, the sort who might play an earnest young doctor. Emma imagined some women would find him attractive, but to her, he seemed self-conscious, too neat, spotlessly attired in white jeans and a plaid shirt rolled up exactly an inch and a half from his bony wrists.

Emma left Jack and Scott at a table drinking double cappuccinos and wandered off through the bargain books and calendars into the literature section. She had the San Geronimo library at her disposal, of course, but the library's collection was spotty in many areas due to budgetary constraints. She glanced curiously from time to time toward the front of the store to see Jack and the willowy graduate student deep in conversation. She couldn't hear what they were saying, but it was fascinating to watch their body language. Scott was the one doing nearly all the talking. He was gesturing with his hands, obviously passionate about whatever it was they were discussing. Jack, for his part, had a mock-sympathetic expression on his face that Emma had seen plenty of times before. It was Jack's tell-me-all-your-secrets mode, an entirely construed state, from the slightly raised eyebrow to the way he

leaned forward and cocked his head slightly, as though to em-
pathize better.

The conversation went on for nearly half an hour. Emma
filled the time by buying a P. G. Wodehouse omnibus of three
Jeeves novels because Howie had declared recently at dinner
that Wodehouse was the funniest writer of the twentieth century—and frankly, between local cannibalism and the mess the
world was in, Emma was in a mood for a funny read. Finally,
the willowy blond graduate student stood up abruptly, shook
hands with Jack, and left the store. Emma carried her pur-
chases over to Jack's table.

"Well?" she asked.

"Well, indeed," he answered vaguely, far away in his
thoughts. His black glasses were pointed at some indetermi-
nate point halfway to the ceiling.

"Is that a good 'well indeed,' or a bad 'well indeed'?" she
inquired.

"Rutherford Hughes," he told her, shaking his head. "That's
the name of the British archeologist."

"You found him? Congratulations, Jack! Do you suppose
he's your Shark Tooth?"

"Possibly. The crazy bastard was certainly asking for trouble . . . Excuse me one moment, Emma. I've got to make a
call."

"Make it in the car while we head on over to Coronado
Mall."

"Emma, for chrisssake, I'm trying to solve a murder here!"

"Yes, but *I'm* trying to buy a new mattress—the old one
happens to have a fatal sag on your side of the bed." She led
Jack ruthlessly to the car. "Remember, dear, when I agreed to
drive you to Albuquerque today, you said I could shop till I
dropped."

"And you're not ready to drop yet?"

"Not by a long shot."

While Emma was unlocking the Subaru, Jack stood on the
curb punching numbers on his cell phone. Over the past few
years, Jack had become a cell phone junkie, racking up huge
monthly bills. Emma liked to tease him that he should have

been a Hollywood producer. Personally, she shared Howie's distaste of seeing people on sidewalks and in restaurants and cars, with one hand to their ear, yacking to invisible friends and mates. It seemed to her somehow impolite, not to mention an intrusion on one's solitude.

Jack was asking the information operator for a Janet Dimas on Polk Street in San Francisco while Emma helped him down into the passenger seat of the Subaru. "Watch your arms and legs, Jack," she advised, slamming the door with enough force to give a normal person a small concussion. Jack didn't notice. By the time Emma was pulling out of the Page One parking lot onto Juan Tabo Boulevard, he had the number he was seeking and apparently had been put through directly, for a modest extra charge that she didn't care to contemplate.

"Janet! Hey, how you doing?" he greeted. "Yeah, it's Jack Wilder! . . . No, I'm not in California, I'm in Albuquerque. How's it going, Janet? How's Doug . . . Oh, I'm sorry to hear that. A younger woman, huh . . . ?"

Jack quickly moved from personal matters—a broken marriage complete with obligatory younger woman—to professional concerns. He asked her to run the name Rutherford Hughes, a British citizen, through a certain computer. Today was Saturday, Janet's day off, but Jack pressed upon her how important this was, that Hughes was a possible homicide victim. This went on for a while, until Janet agreed to do what he was asking. He gave Janet his cell phone number and disconnected.

"So, Janet Dimas," Emma mentioned, now that the little plastic box was no longer pressed to her husband's ear. "SFPD?"

"INS."

"Really? So her husband ran off with a younger woman, did he? What a predictable jerk. How old is Janet?"

"I don't know, Emma. Thirty-five, thirty-six."

Emma was aghast. Thirty-five, thirty-six *was* a younger woman, as far as she was concerned! She shot a worried glance at Jack, wondering if she was safe herself from this scourge of predatory young females who stole your mate.

Surely no one else would want an overweight blind bear like Jack Wilder, but you couldn't be certain. Emma knew that there were a lot of desperate women lurking out there.

"So, Jack, are you going to tell me all the gory details of your conversation with Scott Updike, or are you going to keep me in suspense?"

Jack smiled. "I didn't think you were interested in just another boring murder case."

Emma put on her best *Good Housekeeping* voice, guaranteed to keep any old bear from seeking honey from younger bees:

"Oh, Jack, you know I'm *always* interested in *everything* you do!"

"Here's the story," he told her as they continued through the late Saturday morning traffic to Coronado Mall. "You remember our spacey Professor Lehman said he had a female undergraduate student four years ago who wanted a copy of a satellite photo for a British archeologist, who was a friend of hers and working up north on his own. Are you following me?"

"What I'm doing, Jack, is driving you."

"Patience, Emma, and I'll tell you a romantic tale. Back in the winter of 1998, our young man, Scott Updike, found himself at a party one night with an unusually attractive young woman. Frankly, Scott's lust was aroused to such wild heights that, being a young man, he immediately called it love. Unfortunately, the young woman did not love Scott in return—for that would have been too simple, I suppose, not enough heartbreak and drama. Instead, the young woman fell in love with a man twice her age who didn't care a hang for her."

"Rutherford Hughes?"

"Exactly. Now Scott never actually met 'Ford' as she called him, but he heard plenty of stories because the young woman eventually became Scott's friend—a platonic friendship, alas—and confided all her woes to him. Apparently, Ford was a brilliant, self-centered bastard with a fabulous British accent, just the sort of unfeeling brute any young lady could throw herself at, romantically speaking, without there being any danger of experiencing a real relationship."

"Jack, I really hate it when you act so cynical."

"I'm not cynical. I'm simply a realist."

"You are not—you're a wounded idealist, and there's nothing worse. But go on."

Jack smiled mischievously. "You know, I'm nuts about you. Just in case I haven't told you for a while."

"Yes, Jack. But let's hear the rest of the story."

"Okay. Now I may be blind, but at least I'm not as blind as love. In short, Professor Rutherford Hughes was *not* an appropriate individual for any nice young New Mexico graduate student to set her sights on. He had been thrown out of his teaching position at Cambridge for a whole bunch of hanky-panky—cashing bad checks, getting the head of his department's sixteen-year-old daughter knocked up, showing up at class occasionally drunk and raving, telling all his students what dumb rotters they were."

"I had a poetry professor at the University of Iowa like that once," Emma said. "Women go wild over those bad-boy intellectual types."

"Do they? Not the smart women, I trust. The Rutherford Hugheses of the world aren't exactly in a relationship for the long haul."

"Jack, this is going to surprise you, I'm sure. But when you're twenty years old you don't think about the long haul so much as the long—"

"Don't be vulgar, Emma."

"I'm not being vulgar. I'm simply a realist, unquote. Now what happened?"

The story was thirdhand so Jack advised a grain of salt. According to Scott, Rutherford Hughes came to New Mexico on his own, unemployed, but with enough independent wealth so that this was not a problem. He was determined to write the final word about the Anasazi and show academia how superior he was to their petty ways. The young woman met the ex-Cambridge prof old enough to be her father in the stacks at the

UNM library one afternoon in the fall of '98. They had both been reaching for the same book.

One thing led to another and nature took its course: dinner, bed, the start of an affair. The young woman was currently working on her master's degree in archeology so she was impressed at meeting an actual field archeologist—a brilliant man, she believed, a maverick, Bohemian intellectual.

But it was not a happy romance. Scott met the young woman some months after the start of her affair with Ford and their friendship—hers and Scott's—was based upon him providing a shoulder for her to cry on. Ford left Albuquerque for weeks at a time to do field work and she never knew when to expect him back. She suspected he had other women, that he didn't really care for her at all. Scott kept telling her to leave the bastard and date someone who would treat her better— himself, for example. But the more of a bastard Ford was, the more she was certain that what she felt was true love forever.

"Now here's where it starts to get interesting. As it happens, our young woman is Native American, from the San Geronimo Pueblo—did I tell you this part?"

"No, you didn't."

"Well, she is. And before she came to study in Albuquerque she used to do a lot of hiking up in the mountains above the reservation. Apparently, she had discovered a few Anasazi artifacts in a cave and she wanted Ford's expert opinion about what she had found, and whether there was enough there to do her doctoral dissertation about the site. She finally dragged him up there, but he wasn't impressed. He told her the site was no big deal and that she should forget about it."

"He sounds like a creep. He should have been more encouraging."

"Well, I suspect this is one creep we can talk about safely in the past tense. Unfortunately, Scott's tale comes to an end exactly at the place I'd like to know more. It seems that Scott finally met another woman—her name's Anne and Anne apparently is the jealous type, and not too happy about Scott remaining friends with old loves. So Scott and the Indian girl drifted apart and she didn't confide in him anymore."

Emma pulled into the parking lot at Coronado Mall and began cruising up and down the aisles for a free space among the acres of cars.

"So this young Indian woman—it's the *cacique's* grand-daughter, isn't it? What's her name again?"

"Donna Theresa. Or D.T., as Howie calls her. I gather she's quite a beauty. Howie seems to think so, at least."

"And you think she killed the British archeologist, is that it?"

"Well, I don't know. After all, we haven't entirely ID'd Howie's head, so we don't know for certain if Ford is actually dead. This said, however, it seems to me that yes, it's quite possible D.T. killed him."

"Come on, Jack! Because he treated her badly?"

"No, it's more than that. You need to picture this girl as a woman scorned—and I mean *seriously* scorned, both romanti-cally and professionally. The way I understand it, D.T. eventu-ally went to the tribal council and asked permission to explore the cave she had found—the council said no, so she turned her efforts to some other site outside of Chaco Canyon. D.T. sounds like a complicated person, insecure enough to be a pushover for some selfish son of a bitch, but very determined in her own way. I doubt that it was so easy for a Native Ameri-can girl growing up on a reservation to make her way into the PhD program at UNM, but she's kept at it—I imagine she's had more of an uphill struggle than Howie, for instance."

"It hasn't been so easy for Howie, either. Don't fool your-self."

"No, I'm not saying it was a picnic for Howie. But I think it would be even *more* difficult for a young Native American woman than a man. I'm trying to get at her motivation, Emma. The way I see this, I picture a very stubborn young woman—she's been turned down by the tribal council, discouraged by her archeologist lover, but she's still working away on her doctorate. Then suddenly the council calls and guess what? It turns out that Ford lied to her, the cave she found wasn't such a minor discovery after all, and he's been sneaking up there himself in her absence. A young woman like that who's all wound up anyway, she could snap. This is a huge betrayal, after all. She might confront him and kill him in a rage."

"And the cooked brain? The cannibalism?"

"All window dressing. Just a way to confuse the evidence. Make it seem like something very complicated—the Curse of the Anasazi, indeed! When all the time, it's the same old boy-girl boogie from the dawn of time. I'm not saying that this is how it actually happened—it *is* a little far-fetched that she would actually cook the guy. But D.T. has some explaining to do, at the very least. Meanwhile, to be honest, I'm a little worried about our boy in the field."

19

Howie rode Black Mare over the top of a sloping meadow and found himself with a huge panoramic vista. Spirit Lake lay spread out below him in a natural bowl of land, a lost valley paradise that seemed entirely separate from the rest of creation. The lake was not large, only a hundred yards or so across, but Howie imagined its dark green waters were deep and cold.

On the west shore, there was a field of long grass, the sort of perfect mountain meadow where a person was tempted to linger and stretch out in the sun. The north and south shores were covered with dense pine forest, and to the east, a granite bluff rose directly from the water, reaching upward to a craggy peak high above them that had to be at least 13,000 feet, a good place to be an eagle. All in all, it was a breathtaking view, like something from a tourist calendar, August in the Rockies: the lake, the meadow, and the high mountain that kept watch on the lush valley.

Lewis, Big Carl, and Daryl had stopped on the trail ahead with their packhorses, waiting for Howie to catch up. Even they seemed touched by the beauty of the land, momentarily not so sour.

"Well, there it is, Moon Deer—there's the cave of my ancestors," Lewis said with pride, nodding toward the steep mountain face that soared up from the lake.

"Where? I don't see it."

"About three quarters of the way to the top . . . if you look hard, you'll see a ledge. The cave's behind that."

Howie let his gaze move slowly upward along the jagged

side of the mountain. All he saw was rock and scree, fallen rubble from old avalanche slides. It was an inhospitable mountain face, bare of trees or any kind of vegetation.

"I still don't . . . oh, there!" Howie would not have seen the ledge except for the appearance of a human being in a red shirt against the rocks about a thousand feet up the side of the mountain. From where they sat on their horses, the figure was small and insignificant, unrecognizable. Howie shielded his eyes with his hand from the hard high-altitude glare of sun against rock. The figure raised an arm and waved at them far below and Howie knew at that instant who it was: Donna Theresa. Before he could wave back, the red shirt disappeared from the ledge, stepping back into the opening of the cave.

It seemed incredible to Howie that prehistoric people could have lived in such a high, inaccessible place. His stomach got a little queasy just thinking about how they were going to get there themselves. Howie was just admiring the dangerous beauty of the ancient valley, when there was an explosion inches from his right ear.

Bang! It was gunshot, totally unexpected. Black Mare reared back in terror and Howie only just managed to stay on her back by hugging onto her powerful neck.

"Goddamn!" Howie cried, trying to calm the frightened horse. They danced in a circle and reared a second time. "Easy, girl . . . easy . . . easy . . ."

Gradually, he got Black Mare calm enough so that he was able to worry about other dangers.

"Who the hell's shooting at us?"

"Calm down, Moon Deer. Ain't you ever heard a rifle before?" Daryl asked.

"Not two inches from my eardrum."

He saw now what had happened. Big Carl had just shot a bighorn sheep, firing from his saddle. It was a huge animal with thick wool and curved horns, still alive, writhing on the ground about fifty feet above them on the meadow from which they had just come. Carl dismounted and walked back up the slope of the hill to where the sheep lay dying. Howie thought Carl was going to shoot the animal a second time, but instead he put down his rifle on the grass and grabbed the sheep by its horns.

"My God, Carl, *don't!*" Howie shouted. But Carl didn't pay any attention.

"Mutton tonight!" Daryl said with appreciation.

"Finish him off, Carl," Lewis called from on top of his horse.

As Howie watched, Carl twisted the sheep's head by its horns until its neck broke with a terrible crack, and the animal lay limp and still. Howie turned from the slaughter, sickened; nature did not seem quite as grand as it had only a few minutes before. A distant flash of light caught his eye. It was Donna Theresa once again on the ledge outside the cave high above on the mountain precipice, looking down at them with binoculars, the two lenses reflecting beams of sunlight. Probably the rifle shot had caught her interest.

"Well, let's get riding," Lewis said. "We still have a ways to go."

The trail led around the south side of the mountain, and kept climbing relentlessly higher into the thin air. The way was narrow and steep. Lewis went first, then Big Carl, and Howie in the rear. A dozen huge black vultures circled the ancient valley above where Daryl had stayed behind to butcher the sheep.

Emma Wilder picked out a king-size box spring and mattress at Sears, arranged for it to be delivered to San Geronimo, and then led Jack into women's underwear at JCPenney. Jack did not like shopping malls; he was confused by the strange echoes and dislocating sense of space and smell. He walked with Emma's hand on his arm, in a dreamlike state, feeling that there was something he should be seeing that was not quite apparent yet.

Anasazi, ghosts, cannibalism, Jack repeated to himself, like a mantra; it suggested much, but added up to nothing. What was his brain trying to tell him?

His cell phone rang as Emma was discussing intimate female apparel with a saleswoman. It was Jack's INS friend from San Francisco.

"Jack, it's Janet. I called the office and had a friend run a computer search. Your Rutherford Hughes came into JFK on a three-month tourist visa, May twelfth, 1998."

"So he's illegal now?"

"No, because he married an American citizen on September twenty-fifth, 1998. His visa had expired at that point, but generally we're not too strict with someone like that unless they've had a history of overstaying their visa—he was a university professor, apparently. So when Hughes got married, he was given a green card. It was processed and approved by a J. Edwards in our Albuquerque office, if you want to call and find out more. In a case like this, they'll interview the couple, putting them in separate rooms and asking a lot of personal questions, to make sure it is a real marriage."

"What's the woman's name?" Jack asked, knowing the answer in advance.

"Donna Theresa Concha."

Jack thanked Janet and disconnected. It seemed closer now, whatever it was that his fugal state was trying to tell him: *Anasazi, ghosts, cannibalism, Donna Theresa, Rutherford Hughes.* The separate elements of the puzzle twirled like a kaleidoscope in his mind, but they still did not quite converge.

Jack decided it was best to stop thinking about it, and let his thoughts click away in the dark. Sometimes that was the best way to remember what you had forgotten, or to understand what you were trying to grasp. But he had a problem: Emma was no longer by his side. He had let go of her arm to answer the call and hadn't heard her wander off.

"*Emma!*" he hissed. But there was no answer. Jack felt a dizzy rush of agoraphobia. He was lost, groping around in a women's underwear department. It was funny, he supposed—Howie would laugh about this, certainly. But meanwhile he felt a kind of terror being in a large, unknown public space by himself, with neither his white cane, nor Katya, nor Emma's help.

He couldn't imagine that Emma had gone far. Experimentally, he reached forward with his right hand, but there was nothing except black, empty space.

"*Emma!*" he called again, louder than before. There was still no response from the darkness. Then he heard footsteps nearby. Thank God, Emma was coming back for him. He reached out and was startled to touch a breast. Unfortunately, it was too large to be Emma's. Jack's was just realizing that he had made a terrible mistake when a strange woman began screaming at him. He tried to explain, but a hand slammed against the side of his head, slapping him silly before he could get the words out. Certainly she believed she was justified— Jack understood this very well. But her slap had knocked his dark glasses off revealing his old scars and dead eyes, and now the woman was screaming in earnest.

Jack heard voices and feet rushing his way. One of the voices was Emma. He tried to turn toward her, but all the sounds confused him and, off balance, he tumbled backward into a clothes rack. There was a crash as everything seemed to come down around him, and he found himself in a pile of bras and panties on the floor.

"Jack! Are you okay?"

He nodded, though in fact he was too shaken to speak.

"I told you to stay right there!" Emma scolded. She sounded frustrated, guilty, and frightened all at once. "You were on the phone and I just had to pay for something over at the register. I thought you'd be all right."

"I'm okay," he managed. "I just got a little disoriented."

Emma laughed, releasing her tension. "Jesus, Jack! I leave you for five minutes, and look at you!"

Jack smiled, no longer concerned with any of this. His fall had shaken loose the cobwebs in his mind, and sitting among the panties and bras, he had finally figured out what it was that bothered him. There was simply too much coincidence here: that D.T. was married to Rutherford Hughes; that Howie had discovered Hughes's severed head in an alley; that D.T.'s grandfather, the *cacique*, had hired their services.

Jack still didn't understand the logic behind these events, but it was suddenly clear to him that it was no accident that a severed head, complete with markings of Anasazi cannibalism, had been delivered to Howie in a truck from a restaurant that

called itself the Anasazi Grill. Someone was playing an intricate game, enjoying a sophisticated though gruesome archeological joke. Howie had been *meant* to find the head. This was
not a random act. In all probability, the one-eyed truck had
slammed into Howie's MGB deliberately to get his attention,
because if Howie had not walked down to the Dumpster to investigate, the head would almost certainly have ended up at
the town landfill, undiscovered.

This changed everything. Howie, in fact, had been set up.
And if that was true, then someone had to know that Howie
would be on a stakeout in the alley behind the Shanghai Café
at precisely that time. This presented a new problem. Who
knew about Howie's stakeout? Their client, of course, Mrs.
Eudora Harrington, as well as Jack, Emma, and Howie. And
that was all. It was their policy not to discuss an ongoing case
with outsiders.

"Are you all right, sir?" a nervous male voice was asking.
"Would you like us to call a doctor?"

Jack was so deep in his thoughts and revelations that he
didn't know how he had arrived at a comfortable chair in the
manager's office. All sorts of people were busy making apologies; it was a litigious age, the woman who had slapped him
turned out to be an off-duty employee, and the store was
clearly worried about a lawsuit from a handicapped individual.

"I need to make a phone call right away," he told the invisible people around him.

He was reaching for his cell phone when the male with the
nervous voice hurriedly placed a regular telephone into his
hand. Jack accepted the store telephone, hoping it would mean
a better connection to San Geronimo, but he declined help
with dialing. He felt the keypad with his fingertips, oriented
himself, then punched in Howie's cell number. He waited, but
the line did not ring.

"Answer, Howie!" he muttered. "For chrissake, where are
you?"

Had Howie inadvertently told anyone about the Great
Pussycat Caper? If so, that person was the killer. It was as simple as that. All he needed now was to put together what he

knew with what Howie knew, and they would have this damn homicide figured out! Jack tried the number a second and a third time, fearing he had punched in the wrong digits. But Howie didn't answer. He reached only an electronic void, an emptiness so final it was like placing a call to the moon.

"Goddamn it, Howie! *Who* did you tell?"

PART TWO

———— ⬡⬡⬡ ————

FAT CAT

1

Howard Moon Deer slid down from his saddle onto legs that felt permanently bowed into the shape of a horse. It was nearly three o'clock on Saturday afternoon and he had been riding for almost five hours. His crotch hurt, his butt ached, and his thighs were sore. Nevertheless, he felt magnificent, a tamer-of-horses, climber-of-mountains, man-with-his-head-in-the-clouds.

They had arrived at the top of the world, a broad sloping meadow behind the cliff face, not visible from the lake below, from which there was a view hundreds of miles in every direction: far into the mountains of Colorado to the north, more mountains still to the east and south, and a seemingly endless expanse of desert to the west. The high meadow was green with stubby windswept grass, and scattered with large boulders and strange rock formations that were suggestive of giants and mythological beasts. Donna Theresa had already set up a simple camp here, a single green dome tent in the shelter of a huge rock that resembled a crouching lion.

Howie thought about D.T. as he helped unload the packhorses, piling the gear near a circle of blackened rocks, the cold remnants of an old campfire. He had a pleasant sense of anticipation to see her again, a certain energized, sharply focused interest that he hadn't felt about a woman in some time. *Totally inappropriate!* he warned himself firmly. *I'm looking for a killer, not a girlfriend!* In fact, there were many points against her; among other considerations, she already seemed to have a full gaggle of men in her life, from Lester Wounds Eagle to the Tiwa-speaking guy who had squealed up to the restaurant on Saturday night to spirit her away in his Land Cruiser. Nevertheless, unbidden thoughts of Donna Theresa burned their way through his mind. She worked on him in some way he didn't understand.

Once the horses were unloaded, they were set loose to graze on the meadow. Big Carl said there was water in a small stream just below the tree line so they wouldn't venture far. Howie had just finished unbridling Black Mare when he saw Donna Theresa scrambling quickly toward him from a foot trail that came down over the haunch of the crouching lion. She was dressed in jeans and the red shirt he had spotted earlier in the afternoon, and a baseball cap and dark glasses for protection against the sun. The cap had a logo for the Sundance Film Festival on the front, probably a gift from Lester, and her long black hair was hanging in a ponytail from underneath. There was no doubt about it, she was nice to look at. Howie was struck by how tall and lithe and lovely she was. But she didn't look happy. Even with her face mostly hidden, he could tell she was angry and intent about something.

"Hey!" He smiled in greeting.

"What the hell are you *doing* here, Moon Deer?"

Howie was taken aback. "What do you mean, what am I doing here? Raymond came into the office yesterday and hired us. He told me to ride up with the War Chief and give you a helping hand. So here I am."

She shook her head disgustedly, like the world was a rotten place where everybody got most things wrong.

"*I* didn't ask my grandfather to hire you, Moon Deer. That was his idea, and I thought I'd talked him out of it. It's nothing personal. I just don't want a circus up here."

As she spoke, she glanced anxiously at Lewis and Big Carl, who were some distance away setting up an ugly green rectangular tent alongside her more ladylike dome. Lewis said something to her in Tiwa, she answered, then turned back to Howie.

"Well, since you're here, the most useful thing you could do is keep Lewis off my back. I have a ton of work and I don't want that idiot getting in the way."

"I'll do my best."

"Just keep him distracted. Ask lots of dumb questions. Push him off a cliff, if you want—that would be fine with me."

"Where are you going?" he asked, because she was walking away.

"Back to the cave. I only came down here because I'm out of white gas for the lanterns. I hope Lewis remembered to bring me some."

"I just unpacked two gallon tins—they're over with the rest of the stuff." Howie pointed to the pile of gear near the campfire. "Look, can we talk a second? There's something I need to tell you."

She turned back to him reluctantly. She was different today and it took him a moment to figure out what it was: Her stutter was gone. Archeology seemed to agree with her, lending her confidence. Howie could see his own reflection in the lenses of her dark glasses: an Indian guy with a round moon face she seemed to want to escape from as quickly as possible. Unfortunately, he was the bringer of bad news, and he thought he'd better get it over with.

"Well?" she demanded. "I'm in a hurry, Moon Deer."

"I can see that. It's your cousin Charlie. Your grandfather said I should tell you that he's . . . well, he's been killed. I'm really sorry about this."

Her mouth fell open, but no sounds came.

"K-k-killed?" she managed finally. Her voice was small and stunned and uncertain.

"It was very strange. About ten o'clock last night, I was outside on the sagebrush near where I live when Charlie rode up on horseback. There was something wrong with the way he was sitting in the saddle. Then just as he reached me, he fell dead on the ground. I think he'd been shot, but it was dark and I didn't have a chance to investigate much."

He watched her face crumple. Sorrow changed D.T. from an attractive woman into something primitive, ugly with grief. She turned her face so he couldn't see her, walked a short distance across the meadow, and sat on the ground, hugging her knees. After a moment, Howie followed and settled next to her. She was gulping air, trying not to cry.

"I'm sorry," he told her again.

"Goddamn them all!" she moaned. "Those bastards . . ."

"Which bastards exactly? Who shot him?"

D.T. shook her head, bewildered and overcome. "I don't know. Probably Lewis or Carl or some other Lucero asshole."

"But why?"

"*Why?* There's no why about it. They didn't like him, that's all."

"That's a reason to shoot someone? Look, D.T., right before he died, he said the word 'cop.' He said it twice, actually. I got the idea that maybe a cop had shot him and he was trying to tell me which one, but he was too badly hurt to say."

"Cop? That's what he said?"

"That's it. Then he just tumbled down dead."

They both glanced over at Big Carl in his tan uniform, squatting along the outside perimeter of his tent, pounding stakes into the ground with the butt of his semiautomatic pistol.

"Where's the other one—Daryl?" she asked quietly. "I thought I saw him when you were riding up."

"Daryl stayed behind to butcher the bighorn sheep that Carl shot near the lake. Look, D.T., maybe you'd better tell me about your tribal police department. Just how honest are they?"

"Oh, they're honest!" she said bitterly, wiping away silent tears that had appeared on her cheeks with the back of her hand. "Honestly partisan, anyway. They're Luceros, Moon Deer. Lewis is head of the family, and as War Chief, he's also in charge of tribal law enforcement, so they'll do anything he says."

"Anything?"

She nodded. "Our tribal cops don't have legal authority to do much besides hand out traffic citations on reservation land, but that doesn't stop them from being real shitheads. Daryl's the worst—he's been known to beat people to a pulp when he's in the mood."

"I'll watch my step. Look, there's one more thing about Charlie. He had a box with him when he died that he seemed to be trying to give me. But when I opened it, there wasn't much inside, so it's hard to figure."

D.T. gave Howie a quizzical look. "A box? What kind of box?"

"Just a small white cardboard box, nothing special. There was a kind of twig inside. Only it wasn't really a twig. It was hard, almost like petrified wood, only not quite."

D.T. continued to stare at him. When she spoke, her stutter was thick. "Wh-wh-wh-where did you pa-pa-put it?"

"Put it? I left it in a drawer in my cabin."

"It's . . ." She took a breath to control her stutter and began again. "It's safe?"

"My cabin's locked up and I've never been robbed yet. What's in that box, D.T.?"

"I don't know," she told him, looking away.

Donna Theresa wasn't a very good liar. It was almost an endearing quality, how evasive and guilty she looked.

"Is it some sort of artifact from the cave?" he pressed.

"I told you, I don't *know*." She sighed and shook her head. "Oh, Charlie . . . goddamn you, couldn't you do anything right for a change?"

It seemed a strange thing to say about a dead cousin, but before he could get an explanation, the War Chief walked over to inform them that he and Big Carl were now ready to begin their grand tour of the Anasazi site. D.T. stood up and turned her back on Howie. He had the impression that as far as D.T. was concerned, the interruption was welcome.

From the camp, they walked in single file along a narrow trail to the cave. The trail was terrifying, often little more than a few inches wide, climbing fast and hugging the side of the mountain face. Howie tried to keep his gaze focused upward to where they were going, because the downward view was enough to cause a tight knot in his stomach and his breath to grow shallow.

D.T. led the way, weighed down by one of the gallon canisters of gas in her daypack—Howie had offered to carry the gas himself, but she had turned him down, indicating with a scowl that chivalry was out of place on an archeological dig. Big Carl went second, lumbering along, then Lewis, whose walk seemed very tense—maybe he was frightened by heights like Howie. The younger cop, Daryl, had still not returned from his gruesome task at the lake below, which left Moon Deer behind Lewis, taking up the rear. The hot afternoon sun battered down on them, a hard brilliance that offered no relief. The sky at this altitude was tinged with purple, a color you see only from airplanes or high mountains at the edge of the atmosphere. Howie had to stop every now and then to gulp down a breath of thin oxygen.

The trail continued to climb steeply, snaking its way up the mountain. Occasionally Lewis, Carl, and D.T. spoke to one another in Tiwa, but mostly they hiked in silence, each of them wrapped up in their own thoughts. After twenty minutes, they came to a place where the trail ended abruptly at a steep avalanche chute of fallen scree and scattered boulders. From this high vista there was a stomach-lurching view of Spirit Lake almost directly below them, looking like hardly more than a puddle. The air was bone-dry, but Howie was sweating from acrophobia and effort. They were all breathing hard from the altitude.

"So where do we go from here?" Howie asked, frankly concerned.

"Straight up." D.T. pointed up the avalanche chute to a ledge several hundred feet above them. It looked impossible to climb, too steep and unstable with fallen scree.

"You have an extra pair of wings?" Howie inquired.

"There's a rope," she said. "We'll go one at a time in case any rocks get kicked loose."

Howie hadn't seen the rope. It dangled from the south end of the ledge above and stretched down the chute, ending some distance from where they were standing. The rope had been set away from the trail so if an avalanche started, hopefully it wouldn't kill any other would-be archaeologists waiting their turn below.

D.T. offered the first turn up the rope to Lewis. It was hard to read the War Chief's expression, but Howie thought he had turned just a little pale. From the conversation earlier, Howie gathered that Big Carl had climbed this before, but it was Lewis's first time.

D.T. smiled innocently. "If the climb's too much, you can just read my report," she told him in English.

Lewis said something sharply in Tiwa and D.T. shrugged her shoulders. "Whatever," she said. "I'm going to go first, Moon Deer. Then you can follow in any order you like. It's no big deal once you've done it a few times. You just go slow and steady and don't let go of the rope."

The three men watched her scamper across the boulders to the end of the rope. She was agile and fearless, and Howie felt his age just watching her. She made it look easy, even with a heavy pack. She simply walked up the chute, pulling herself hand over hand along the rope. A few minutes later, she disappeared over the ledge above.

Down below, Lewis and Big Carl began conferring between themselves. Every now and then Howie heard his own name mentioned. At last, Lewis turned to him with a weak smile.

"Go ahead," the War Chief said. "Give it a try."

Howie studied the dangling rope. He was scared silly, but there was no way out, and he had his pride, after all: He didn't want D.T. to think he was someone who couldn't get it up, so to speak. He climbed over the boulders and pulled the rope taut, testing to see if it would hold his weight. It seemed strong enough, but who could say what tiny threads were on the verge of snapping? Howie began to climb, leaning back against the rope as he had seen D.T. do, pulling himself up hand over hand, walking up the side of the mountain. It wasn't as hard as it looked, though he needed to stop several times to breathe. There was only one bad moment halfway up when his feet slid out from under him on loose scree. He held on tightly and after a few moments of dangling terror, he managed to get his feet on the ground again and continued to climb.

Howie rappelled himself over the top and stepped out of time onto the high mountain ledge that the ancient Anasazi had once called home.

2

It wasn't exactly Machu Picchu. The ledge itself was a natural outcropping of rock seventeen feet wide at its widest point, and seventy-four feet long. The opening to the cave beyond was partially blocked by huge boulders that had fallen at some time in the past. There had obviously been a landslide here, some cataclysmic event long ago that had hidden the cave, probably for centuries. D.T. estimated that originally the mouth of the cave must have been nearly twenty-three feet tall and thirty-eight feet wide, but today there was only a narrow entrance, a crawlway four feet high by almost three feet wide that had been cleared of fallen debris. A number of heavy timbers had been strategically placed to frame the modern entrance so that the rocks, hopefully, would not slide again.

The cave had a southern orientation, which was a common feature of Anasazi cliff dwellings, allowing for sunlight and maximum warmth. Howie crawled through the opening and found himself in a large vault that was lit by a narrow shaft of sunlight and two Coleman gas-burning lamps. Donna Theresa was on her hands and knees filling a third lamp, pouring fuel through a plastic funnel. The lamps sizzled and made a harsh white light that cast huge, strange shadows upon the sides of the rock, making it all look like some fantastic underground world of the damned.

The Anasazi structures inside the cave were mostly in ruins, such a jumble of fallen rock that Howie could not immediately discern what was man-made from what was simply nature. There was a partially excavated circle of stone near where

Howie was standing, an old wall, possibly a kiva. As his eyes adjusted to the light and shadows, he noticed two larger walls a dozen feet behind the kiva that came together at a right angle, jutting out from the rear of the cave. The walls had two levels of windows set in them, an upper and a lower floor. The building had obviously once been a kind of apartment complex where the cave dwellers had lived. There were signs of modern activity here as well: A wire mesh had been set up in front of one of the walls where debris could be sifted in order to search for artifacts. Howie saw a variety of tools neatly stacked near the cave entrance: picks and shovels, trowels and buckets, a wheelbarrow, a metal chest, measuring instruments, balls of string.

"So what do you think?" D.T. asked, coming up behind him.

"It's incredible! My mind is truly boggled. But how in the world did you ever find the cave?"

"I used to wander all over this land, mostly to get away from people. I was a lonely child, Moon Deer."

"Were you?" It was the most personal thing she had ever revealed about herself. "Still, you'd pretty much have to be an eagle to wander here."

"The first time I came here, I was twelve years old. I remember it was a late-summer morning and my stepfather was asleep drunk on the living room sofa. All I wanted to do was get away to someplace that was high and wonderful, where I could be free . . . everything seemed perfect up here, and lousy down below."

"I can imagine that," Howie told her.

"So I packed a lunch and I just kept climbing higher and higher into the mountains. I didn't want to stop, not ever. And then I saw a big old ram on the rocks and I started following him. We played a game together where he'd let me get within maybe thirty feet of him, then he'd start walking away and I'd have to catch up. He didn't seem afraid of me, but he wasn't going to let me get too close, either."

At the age of twelve, Donna Theresa still believed in miracles: She thought it was a magic sheep, a powerful animal god who was going to deliver her from her evil stepfather. Magic or not, the ram led her to the cave. She followed the animal for nearly two hours, far up into the scree where she had never gone before, to some dangerous places where she could easily have fallen to her death—but she didn't care, she was in a reckless mood. Then she turned a corner and the ram was gone. She looked around, but this time she had really lost him. At last, she sat down on the high ledge where she had been led and peeled an orange she had brought for her lunch. One of the sections fell on the ground, and when she reached to pick it up she saw a large pottery shard near her knee. The opening to the cave was almost directly behind her. It didn't look like a cave at this point, only a very small hole—a rock must have been blocking it at one time and had since fallen away. She moved a few more rocks, and after a while she was able to poke her hand through. And that's as far as she got that first afternoon.

"But you came back again?"

"Sure. Whenever I could sneak away. It was my special place. By the end of the next summer, I had pulled away enough rock so I could get inside."

"Wasn't that dangerous?"

"Of course it was dangerous! But it was wonderful. I could be anything I wanted here. This was my own private world, Moon Deer."

"Did you know it was an Anasazi cave?"

"Well, I didn't know that name, not until sometime in high school when I started taking books on Southwest archeology out of the library. I just knew it was an old place, a place of my ancestors. I believed my ancestors had singled me out specially in order to give me their power. When I went to the big high school in town, I always kept the first pottery shard I'd found in my pocket, and whenever I was afraid of something, I'd put my hand inside my pocket and touch the shard, and then nothing could hurt me . . . maybe that sounds crazy to you."

"No, I understand." And, in fact, Howie understood perfectly well the longing to get away from adolescent troubles into a high, beautiful world that was all your own; he had done the same thing in his own way through books. Still, he found himself wondering just how troubled Donna Theresa's adolescence had been.

"So your stepfather . . ."

"Frank," she said, unpleasantly. She said the name like a swear word. "Frank Lucero."

"*Lucero*?"

"Oh, yeah, my mother crossed family lines! God, I hated her for doing that to me! Frank's mother was a second cousin to Lewis, only a distant relation, not part of the inner circle. But it was bad enough. When he was drunk, he used to b-b-b-b . . . b-b-b-b . . ."

D.T. tried to get the word out, but was unable.

"Beat you?" Howie asked.

She nodded. Outside the cave opening, they could hear Big Carl who had arrived on the ledge and was calling to Lewis below. They didn't have much more time to talk, but Donna Theresa finished her story with devastating speed, speaking in a flat monotone, rushing through to the end. Her stepfather had beaten her whenever he was drunk, or simply in the mood. He broke her arm, a rib, and gave her concussions on two separate occasions. Her mother did nothing to stop it, nor did the adult world come to her rescue. These were years in which poor states like New Mexico did very little about domestic abuse; a man was king of his castle, after all. The situation in San Geronimo was only marginally better today—there were counselors and a shelter, and occasionally the men even went to jail, as long as they didn't have well-connected relatives.

"I hope your mother finally got rid of the guy," Howie said angrily.

D.T. shook her head. "My grandfather did. I went to him finally when I was fifteen and told him what was going on. At first, I was ashamed, you know. I thought it was my fault somehow. But there came a time when I couldn't stand it any more."

"What did Raymond do?"

"I don't know. But the next day, Frank was gone and I never

saw him again. He left his car, his clothes, even the money in his bank account."

"He just vanished?"

"Forever," she said, smiling thoughtfully.

3

Howie spent the rest of the afternoon with a trowel and a plastic bucket digging inside Room 4 of the ancient Anasazi apartment building, whose half-crumbling walls jutted out from the rear of the cave. D.T. had started him on this project before giving her attention entirely to the War Chief and Big Carl.

D.T. told Howie she had identified sixteen rooms inside the old two-story complex, estimating that there had been another seven before the roof had collapsed. The majority of the inside rooms were claustrophobic, windowless rectangles, hardly larger than a tomb, and it was D.T.'s opinion that these were storage areas rather than living quarters. Room 4, however, was a corner suite, choice real estate with two windows, probably the apartment of some important personage, a priest or clan leader. The walls were cleverly built: banded layers of large chipped rocks alternating with layers of smaller fitted stones, which D.T. described as Type Three Masonry of a late Anasazi period. One corner of the room was blackened from an ancient hearth. D.T. had counted only three other rooms in the complex that showed signs of once having had a fire, and she based her estimate of the population partly on this fact. Howie was impressed by her knowledge. When it came to archeology, she was brisk and articulate, and she never stuttered over a single technical term.

D.T. warned that she was planning to work until the last possible moment before darkness made the trail back to camp too dangerous to navigate, finishing up around eight o'clock. Meanwhile, Howie soon found himself tired from bending, stooping, and carrying. His job was to dig carefully with the trowel in the area near the hearth, fill the bucket with rubble, carry the load to the screen mesh set up toward the front of the cave, then strain the rubble for human artifacts. It was hard, painstaking work, but interesting. Howie found several fragments of an old pot that had a black geometric design of triangular waves on one side. It really was a thrill to come across a pot like this *in situ*, and imagine the people who had used it in their daily lives centuries ago. Howie only wished he had a couple of months to find all the pieces and glue them together like a giant jigsaw puzzle. If he did it right, maybe it could be displayed one day at the Indian museum in Santa Fe with his name on it. Moon Deer's Pot.

As Howie dug and sifted and carried his buckets of rubble back and forth from Room 4, he also kept a close eye on D.T. She was giving Lewis and Big Carl an extended tour of the site, disappearing from time to time into various parts of the cave where Howie's eyes could not follow. When he did see them, the War Chief and cop didn't seem happy. They had the look of Christian Fundamentalists examining photographs of aborted fetuses. D.T. was obviously on the defensive. The lecture she gave went back and forth from Tiwa to English, sometimes several times in a single sentence. Howie was able to overhear the fact that the main vault of the cave was approximately twenty-four feet tall, forty-four feet wide, and thirty-seven feet deep, large enough for an extended family to live in rough comfort. D.T. had discovered water marks from an ancient spring, which would have added somewhat to the comfort. Nevertheless, it must have been a desperately hard, cold, brief existence for the people who had lived here. The life expectancy of an Anasazi person in Chaco Canyon at the height of the empire was thirty-five to forty years—and Chaco would have been the posh life compared to a high mountain cave.

D.T. was full of facts and figures, and quite the tour guide. She estimated that from ten to fifteen people would have lived in this cave at any one time, but that it was most likely used for only a short period of time, fifty years or so starting about 1200 A.D. Howie found it amazing to think that human beings had been born in this place eight hundred years ago, eaten simple meals, huddled close to fires for warmth, had sex, and died. Maybe there had been children frolicking in the very dirt where he was standing now, playing games much as children did today. Fascinating as it was to Howie, Lewis and Big Carl did not seem impressed. It was clear that they didn't approve of disturbing the ghosts of their ancestors. They grunted, shook their heads, and made sour noises as D.T. led them around.

Once or twice, Howie was tempted to interfere when the two men seemed to be bullying her. He wanted to come to her aid, but he sensed it wasn't appropriate, that this was her battle and she would be both furious and embarrassed if he tried to act out some politically incorrect chivalry on her behalf. She was a complicated woman, there was no doubt about it. On one hand, D.T. seemed to him so horribly vulnerable that it was almost painful to watch her, a wounded creature trying to survive. Yet she was feisty too, certainly no pushover. Howie spent a great deal of the afternoon trying to figure her out, but he arrived at no easy conclusions. The best he could say was she was someone who had been beaten and bullied maybe one too many times, a person who had reached her limit and now was fighting back.

Toward the end of the afternoon, Howie noticed that D.T. was becoming increasingly exasperated with the War Chief. Her voice rose in anger from time to time. They spent a long time in conference at the far end of the cave next to a pile of something that was covered by a blue canvas. She lifted a corner of the canvas and Lewis and Big Carl examined whatever it was underneath with extremely sober faces. The conversation had reverted solely to Tiwa, so Howie didn't know what they were saying, but the mysterious mound was clearly the center of some disagreement.

Their voices rose and fell and nothing seemed to be getting resolved. Then Lewis turned abruptly and left the cave with Big Carl in tow. Apparently, negotiations had broken down. The two men sat on the ledge, lit cigarettes, and began talking among themselves in low voices.

"Assholes!" D.T. muttered. Seething with frustration, she disappeared into one of the man-made structures at the east side of the cave. Howie tried to get back to work but the canvas-covered mound intrigued him. When he was certain D.T. wasn't anywhere nearby, he strolled over to the mound and pulled back the canvas. He wished he hadn't.

The mound was a pile of human bones. There were thighbones, hipbones, ribs, femurs, and every other kind of bone, too, often in small pieces. There were at least a dozen skulls as well, of differing sizes, disconnected from the bodies they had once shared in life and lying in a separate pile of their own. All the skulls had been smashed open in front by some heavy blunt instrument.

Howie overcame his squeamishness and picked up a small head that must have once belonged to either a woman or a child. The back of the skull was slightly blackened, charred and flaky from where it had been set on some long ago fire. He put down the small skull and picked up a larger one to see if the markings were the same. These skulls reminded him of something he couldn't immediately place, something he had read years ago. He examined a third skull and it, too, was the same, smashed in front, blackened and flaky on the back. What remained of the skull looked almost like a bowl. Like a casserole dish you might bring to some prehistoric potluck Tupperware party . . .

"They're *all* like that," D.T. told him, coming up behind him.

Howie was so startled by her voice that he dropped the skull he was holding back onto the pile, causing the jawbone to break off and the head to split in two. He wished he could apologize to whoever's head he had just shattered.

"You know what this is all about now, don't you?" she asked him.

Howie nodded unhappily.

4

Dinner was not much of a social event that night around the campfire. Donna Theresa sat rigidly between the War Chief and Big Carl, looking more like their prisoner than a would-be archeologist. Howie was on the opposite side of the fire, where the smoke kept getting in his eyes no matter where he moved, shifting with malicious cunning to follow him. Daryl, the younger cop, had been busy butchering and cooking the bighorn sheep while the others were at the cave. Howie said he would pass on the murdered mutton, thank you. He filled up as best as he could on tortillas and beans.

It was a grim, silent meal. The temperature had plunged with the setting sun, and in the absence of scintillating dinner conversation, Howie hovered as close as possible to the fire and tried to remember everything he could about Anasazi cannibalism. Nearly all of his knowledge on the subject came from a *New Yorker* magazine article he had read several years ago in a dentist's office, and a conversation he once had with an anthropologist at Princeton. As Howie remembered it, the notion that the Anasazi had succumbed to eating one another was one of a handful of theories referred to in academia as "fringe archeology," a corner of thought that included tales of marvelous underwater cities and Zen monks coming from Japan to the New World a thousand years before Christopher Columbus.

The theory was that the wonderful, peaceful Anasazi who built the marvels at Chaco Canyon weren't really Anasazi at all but Toltec invaders from Mesoamerica. The Toltecs were the precursors of the Aztecs and flourished in Old Mexico from about 800 to 1100 A.D. Unlike the Anasazi, no one had ever been inclined to regard the Toltecs as anybody's utopian ideal. They were a highly advanced people with many skills, but their civilization was a harsh theocracy ruled by priests who had an unpleasant habit of demanding human sacrifice.

From what Howie could remember, these warlike people supposedly sent a raiding party north around the year 900, where they encountered a backward, pliant group of natives living in the San Juan Basin in the area now called Chaco Canyon. The Toltecs were like sharks moving into a pond of guppies and they easily conquered the hang-loose New Mexicans, using the aborigines as slave labor to build the various technological marvels that archaeologists still puzzle over today—the Great Houses, the irrigation systems, the roads, and the like. Despite their easy conquest, the Toltecs remained a minority and in order to rule effectively they took to terrorizing the local inhabitants, eating people from time to time just to show how totally they were the masters of their domain.

All that was known for certain was that the Toltecs and the Anasazi existed around the same time chronologically, a mere thousand miles or so apart from one another—not an insurmountable distance for a raiding party—and that the ancient cultures of Mesoamerica were in fact more technologically advanced than the prehistoric people of the American Southwest. The idea was that cannibalism was first used as a kind of inventive crowd control, but then it got out of hand, setting off a great terror in which Chaco Canyon was abandoned and the citizens fled to the hills.

It was an interesting theory, but whether it was true or not was a subject most academics avoided like the plague. Political correctness was a requirement of university life these days, and as all politically correct people knew, Native Americans were the First Environmentalists, and many other lovely things also—but certainly not cannibals. Howie had great love and respect for the wisdom of his Native American ancestors; he, too, did not cherish the notion of Indians eating one another. Nevertheless, it disturbed him whenever the truth of certain matters was decided in advance.

All in all, it would take a lot of nerve, anger, or plain stupidity for D.T. to be investigating Anasazi cannibalism—if in fact, that was what she was doing. Not only did the San Geronimo Pueblo regard themselves as descendants of the Anasazi, but Howie knew from local reports that Lewis Lucero and the present tribal council had been elected as "traditionalists," taking power by making pompous statements about the need to return to the moral ways of yesteryear—a common tactic, Howie had always observed, of politicians who were generally stealing everything in sight. Howie just hoped that D.T. knew what she was doing, because this was archeology a person could die for. And maybe two people already had.

He finished eating and stretched out more comfortably on his elbows, leaning back from the fire. The summer night was lovely with a billion stars overhead, twinkling and winking at him. A coyote began to howl close by. It was a high, plaintive wail, very human and sad. The sound rose louder than before, full of dreadful remorse. Howie felt a small tingle of concern. He had never heard a coyote call quite like this.

"Sounds like a soprano I once heard at the Santa Fe Opera," he remarked.

Lewis snorted scornfully and replied in Tiwa, which Howie thought was rude.

"What did he say?" Howie asked D.T.

She shrugged. "He says it's not a coyote. It's a ghost. And that you're a very stupid Indian not to know the difference."

Howie grinned. "So what's the ghost saying, Lewis?"

"He's saying maybe he'll come and steal your soul tonight, Moon Deer, just to take that dumb smile off your face. Carl, I think you should tell our Lakota friend the story."

"I'm always up for a campfire story," Howie said agreeably.

Big Carl was leaning against a rock, rolling himself a cigarette from a pouch of tobacco.

"Well, there are ghosts on this mountain, that's undeniable," he said in his slow drawl. "I will tell you a story that all our children know. A long, long time ago, Moon Deer, the people became evil and God punished them by spreading famine upon this land. The corn died on the stalk, the beans and the squash shriveled on their vines. The people went hungry."

"What about game?" Howie asked. "Couldn't they hunt deer and rabbits?" This had always been Howie's problem when people started to tell stories of this nature: He asked too many questions.

Big Carl shot him a disapproving look. "The deer and the rabbits and all the game died from disease and pestilence. In those days, the tribe was ruled by an evil chief whose name, in English, would be called, Waits-For-Evening. Waits-For-Evening lived in sin with his eldest daughter, Cloud Woman, with whom he had three sons—Fox Boy, Gray Bear, and Hungry Wolf. When the famine became very bad, Cloud Woman said to Waits-For-Evening, 'Why should we be hungry, my husband, when we have three large sons? I will slaughter and cook our oldest son, Fox Boy, for our dinner tonight.' Waits-For-Evening agreed and that night they had a large feast. Cloud Woman dried the rest of the meat and she and her husband fed on Fox Boy for nearly the next two weeks. But eventually the food was gone and they became hungry again. So Cloud Woman said to Waits-For-Evening, 'Here we are hungry again when we have two large sons, my husband. Why don't I slaughter and cook our middle son, Gray Bear, for our dinner tonight?' Waits-For-Evening agreed, because in fact he had developed an inclination for human flesh. So they killed and ate Gray Bear, who was so large that they were not hungry for nearly a month."

"I think I can see where the plot is heading," Howie said. "So they decided to kill the third son as well, I bet, Hungry Wolf?"

"Do you want to hear this, or don't you?"

"I want to hear."

"Well, then, yes, they decided they would kill and eat Hungry Wolf. But meanwhile, Hungry Wolf had watched as his two older brothers disappeared. His mother, Cloud Woman, was an expert in witchcraft and she had made all the people in the Pueblo believe that Gray Bear and Fox Boy had only gone away on a long journey. But Hungry Wolf was not fooled.

Now I could give you the long version of this tale, Moon Deer, but since you're such a know-it-all, I'll make the story short. After many dangerous adventures, Hungry Wolf killed his parents and rid the people of the great evil in their midst, and soon the fields began to grow again and the game in the forests returned. But because Cloud Woman was a great witch, she couldn't be killed completely and it is said that she and Waits-For-Evening haunt the part of the mountain where we are sitting right now. You can hear them call to each other at night, and sometimes people who have strayed up here have disappeared. It is said that the people who disappear are killed and eaten."

"Eaten?" Howie was particularly interested in this point.

"Maybe you won't think it's so funny if *you* end up as dinner, Moon Deer!"

Howie laughed, trying to dispel the disquieting image of being eaten by a ghost. He had grown up on stories like this that were designed mostly to scare the crap out of small children so they'd behave. The stories always seemed to have a witch in them, an evil old woman who beguiled her witless husband into doing something terrible, usually to the kids. Like all Indian children, Howie could remember lying in bed at night in mortal terror, certain that the moment he closed his eyes some evil old witch would get her claws into him. Even now, he felt just a twinge of the old childhood terror. He wondered if the story he had just heard had any basis in fact, a whispered collective memory of an evil time when the ultimate taboo of cannibalism had been broken.

When the story was finished, D.T. rose to put away the food and clean up. One thing Howie had always noticed about traditionally religious people—whether Native American, Christian, Jewish, or Muslim—is that they always let women do the dishes. God apparently had decreed a universe in which males had all the perks. Fortunately, Howie was a doubter when it came to religious matters (except when he was flying in airplanes), and he rose to give D.T. a hand. He cleaned the pots with an orange plastic scruffy and a small amount of water from a jug while D.T. took care of the food, putting it away into various bags and boxes. The plates they had been using were paper and these were simply tossed into the fire, making a bright flare of light.

Just as they were finishing the cleanup, an argument in Tiwa broke out between Lewis, Big Carl, and Daryl. Howie couldn't imagine what the trouble was. The three men had been sitting together smoking and talking quietly near the far end of the fire when their voices suddenly rose in anger. After a few moments, D.T. turned from what she was doing and joined in the fray, and this made things even more heated. After a good deal of angry conversation, Daryl rose unhappily and stomped off by himself, leaving D.T. and Lewis shouting at each other. Howie was poised to interfere, but the mysterious argument ended as abruptly as it began: Lewis made a rude gesture in D.T.'s direction, then he and Big Carl retired with stern faces to their big ugly rectangular tent.

"What was *that* all about?" Howie asked when he and D.T. were alone by the fire.

"God, they're such idiots! They're making Daryl sleep at the cave tonight to stand guard. I guess they think I'm going to steal those old bones, maybe sell them to the Santa Fe Indian Museum. Big macho stud Daryl, of course, is terrified to be there alone at night, thinking the ghosts will get him. Carl had to threaten to tell everybody in the Pueblo what a sissy he was."

"What did you say to them?"

D.T. was all revved up still with her anger and disappointment. "This is such a disaster, Moon Deer, I can hardly bear to talk about it! That asshole Lewis said he's seen enough, that he's decided to recommend to the council to close up the cave and not let anyone else go there—including me, starting immediately. That's when I weighed in. I reminded Lewis that the council has asked me to make a complete inventory of what's inside, and that I haven't had time to do that yet. It's ridiculous—I need at least a month to even *begin* to make an inventory! But Lewis hates me and he has a real feather up his ass. He went on and on about how he's the voice of the council up here, and that his word goes, and this whole thing is under his jurisdiction as War Chief. I got angry and told him if he didn't let me back in the cave I was going to tell everybody about all the money he's been stealing from the tribe. He got angry back and said that from now on there was going to be a guard twenty-four hours a day at the cave, and if I try to go back there, he'll arrest me."

"What's this about Lewis stealing?"

D.T. sighed. "Gossip, mostly. I just threw it at him because I was so pissed off. It's something my cousin Charlie told me, but there isn't any proof."

They had been speaking in low voices, but Carl had just stepped ponderously from the tent to glare at them, making it difficult to continue.

Howie led D.T. a little way from the fire. "You need to tell me about this," he whispered. "If Charlie thought Lewis was stealing, it could have something to do with why he was killed."

D.T. shook her head wearily. "Well, we can't talk here," she said reluctantly. "Meet me out on the meadow in five minutes. I'll just get something warm."

Howie watched Donna Theresa climb into her dome tent. He waited near the fire until he felt he wasn't attracting attention, then he wandered off into the darkness, trying to make it appear that he was merely obeying a call of nature. D.T. appeared a short while later with a small silver flask of something that looked very warming indeed.

"Come on," she said, leading him out onto the dark grass beneath a zillion stars.

5

Howie sat next to D.T. on a boulder as smooth as skin. Far away in the western desert, the lights of a small town twinkled in the darkness. It was the sort of night you could stare upward at the swirl of distant galaxies and almost figure out the logic of the universe. Meanwhile, back on Planet Earth, matters were not so easy to comprehend.

D.T. took a hit from the flask and passed it to him. Their hands touched during the transaction and Howie couldn't help but wonder about the possibility of maybe the two of them exchanging more than just firewater tonight. *Down, boy,* he told himself. He hated being so predictably at the mercy of guy-thoughts: pondering a pounce, just because he was sitting with a beautiful woman alone on a high mountain meadow on a gorgeous summer night.

He took a drink from the flask, hoping to quench his reckless libido. The flask contained brandy and it burned a pleasant path down Howie's gullet. It was always good fortune to find an oasis of depravity in an otherwise drug-free, alcohol-free reservation.

"Good stuff," he told her.

"I shouldn't be drinking up here, but Lewis and Carl are driving me nuts. Can I ask you something, Moon Deer? . . . No, it's stupid. Forget it."

"Go ahead," he encouraged. "Maybe it's not so stupid after all."

"Well, it's just this. Do you think I'm too modern?"

"Modern? Well, it *is* the twenty-first century. I suppose you could pretend it was the nineteenth century, but that would be a lot of work, and it would probably make you grouchy."

"I'm sick of everybody telling me I'm not traditional enough! Even my grandfather's been on my case, saying I care more about archeology than the interests of the tribe."

"Is he right?"

"I'm not an idiot—I know very well that this dig could make my reputation if I play my cards right, and the council lets me continue to work, and if eventually I publish the right sort of paper. I won't pretend that doesn't interest me. But I *do* care about this damn tribe of mine, even if sometimes I wonder why. What I believe is that we need to know the truth of what happened here. That's all. The simple truth. If our ancestors were cannibals, we need to know that. If not, better yet. Honestly, I'll be relieved. But you can't pretend the past didn't happen, just sweep it under a rug, because then humans will never stop making the same mistakes."

Howie studied her. She was an interesting woman and he hated to be obnoxious, blowing any chance he might have with her. Still, he was being paid to do a job and he thought held better get on with it. "Speaking about the past," he said, "I really need to ask you about the British archeologist. You knew him, didn't you?"

"Moon Deer! For chrissake, my grandfather hired you to help me, not to ask a whole bunch of dumb questions."

"Raymond hired me to find out what's going on up here. Now, look, when you came to my cabin Wednesday afternoon, you knew about the earring on the head I'd found. How did you know that?"

"I told you. I heard it on the radio."

"No you didn't, because it wasn't *on* the radio. I checked. Now what's going on, D.T.?"

D.T. took a sip of brandy. "All right, Charlie told me. He said Shark Tooth's head was found in a garbage Dumpster in town. I don't know how Charlie knew that, and I guess we're not going to be able to ask him about it now, are we?"

"Why didn't you tell me this on Wednesday?"

"Why should I? I wasn't sure I trusted you. I came to you

because I wanted to find out what you knew, that's all. I needed to know if he was really dead or not."

"*He*? Come on, D.T., give me a name. I'm on your side. I'd like to help you."

She shook her head. "If you were on my side you'd just leave this alone, Moon Deer. It's not something I like to talk about."

Howie gave her a small lecture about how some things in life are hard to do, but necessary. Like cutting your toenails, or going to the dentist, or standing in a long line at the bank.

"All right, all right!" she cried, putting an end to his dismal lecture. She took a deep breath, like a person about to dive into deep waters. "His name's Fa-fa-fa . . ." It took her three times, but she got it out: "Ford."

Howie nodded, glad to be getting somewhere at last. "Good. Ford. How well did you know him?"

She turned and gave him a shrewd, womanly look. "You want to know if I went to b-b-bed with him? Is that it?"

Howie hadn't thought of this, actually. But since the very name of the man brought her stutter back, it didn't seem like a bad place to start.

"All right, did you go to bed with him?"

"You want the details, huh?"

"D.T., I *don't* want the details. I'm looking for the overview here. What was your relationship with this guy?"

"He was my ha-ha-ha . . . my ha-ha-ha . . ."

Howie could often finish her words when she was caught in a stutter, but in this instance he was clueless.

She took another long swallow of brandy. "We were married," she said, exhaling a long breath that could have been lit with a match.

In the end, Donna Theresa seemed relieved to tell Howie about her unlikely marriage. She spoke hesitantly at first, but with increasing speed and involvement as she went on.

His full name was E. Rutherford Hughes. He had a gaunt, weathered face, wicked blue eyes, and long white hair that reached his shoulders. Physically, you might take him for an aging hippie, except for his precise, extremely upper-crusty British voice—one of those smooth BBC voices, as Howie imagined it. With his shark's-tooth earring, E. Rutherford Hughes was a cross between a pirate and a professor. And if this wasn't enough to whet any graduate student's romantic fancy, he came from one of the oldest families in England: He had money, self-confidence, spoke five languages fluently, had traveled everywhere, and had vividly interesting opinions about nearly everything.

D.T. had been no match for a pirate professor with shrewd blue eyes and a fabulous British accent. He picked her up in the stacks of the UNM library, whisked her off to bed, and soon convinced her to give him a crash course in Tiwa, the language of the northernmost New Mexico Pueblo Indians that was supposed to be kept secret from outsiders, particularly archeologists working on books. D.T. was flattered by his interest, the way he wanted to know every last thing about her— with a special emphasis on her language and culture. In her entire life, no one had ever focused such minute attention on her before. She wasn't a virgin, but this was her first real affair. It only came to her much later that he had been using her ruthlessly, mining her as a kind of living Native American artifact.

"I was so naive, Moon Deer! I remember thinking, here's this guy who's taught at Cambridge and who's been to China and Paris and Tahiti and Egypt, all the places I've always wanted to go—and he's fascinated with *me*! I couldn't tell him enough about boring little San Geronimo, New Mexico! I was so eager, so horribly eager . . ."

"Was he teaching at UNM?"

"No. At first he told me he was on leave from Cambridge, but later I found out that he'd been given the boot. He was too much of a rebel for academia, but I loved that about him. He was brilliant, really. Totally ruthless and egocentric, but a genius in his way."

They began their affair in the spring, and all summer long she worked hard to answer his questions and teach him her language. By fall, she had pretty much used up her store of fascinating native secrets, and it was at this point that she felt his interest in her wane. She tried everything she could to keep him, even making up Indian customs out of the blue just to have something to talk about—a common tactic, in fact, of natives when forced to deal with inquisitive archaeologists. But in this case, Ford seemed to have a sense of when she was lying, and she felt him slipping away.

Then in the fall, miraculously, he asked her to marry him. Even at the time, she understood he was having problems with his visa and that marriage to an American citizen was a way for him to stay in the country. Nevertheless, she was willing. She thought that if they were married, she'd have a hold on him, that a marriage of convenience might gradually evolve into a marriage of love. Unfortunately, a week after her marriage, she came home to their apartment in Albuquerque and found him in bed with a waitress from the Double Rainbow Café. D.T. was devastated. Yet she believed it was somehow her own fault, that she only needed to be sexier and more interesting to lure him back. She read books on everything from advanced sexual techniques to French cooking, hoping to become a fascinating sexpot gourmet that any eccentric genius would be glad to have as a wife.

"You must have scored some points with him when you showed him your cave," Howie suggested.

D.T. was momentarily quiet.

"You *did* show him the cave, didn't you?"

"Well, not at first. Ford was such a strong personality, I guess I was afraid he'd take it away from me somehow. Not in the actual way he finally did, but intellectually—I mean, he knew so much more than I did about the Anasazi. It was the only thing I ever had that I felt was totally mine . . . do you understand?"

"I'm not sure," Howie admitted.

"Well, he got it from me anyway. It's my own fault. The marriage just got worse and worse. Ford did anything he liked. Sometimes he'd disappear for weeks at a time, then come back and laugh at me when I'd ask him where he'd been. He didn't even bother to hide his affairs. By that spring I was a real basket case. One night in May, he was off somewhere and I was so depressed I swallowed a bottle of sleeping pills. I called 911 just before I passed out, and an ambulance came and they pumped my stomach. I woke up in the hospital and that's when I knew I had to do something for myself. I'd had enough, I really had. It was a turning point. What saved me was work—I was just finishing up my master's that spring, and I really threw myself into it. It gave me my self-respect back somehow."

"You were still living with Ford then?"

"Well, he was in and out. I got so I didn't even ask him where he'd been. I just kept plugging away on my thesis, shutting everything else out. Then in June, I decided I'd apply for the PhD program and come back to San Geronimo and excavate the cave. That was when I finally told Ford about the site. All I wanted was his professional advice, how I should present the find to the archeology department, and what was the best way to organize a dig—how many people I'd need, how much money I should ask for, that sort of thing. I thought he owed me that much, at least, after I'd gotten him his green card. Anyway, I trusted him when it came to archeology."

"So you brought him here?"

"Yeah. It was late June and there was still a lot of snow. I had to sneak him up a back way on an old logging road, because non-natives aren't allowed on this part of the reservation. But when he saw the cave, he laughed and said it wasn't much. He was very condescending about it, actually. Of course, it wasn't much back then—you could barely get inside and most of the structures were hidden by all the collapsed rubble. Ford said the altitude was way too high for any prehistoric people to live here, so at most it was a place where hunters might have come for shelter during the summer. He did his best to discourage me. He said if I wanted to be an archeologist, I should get myself involved with an established project and not waste my time on a very minor site, and that the cave would be impossible to excavate anyway unless I had some multimillion-dollar grant. He even convinced me that it would be dangerous to do any more clearing without a structural engineer and a whole lot of help and materials—that caves were no places for amateurs and that I could set loose a new slide and kill myself."

"And you believed him?"

"Of course. He was the big archeologist, I was only some grad student. So we went back to Albuquerque and a few weeks later I came home and he was in bed with my best friend, a girl named Carol. Somehow, that *really* was the end. It was cumulative, Moon Deer. I'd had it. So I moved out, got my own place, got accepted into the PhD program, and put my life back together. The council turned down my request to excavate the cave here—I was pissed off, sure, but my adviser at UNM helped me come up with a new dissertation topic about the evolution of prehistoric irrigation techniques at Chaco. It wasn't as exciting as having my own cave to explore, but I put my energy into it. I didn't see Ford, and I didn't plan to come back to San Geronimo, not ever. And then Don Lucero, the tribal governor, called and asked for help—surprise, surprise, it turned out that Ford had been excavating my cave during the year I was gone."

"You must have been angry."

D.T. nodded. "Well, I was . . . I don't even know how to put it into w-w-words. The cave was mine, I found it, I felt vi-violated."

"I can understand that."

"I couldn't . . . it wasn't only Ford . . . I c-c-couldn't understand how he did it, why they'd let him up here."

"The council?"

"Even Ford, tricky as he was, he couldn't have done it alone."

"I want to get back to that point. But first, I need to know just how angry you were, what you thought you were going to do when you saw Ford again?"

She smiled in a very disarming manner. "Kill him, naturally. What would you have done in my place? I bought a .22 automatic at a dealer in Española, driving home from Albuquerque. I wasn't even angry, really, not at that point. More just sort of businesslike about the whole thing. I thought Ford needed to pay for the way he had treated me, that's all. I couldn't let him get away with it. The only problem was, I couldn't find him anywhere. When I first got back home two weeks ago, I rode up to the cave—I saw the work he'd done, and that pissed me off all over again, but he wasn't here. Maybe I'd just missed him, I don't know. I rode back down the mountain, but I couldn't find him at the Pueblo or in town. The next few days I had a lot of things to do, so I put my gun away and let it go. I had to spend some time with my grandfather, and also my mother, who's not in very good health. The council wanted to talk with me as well. It's hard to kill someone when you have so many interruptions."

"But you found him finally?"

"He found me. You were there, Moon Deer—it was last Saturday night. That was Ford who came to pick me up just as we were leaving the restaurant."

"*That* was Ford? In the Land Cruiser?" Howie found this surprising. "But it was an Indian, I heard him. You were speaking Tiwa together."

She laughed without humor. "After the first day or so, Tiwa was the only language we ever spoke together—it's how he picked it up so fast. He'd heard I was in town and he wanted to talk with me. He had gone to the Pueblo first, to my mother's house. She told him I was having dinner at the Anasazi, so he came there. Ford's always impatient when he wants something."

"What did he want?"

"You'll never guess the guy's nerve! He wanted me to come back to him, help him up at the cave, be his little pushover wife again. He said he was really on a roll and thought he might be able to finish up the whole operation before the snow came this fall. All he needed was the help of a good assistant. He even tried to put the make on me, give me a shot of the old Rutherford Hughes charm. I told him to forget it, that I was involved with someone else."

"Really?" Howie couldn't resist asking. "Who?"

She smiled. "You, of course."

"*Me?*"

"Well, I just made it up. We'd been talking at dinner and you were the first person I thought of."

"You could have said Lester," Howie suggested.

She shrugged. "I don't like Lester. I told Ford you were really smart and nice, a private detective even, and that you were totally hot in bed. I hope you don't mind. It was a way to keep him off me."

Her eyes were glistening in the moonlight, and Howie wasn't certain if perhaps she was flirting. He cleared his throat and thought of different things to say, some of them clever. But it seemed best to get off the topic of sex.

"So what did you say about his offer to assist him on the dig?"

"I said I needed to think about it. Believe me, I *wasn't* planning to work with Ford. But I wanted to find out more about what he'd been doing up here, maybe lead him on a little. The way we left it, I was supposed to meet him up at the cave on Monday afternoon and he'd show me what he'd found. He gave me a couple hundred dollars and told me to drive to Albuquerque and get some supplies he needed—surveying equipment and a new sleeping bag and some other camping stuff at REI. I guess he'd been roughing it for a while."

"You agreed to run errands for him?"

"Well, yeah. I wasn't thrilled, but I wanted to butter him up. If I was his stupid pushover wife, you see, he would let his guard down and tell me all the things I wanted to know—not only about the cave, but who was helping him. I was more than a little curious about that."

Howie looked at her sternly. "D.T., let's stop playing games. Did you kill him?"

She returned his stare. "What do you think?"

Howie sighed. "I don't know, I never think *anybody* did it—Jack says that's one of my problems as a PI, that I'm too trusting."

"Well, you'd be right in my case. I just couldn't stay angry long enough. I went down to Albuquerque on Sunday, did the shopping Monday morning, then drove back north on Monday afternoon. But the water pump on my truck broke as I was driving through Santa Fe and I had to spend the night there until someone could put in a new one early Tuesday morning. By the time I got home to San Geronimo, saddled up one of my mother's horses, and got to the cave, it was late Tuesday afternoon. But Ford wasn't there—I'd missed him again. It was too late to ride back down the mountain, so I camped up here on Tuesday night, then rode down Wednesday morning. And that's it, the whole story. I never saw him again."

"Tuesday's the night I found Ford's head in the Dumpster," Howie added.

"I have an alibi, then—you can ask my mother, Moon Deer, what time I rode up here on Tuesday morning. Even if I'd wanted to, there's just no way I could have reached the cave, killed Ford, then got his head down to your alley by Tuesday night."

She didn't seem to understand how leaky her alibi was. Howie could see a number of possibilities: She could have murdered Ford on a different day than Tuesday—Saturday night, for example—or killed him in a different place. But he let it pass for the moment.

"All right," he said. "I'm starting to see this just a little more clearly, but there's still a whole bunch of stuff I need to know. Let's talk about your cousin."

"You want me to tell you about Charlie?"

"I think you'd better."

Cousin Charlie grew up in the house next door to D.T. and was her closest friend when she was a child. They were inseparable, only four months apart in age. They rode their bicycles together, made up games in the woods, got into trouble, went fishing, built a treehouse, and sometimes on summer afternoons walked into town from the reservation to gape at the white people and spend fifty cents apiece getting an ice cream at the drug store that used to be on the San Geronimo Plaza

before all the shops there got turned into art galleries and
T-shirt emporiums.

Around thirteen years old, they became more conscious of
the separation of girl things and boy things, and they weren't
as close as before. D.T. went off to the big public high school
in town, taking the yellow bus every day, while Charlie stayed
on the reservation, attending the small day school that was run
by the Pueblo. They were still friends, but life and different interests had begun to tug them apart. D.T. was nearly desperate
with longing to get off the reservation and go to college in the
big city of Albuquerque; Charlie was content to stay closer to
home. He and his friends smoked a lot of dope and started a
rock band that fell apart after a while because no one felt
much like rehearsing. When she saw him, Charlie always
made her laugh, but after a while she realized she didn't know
him anymore.

Howie had heard some of this from Raymond: how Charlie's father was killed a few years ago, run over in a drunken
mishap by Anthony Lucero, the War Chief's oldest boy.
From that moment, Charlie began drinking, along with
smoking dope, going from bad to worse. There was an anger
in him now, giving his jokiness a bitter edge. D.T. finally understood that her old playmate had become a serious partisan
in the Concha/Lucero feud. He wanted to avenge his father's
death.

"A few nights after I got back, Charlie and I went out for
some burritos in town," D.T. said. "We hadn't really talked in
years, so we spent some time just catching up. He went
through four beers at dinner, sucking them down one after another, which worried me a little since he was driving. Then out
of nowhere, he started talking about Ford, saying he'd taken to
riding up to the cave once or twice a week, helping Ford with
some of the work up here, just on a part-time basis, whenever
he had free time."

"How did Charlie know about the cave?"

"I showed it to him when we were kids, making him
promise not to tell anybody. We must have been thirteen or
fourteen, and he was just putting on a bunch of weight. He

only hiked up with me one time, and he said it was too much trouble just to see a few old pottery shards. He didn't feel the magic of the place like I did."

"Okay. What else did you talk about at dinner?"

"Well, he went on about how he and Ford were buddies. I wasn't sure I believed him at first, but he knew about my marriage—and only Ford could have told him that. I sure as hell haven't told anybody around here about *that* mistake! Charlie was on his fourth beer by this time and he started acting kind of cagey, like he knew something he was dying to tell me. Finally, the weirdest story came out. I wasn't sure whether to laugh or cry—he thought he was some kind of detective, finding out all kinds of dirt on Lewis Lucero that he said was going to destroy the entire family. But it was all half incoherent, Moon Deer, and I'm not sure how much of this Charlie was imagining. He said he was certain it was Lewis who was allowing Ford to work up at the cave, and that the rest of the council didn't know."

"But that doesn't make sense," Howie objected. "Lewis is totally opposed to anybody working up here, much less a white person."

"I said the same thing. But Charlie was convinced Lewis didn't have any choice in the matter, that Ford was blackmailing him in some way. That's the reason Charlie was hanging out up at the cave, hoping Ford would tell him whatever his leverage was."

"Really? So did Ford tell Charlie how he managed all this?"

"No, of course not. Ford was an arrogant bastard, but he wasn't a fool. If he was blackmailing Lewis, he wouldn't have given away whatever it was that he knew to some stoner like Charlie. But Charlie didn't give up. His theory was that Lewis was stealing tribal money, and that somehow this was what Ford had discovered. Lewis has been on the tribal council for probably the last decade. One year he'll be elected Governor, the next year War Chief, then Lieutenant Governor, back and forth—but whatever position he has, he's the real power behind things. The way it's set up, the tourist operation is under the jurisdiction of the War Chief's office, which is maybe why

Lewis keeps running for that particular position. There's a lot of money involved here—all those ten-dollar admissions add up. The money is supposed to go into a special fund for scholarships, but there's never been any kind of oversight, not even an accurate record of daily receipts. Meanwhile, Lewis and his family tend to take vacations in Florida and his oldest son, Anthony, always has a brand-new truck . . ."

"I'm surprised people don't demand an outside audit," Howie said.

"It's just not in our culture to demand things like that. We're very traditional, you know—it's considered disrespectful even to question what the elders decide. Charlie tried to crash a few of the council meetings, but he didn't get anywhere. The way he described it, Lewis just got this very stern, constipated look on his face and told Charlie if he was a good Indian, he'd forget all this white-man's nonsense of keeping books and having an outside accounting. The idea was that non-natives need policing like that because they're so evil, but not us, of course, because the elders are such spiritual beings that they can be counted on to always be just and fair and honest and keep perfect records in their heads. I'm sure you get the picture."

"Sounds like a good line," Howie said. "But I still don't understand how Charlie got onto this."

"Well, the way I understand it, Charlie just kept his ear to the ground, listening to rumors. Of course, he's been trying to find some way to destroy the Luceros ever since his father was killed. Then about a month ago, he got a job as a dishwasher at the Anasazi Grill. He had the idea that Lewis was an investor in the restaurant, that this was what Ford had discovered, providing him with leverage over the War Chief. If Ford could find out something like that, Charlie was certain he could do it, too. All he needed was some proof, a paper trail to show Lewis was diverting Indian money into a restaurant that served alcohol, and that would be the end of Lewis and the entire Lucero hold on the council."

Howie shook his head. "If this is true, I can see why Charlie got killed. And Ford, too—my God, what a nerve that guy had! But it's impossible, isn't it? I mean, how could a white man, an outsider, learn so much about tribal affairs that he'd be able to blackmail the War Chief?"

"Remember, this is a white man who knew fluent Tiwa and all kinds of confidential stuff about us. Plus he had money for bribes and God only knows what else. During the time we were together, Ford used to ask me incredibly detailed questions about the Pueblo, and I answered him—how the council was set up, who was responsible for what, where the money came from, where it went, stuff that probably ninety-five percent of the people who live at the Pueblo don't even know. I knew these things because my grandfather was the *cacique* and I used to ask a lot of questions myself. Ford's the only person I know who's smart and ruthless and arrogant enough to have pulled a stunt like that and actually gotten away with it. To tell the truth, I may have been the one to give him the idea that someone was stealing—I remember complaining once that when I tried to get money from the scholarship fund to go to UNM, I got turned down. And hell, I was a straight-A student in high school! A lot of us have suspected for years that the scholarship fund just doesn't exist."

"So you think this is all true, then? That Ford was blackmailing Lewis?"

D.T. shrugged, helplessly. "I don't know. It makes as much sense as anything else."

"I understand someone wrote an anonymous letter to the governor, saying that there was a white archeologist working secretly on the mountain. That was Charlie, I imagine?"

"Yeah. He admitted that to me just as we were finishing dinner. He hadn't been able to find any proof of anything, so he wrote the anonymous letter just to shake things up. He thought that Ford would be really angry if it looked like he was going to get shut down, and maybe then he'd tell Charlie what he knew. But it didn't work out that way. The governor sent Carl up here to investigate, and Carl is Lewis's man, a hundred percent—he reported back that there was no sign of the white man, but actually if he saw Ford, he probably just tipped him off that the gig was up. Maybe that's the reason Ford came to me on Saturday night to ask for help. He knew he didn't have much time left."

They fell silent. The flask was empty and the cold night was starting to penetrate Howie's clothes. All the information swirled in his mind inconclusively. There were some possible motives for murder in what D.T. had told him, but he still couldn't see how Ford's head had ended up in a Dumpster in town, cooked and cannibalized. That was the part of this that just did not fit.

"D.T., did you tell anyone what I told you on Saturday night—about my stakeout behind the Shanghai Café?"

"Well, yes I did. I told a couple of people. Was it supposed to be a secret?"

"Who did you tell?"

"I told Raymond. It was when he was discussing whether to hire you or not. Like I said this afternoon, I was against Raymond bringing you up here—I thought it would just complicate things and I didn't see the point of him spending so much money. So I told him about your Great Pussycat Caper, to put you down, I guess. Show what sort of cases you usually handled."

Howie sighed. "Okay, so you told Raymond. Who else?"

"Ford. That Saturday night in his car, when I was pretending you were my boyfriend."

"And Charlie? Did you tell him, too?"

"No. I didn't see Charlie again after that night we had dinner. But I guess Ford could have told him, or Raymond."

"And you still don't have a clue why Charlie was bringing me that strange box with some prehistoric twig inside."

D.T. shook her head. "Honest, I just don't have a clue, Moon Deer."

It was the word *honest* that didn't ring true. Howie looked at her profile in the dark and he felt certain that she was holding something back. Just at that moment, while he was looking at her, she turned to look at him with a meaningful stare. A sly half-smile fluttered across her lovely lips, loaded with innuendo.

"What?" he asked, slightly alarmed.

"You know what," she told him.

Afterward, Howie wasn't sure exactly how it happened, if she moved to him, or he to her. Like magic, suddenly they were kissing. Her lips were cracked from the New Mexico sun but her tongue was soft with insinuation.

Everything about her felt good. Howie stroked her graceful neck, her warm skin. Experimentally, he ran his hand underneath her sweater and discovered she wasn't wearing a bra. Her breasts were perky and firm, about as perfect as breasts could be. Still, he fought with himself, the cautious Moon Deer versus the horny devil. He was thinking this wasn't a good idea, he should stop this foolishness, step away, when she unbuckled his belt and slipped her hand down his waistband into his underpants.

He was in a hard bind, certainly. What could a guy do but return the gesture, snap open the top of her jeans and let his own hand drift down the smooth contour of her stomach to the soft gooshy splendor below? Howie gave in to the urgent call of the birds and the bees, overwhelmed with desire. They tore at each others clothes, gasping loudly, until they were half naked despite the chill.

"This is crazy!" he managed.

"Mmm," she agreed. "But don't stop."

She lay back on the rock and, with a sharp tug, Howie pulled one leg of her jeans free of her shoe so that she could open herself to him. He was positioning himself on top of her for the final entry, when Howie was startled to feel something very strange touch against his naked rear end: whiskers, it seemed, that were attached to some huge, hotly breathing creature.

"*Yeaahh!*" he screamed, forgetting sex. He could almost swear he had just been goosed by a monstrous warm nose.

D.T. was laughing wildly.

"It's only Saze," she cried.

"What?"

Howie spun around defensively and saw that a horse had wandered quietly over the meadow to the rock where they were about to mate. It was a black horse with a familiar star on her forehead, and she had just given Howie an affectionate nudge in the ass. D.T. seemed to think it was the funniest thing she had ever seen. Howie personally wasn't so sure. His heart was beating at a panicked speed, recovering from the surprise, and he felt ridiculous, frankly, with his jeans down around his ankles and a dwindling erection.

"I didn't hear her," Howie admitted.

"I saw her over your shoulder. I didn't expect her to nudge you like that, though. She must like you, Moon Deer . . . Hey, what are you doing up here, Saze?" she said to the horse affectionately.

"Saze? What are you talking about? This is Black Mare, the horse I rode coming up here today."

"Her name's Anasazi. It's Ford's horse, Moon Deer. He used to keep her stabled down in Albuquerque when we lived together . . . Come here, Saze!"

From where they were positioned on the rock, the horse's head was at eye level and she was studying the two humans with meditative interest. Howie stood and pulled up his pants, bothered by this news.

"This is *Ford's* horse? Are you sure?"

"Of course I'm sure. I used to ride her all the time. We're old friends."

D.T. climbed off the rock and stood with one leg of her jeans dangling free to stroke the mare's neck. It was a touching reunion, Howie supposed: half-naked woman and beast. Nevertheless, he liked the horse he knew as Black Mare, and it upset him to think she had belonged to Ford. Most of all, he couldn't imagine how Ford's horse had ended up stray with a broken halter outside of Lewis Lucero's corral . . . or at least that was the story Lewis had told him. Maybe Lewis had simply stolen the horse after he had killed the blackmailing archeologist. That was the more likely scenario.

Meanwhile, Howie had himself a serious case of *passion interruptus*. He joined D.T. on the meadow and they regarded each other warily over the horse's nose. The moment between them was over, and they both knew it. Her lips were blue-white in the moonlight, slightly parted, and she was every bit as beautiful as before. But now the specter of Ford stood between them—along with Ford's horse—not to mention Howie's suspicions that D.T. had been less than honest. All these things made it difficult to jump back blithely into lustful innocence.

She smiled a little sadly, acknowledging that some moments are fragile, and when they're gone, they never come again.

6

Howie had his one-man pup tent set up on a level patch of meadow about thirty feet from the campfire. It was the latest in camping technology, but he had a difficult time falling asleep. His mummy bag was warm, but the ground was hard and rocky and he wished he had thought to bring along a foam pad. Meanwhile, he had made a makeshift pillow out of his jeans, but no matter how he arranged things, his belt buckle pressed into his neck. There were also two pebbles that some-how managed to poke into the small of his back, and no matter where he wiggled, he was a fairly good example of a guy caught between a rock and a hard place.

He read by flashlight for a while, the thin volume he had packed this morning on Zen Buddhism hoping for woodsy in-spiration. Zen appealed to Howie because it attempted to look squarely at how the world actually was, without dogma—no rules or regulations, no nailing of people to crosses, no ghosts, no magic shirts that guaranteed protection from the white man's bullets, no slick-talking dudes on TV trying to get your money. When he was in the proper frame of mind, Howie could get very Zened-out with the *is-ness* of things. But not tonight. Tonight the *is-ness* was lumpy with the twin torments of desire and regret, thinking about Donna Theresa and wish-ing that they had finished what they had started earlier on the meadow.

He switched off his flashlight and lay in the darkness full of smoldering images of smooth skin and curves: a tactile mem-ory of how his finger had slipped up inside of her, where the rest of him longed to go. It was a bad idea to have sex with

D.T., he knew that rationally, and he forced himself to think about murder instead. He wondered if she had killed her husband. Or was it Lewis Lucero, the War Chief, forced to kill in order to get out from under some undefined blackmail attempt? *Eeney, meany, miney, moe . . . do I want her, do I want her not?* Howard Moon Deer's thoughts circled like hungry vultures until he burned himself out. At last, despite pebbles and desire, he fell into a troubled sleep.

Something woke Howie. Was it a whisper, a dream, a footstep? He didn't know. He lay curled on his side listening, his cheek against the rough material of his mock pillow, his rolled-up jeans that smelled of wood smoke from the campfire. But he heard nothing except a restless mountain wind that alternately billowed and collapsed the material of his pup tent, turning his small shelter into a kind of living lung.

After a while, Howie propped himself up on one elbow to check the time with his flashlight. The hands of his Swiss Army watch reported the depressing news: It was approximately halfway between 2:20 and 2:25 A.M. At this hour, greater accuracy would only be an unnecessary punishment. He was snuggling back down into his mummy bag, when he heard a cry from a great distance:

"*Aiiiieeeee!*"

Howie sat up, terrified. It was an awful sound, enough to make a person's blood run cold. Howie didn't know if it was a scream, the wind, a ghost, a coyote, or only his imagination. He reached to his backpack stuffed inside the tent near his feet, and pulled out his .38 revolver. The gun was cold and heavy in his hand, but it didn't offer much protection against nightmarish screams in the night.

He waited, listening intensely, but the scream did not come again. Some time passed and Howie decided it must have been a coyote after all. He slipped the gun into the netting overhead, a pocket for personal items that dangled conveniently nearby and tried to get back to sleep. He was just settling down when the front of his tent was unzipped and a flashlight glared into his eyes.

"Where the hell is she?" a voice demanded.

Howie raised a hand to shield himself from the glare. He could just make out the shadowy figure of Lewis Lucero behind the beam of light.

"Where is who?"

"You know who I'm talking about. Where is Donna Theresa?"

"She's not in here," Howie said. "Look for yourself if you don't believe me. Isn't she in her tent?"

"The bitch is gone."

"She's *not* a bitch, Lewis. She only has a different point of view than yours," Howie explained, very reasonably, he thought. "Maybe she's just off taking a pee. You know how women are. They have small bladders."

Lewis seemed to consider this. "Don't go anywhere, Moon Deer." The flashlight clicked off and Howie listened to Lewis's footsteps moving back toward the campfire. Howie didn't wait. He unzipped his mummy bag and wiggled into his clothes, a gymnastic feat in a small tent. He checked his shoes for creepy-crawlies, grabbed the .38 from the netting overhead, and bolted outside. The night was cold and dark and alien at this high elevation, with a thin crescent moon that had risen in the east. In the distance, he could hear Lewis and Big Carl talking to each other in low voices near the campfire. Howie stuffed the revolver into the waistband of his jeans and made his way carefully around the back side of the crouching lion rock to where the trail to the cave began. He moved quietly, keeping his flashlight off until he was safely out of sight from the camp. The cave was off limits now, guarded by Daryl, but Howie was almost certain that if D.T. was gone, this was where she would be.

Howie hiked as quickly as he dared, but his batteries began to dim after only a few minutes, causing him to move slowly. The trail was lonely and dangerous at night. The wind made an eerie sound, shrieking through the rocks. Howie's apprehension grew as he approached the cave. In the daytime, this high mountain perch was scary enough, but in the dark the terror was more subtle, full of a whispering evil. He forced himself onward, following the fading yellow circle of his flashlight beam up the steep path.

He turned a corner of the switchback trail and was startled by a bright flash of light that seemed to come from the mountain overhead. It happened so quickly it was difficult to say what it could be. Lightning perhaps, except the sky overhead was clear with stars. The flash came a second time, a magnesium spark, just for an instant.

This was getting a little freaky. Howie was tempted to turn back, but that would be ridiculous, and embarrassing to explain to Jack. Surely there was a reasonable explanation for the flashing lights. It could be a flying saucer, for instance—aliens often landed in New Mexico, after all. He kept hiking with reluctant footsteps until he came at last to the end of the trail where the rope dangled from the ledge overhead. There was another flash of light; it seemed to be coming from the cave itself, from the opening. Howie could think of only two possibilities: Either the Anasazi ghosts were having themselves a jamboree, or someone was using a camera up there with a flash attachment.

He turned off his dying flashlight and stuffed it down into his waistband next to the gun. Howie took a deep breath, grabbed hold of the rope, and began to pull himself upward. The one blessing of climbing a mountain at night, he supposed, was that he couldn't see the vertigo-inducing view below. He climbed cautiously, making certain his feet were solidly set before rappelling onward. Before long, he was sweating freely despite the cold. His sweat was clammy on his forehead and neck.

He kept going, hand over hand, breathing hard. He was starting to get into a rhythm when his left foot came to rest on something squishy that didn't feel like a rock. He looked down and nearly died of fright. He was standing on a hand. A *human* hand . . .

"Yah!" he cried, stepping away violently. The hand was attached to an arm, which in turn was connected to a shoulder, but beyond that, Howie could see nothing more in the darkness. He was so scared that he dangled for some time on the rope, his teeth chattering, unable to move up or down. At last, he reached for his flashlight, thinking that this was a situation in need of further illumination. The beam was very dim now, but it showed Howie more than he wanted to see, ever. The flashlight dropped from his hand and clattered down the mountain, bouncing over the rocks until it landed far below. In the brief glow of light, he had seen a dead man on the scree, his body arched backward over a sharp rock in a horribly un-natural way. It was Daryl, the sentry, no longer fit to guard anything except the route to hell. His arms were spread apart, as though he had been crucified, and his head was smashed in like an overripe melon. Howie reached for his .38 revolver, not certain what other horrors might be near at hand. It was possi-ble that Daryl had fallen from the ledge above, but it was a lot more likely that he had been pushed.

Howie hung to the rope, listening, not certain whether to go forward or back. Meanwhile, the bright flashes of light contin-ued from the cave overhead. Howie decided to go on. Going back would be difficult without a flashlight and meanwhile there was someone at the cave, almost certainly Donna Theresa, and he wanted to confront her.

He was shifting his weight, getting ready to continue up-ward, when his legs slipped out from under him on the scree. He managed to hold on to the rope, but the .38 fell from his hand and bounced down the rocks, joining the flashlight below. *I'm not doing this very well!* he said to himself, dis-gusted. His left knee throbbed with pain from banging against a rock and his arms were sore from rappelling. With diffi-cultly, he got his legs set underneath him once again and he continued hauling himself up the rope. He was very tired now and had to stop to rest every few feet. With a final effort, he pulled himself over the ledge and lay on his stomach panting and scared, his cheek against rock that was cold as a mortuary slab.

As Howie lay panting, he saw another bright flash of light come from inside the cave. This time he heard the electronic whir of film advancing. It was a camera after all. With an ef-fort, he picked himself up and crawled on his hands and knees toward the opening to the cave and poked his head through. At first he saw nothing, only the harsh glare of a single Coleman lamp that had been lit and set on the ground. The light cast a huge shadow of a moving giant on the back wall and made the ancient Anasazi buildings appear frozen in time, unreal. The moving shadow belonged to Donna Theresa. She was standing between the lamp and the rear of the cave methodically photographing different angles of the old apartment complex. Her back was to Howie and she was so involved with what she was doing that she didn't appear to notice that she was no longer alone.

Howie watched her, fascinated, a woman and her obsession. It bothered him that she could go about her archeological business so calmly with Daryl dead on the rocks below. It wasn't that he expected her to tear her hair and weep, but this seemed a little cold. She was taking precise pictures of the main doorway into the apartment complex when Howie stood up and said, "Well, well."

D.T. cried out in surprise, a high little yelp, and spun around.

"Moo-Moo-Moon Deer," she managed, pale as the light on her face. "Wh-wha-wha . . ."

"What am I doing here?" Howie tried to speak reasonably, though it didn't seem much like a reasonable occasion. "The better question is what are *you* doing here with Daryl dead on the rocks below, his head smashed in."

"I . . . I climbed over him. He was dead when I got here. I don't know how . . ."

"Maybe he had to pee, and he just got too close to the edge," Howie suggested. "A urinary accident, so to speak."

"Howie, honestly—"

"Or a ghost got him. One of those restless Anasazi spirits who's been disturbed by modern science."

"Listen, Howie, please. I came here to finish up a few things, that's all. You heard Lewis—I'm not going to be allowed here anymore. I wanted to document everything with pho-pho-photographs. It was my last chance and Daryl was already d-d-dead. I'm sorry about him, but there's nothing I can do about it. He was a real asshole, frankly. But I never wished him any harm."

"When did you get here?"

She glanced at her watch. "About two. A little over an hour and a half ago."

"Let me get this straight—you came here knowing Daryl would be standing guard. Right?"

"Well, sure."

"So what did you plan to do? Soft talk him a little, then give him a push when he wasn't looking?"

She shook her head sadly at Howie's unpleasant insinuations. "Moon Deer, please, there just isn't t-t-time to explain. I've got to finish what I'm doing and get out of here before Lewis and Carl show up."

"First, convince me you didn't kill Daryl. How did you plan to get past him, for instance?"

"Do you really think I could kill anybody?"

"Yes," he told her. "It scares me a little to say it, but I think you could."

"Well, you're wrong. I thought I'd flirt a little, that's all. He's come on to me a bunch of times over the years, always looking at me like he's undressing me in his mind. I thought . . . well, you know, make him think he could get somewhere with me if he'd just be nice and let me look around the cave a little. You saw how Lewis and Carl were treating him around the campfire tonight—I was hoping he'd be angry about that and maybe feel a little rebellious. But I swear, I found him dead on the rocks when I was climbing up. It scared me half to death. Moon Deer, you've *got* to believe me!"

"I've been trying to believe you all day, but frankly my credulity is stretched just a little thin."

Howie was about to enumerate the list of her many untruths when a new problem caught his eye. The blue tarp he had seen that afternoon covering the mound of bones was now lying flat on the ground, no longer a mound. With a quick motion, Howie walked across the cave and yanked back the tarp. There was nothing underneath.

He turned to her with an accusing smile. "Now, isn't that something—the bones are gone! Do you know where the bones have gone, D.T.?"

"I d-d-didn't . . . I didn't take them."

Howie laughed bleakly. "For chrissake, D.T., you *stole* them. If the War Chief wasn't going to allow you back here, you wanted to be damn well sure you had all the material you needed to write your paper. You know, you're going to be a great success in academia—you've got the killer instinct. It's a shame you had to kill Daryl, though. I bet he was a real pushover, wasn't he?"

"I didn't kill him—I keep telling you that! And the bones were gone when I got here."

"They just danced away, huh?"

"Moon Deer, be realistic. There wasn't time for me to steal them. Think about it. It'd take at least two trips up and down the rope to remove them, maybe three. And where would I hide them? We were on the meadow until at least eleven. There's just no way I could have done everything, even if I'd wanted to."

"No, I think you could have done it, D.T. No problem at all. You've been coming up here since you were twelve. You know this mountain inside out. You could have taken the skeletons and hidden them away close by, someplace handy where you can return for them later. The fact is, there's just no other explanation. Either you took those bones, or they danced off on their own—that's what it boils down to."

"All right, it's mysterious, I admit that. But I *didn't* do it. Look, can I show you something?"

"Show me what?"

"Just trust me for a second, okay? I thought we were f-f-friends."

Howie raised his left eyebrow very slightly.

"This will only take a second," she said briskly, picking up the Coleman lantern from the ground. Howie thought she was going to lead him somewhere interesting, like up some Anasazi version of the garden path, but that's not how it worked out. What she did was very simple: She turned the little wheel on the side of the lantern, cutting off the flow of gas. The wick flickered, glowed orange, then died, leaving the cave in a thick, velvety darkness that was like being buried alive.

"That's clever," he told her. "Now I can't see a thing."

"I'm sorry, Moon Deer. I really am." And indeed, there was a note of honest regret in her voice.

Howie sighed, understanding that she had taken advantage of his trusting nature. "So that's it, huh? You're just going to leave me in the dark?"

"I have to. There's too much to do, and I'm not going to let you stop me. You don't give me any choice."

"I gave you lots of choices. All I wanted was the truth. Now, please, light the lantern."

"I told you the truth and you didn't believe me. Good-bye, Moon Deer. Do yourself a favor and don't try to climb out of here until morning. I'd hate to see you end up like Daryl."

Howie felt a wave claustrophobia. "Come on, D.T.! Light the goddamn lantern!"

She didn't answer. Howie's eyes had adjusted somewhat to the velvety gloom and he could see a faint afterglow from the wick hovering in the darkness. He began to walk toward it before it faded completely, thinking it still might light if he could turn up the gas in time. But the floor of the cave was uneven and he tripped after just a few steps, sprawling out painfully onto the rock. The wick's glow, his last bit of orientation, was gone now. The darkness was so final it was hard to say what was up and what was down.

"D.T! This is not funny!" he cried furiously.

He was angry and terrified in equal measure, and he shouted a lot of things, many of them not nice. But it did no good. This was her special place, after all, and unlike Howie she knew her way even in the dark.

After a while, Howie realized he was alone.

7

Howie spent the rest of the night lost and disoriented in the dark, crawling into things, trying to find the exit. He bumped into man-made walls, shovels, ancient rubble, the wire mesh, and all three sides of the cave, several times. Everything he crawled into was hard and cold and hurtful, and when he got tired of crawling into things, he fell down a hole into the partially excavated kiva and almost broke his neck. It was humbling. He attempted to learn from his mistakes, like a mouse in a maze, but he got nowhere at all.

Time passed slowly without any light to give it reference. After a small eternity, Howie noticed a hole in the darkness, a lighter shade of black—a very subtle gray. He studied the phenomenon without comprehension until it dawned on him that this was, in fact, the dawn, a small hint of morning showing itself through the cave opening. Howie guided himself toward the crack of daylight and crawled through to the ledge. It was a relief to be outside and breathe lungfuls of open air and watch the morning come alive. A line of clouds to the southeast caught fire, glowing red and orange. He remembered the saying his Uncle Two Arrows had taught him: "Red sky in the morning, red man take warning." The weather was changing.

He waited until there was more light, then Howie climbed down the rope to the trail below. He felt bruised and cold and discouraged, and he wished now that he and D.T. had not kissed on the meadow. Howie was pouting about this, thinking he'd be more careful about whom he fondled in the future, when he came around the bend of the trail and nearly ran into Lewis Lucero. The War Chief was as startled as Howie. His eyes opened wide and he nearly dropped the rifle he was carrying. After some fumbling, he pointed the gun sternly in Howie's direction.

"Where's Officer Fernandez?" he demanded.

"Daryl had an accident. It looks like he fell off the ledge."

Lewis squinted and moved back a little on the trail. "He's dead?"

"Probably. His brains are scattered on the scree."

Lewis said a long string of incomprehensible words in Tiwa.

"I'm sorry?" Howie said.

"I said you're under arrest, you Lakota shithead."

"*I* didn't kill him!"

"Sure. Now let's get going. And don't try anything, because I haven't had any coffee yet this morning, and I'd just as soon shoot you as look at you."

Lewis backed down the trail until there was a wide place where they were able to change positions, and from here he herded Howie back toward camp. Howie was surprised to see Donna Theresa sitting near the campfire with handcuffs around her wrists and Big Carl guarding her with a pistol. Howie smiled at her. She shook her head bleakly. She had gotten away from him at the cave last night, but clearly she hadn't gone far.

Howie dozed, sitting on the ground near the campfire, leaning against Donna Theresa. They were connected back to back with two pairs of handcuffs: his right wrist attached to her left wrist, her right wrist to his left. As positions went, it was far from comfortable, a small agony to be unable to scratch an itch at the tip of his nose. Nevertheless, he was exhausted and he managed to sleep in little catnaps. D.T. was dozing, too. Sometimes she woke him by yanking on one of their common wrists, other times he woke her. As sleeping partners, they were not a great success.

Each time he started awake, the morning seemed further along. Overhead, the sun was coming in and out of fast-moving clouds. When the sun was out, it was warm on his face, delicious; when it disappeared behind the clouds, there was an unseasonable chill in the air, adding to his torment. Hours passed in which Howie lingered in some fuzzy netherworld between sleep and waking. He dreamed of his greatuncle Two Arrows, that they were sitting together in Two Arrows's old pickup truck on one of those endlessly long summer reservation afternoons of childhood. Then Two Arrows turned into Raymond Concha, following the logic of dreams, another cagey old man. In the dream, Howie remembered that someone was supposed to help him on this mountain if he got into trouble. Be prepared to accept help from an unlikely source when least expected—this is what Raymond had told him. Howie sensed that this wouldn't be a bad time for help to appear.

"Come on, I'm ready now for an unlikely source," he muttered. But no help came from any source, unlikely or not.

The sun was higher, muted and melancholy in a dark sky. Howie woke, stiff and miserable, to find Big Carl studying him. Having nothing else to do, Howie studied Big Carl in return. Big Carl had a fat face and a fat gut, and a woeful expression in his fat brown eyes.

"You need to go on a diet," Howie told him.

Carl shook his head. "Let's talk about Daryl. Which one of you killed him?"

Howie thought hard, trying to remember last night, a long time ago. "He was dead when I climbed up the rope," Howie explained. "And I don't think it could be D.T., either," he added, chivalrously. "There wasn't enough time. And anyway, how could she get the jump on a cop who was armed?"

"It doesn't take much time to kill somebody, Moon Deer. And a pretty girl can get the jump on any man."

Carl began to question D.T. in Tiwa. It went on for a long time. Howie knew it must be important, whatever they were saying, but meanwhile, he couldn't keep his eyes open. He fell asleep and the next time when he woke, he was surprised to see someone riding into camp on a gray horse. The newcomer was a bulky Indian man in his late thirties with a flat, wide

face and a body shaped like a penguin. He was wearing a
tribal police uniform with a gun on a holster on his hip. Lewis
and Big Carl walked out onto the meadow to meet him. The
new arrival dismounted and he and Lewis and Big Carl sat
down in a three-pointed circle and spoke among themselves in
low voices.

"Who's the penguin?" Howie asked D.T.

"You're hallucinating, Moon Deer."

"No, really—look."

The way she was facing, she had to strain her neck to see.
"Oh, that's Johnson Trujillo. He's a tribal cop."

"I can see he's a cop. But what's he doing here?"

"How should I know? Johnson likes to beat up people—he
was brought up before the tribal council a few years back for
nearly killing some guy who went through a stop sign on Indian land. Offhand, I'd say this isn't looking g-g-good."

"Well, he won't hurt you—you're the *cacique's* granddaughter," Howie said optimistically. It was odd to have a conversation with someone tied to your back. He couldn't see her,
but he could feel her vocal chords vibrate against his back.
"And he won't touch me, either. After all, I'm here in a sort of
semiofficial capacity, hired by Raymond."

D.T. chuckled. "Boy, you're dumb, Moon Deer! They're not
going to beat us—they're going to *kill* us. Haven't you got that
yet? Right now they're probably figuring out what sort of fatal
accident we're going to have. Lewis won't dare let me live,
not after the way I threatened to expose him last night. He's
afraid I know too much. And if they kill me, they have to kill
you too so you won't talk."

Howie spent some time absorbing this information. It didn't
seem fair somehow. "Maybe you should have kept your mouth
shut," he mentioned.

"Well, I get m-m-mad . . . and I can't help myself."

"Next time, practice self-control."

"There isn't going to be a next time, asshole."

"I was speaking rhetorically," he told her.

They fell silent after that. Howie kept an eye on the three
men having their powwow on the meadow. After a long con-

versation, Big Carl and Johnson the Penguin picked up several halters and ropes from a pile of horse gear near the big rectangular tent, then disappeared over the meadow—Johnson on his horse, Carl on foot—apparently to round up the rest of the horses. Lewis walked back to where Howie and D.T. were handcuffed.

"Well, you two have caused us some big problems," he said cheerfully, sitting down cross-legged a few feet away, and placing his rifle onto the ground. "Luckily for you, I'm going to let you go. All you gotta do is answer a few questions first."

"Oh, sure!" D.T. taunted.

"This is the deal," Lewis continued. "Neither of you will be allowed back onto Pueblo land, not ever. And if you break your word, you'll regret it. Believe me, I'd much prefer to send you both to the white man's prison for killing Daryl, but a person in my position, you see, I have to consider the interests of the tribe first, take in the whole picture here. A murder investigation would bring in a lot of outsiders, and give our tribe a bad name, and we don't want that."

"Yeah, you especially don't want an outside audit of tribal funds!" D.T. said.

Howie yanked on her handcuffs. "Let's just listen to the guy, okay?"

"You tell her," Lewis agreed pleasantly. "We've had enough trouble, and it's time to put all this to rest. Like I said, all I want is just a few answers."

Lewis smiled hopefully, quite the friendly guy. Howie studied him, not believing a word of what he was saying but wanting to hear more.

"All right," Howie said. "I'm into answers."

"Good. Well, let me lay my bingo card on the table, so to speak. As you may have noticed, one of our tribal officers rode up just now, a very fine young man by the name of Johnson Trujillo . . ."

"Do we really have to listen to this crap?" D.T. muttered.

Howie jabbed her in the back with his elbow, and she jabbed him back. Tit for tat.

"Relax, you two," Lewis told them. "Now Johnson's been

investigating a homicide down in the Pueblo—one of our young braves, Charlie Concha, was found shot to death early Saturday morning, strapped to his horse. You wouldn't know anything about this, would you, Moon Deer?"

"Why should I?"

"Well, Charlie had a girlfriend, you see. Darlene Reynaldo, a very nice young lady. Now in the course of the investigation, Johnson had a talk with Darlene and she said that Charlie stopped by her house late on Friday afternoon and he was in a very good mood. He told her he had something very valuable from the cave in his possession, and that he was going to take this thing to you for safe-keeping."

"Why me?" Howie asked, truly curious.

"Because you'd been hired by the *cacique* and he wanted to get it off Indian land."

"Did he tell her what this thing was?"

"Yes, he did," Lewis agreed, nodding vaguely.

"Well? What was it?"

"I think you know perfectly well. Now where is it, Moon Deer? I'm tired of playing games. All the artifacts in that cave belong to the tribe, not to you or Donna Theresa. And I'll be damned if I'll stand by and see our sacred tribal relics end up in some museum. You understand me, boy?"

Howie *did* understand. And, in fact, what Lewis was saying seemed perfectly reasonable to him. But D.T. spoke before Howie could answer.

"Don't tell him, Moon Deer, he's going to kill us anyway."

"That is a lie!" the War Chief said coldly. "You have a very wicked imagination, girl."

"Howie, don't believe him—"

"Shut up," Howie told her. Frankly, he was heartily sick of her and this entire business, and nothing in the little white box seemed worth anybody getting hurt over. "Lewis, you can have the thing, gladly, whatever the hell it is. It's just some sort of petrified twig, that's all. Charlie brought it to me on Friday night, though I don't know why. He was shot pretty badly and he tried to tell me about a cop—the person who shot him, I guess, though he wasn't able to finish what he was saying."

"A cop?" Lewis frowned and shook his head. "Go on."

Honesty seemed the best policy under the present circumstances, and Howie spent the next ten minutes telling Lewis all the details he could remember about Friday night—how Charlie had appeared on horseback only to slide off his saddle, a mysterious white box in hand, and how Howie had sent the body back toward Indian land. Howie laid in on a little thick, how he had done this last act for the sake of the tribe, to spare them the invasion of federal law enforcement.

"And this white box—where is it now?" Lewis asked.

"I left it in a drawer. It didn't seem so important."

"Goddamn you, Moon Deer!" D.T. moaned.

"And where is your house? Tell me exactly."

By Howie's reckoning, the tribe had a perfect right to the petrified twig, if it came from the cave of their ancestors, so he gave Lewis exact directions to his cabin.

"Asshole!" D.T. muttered behind his back, once he was finished.

"Okay, now what about the human skeletons from the cave?" Lewis went on. "They seem to have gone missing."

"Sorry, I can't help you there," Howie answered. "I don't know anything about the bones."

"Don't start lying to me now, Moon Deer!"

"I'm not."

Lewis's mouth opened to ask another question, but then he squinted and peered across the meadow to where Carl and Johnson were bringing in the horses, coming their way. Lewis stood up stiffly from the ground with an old man's sigh, picking up the rifle and cradling it in his arms.

"Well," he said, "maybe we'll never know the whole truth of this matter. I told you there were ghosts on this mountain. But you've kept you're part of the bargain, so I'm going to keep mine. I'm going to unlock you now, and I want you both to just get the hell off this land and don't come back. We'll put this whole thing down as a learning experience for both of us. You got that?"

"Okay," Howie said. But he felt a chill. This was just a little too easy.

"You're such an idiot, Moon Deer!" D.T. said in a low voice.

The War Chief leaned between them and in a moment Howie heard the click of first one pair of handcuffs and then the other coming free. Lewis stepped back quickly, taking no chances.

"Just one thing," he said, raising the rifle in their direction. "You're going to have to get yourselves down the mountain without your horses. Carl won't quite understand this, being a lawman—how you gotta do some things for the interest of the tribe. So what I'm gonna do, I'm just going to tell him you got away."

Howie's mouth was dry as sawdust. It didn't take a genius to see that Lewis was going to shoot them as they were getting away. Lewis raised the rifle to his shoulder, seeing that Howie knew, and D.T. knew, and there was nothing more to pretend.

"It was you all the time, wasn't it?" Howie asked. "You killed the British archeologist."

Lewis shrugged. "Yep, I had it done, all right. Old Shark Tooth needed to die, just like the two of you. For the sake of the tribe."

"It wasn't for the tribe, it was for you," Howie told him.

"Well, it doesn't matter now, does it? . . . Go ahead, run," Lewis said with a sleepy smile. "What have you got to lose?"

8

Howie glanced longingly at the huge sky overhead and saw that the small clouds of early morning had transformed into bigger, more ominous clouds, dark as charcoal, rushing past the sun. A storm was certainly coming. Howie loved storms, along with sex, food, wine, and all the other living pleasures. He didn't want to die. His mind darted around trying to figure some way out of this. But there was nothing he could see, not with Lewis and his rifle five feet away.

D.T. stood silently next to him. She seemed resigned to death, sulky and petulant, like the world had always been a lousy place anyway, and she wasn't surprised much at the prospect of a nasty ending. Howie felt a little responsible for her attitude. He had fumbled the ball, so to speak.

"Go on, what are you waiting for?" Lewis asked.

"I have to tie my shoelace," Howie told him, glancing at his left sneaker.

"It doesn't matter about your shoelace."

"Sure it matters. I'm *not* running with a goddamn lace flapping around."

Lewis shrugged. "Okay, but do it quickly."

Howie bent over and fiddled with his lace, his back to Lewis, not wanting to finish too quickly because it was likely that this was the last time he would ever do such a homely, familiar act. He could see the War Chief upside down between his legs, about six feet away. Blood rushed to Howie's head along with a crazy half idea. His right foot was only inches from the fire pit that was ringed with blackened rocks. There was a particular rock the size of a softball not far from his right hand. Howie wondered if it might be possible to scoop up the rock and do a kind of backward bowl, propelling it at Lewis, getting him off guard. He knew it wasn't a good plan, as plans go. The rock could easily miss, or glance harmlessly off his shoulder.

"Hurry up," Lewis told him. "We don't have all day."

I have all eternity, thank you, Howie thought sourly. In the end, he figured this was the only opportunity he was going to get. He finished tying his left shoelace and, still bending over, pretended to check the right one. Then he made his move. Aiming between his legs, he scooped up the rock in a single fluid motion and sent it backward at Lewis as hard he could.

Lewis cried out. The rock grazed his left arm, not hard enough to do much damage, but Lewis lost his balance trying to get out of the way. He did a little dance on one leg, trying to regain his footing, firing the rifle harmlessly at the sky. Howie had started to spin around even before gun went off, and he threw himself on the War Chief just as the explosion came. They fell onto the ground together and rolled toward the fire pit. D.T. was trying to help, beating on Lewis with her fists, but many of her blows landed on Howie instead. In Howie's limited experience, real-life violence was a strange combination of tragedy and farce. Meanwhile, Lewis was a scrappy fighter for a middle-aged man, wiry and hard to pin down.

"Moon Deer, hurry up!" D.T. shouted at him. Frankly, it pissed Howie off since he was doing the best he could. But then a shot rang out from some distance across the meadow and he understood why she was anxious to leave. In a blur of motion, Howie saw that Carl and Johnson were about fifty yards away on horseback, galloping to Lewis's rescue. Johnson had fired from the saddle at full gallop and it looked as though he were aiming to fire again.

Howie left Lewis dazed on the ground. The War Chief's rifle was about a dozen feet away, and he thought he might take it along for a souvenir. But Johnson got a second shot off and the bullet was close, making a sound like an angry mosquito as it ricocheted against a stone in the fire pit. The riders were closing fast and there wasn't time now to do anything but run.

D.T. led the way, sprinting around the side of the crouching lion rock and up the trail toward the cave. The rock protected them momentarily from gunfire, but Howie suspected it wouldn't be long before the three men were after them.

"This is a dead end!" he shouted at D.T.'s back. "Where the hell are we going?"

"Just shut up and follow me. They can't ride their horses here. I know a way down, but we have to hurry."

Howie was dubious, but he followed her anyway, not having much choice. They ran along the trail nearly halfway from the camp to the cave. "Here!" she said, panting for breath. She stopped abruptly at a place where a dry creekbed crossed the trail and cascaded down the side of the mountain in a series of giant footsteps over huge boulders. D.T. climbed onto the first boulder and began descending quickly.

"For chrissake, it's too steep!" Howie objected, studying the terrain. "We'll never get down there."

"I've done this before. Stop worrying and just do it."

Howie shook his head at the folly of what they were doing, then he followed her down into the cleft of the old creek bed. The boulders were smooth, sometimes slippery. He stayed close to D.T., often sliding down the rocks on his ass. The descent was nearly vertical, scary as hell, but the boulders made a sort of natural ladder. Occasionally they zigzagged back and forth to a different side of the creek bed to find a better footing. After a while they passed from the bald mountain face into a new ecological zone below the tree line, where they were sometimes able to use roots and branches as footholds. There was a final stretch where they had to straddle a V-shaped crevice between two huge rocks, then they came out onto a wide flat trail nearly a thousand feet down the mountain from where they had started. Howie saw some old horseshit and was surprised to recognize where they were. This was the trail where they had ridden Saturday afternoon from Spirit Lake to the mountain camp.

They were catching their breath when they heard hoofbeats coming their way from above them on the trail. Howie grabbed D.T.'s arm and led her quickly into the trees. They reached shelter just in time. The hoofbeats grew louder and from their concealment in the woods they soon saw Lewis and Big Carl riding by, side by side. Lewis had his rifle propped in the shoulder of his saddle horn. There was no sign of Johnson Trujillo, the penguin-shaped cop; he had probably been sent on foot up the trail to the cave. Unfortunately, Lewis and Carl had guessed correctly that Howie and D.T. would try to climb down in this direction.

Howie waited until the hoofbeats faded down the trail. "You know any more tricky escape routes?"

There was a cagey look in D.T.'s eye. "Sure. There's a back way off reservation land that not many people know about. But we have to go down the main trail here just a little farther, until we get past the lake, maybe another quarter mile or so. That'll be the dangerous part. Once we're past the lake, we can take an old logging road I know that was made back when this mountain was still national park land eighty years ago. The road's overgrown but passable . . . it's the way I brought Ford when we came together."

"Okay, but I wish we could avoid the main trail from here to the lake."

D.T. shook her head and told him that there was no way they could manage this, not unless they were up for some serious technical climbing with rope and a lot of gear they didn't have. Howie followed her onto the path where they had just seen Lewis and Carl go by. They walked silently in single file close to the trees, so they would be able to jump to safety if they needed to. Every twenty feet or so, D.T. stopped to listen, trying to scope out what was ahead. The forest was noisy with birdcalls and chipmunks chattering at them from the branches above. It was nearly one in the afternoon according to Howie's watch, but the storm clouds overhead made it seem closer to evening.

They moved slowly, taking their time. There was one bad moment when they jumped into the trees thinking they had heard something, but it was only a marmot coming out of its hole to ogle them, one of the fat bushy rodents nearly the size of a beaver who managed to live at this high altitude. The sun briefly broke clear of the fast-moving clouds just as they were arriving at Spirit Lake. It was the same postcard view of lake and mountains that Howie had seen on the way up, though from a different angle. Howie studied the narrow trail they would have to take from here that followed the eastern edge of the lake along a granite bluff. This was the trickiest part of their escape because there would be no place to hide. They would be totally exposed for nearly a hundred feet, hemmed in between the mountain on their right, rising in a steep unbroken line to the cave above, and to their left, the green-gray water of the lake stretched out twenty feet or so directly below them.

"I think we should wait," Howie suggested. "We can hide in the woods until night, and try it then."

"There's no time. You can wait if you want to, but I'm going now."

"What's the hurry? Better safe than sorry, my mother always said."

D.T. turned to him bitterly. "The hurry, Moon Deer, is that you were such an asshole that you told Lewis where that white box is. So we have to get to your cabin before Lewis and Carl do. *That's* the goddamn hurry, all right?"

"You're going to risk our lives for some old Anasazi twig? No, thank you."

"I told you, you don't have to risk anything."

Howie studied her right shoulder with a dawning suspicion. "What's in that box? You know, don't you?"

"I don't know. It's probably just some ar-ar-artifact. But I want it."

She shrugged, trying to be nonchalant, but Howie didn't buy it.

"My God, you've been jerking me around this whole time! You know *exactly* what's in that box. It's the reason you ditched me in the dark last night. You were trying to get down the mountain to get your hands on that thing. Tell me I'm wrong, D.T."

"It's none of your business!" she said savagely. "This is my life, not yours."

"No, it's my life, too, at the moment. And I want you to tell me what's so important about a prehistoric twig."

"You wouldn't understand. Now let me go," she demanded, because he was holding on to her arm. She pulled free and began walking toward the exposed part of the trail.

"Don't do this," he pleaded. "Be reasonable. All we have to do is wait a few hours."

Howie supposed he could physically tackle her, but short of that, there didn't seem to be any way to stop her. In the end, he couldn't see what else to do but follow her once again. They came out of the trees and began walking along the exposed part of the trail along the cliff face above Spirit Lake. Howie had an uncomfortable sense of a hidden rifle barrel pointed between his shoulder blades. His fear was well founded. They were walking quickly, halfway to safety, when there came a sound from behind.

"Stop right there," a voice said.

Howie and D.T. stopped and turned to face Lewis Lucero. He was standing on the trail with his rifle. The War Chief had been waiting in ambush in the trees, just like Howie had imagined he might be doing, waiting for Howie and D.T. to pass this way. There wasn't any sign of Big Carl or the horses, but Lewis's rifle more than made up for the fact that he was alone. D.T. swore at him in English and Tiwa, but Lewis only laughed. He was in a good mood, outsmarting them so soundly. Howie was sick with disappointment, hating to come so far only to meet defeat.

"What I think I'll have you do, Moon Deer, is cuff the little lady's hands behind her back so she'll behave herself," Lewis said happily, holding up a pair of handcuffs in his free hand.

"Hell with you, Lewis!" D.T. told him. "You'd better just shoot me now, if you dare."

Lewis wiggled his rifle at her. "Well, maybe I will at that."

D.T. was standing at the edge of the trail close to the sheer drop-off to the lake below. With casual contempt, she forked Lewis the finger, then she turned and jumped. It was a simple move but unexpected. She hit the water with a great splash and sank like a stone. Howie was stunned. He stood at the edge of the precipice and stared stupidly at the water below, waiting for her to come up. She rose once, flailed her arms, and then sank again in a foam of bubbles. This time she didn't come back up.

"Goddamn!" Lewis muttered behind him. "That girl is plain crazy!"

Howie knew he had to move quickly if he was going to jump after her. Frankly, he wasn't overly fond of heights, and from where he stood, the twenty-foot drop to the lake looked like a very long way down. He took a deep breath and leaped off into empty space as far from the precipice as he could. There was a second of free fall and then he landed in the icy water with a loud splash, stunned and disoriented, sinking into the bitter depths. The cold was a shock, almost unimaginable; these high mountain lakes froze solid in the winter and barely warmed to liquid in the short summer months. Howie sank until he reached a point of neutral buoyancy and then he began to rise again toward the daylight above. On the surface, he looked around wildly for D.T. but she wasn't anywhere.

Howie had come up directly against the cliff, making it a difficult shot for Lewis on the trail above. Before the War Chief could give it a try, Howie filled his lungs with air and dove under the surface of the lake once again, hoping to find some sign of D.T. He turned in every direction but saw only green-gray water, a world that was ghostly and dank. The cold hurt his eyeballs, and Howie realized he could soon die down here from hypothermia.

He came up again to the surface, breaking water and taking a mighty gulp of air. A shot exploded and there was a plip nearby as the slug hit the surface. He dove again quickly and heard a second shot more distantly while he was underwater. He kept looking about frantically for D.T., but she was nowhere. Something took over in Howie that was not entirely conscious, a boundless desire to live, to get away from this terrible cold. He swam underwater with all his might toward the far shore, away from where Lewis was taking shots at him. There was nothing more he could do here.

He broke surface, gulped air, then continued underwater desperately, trying to work up some body heat in order to survive. He came up again and now he stayed on the surface, hoping he was far enough from Lewis's rifle that he'd have a chance. He clawed at the water, pulling himself toward a rocky beach he could see on the far shore about a football field's length away. He couldn't tell if Lewis was still shooting at him above the noise of his frantic swim.

His hand touched land and he staggered to his feet, stepping through slimy muck toward the bank. His hair had come loose into his eyes and he was breathing in hard, rasping breaths. He heard footsteps nearby. *God!* he prayed. *God don't let that vicious bastard kill me!*

He ran, tripping over a dead branch on the bank. Howie was picking himself up when he felt two powerful hands take hold of him. He was going to die now, he knew that clearly. It was all over. He hoped that it would be simple and fast.

But it wasn't the War Chief who was holding him, dragging him from the beach. It was Big Carl, stronger than Howie had ever imagined. Howie thrashed his arms and tried to get away, but Carl got his arms firmly around Howie's chest and dragged him over the meadow. Howie had not felt so helpless since he was a child.

"Relax," Carl said, hauling him across the meadow toward a stand of trees. "We've got to get away from here

Howie didn't understand a word. He was half drowned and nearly delirious with cold and fear. The big cop set him down in a forest glade among many small blue flowers. Howie scrunched his eyes shut and tried to curl into a protective ball.

"Murderous bastard! Leave me alone!" he screamed.

Carl watched him calmly from where he was sitting nearby in the tiny blue flowers. A number of minutes went by and when Howie found himself still alive, he opened his eyes to see what was happening. Carl was studying him with interest, chewing thoughtfully on a piece of grass.

"You're kind of slow in the brain department, aren't you, boy?" Carl said, taking the grass from his mouth. "I just saved your worthless Lakota ass."

"*You?*" Howie said in astonishment.

The big cop shrugged modestly. "Me," he agreed.

9

At nine o'clock on Sunday morning, Emma Wilder drove to the San Geronimo Public Library in order to squeeze in a few hours of work. She left Jack alone in the house with Katya and the two cats; he planned to spend the day methodically calling every motel, hotel, inn, lodge, and bed-and-breakfast in the county to inquire after a British guest, past or present, registered under the name of Rutherford Hughes. Emma had gone through the phone book earlier at breakfast to record the names and numbers on Jack's miniature cassette player so that he would have them handy, from Auntie Amy's Bungalows (rustic family vacations, kitchens, no TV) to The Zuni Lodge, a low-rent mecca of local sin that had vibrating beds if you put a quarter in the slot, and a reputation for customers who stayed only an hour or two.

Emma theoretically had two days off a week, Sunday and Monday, the days the library was closed. But she had missed work yesterday to be Jack's chauffeur so she knew there would be a backlog sitting on her desk, waiting for her attention. Jack was not happy to lose his seeing-eye help today—he seemed a little lost with Howie gone. But Emma had her career, too.

The San Geronimo Public Library was housed in a half-crumbling two-story adobe house that had been bequeathed to the town fifty years ago by an eccentric and wealthy old woman. The building was a warren of small rooms, quaint but inefficient. Emma's office was up a creaky flight of stairs, past the Southwest Art room and the psychology section. Emma opened a window to let in the summer day. She turned on her computer, found a classical music program on her radio from the public station in Alamosa, Colorado, and set to work.

As a young woman, Emma had been a crusader for large causes; today, more modestly, she had narrowed her efforts to local concerns. Her project this Sunday was to finish writing a grant proposal for an adult literacy program that she had begun several years ago and wanted to expand. According to a recent study, thirty percent of the adults of San Geronimo County were functionally illiterate, an astonishing figure. For Emma Wilder, librarian, this statistic had become her personal battle cry. She told everybody who would listen that illiteracy in northern New Mexico was the real killer, at the root of other more publicized ills: alcoholism, domestic abuse, poverty, and hopelessness. All she wanted was $50,000 a year from the state, plus another $25,000 from a private foundation, and she was convinced that she could knock the thirty percent figure in half within five years. As causes went, this seemed to her an eminently reasonable one.

After an hour of fierce concentration, Emma paused to stand up from her desk and stretch. Grant writing was not easy. From her second-story window, she could see a corner of the historic town plaza that was clogged with tour busses and out-of-state cars. Placed in the high desert against the mountains, San Geronimo was a gorgeous, dysfunctional place where nothing quite worked—Third World was the phrase Howie generally used. The town had terrible schools, a county government that was paralyzed with corruption, a police department that was inept, a high incidence of violence, often against women . . . and now cannibalism. Yet Emma couldn't imagine living anywhere else. It was hard to say where exactly the charm lay. Maybe it was the fact that San Geronimo was so poor, though Emma did not like to admit this thought aloud. There was something terrible about rich places, arrogant and empty and crass—a problem San Geronimo did not have, not with an average annual family income of $23,000. People were earthy here, and painfully real; they sang and wept and, yes, killed each other in fits of operatic violence. But at least they weren't plastic dolls. Best of all, there wasn't a single

shopping mall in the entire county. For Emma, it was a relief
to escape turn-of-the-millennium America, the richest unhappy
nation on earth.

But, my God, cannibalism!

Emma's fingers stopped in midflight across the computer
keyboard as she tried yet again to absorb the horrific nature of
what had been done to the British archeologist whose death
Jack was investigating. Jack was always careful to use the
phrase, "possible cannibalism," since as far as he was concerned, the matter was unproved. Still, it was her understanding from overheard conversations that there was really very
little doubt about it. Emma tried to get her mind back on her
grant proposal, but ten minutes later, an idea occurred to her
that had little to do with adult literacy. Rutherford Hughes,
whoever this person was—and offhand he didn't sound like a
very *nice* person to Emma—was an educated man, the type
who might visit the local library and perhaps even have a library card. It was simple enough to check out. Emma closed
down her word-processing program and looked in her file cabinet for a disk with the database of all the current library-card
holders. She slipped the disk into her zip drive and typed
HUGHES into the search field.

"Wouldn't this be too absurdly easy!" she muttered. The
name Hughes brought up fourteen entries from the database,
starting with Alice Hughes, 23 Mesa Drive. Poor Alice had
died two years ago and Emma took a minute to delete her
name from the list. She continued scanning and, unbelievably,
Rutherford Hughes was the ninth listing. He had applied for a
library card ten months ago. There was an address, 29 Lhasa
Road, and a telephone number. His Social Security number
had been left blank—occasionally people did not fill in all the
required information, and as a small-town library, they were
not sticklers when it came to paperwork. Hughes had described himself on his application as "self-employed." He had
received his library card at a time when Emma had been working hard to modernize the computer system in the library,
wanting to keep track of the books that people checked out in
order to better understand what the local population wanted to

read. Rutherford Hughes had checked out nearly a dozen volumes on his card, all nonfiction, all various histories of the Southwest and Colorado. The last book Hughes had checked out was on January 17 of this year, *People of Chaco: A Canyon and Its Culture,* by Kendrick Frazier. The book had never been returned.

"You know, somehow I don't think that volume is ever coming back!" she said aloud to herself, picking up the phone on her desk. Jack's voice answered on the third ring, but it was the answering machine in the kitchen, not the actual old bear in person.

"Guess what, O Great Detective." she boasted to the machine. "You aren't the only snoop in the family. It occurred to me that your Shark Tooth might have taken out a library card, so I poked around in my database and there it was—Rutherford Hughes. I have an address, the phone number, the works . . . just thought you might be interested," she added breezily.

Emma put down the phone with a smile. She imagined Jack outside in the garden with Katya, weeding his beloved tomatoes. She returned to her grant proposal but half an hour later Jack had still not returned her call and this surprised her. She decided to try his cell phone because, all kidding aside, she was aware that she had made an important discovery in the case.

Jack answered on the second ring, but he didn't let her say more than two words before he cut her off.

"Emma, I'm in a meeting with Ed Gomez and his cousin. I can't talk right now."

"But Jack—"

"Not now," he repeated impatiently. "You can tell me everything tonight. Oh, by the way—would you mind picking up a pound of ground round on your way home? I need it for my spaghetti sauce."

The line went dead. Emma was speechless. *A pound of ground round!* She went through a slow burn as she imagined Jack and Captain Gomez and some cousin all huddled together having their self-important "meeting." Then the little wife calls on the cell phone. How inconvenient!

Jack had brushed her off!

"Yes, I *do* mind, Jack!" Emma said aloud to the dead receiver. She stood up and paced about her office, hurt and angry. Storming up and down the carpet, she was startled to catch sight of an unknown woman in the full-length mirror mounted on the back of the door. The woman was unrecognizable: stubby, middle-aged, short gray hair, at least twenty pounds overweight.

Who *was* that strange person in the mirror?

My God, it was *her*! It was unbelievable how old and shapeless she had become! The shock for Emma was that in her mind's eye, she didn't see herself like this at all, but rather as the attractive, energetic, eternally twenty-something creature who had once so confidently caused every male eye to turn her way. She had never worried much about her appearance, not needing to, knowing she was pretty. Unfortunately, the image in the mirror and the self-image she carried in her mind were about twenty years out of sync. It was silly, really—she had been so busy with her life that somehow the years had slipped away without her noticing how much she had changed.

She shook her head thoughtfully. *Well, my God! I've become an old woman! No wonder Jack doesn't treat me like he used to!*

Emma was suddenly energized. Tomorrow she would join the local health club and lose twenty pounds. She would make an appointment with a hairdresser and consider tinting out the gray. And look out, Jack!—she was going to spend a whole bunch of money on clothes!

"So, my dear, you think your frumpy little wife is only good for picking up a pound of ground round, do you? Why should you listen to anything I have to say?"

Emma knew quite well that she was overreacting, but this only fueled her irritation. She had always been an impulsive woman, quick to anger, quick to forgive. She picked up her telephone and dialed the number for Rutherford Hughes that was on her computer screen. The number rang three times and then an answering machine cut in. There was no voice, no announcement of any sort, only a few bars of music, a Mozart overture, and then a beep. Emma disconnected without leaving a message, not knowing what to say. She stared at her computer screen as the cursor continued to blink hypnotically under the R of Rutherford Hughes, 29 Lhasa Road.

"All right!" she announced decisively to the world at large.

She shut down her computer, locked up her office, and walked downstairs out of the library to her car. It took her nearly five minutes to locate Lhasa Road on the map of San Geronimo County she kept in her glove compartment, for the road was hardly more than a squiggle in the mountains east of town.

Emma Wilder gunned her Subaru station wagon out of the municipal parking lot with a sense that she was on a mission for truth, justice, and a woman's basic right not to be taken for granted by any big oaf of a meat-eating husband. Was this her business? You bet it was! Rutherford Hughes had a library book that was more than seven months overdue, and that really pissed her off!

10

The moment Jack Wilder made his request for Emma to pick up a pound of ground round, he sensed he had made a serious mistake, marriage-wise. Unfortunately, he didn't have a clue why.

Jack had been the family cook since the early days of losing his eyesight. There had been a few initial disasters, certainly, like mistaking a can of Katya's dog food for refried beans, and once cutting himself so badly that Emma had to rush him to the emergency room. But he had persisted and for years now he'd been a master of blind cooking, with the kitchen organized in such a way that he always knew where everything was located. Jack did a once-a-week bulk shopping with Howie's help, but it was not unusual for him to ask Emma to pick up a last-minute item at the supermarket and she had never objected before. So he couldn't imagine why his request today had seemed to send them into some vast man/woman nowhere.

At 1:15 on Sunday afternoon, Jack was seated on a fake leather sofa with Captain Ed Gomez at the office of Ed's cousin, Jimmy Gomez, the local attorney who paid the bills at the Anasazi Grill. Jimmy had agreed to come in to his office even though it was Sunday, after discussing and rejecting a number of other possible meeting places—his home and various restaurants—apparently he did not relish the idea of people in town seeing him getting the third degree by his cousin the state cop. Ed had picked up Jack earlier in the morning and the meeting was well underway when Emma had called. Unfortunately, her call had come at an awkward time, just as

Jimmy been about to answer an important question. This was a shame because the attorney had been hedging and now he had time to rethink his response.

"What's wrong?" Ed asked, seeing Jack with a puzzled expression on his face.

"You tell me! I asked Emma if she'd pick up a pound of ground round on the way home from the library and it was like I'd suggested three-way sex with a teenage hooker . . . Emma's my wife," Jack added in the direction of the attorney, since this was the first time they had met.

"I had three-way sex one time in New Orleans," the lawyer bragged. "Did I ever tell you about that, Ed?"

"No, you didn't," Ed replied warily. "You sure this wasn't just some fantasy you read about in *Penthouse*, Jimmy?"

"No, this happened, swear to God! It was with these two college girls I met in a bar. At least they *told* me they were college girls. The next day, my wallet was gone, so maybe the school they were attending wasn't exactly Bryn Mawr."

Jimmy Gomez began recounting the graphic details of the night in question, who did what and to whom. Jack managed a thin smile concealing his disdain for this particular variety of guy talk. Jimmy Gomez was a sleaze all the way. Jack had spent much of his professional life in the company of people like this and worse, but he had always kept his own home life with Emma strictly separate. It was another reason he had been curt with her just now on his cell phone—and he saw, belatedly, that he *had* been curt. He didn't intend to have a personal conversation with his wife while someone like Jimmy Gomez was listening in.

"Let's get back to who owns the Anasazi Grill," Jack suggested, interrupting the pornography.

"The Anasazi? Look, amigo, ask me anything else! It's a corporation, that's all I can say. They're very shy people, you know. They don't want the spotlight. I mean, to be completely truthful, I don't even know myself *exactly* who they are. And even if I *did* know, I couldn't betray client confidentiality, not even for my favorite cousin here."

"Jimmy!" Ed laughed softly. "I can't believe you're holding out, cuz!"

"Ask me anything else!" Jimmy swore.

Ed turned to Jack and spoke in a confiding way, as though Jimmy wasn't there.

"You know what gets me, Jack? Here's my cousin who hits me up for favors all the time. And generally I oblige him, seeing as how he's family. That's what makes this all so discouraging, to do all that for him, and then have the guy jerk us around."

"Yeah, but the favors are never for myself!" Jimmy objected, an altruist.

"They're for his kids," Ed continued to Jack. "There's Jimmy Junior, for instance. Back around the start of the summer one of my troopers caught Junior in a car with a bag of marijuana and a fourteen-year-old girl who didn't have too many clothes on. I got a call about this in the middle of the night, woke me up. Well, this was the first time this particular thing had happened so I told my officer to just scare Junior a little, give him a heavy warning, then let the little bastard go . . . that's the sort of thing you do in a small town for a cousin, Jack."

It was the sort of thing cops did in big towns, too. But favors like this come and go, depending. Jimmy was getting the message.

"Ed! You know how I appreciate what you did for that lousy kid of mine!" the attorney cried. "But don't ask me this one thing. I've been sworn to secrecy, and if those guys ever get wind of me telling stories about them, I'm history, man."

Ed was sighing and clicking his tongue, making a big show of regret. "Jimmy! I gotta know this! Who are these guys? Are they paying taxes? I'm not sure I like the sound of this!"

Jack sensed that they could go back and forth indefinitely, getting nowhere. Fortunately, he had an idea. It was hard to say precisely where it came from, a convergence of fact and intuition, but suddenly he had a feeling of why Jimmy Gomez was hedging.

"Excuse me, Ed. But I think I can cut to the chase here. Do you mind?" he interrupted.

"Go for it," Ed told him. "To tell the truth, this cousin of mine's starting to piss me off."

Jack smiled knowingly at the place in room where he imagined Jimmy Gomez was seated. "As it happens, I *know* who owns the restaurant, so let's not waste any more time. What I need from you is corroboration, that's all. It's the Indians, isn't it? The Anasazi Grill is owned by the San Geronimo Pueblo?"

Jimmy sighed, full of loud self-pity.

"Look, you can't tell anybody this came from me. Those guys are crazy mothers, I swear to God. They'll do something terrible to me if this gets out."

"It's the *Pueblo*?" Ed said in astonishment. "How the hell did you know that, Jack?"

Jack shrugged. It was a lot of things, starting with the fact that Jimmy had been sworn to secrecy, just like he and Howie had been sworn with Raymond. And beyond that, it made sense: It was a line that happened to connect a number of dots in this case.

"It's not really the Pueblo per se," Jimmy was saying, eager now to show his new spirit of cooperation. "It's Lewis Lucero, the main man on the tribal council—he keeps getting elected to different positions. Right now he's the War Chief."

"And I thought you didn't know who owned the restaurant!" Ed mentioned.

"What I said was, I don't know *exactly* who is involved—who *else* besides Lewis, whether it's the entire council or just one or two guys. The last couple of years, most of my dealings have been with Anthony Lucero, Lewis's oldest son. He's sort of the point man, you know—a scary kid, as a matter of fact. Frankly, there's a lot of bullshit happening on that reservation right now. Some of them want to invest their money in restaurants and stocks and bonds, stuff like that. And the others want to cling to the old ways and have nothing to do with the white man. So they fight a lot among themselves. But that's fine with me, as long as they continue to pay me two grand a month."

Jack nodded, imagining the situation. Howie had been telling him not long ago about the new spirit of entrepreneurship on reservations around the country. The Lac du Flambeau Chippewas of Wisconsin owned Ojibwa Brand Pizza, a chain in seven states. The Choctaw tribe of Mississippi manufactured circuit boards and automobile speakers. Here in New Mexico, the Santa Ana Pueblo north of Albuquerque grew tons of blue corn every year to sell to a British company, The Body Shop, which used the corn as a major ingredient in a blue-tinted facial cream. Other tribes made rocket engines, greeting cards, cotton clothing—and of course made lots of money from casino gambling. So why shouldn't the San Geronimo Pueblo own an upscale Southwestern restaurant?

In a few minutes, the entire story spilled out, as much as the attorney knew. The Anasazi Grill had been built and operated during its first year by two gay California businessmen who liked to start up trendy restaurants and then sell them quickly for a profit. The California men had the right touch and as soon as they had turned the Anasazi Grill into an apparent gold mine, they put it up for sale. It was at this time that Lewis Lucero, then tribal governor, contacted Jimmy Gomez and asked him to act as a middleman between the tribe and the Californians. He wanted to buy the business but keep the Indian involvement secret. Jimmy was the sort of small-town dealmaker who knew all the ins and outs of getting things done without attracting undue attention; he was personally related to most of the people who needed to be paid off in order to transfer the liquor license and get the necessary permits, while keeping everything out of the public eye. The sale was effected, *no problema.* Unfortunately, Lewis did not have the same magic touch as the gay Californians when it came to running a trendy restaurant serving minuscule portions of froufrou food; the Anasazi Grill was soon deep in the hole, losing money hand over fist.

"How much did Lewis pay for the business?" Jack asked.

"Half a million bucks."

"Do you believe it was tribal money?"

"Where else would it come from? Lewis and whoever his

partners are don't have that kind of bread on their own. I always suspected he stole it from BIA funds, or maybe from the tourist operation. That's the big reason it was all kept so secret, of course—not to mention the fact they're selling booze there, which would offend a whole bunch of people at the Pueblo as well. The thing with Lewis is he's kinda greedy—I know for a fact he's been siphoning off cash receipts from the restaurant for his own personal expenses, which is one of the reasons the place is running at such a loss. *All* restaurants do that to some extent, of course, but with Lewis the practice has gotten out of hand. I had to tell him, watch it, man, or you're going to have big trouble with the IRS."

"So now Lewis is in trouble?" Jack was thinking out loud. "If the restaurant had kept making money like it did under the Californians, he would have been able to pay back whatever he stole and nobody would have been the wiser. But since it's losing money, he's probably hoping like hell that nobody demands an independent accounting of tribal funds."

"Lewis *has* seemed a little tense the last few times I've spoken with him," Jimmy agreed.

Jack's mind was racing. Tribal elections were coming up in the spring, the various positions chosen by the elders. If the misappropriation of funds became general knowledge, the War Chief and his son would be out on their collective asses fairly quickly, he imagined. The question was: What did the theft of tribal money have to do with an Anasazi cave, a British archeologist, and a severed head left in a Dumpster in town? Jack had the frustrating feeling of almost being able to fit the pieces together in his mind, but not quite.

"Tell me something, Jimmy. Have you ever had any dealings with a Englishman named Rutherford Hughes?"

"Hughes? Strange you mention him. He came to see me once. He said he represented a European consortium that made investments in the United States. Somehow he knew about the tribe owning the restaurant and he said he was very interested in acquiring it. He told me his group was willing to offer one million five and they'd give me a five percent finder's fee if I could arrange it with the Pueblo."

"When was this?"

"A little less than a year ago. Five percent, hell—that would be seventy-five thousand bucks for me. So I told him, sure, I'll check it out. I went to Lewis, and man, he *jumped* at the offer! He knew by then he'd made a bad investment. I mean, the guy was just about drooling at the thought of unloading the place at that kind of profit. But when I tried to call Hughes back at the hotel in Santa Fe where he said he was staying, they told me they'd never heard of him. So he scammed me. I never did figure out how he found out there was Indian money in the restaurant."

Jack smiled. "*You* told him."

"*Me*? I didn't, I swear to God!"

"Sure you did. Hughes must have *suspected* the tribe owned the restaurant, but that was all. When he came to you and you agreed to take his offer to Lewis, then he knew for certain. All he wanted was that information, and you gave it to him. That's why you never heard from him again."

Jimmy Gomez appeared stunned. "Man!" he sighed. "If the guy didn't want to make an offer, why did he go to the trouble to con me?"

Jack pointed the lenses of his dark glasses halfway to the ceiling, wondering the same thing himself.

11

Captain Gomez drove Jack to the supermarket, guided him through the busy aisles into the meat department, and helped pick out a good lean pound of ground round. Jack was oddly moved by the gesture, though in fact he had lost all interest in the spaghetti sauce he had been planning to make tonight.

For Jack, the supermarket was a harsh place full of hard sounds and imminent danger. The possibilities for disaster were nearly endless for a blind man in a crowded public place such as this: crashing into stacks of display boxes, getting mowed down by reckless shopping carts, terrifying small children. He held on to Ed's right arm, and drifted among the other hungry hunter gatherers, his mind on other matters: Rutherford Hughes, or Ford, according to his nickname. Jack was starting to imagine the man more clearly. He could probably be extremely charming when he wanted to, a skill he had acquired to camouflage his basic ruthlessness. This was a person intent on getting his way, who had the ability to bend other people to his will. An evil genius of a sort. Donna Theresa, the *cacique's* granddaughter, had been in love with him, willing to give him nearly anything. And now it appeared that Lewis Lucero, the War Chief, had allowed him access to Indian land, which was unthinkable.

"So what's the story about the phony English investor?" Ed asked while they were waiting in a slow-moving express lane from hell, half a dozen people ahead of them with coupons and disagreements about the prices.

"It's just a case Howie's taken on," Jack replied carefully.

This was awkward. He didn't enjoy misleading Ed, but he had to honor his deal with Howie.

"I didn't realize Howie took cases on his own."

"Well, he's been out at the Pueblo the past couple of days looking into a few matters for them. It's an Indian thing, which is why Howie's involved and I'm not. I wish I could tell you more about it, but the fact is, the very little I do know I've sworn to keep to myself."

"You know, Jack, I feel like I'm getting a kind of echo here. Like I'm hearing the bullshit line my cousin was giving just now."

Jack smiled. "I tell you what—when Howie reports back, if there turns out to be any relevance to your murder investigation, I'll tell him to give you a call. Okay?"

Ed didn't answer immediately. "Jack, you're not holding back anything important, are you?"

"Ed, please, I'm only a newcomer to this part of the world—to tell the truth, I'm not up to speed when it comes to all the local sensitivities between Anglos, Hispanics, and Indians. You're going to have to talk to Howie if you're curious about Rutherford Hughes."

"You're saying this has to do with Indian sensitivities?"

"Yes."

"And when will Howie be back?"

"In a day or so," Jack told him, optimistically.

"Can't you raise him on your cell phone?"

"No. He's way the hell up in the mountains somewhere."

Ed laughed. "*Howie?* I hope that kid's surviving Mother Nature! What are those damn things he always has to have for lunch?"

"Wraps," Jack told him. "In my day, a wrap was what we called a lady's coat."

"In *my* day, we ate sandwiches, not goddamn *wraps*. With plenty of meat in 'em, too. And cheese and pickles and mustard and onion and all sorts of shit. We ate like men are supposed to eat, Jack."

"It was a rite of passage just to survive the heartburn." Jack was glad to change the subject. Mourning the good old days when men ate like dinosaurs, Ed let the matter of Rutherford Hughes slide, at least for the moment. They had just reached the cash register when Ed's cell phone beeped. He listened for a few seconds then fired off several questions in Spanglish, a local blend of Spanish/English that always amazed Jack by how easily the two languages flowed together.

"Well, miracles *do* happen," Ed said, stuffing his phone back into his shirt pocket. "That was a buddy of mine. It seems two off-duty cops came across the white GMC pickup that belongs to the Anasazi Grill."

"Where did they find it?"

"It's in the sacred river getting a bath. We'd better take a drive, amigo."

The Rio Pueblo flowed down the mountain from Spirit Lake, passed through the reservation, then meandered westward into the desert where it eventually joined the Rio Grande. The white GMC truck was upside down at a shallow bend of the river in a steep canyon about five miles outside of the reservation on public land. Off-duty Officers Sammy Trujillo and Billy Whitman came across the vehicle late Saturday afternoon while wading their way downstream on an overnight fishing trip. Fortunately, they had remembered that there was an APB out for a stolen truck like this with a connection to an ongoing murder investigation. Unfortunately, the two off-duty cops were so drunk that they had been physically unable to climb out of the canyon to report their find until the following morning.

Sergeant Ted Rodriguez, the morning duty officer at the San Geronimo Police Department, got the call about the truck at 10:07 Sunday morning from the two hungover cops, but with one thing and another, he hadn't gotten around to phoning Ed about it until just now.

Ed drove on a dirt road along the canyon rim and parked alongside several law-enforcement vehicles. He left Jack in the passenger seat for nearly twenty minutes while he hiked down to the river to see what was up. Jack spent the time listening to the familiar squawk of police radios and worrying about how Howie was doing up at the Anasazi cave. Howie was very bright, but he wasn't a professional, at least not in the sense that Jack understood it.

Five years ago, Jack had hired Howie for part-time work around the house: chopping wood, helping with the garden, driving Jack to the supermarket and bank. In those days, Howie had been experiencing writer's block with his PhD dissertation, wondering if the thing was worth doing at all, in need of some extra income while he figured out the direction of his life. It had been Jack's idea to start a detective agency using Howie as his eyes, but recently he had begun to wonder if this hadn't been selfish on his part, and that he hadn't necessarily done Howie a favor by luring him away from academia. In this case, there were dangerous forces at work, even the possibility of new violence. Howie was a thinker, a dreamy kid, and Jack worried that he was way over his head.

He took out his cell phone and tried Howie's number for probably the tenth time today, hoping Howie would answer. But the number still wouldn't ring. He was turning off his phone when Ed returned to the car.

"Well?" Jack asked.

"Well, there's no headless body down there, but I guess I didn't expect there would be. It looks like the inside of the truck was wiped clean of prints. There's a stain on the floor mat on the passenger side that might be blood, and that's about it. Luckily, there's a visiting expert from Denver, a hair and fiber guy—he's vacuuming the cab right now. So maybe he'll find something."

"How did the truck get into the river?"

"It looks like it was rolled off into the canyon from about where we're parked now."

Ed was clearly discouraged. This case had brought him a lot of pressure and he had been hoping for a breakthrough. Thunder echoed lazily down from the mountains and Jack felt a cool shadow on his face as a cloud blew across the sun.

"Well, there's not much more we can do here," Ed said wearily. "Come on, Jack—it's going to start raining like crazy any moment and these dirt roads will turn to shit. I'll drive you home."

It started to pour just as Jack was hurrying with his groceries from the police car to his back door. Katya greeted him noisily in the kitchen, but he was surprised Emma wasn't home. It was nearly 5:30. He fed Katya, turned on the public radio news, and began mincing and chopping in a distracted manner, making his spaghetti sauce. By six o'clock, Emma was still not home and he tried calling her at the library. There was no answer, only a recorded message saying that the library was closed and relaying the hours when it was open. Most likely she was driving home, perhaps even stopping off to get a pound of ground round—well, he would put it in the freezer for another meal.

At 6:30, Emma still had not arrived and Jack was starting to worry about her in a nagging way—added to his worry for Howie, this was starting to feel like serious stress. He tried to remind himself that Emma had her own life, after all, and he had always encouraged her to do things, not just stay at home taking care of a blind husband. If it had not been for their slight misunderstanding on the phone, he wouldn't have thought twice about her absence.

At close to seven, the telephone rang and Jack picked it up eagerly before the second ring, certain it was Emma. But it wasn't. It was a telemarketer for a long-distance phone carrier touting a new nickel-a-minute plan. Jack didn't like telemarketers under the best of circumstances, and even less so when he was expecting to hear from his wife. He put down the receiver without bothering to speak, and his hand accidentally brushed against the answering machine. With all his preoccupations, he had somehow forgotten this simple electronic device. He pressed the play button and immediately heard Emma's voice. But he was not reassured at what she said.

"Guess what, O Great Detective. You aren't the only snoop in the family. It occurred to me that your Shark Tooth might have taken out a library card, so I poked around in my database and there it was—Rutherford Hughes. I have an address,

*the phone number, the works . . . just thought you might be in-
terested.*"

Rutherford Hughes! This man was the devil himself. Even
Emma couldn't leave him alone.

With sudden clarity, Jack got it, the one explanation that
made all the puzzling facts make sense. What had been a low-
level anxiety roared into high gear. God, how stupid he'd
been! He'd simply been looking at this case backward, from
entirely the wrong angle. For a few moments he stood in dumb
astonishment, nearly paralyzed with understanding. Then he
phoned Captain Gomez and asked him to come over immediately.

12

The storm hit when Emma Wilder was half lost on a treacherous, narrow little road in the mountains east of town. The rain was furious and sudden, throwing a nearly impenetrable curtain of water against the windshield. Though it was early afternoon, the sky had turned dark as night. Lightning flashed and the thunder that followed shook the fillings in her teeth. Emma wasn't expecting the ferocious change of weather. Thunderstorms were common in the mountains during the late summer, but her mind had been on other things.

She was following a road that had climbed quickly from the desert up the southeastern slope of San Geronimo Peak, passing through a steep forest of aspen and pine. This was a remote part of the county that Emma did not know, and occasionally she had to stop and consult her map. Somewhere ahead, Lhasa Road supposedly branched off from County Road 74, the barely paved mountain road she was doing her best to negotiate. The storm made everything more difficult. She turned on her headlights, defroster, and windshield wipers all at once—everything at their highest, fastest, brightest setting. For good measure, she put the old Subaru into four-wheel drive as well; it wasn't strictly necessary, but Emma was a nervous driver under the best of conditions and wanted all the technological support her car could give her.

Her anger with Jack faded as the storm gained force. She knew Jack very well, after all. He was an obsessive workaholic, following leads in even minor cases as though the entire fate of the world depended on the outcome; that was just the way he was. Still, he was almost always courtly and kind with

Emma. Old-fashioned, even. He would never have brushed her off unless she had phoned at a moment when he truly couldn't talk. She knew that now. And in fact she'd known it back in her office. This whole outburst was nothing but an indulgence.

"Face it, you just got pissed off you're not a slim little sexpot anymore!" she told herself sternly.

Of course, Jack wasn't exactly a slim little sexpot himself these days, but that didn't seem to matter so much for men. It wasn't fair, but unfairness was the way the cookie crumbled, she supposed, this side of paradise. Emma peered ahead through the windshield, feeling all the tension of driving through heavy weather in her neck and shoulders. She considered turning around and going home, but that would make the afternoon a total waste. She decided she might as well go ahead at this point and finish what she had started.

The road continued to climb into the mountains. Emma passed an occasional driveway and summer cabin, but there were no other cars on the road and signs of people were few and far between. A road marker told her that she had arrived at an altitude of 9,000 feet. From here she descended into a steep canyon, then climbed up the other side—up and down and all around, maneuvering so many hairpin curves that soon she had no idea which direction she was headed. She supposed wherever she was, she couldn't be too far from Indian land.

Ten minutes later she came to a dirt road that turned off to the left, following a fast-moving stream. The road was marked by a collection of mailboxes and a small hand-painted sign:

LHASA ROAD
PRIVATE
BRAKE FOR MIRACLES

At the bottom of the sign, someone had painted a vaguely Tibetan squiggle that Emma recognized as the symbol for *om*. Apparently there were advanced spiritual beings living in this far-flung region of San Geronimo County. She drove cautiously from the main road onto the gravel, watching for puddles and fallen tree limbs. It would be a miracle if she didn't get stuck in the mud. The road followed a raging mountain stream up into a steep, thickly wooded canyon. She passed several small cabins, all apparently empty of life, vacation homes that might be used one or two weekends a year. There were occasional house numbers, often half hidden by bushes or trees: 2, 7, 10, 13, 18. Emma was encouraged she was going in the right direction, but then both the numbers and the houses became more sparse.

The rain continued to beat fiercely against the windshield. Emma passed 21 Lhasa Road, a short driveway leading to an ancient Airstream trailer, and from this point on, the road deteriorated sharply to hardly more than a Jeep track. She downshifted into first gear and continued over the ruts and running water. Fifteen minutes later, when Emma had not passed another driveway or house, she decided enough was enough. This was hopeless, and a little scary, too, and she resolved to turn around at the first opportunity and go home. Unfortunately, as she continued driving she really couldn't see any place that looked wide enough for a U-turn.

This was turning into more of an adventure than she had bargained for. Belatedly, Emma thought of setting her mileage counter to zero in order to get a better idea of how far she was traveling. 2.3 miles later, she still had not come to a house, a driveway, or any reasonable place to turn back. At 2.9 miles she arrived at the top of a small rise and was forced to stop. The road ahead, such as it was, dipped down into a muddy bog, an extended puddle that was a result of the sudden rain and overflow from the stream. Emma would certainly have turned around, except for the fact that the stream was very close to her left-side tires, and on the right there was an impenetrable tangle of wild berry bushes.

Forward appeared the only viable direction.

"Should I try it?" she wondered. The water ahead didn't look terribly deep and if she could only get across to the other side, the road appeared much better. Emma had a semireligious faith in the power of four-wheel drive, based on television ads and the assurances of a salesman in Albuquerque who had declared that her Subaru "could just about climb Mt.

Everest." She decided to give it a try. She gunned the engine, tore down the small rise in first gear, and managed to get almost all the way across before the station wagon sank to its axles in mud so thick it was like being in quicksand. Emma tried moving forward, then backward, but the wheels only spun hopelessly. She was stuck.

"Damn!" she swore, wondering what in the world she was going to do now. At least the rain had stopped and the sun was momentarily peeping out from behind a black cloud, brilliant and warm. Emma undid her seat harness and stepped out into a deep gloppy mess of mud that sucked her left shoe off her foot.

"Really, this is too much!" she cried, at the end of her patience. By the time she managed to retrieve her lost shoe, her dress and arms and legs were totally splattered with mud. At last, with one shoe on her foot and the other shoe in her hand, she succeeded in wading across the bog to where the road was reasonably dry on the other side. From here, she was able to survey her car. The tires were buried in mud all the way up to the doors. For the first time in her life, Emma Wilder wished she had a cell phone. Jack had always encouraged her to carry one, but she was like Howie in this regard, a militantly anti–cell phone type who often declared that wireless technology was the final assault of the modern world against solitude and sanity. Of course, she had never quite imagined a situation like this: stuck in the woods, miles from nowhere.

Emma debated her choices. It was 3:35 according to her watch and this time of year she would have a few more hours of daylight. One possibility was to walk back to the last inhabited house she had passed on Lhasa Road and call AAA. But that would be a long walk, possibly four or five miles—she wasn't sure how far she had traveled from the last house that had a car in the driveway before thinking to set her mileage counter. The other choice was to continue onward. Surely 29 Lhasa Road could not be too much farther ahead. She knew there was a telephone there from listening to the answering machine pick up earlier in the afternoon. It was doubtful that anyone would be home, so she'd simply break a window, get

inside somehow and call for help. Emma did not normally
break into houses, but this was an emergency, after all.

Emma was debating her choices, backward or forward when
a rainbow appeared in the sky, one end touching a high green
meadow above her on the road, the far end disappearing into
the dark storm clouds that still shrouded the nearby mountains.
To Emma, it seemed like a sign from heaven. An optimist at
heart, she went forward.

The branches of the pine trees overhead heaved and sighed
in the wind and seemed to be whispering evil things. The air
was fluttery and restless. One minute the sun was shining, and
Emma was thinking of shedding a layer of clothes; the next
minute, black clouds had crept in once again from the west,
bringing a sudden unseasonable chill. There was a low grumb-
ble of thunder in the near distance. It sounded like cosmic indigestion, which reminded Emma that she had missed lunch.

She walked briskly on the muddy road, humming an old
Bob Dylan song, the poetry of her generation. She had thought
to bring along the big golf umbrella she always kept this time
of year in the back seat of the car. The umbrella was comforting and multipurpose: a stout walking stick when carried
furled; protection from the weather if the rain came again; and
a possible weapon, if she met with danger.

The road came out of the trees and passed along the curve
of a wide mountain meadow. The wind picked up and the sky
grew increasingly dark. There was a flash of lightning and a
few seconds later a mighty peal of thunder nearly shook her
off her feet. Fat drops of rain began to fall, widely at first but
then closer together. Emma unfurled her umbrella and raised it
above her head. She walked more quickly now, singing songs
from her youth, moving from Dylan to Janis Joplin and on to
Richie Havens. *If I could survive the sixties,* she thought,
surely a mountain thunderstorm is nothing to be frightened of!
The thought made her laugh. She was glad that no one saw
her: a middle-aged woman with a raised golf umbrella singing
in the rain.

The road led around a bend and Emma was suddenly confronted by a small wooden cottage nestled in a grassy clearing at the edge of the woods. The road itself seemed to end here. There was a beat-up gray Land Cruiser near the front door, an expensive vehicle, but it was dented and muddy and looked as though it had seen better days. The windows of the house were dark and lifeless. Emma stopped a few feet from the vehicle, the rain pelting down harder now, swirling around her legs. There was no sign to tell her that this was 29 Lhasa Road, but she sensed that this had to be the house. A flash of lightning filled the sky so close at hand that Emma could see the jagged pulse of electricity, like the filament of a giant light bulb. Almost immediately there followed a deafening boom of thunder. Emma was so startled she bit her tongue. The rain slashed down at her with new force; the wind nearly blew the umbrella from her hands.

"Hello!" she called in a small, frightened voice. "Anybody home?"

The cottage worried her in some primal way that wasn't strictly rational. Her legs were reluctant, but she forced herself to walk along a soggy overgrown path to the front door and knock.

"Hello!" she cried again.

She waited, but there was no response.

"Hi! My car got stuck down the road . . ."

She left the path and walked along the side of the house to an uncurtained window. Peering inside, she could see a small living room/kitchen. There was a cast-iron stove for heating, a refrigerator, lamps, an overstuffed armchair. The room wasn't messy, but it wasn't clean, either. There were stacks of papers on the floor and disorganized piles of books on every surface. Emma chanced to see her own library book, *People of Chaco: A Canyon and Its Culture*, its spine open, lying facedown on the floor near the stove. This made her blood boil.

Emma had seen enough. A person who didn't return library books deserved no mercy. She closed her umbrella and used it as a spear to smash in the window. Glass tinkled and fell everywhere. She tried to clear away as much glass as she could, using her all-purpose umbrella and the sleeve of her sweater. When it seemed safe, she reached inside, opened the latch, and pulled up the window frame. At last, she stepped through carefully, feet first, doing her best to avoid the broken glass. She cut herself a little on her hands and ankles, but not badly.

She was soaked to the skin by the time she got inside. The cottage smelled stuffy and claustrophobic, as though it had been closed up for a long time. She didn't see the telephone or answering machine, but perhaps they were in another room. There were two doors, both of them closed, leading off from the kitchen/living room area. Emma tried the door to the left, which opened into a dark, windowless bathroom. She found the switch just to the side of the door, turned on the light . . . and screamed.

"Dear God in heaven!" she cried.

The bathtub was full of human bones! Skulls, legs, ribs, all of them whitened and stripped of flesh, but hideous! There was more than one skeleton here, at least six or seven dead people, maybe more.

Emma was stepping closer to the bathtub in horrified fascination when she heard a sound behind her. Before she could react, the bathroom door slammed shut and she heard a key in the lock.

"Hey!" she cried. She pulled on the door, but it wouldn't open.

"Please!" she whispered, almost too frightened to speak. "My car is stuck down the road . . . I was only looking for a telephone . . ."

From the other side of the door came the most terrifying sound of all: ghostly laughter.

13

At two o'clock on Sunday afternoon, the weather just below tree line was threatening but not yet the dangerous mountain storm it would become within an hour. Howard Moon Deer sat cold and wet and miserable in a forest grotto on spongy grass and a carpet of tiny blue flowers watching Big Carl make a small fire of gathered branches.

"Snow's coming. I smell it," Carl said, casting a dour eye at the sky.

"Gimme a b-b-break," Howie shivered. "It's August."

Carl shrugged, not a talkative man. At the moment, the wind was blowing, but the sun was out and snow seemed unlikely. A single beam of light shone down upon Howie through the tall trees, seeking him out like the eye of God. It was an intimate grotto, yet there was a grandeur here as well, like being inside a cathedral. The sun had little warmth and Howie's teeth chattered in violent spasms, a memento of his dip in Spirit Lake. Carl blew the sparks of his small fire to life until a plume of smoke rose into the trees.

"Warm yourself, boy. Hypothermia ain't no joke."

Howie moved closer to the fire while Carl disappeared into the forest to gather more wood. He wasn't sure why Carl was helping him, but he was too dazed to question the appearance of help.

"Donna Theresa," he managed, when Carl returned. "What happened? Did she . . . ?"

"Naw, she's not drowned. That girl is reckless, but she has more lives than a cat."

"Cats don't swim," Howie observed. "I looked for her in the water, but I didn't see her."

"Well, you were thrashing around like a trout on a hook, Moon Deer, and that got in the way of you seeing much. Donna Theresa swam out on the north bank and Lewis nabbed her."

"Then she's alive?"

"Aren't you listening? Of course she's alive. Probably pretty damn cold, just like you are."

Howie hugged himself and turned sideways to the fire, hoping to get another part of himself warm. It took a few seconds for Carl's words to penetrate. He stood up abruptly from the fire. "Damn! If Lewis has her . . . I've got to do something . . ."

"Sit down, boy, and get yourself warm first, or you ain't gonna rescue nobody. Now listen to me—Lewis isn't going to do anything for a while yet. I know how his mind works. I should, since we grew up together. He's not going to do anything until I bring *you* in, Moon Deer. He has to kill both of you, or neither of you at all. If one of you gets away, that person will talk and then Lewis gets himself convicted of homicide, which he wouldn't like. As long as you're free, he'll figure it's better to wait. If he has to, he can always take Donna Theresa down to the tribal lockup and charge her with killing Daryl. If she talks about what's been happening up here, no one will believe her, and if they do, the worst that can happen is he'll be convicted of embezzlement. Lewis is someone who's always weighing the odds."

It was the longest speech Howie had ever heard Carl make. "So why are you helping me?" he asked finally. "Raymond said I should expect help from an unlikely source. But, Carl, you really *are* about the last person I was expecting."

Carl's face lit up with a slow smile. He was a big, stolid old Indian, with a face that was generally set like a closed door; but the smile made him accessible, opening the door a crack.

"Well, it's a long story. When I was a boy, I showed an inclination for the sacred life, and I was put in kiva, as we say. It's a time when certain boys are taken from their families to live with a teacher who passes on the old ways. I'm not sure what kind of student I was, but Raymond was my teacher and I've always honored him."

"Even though you're a Lucero?"

"Well, that came between us when I got older. When I was young, I didn't think of Raymond as a Concha—he was a wise man, that's all. But then I grew up and I saw that I was one family, and he was another, and there was bad blood between us. My life went along a different path. I didn't become a holy man, I became a cop."

"It happens," Howie agreed.

"Nevertheless, I've been troubled about a number of things, and finally, when my heart became so uneasy that I couldn't sleep at night, I went to my old teacher for advice. I told him some of the things I knew, though not everything. To be honest, Moon Deer, I've gotten so I'm fed up with Summer People and Winter People alike—Luceros or Conchas, it's all the same to me. I'm tired of all the squabbling and people not getting along."

Howie turned his other side to the fire without taking his eyes off the tribal cop. "So what is it that's been troubling you, Carl? What's happening here?"

Carl didn't answer for such a long time that Howie was afraid he had forgotten the question. But finally, he spoke:

"A dozen years ago, the San Geronimo Pueblo was declared a United Nations Cultural Heritage Site, along with the Pyramids and a number of very famous places. It was a great honor, but things like this do not happen by accident. Lewis was the one who did this, working hard on our behalf, writing letters, inviting important people to visit our tribe. Lewis wasn't always as you see him now. He was a better man once. I wish you could have met him then."

"Me, too," Howie said, without enthusiasm.

"We've always had tourists, of course, but once we had the UN designation, suddenly there were hordes from all over the world. Lewis created the system we have today, that visitors must pay to come into the Pueblo—at first it was three dollars a car, then five dollars, and now it's ten. The money was sup-

posed to provide for the tribe. A new health center, an addition
to the school, scholarships so that our young people could go
to college and come back to us as teachers and doctors. . . ."

Carl's words faded off with a sigh.

"When did you become aware that Lewis was stealing?"
Howie asked, feeling a little awkward about the question.

"Not for some time. In the first years, we built the new
health center and a new school, and it seemed like we were a
very rich tribe. But there was no accounting for the money,
and after a while, it seemed to vanish. When people dared to
ask, Lewis spoke about overhead and interest on loans and
balloon payments and other things that few could understand,
and were hard to prove or disprove, since Lewis had created
all these things himself."

"He was in charge of the tourist operation whether he was
Governor or War Chief?"

"Yes. No matter what his position on the tribal council,
Lewis had begun the operation, and it was left in his care. In
the last four or five years there have been rumors and com-
plaints, mostly from the Winter People, naturally. People
began saying that the money was disappearing. At first, I paid
no attention because people will always say these things,
whether they are true or not. But about a year ago, Charlie
Concha came to me and he said, 'Think about this, Carl, we're
averaging five thousand visitors a month to the Pueblo—you
can count the cars like I did if you don't believe me. That
means we're taking in fifty thousand dollars a month, not
counting the separate camera fees. Where's the money going?'
he asked."

"So what did you tell him?"

"Well, I couldn't tell him much. Just the usual stuff about
interest payments on the health center, and things that I had
heard Lewis say, and that he shouldn't worry about it. But for
my own curiosity, I started having my officers do a rough
count of the tourist cars over the course of a month, and also
estimate the camera fees. This was July, a busy time of year so
maybe it wasn't average. We came up with 6,500 cars, which
meant $65,000 and another $15,000 for cameras—so we're

talking about $80,000 for a single month! I guess it's silly, but a few hundred cars a day don't seem like that much in a big place like the Pueblo, and I'd never really bothered to add up how much money was coming in. I went to Lewis and asked what the tribe had made in July, just curious to hear what he'd tell me. Lewis is my cousin, you understand, and we've been close all our lives. He said, oh, about $40,000, almost exactly half of my estimate. And that's when I understood he was stealing big-time. Cousin or not, I felt I had to confront him. It wasn't a very comfortable conversation, but finally he admitted, yes, he'd been taking money."

"He *admitted* that?"

"Oh, yeah. But he made me see it in a different way. Lewis is very clever, you understand. He told me that the money he had taken was for the sake of the tribe, that he had been investing it in various ways—a stock portfolio, a motel in Albuquerque, a convenience store in Santa Fe, a restaurant here in San Geronimo—"

"The Anasazi Grill?"

"Yes. He said he had kept these things secret, knowing that many people would not approve, particularly of the restaurant where alcohol was sold. Nevertheless, Lewis made me see that this was the modern way, and that we must do these things if the tribe is ever to be independent of handouts from the federal government. The rest of the council, of course, is very conservative. Very traditional. He could not tell them what he had done, but one day in the future he hoped to present to them the deed to a 20,000 acre ranch that adjoins the northeast corner of our land. This land is for sale for $8 million and for a long time, many of us have wanted it for the tribe."

"In other words, you believed Lewis was acting in the best interest of the tribe?"

Carl sighed. "I believed Lewis had convinced *himself* of this, that he was acting correctly. But meanwhile he and his family were living well. It was a difficult matter for me, so I let it pass. I did nothing. And then the British archeologist arrived. This was when everything became very bad."

"Shark Tooth?"

Carl snorted contemptuously. "Dr. Rutherford Hughes had found out that Lewis and his son Anthony owned the dummy corporation that owned the Anasazi Grill, and he presented a simple case of blackmail—either let me explore the ancient cave on your land, or I will go to the newspapers and the council and tell everyone that you've been stealing tribal funds. Lewis believed he had no choice, so he allowed the Englishman to do what he wanted."

"But how could Hughes have found out about the restaurant?"

"Well, he spoke Tiwa—it's a mystery how he learned. Perhaps he was able to overhear people gossiping. You know how it is. We talk freely in our language when white people are around, believing that they can't understand us. He may have heard a rumor about the restaurant, and then set out to investigate the financial trail. He was very smart. Maybe the county has all the paperwork on file somewhere and it was just a matter of looking very patiently. I don't know."

"But how did he work up here without people finding out?"

"Lewis came to me and asked me to make this possible. I showed Hughes how he must get in and out of reservation land secretly, as well as where he could go and where he could not go. This was our agreement with him, that he must keep himself hidden, because if the council found out there would be an inquiry and Lewis would not be able to help him any longer. Also, one of my officers was assigned to help him because we did not want this archeologist on Indian land without supervision—either myself, Daryl, or Johnson were supposed to be with him at all times. Among other considerations, we wanted to prevent him from stealing any of our treasures. But in fact, we are only a small police department, spread thin, and there were many times when the Englishman was by himself, left to do as he liked. Toward the end, one of us would ride up to the cave maybe once a week for a few hours, that was all."

"But the council found out about Hughes eventually. I heard they received an anonymous letter."

Carl nodded. "Yes. I believe this was written by Charlie Concha, though I'm not sure. It has been a problem for Lewis.

As War Chief, the council gave him the task of investigating how a white archeologist managed to be here for nearly a year without people knowing. Lewis knew the answer very well, of course, and he was frightened it would ruin him. And this is where he crossed the line. He decided to kill the Englishman so he couldn't talk. It was the only way he could think to save himself. He sent his son Anthony to do the job. Anthony . . . well, Anthony enjoys these things."

"I've heard that Anthony hasn't been seen recently."

"Yes, but this was part of Lewis's plan. Anthony was to do the thing, then disappear for a while with a girlfriend in Gallup. Lewis is a little afraid of his son, actually. He was worried the boy might start boasting of what he'd done. Distance seemed like a good idea after such a deed."

"All right, but how did Hughes's head end up in a Dumpster in town? This is the confusing part, Carl. I mean, why didn't Anthony just bury the guy in the woods? I don't know if you've heard, but there's some evidence to suggest the head was cannibalized, too."

Carl nodded gloomily. "I've heard this, but I don't know anything. It's very strange. The only thing I can think is that perhaps Anthony went a little crazy. He's not a normal young man."

"And what about Charlie Concha? Who shot him on Friday night?"

Carl's expression became gloomier still. "I don't know the answer to that, either. Charlie was interfering for his own reasons—Anthony killed his father in a car accident a few years back and he had no love for the Lucero family. Maybe Lewis shot him, I don't know. Lewis keeps some of these things from me, knowing I don't approve. I am in a difficult situation, Moon Deer . . ."

"Family values, I guess," Howie said. A silence fell between them. It was nice that Carl had been so forthcoming, but Howie wasn't certain how far he would go to help. "Well, what do we do now?"

"I have an idea how you can help Donna Theresa. I don't want to see any more killing. If you're dry, we can go."

"I'm dry enough."

But just then, as if on command, there was a flash of white light, the earth shook with thunder, and sheets of rain came down in a sudden torrent. Carl clapped his hands and laughed uproariously. It was Indian humor to find this funny, that Moon Deer should spend an hour around the fire getting dry, only to become drenched to the skin once again in an unexpected deluge from the sky.

Howie had to agree: The futility of it was profound.

14

Carl pulled apart the remains of the fire so that the burning branches would sputter and die out in the rain. Once this was done, he turned and led the way deeper into the woods. Howie followed, not certain where they were going. When he asked, Carl's answer was vague. "You'll see," was all he would say. "First we need the horses."

They walked steeply uphill through a dense forest of pine. Carl was agile for an overweight, middle-aged man, and Howie had to struggle to keep up. Meanwhile, the rain turned to hail and the lightning and thunder were coming so fast and furious, it seemed as though the sky was in danger of cracking apart. The trees overhead deflected most of the hail, but every now and then a hard icy pellet slapped against Howie's exposed face and hands.

They came to Spirit Lake, whose gray surface was pockmarked with thousands of tiny ringed splashes. There was no sign of Lewis, D.T., or Johnson, the newcomer cop who had arrived in the morning. They kept climbing a nearly vertical rocky path up the face of the cliff to the main trail where Howie and D.T. had been earlier. Carl had left his Appaloosa tethered to a tree limb in a clearing just off the trail. The Appaloosa was a small horse, unfit to carry two large men, so Carl told Howie to wait while he went to get the black mare—Saze, D.T. had called her, Ford's old horse, though Howie was reluctant to call her by this name.

Howie sat on wet pine needles, leaning again the trunk of a tree, listening to the hail batter down on the branches above. The temperature was plunging. After a while, when Carl had still not returned, he stood and began walking in circles to get warm. Without warning, the loud assault of hail stopped and a dense silence settled upon the woods. Howie was thinking the storm was over when the first snowflake floated down upon his nose. Unfortunately, it was a flake with plenty of brothers and sisters. Snow was silent but deadly at this altitude if you were unprepared. Howie flapped his arms to get his circulation moving. This was starting to look like a problem.

There was nearly a half inch of gloppy wet snow on the branches of the trees by the time Carl came back, leading the black mare on a rope. Howie stroked her powerful neck.

"Well, girl—I wish I had some Godiva chocolates for you, but we're fresh out of treats." She was saddled and bridled. Howie put a foot in the stirrup and hoisted himself upward. He felt more optimistic about survival once he was on her back.

"Lewis arranged for us to meet at a place about half an hour from here," Carl said. "I was supposed to bring you there once I caught you. He'll be wondering why I took so long, but I'll say you got away and that I had trouble finding you in the forest."

"What's your plan, Carl?"

"I'll tell you when we're closer," Carl said. "Now stay close behind me, Moon Deer, and keep your horse's head up. The snow will make the way dangerous."

They rode out of the trees and along the narrow trail that crossed the cliff at the east end of Spirit Lake. Once they were on the other side, the footing was more reliable and Carl broke into an easy canter. Howie followed, pulling back a little on the reins because Black Mare was anxious to run. They made their way up the meadow that rose from the valley. Carl came to a halt when they reached a flat open place at the top. Lightning crackled in the sky. Snow and thunder, an unusual combination. The afternoon was already fading into night. Howie checked his watch. It was 3:40.

Carl pointed to a meadow below them, perhaps a thousand feet lower in altitude. With the snow and darkness, Howie couldn't see more than a ghostly break in the trees.

"That's where Lewis and Donna Theresa will be waiting. How brave are you, Moon Deer?"

Howie considered the question while he squinted through the snow. The scene below looked like an old black-and-white movie, *Nanook of the North*, and Howie found himself wishing fervently that he was in some nice warm cabin (his own, for instance) with a fire burning in the woodstove, and a cup of steaming grog. He was moderately brave, he supposed, though generally the dangers he had faced of modern life were of a more subtle nature: heartbreak, spiritual confusion, and wondering what he dared leave off from his tax returns.

"I can do what needs to be done," he told Carl judiciously. "But I probably won't beat my chest in glee at the prospect."

Carl smiled thinly. "That'll do."

They continued to ride toward the lower meadow while Carl explained what he had in mind. Howie was going to pretend that he was Carl's prisoner, which was what Lewis was expecting to see. They would ride to where the War Chief was waiting, Carl leading the black mare on a rope with Howie's wrists apparently handcuffed on the saddle horn. Then, as soon as they were close enough, Carl would create a distraction, leaving Howie free to scoop D.T. up on his horse and gallop away. It wasn't much of a plan, and a lot of it would depend on Howie's abilities as a swashbuckler. If it worked, they would each get what they wanted. Howie would rescue D.T., and Carl could pretend he was still the War Chief's loyal cousin, that the egregious Moon Deer had simply pulled a fast one. However, a lot of things could go wrong.

Howie had a thought; it wasn't that he was a coward, but he was anxious to avoid the swashbuckler option if at all possible.

"Look, Carl, you said D.T. was safe as long as Lewis didn't have both of us. So what say we just give them a miss, ride on by. We can spring her later down in the Pueblo with no danger of anybody shooting anyone."

"Good thought," Carl agreed, nodding in his slow, ponderous way. "Except for the fact it won't work."

"Why not?"

"The way the land is here, it's too narrow. We can't get by Lewis without him seeing us."

"No way at all?"

"Maybe if it wasn't snowing, there's a hill we could try riding down where we'd be out of sight. But it's steep and I wouldn't try it on a day like this. Not unless suicide has an appeal for you, Moon Deer."

"Not much," Howie admitted. They continued riding through the blowing snow. Howie's lips and nose were numb with cold, and his eyebrows were positively frosty. "Here's another thought," he said after a while. "How about we just ride up to Lewis, and you take out your gun and arrest him. You're the head of the tribal police department, and Lewis is a thief and a killer. I mean, come on, Carl—it's time to get real here."

Carl shook his head. "No, I won't do this to my old friend. You must take Donna Theresa on your horse and try to get away. It's the only way."

"Then what? I'm supposed to keep quiet afterward that you helped me?"

"I would prefer that. But you have to do what is right for you, just as I have to do what's right for me."

"Okay, but I gotta tell you, this is totally crazy. The council's going to figure out that Lewis has been stealing, and then they're going to understand why he allowed Hughes onto Indian land. So why go down with a sinking ship? You didn't break the law, *he* did."

Carl shrugged, a fatalistic Indian gesture Howie had seen many times and in many places. There was no arguing against such an attitude. Shortly before they reached the lower meadow, Carl attached a lead rope to the black mare, and Howie pretended to put his wrists into handcuffs so that it would appear that he was Carl's prisoner. It seemed to Howie that Lewis would eventually figure out that the handcuffs weren't closed properly, and that Carl had helped him. But Howie had enough problems of his own at the moment without taking on Carl's future with his cousin.

Up ahead, Howie could see two small figures in the snow, the War Chief and Donna Theresa standing at the edge of the meadow in the shelter of some trees. Riding closer, Howie noticed that Lewis had his rifle pointed at D.T. There was no sign of their horses.

"Ready?" Carl asked.

Howie supposed he was, more or less.

15

The first thing that went wrong was that Donna Theresa saw Howie and was so disgusted by the very sight of him that she sat down on the ground and began to sulk. It was going to be more difficult, Howie suspected, to scoop up a sitting, sullen maiden than a standing one.

Carl kept riding across the meadow, leading his prisoner directly up to where the War Chief was waiting at the edge of the trees. Both Lewis and D.T. were covered with a heavy dusting of snow on their heads and shoulders, starting to look like some Native American Christmas card. Lewis said something to Carl in Tiwa that Howie interpreted loosely as, "Good work! You caught the Lakota shit after all. I was starting to worry."

Carl began to swing himself off the left side of his Appaloosa, doing a pretty good imitation of a half-frozen middle-aged man who had been in the saddle a long time. Howie saw that this was his moment, and he'd better make it good. Carl's left foot caught in the stirrup and he tumbled clumsily against Lewis, knocking the War Chief momentarily off balance before his foot came free. Howie jerked his wrists from the handcuffs, grabbed hold of his reins, and moved in next to D.T., reaching down for her.

"Come on," he cried, "jump on the back."

She hesitated; this was the second thing that went wrong. She didn't understand that the confusion had been orchestrated. By leaning over far in the saddle, Howie was able to take hold of an arm, but she jerked away, probably thinking he had lost his mind.

"What the hell are you doing?" she demanded.

"Jump on!" he hissed.

Lewis was shouting in Tiwa, and that seemed to rouse her at last from her sullen stupor. Moving quickly, she got her foot into the left stirrup and hoisted herself upward while Howie helped by pulling her arm. The black horse was already in motion, frightened by the commotion. D.T. was still swinging her leg over the horse's rump when they took off at a gallop across the snowy meadow. D.T. almost pulled Howie out of the saddle trying to stay on, but at last she settled behind him, her arms around his waist. They were riding away when Howie heard a gunshot. A bullet whizzed past his right ear with a whine. Big wet snowflakes slapped against his face, making it hard to see. He gave the mare a kick, urging her on, pointing her toward the top of the meadow where a snowy cloud had enshrouded the hill. He thought they might be safe if only they could get that far.

The mare was straining upward in a lopping gallop, as fast as she could manage with two riders on difficult terrain. Howie heard another gunshot, but this time there was no whizzing bullet. Then they rode into the cloud and became hidden in a whiteout so final it was like being erased from the planet. Howie could barely see the horse's ears in front of him, and had no idea where the ground was beneath him; cleverly, the mare slowed to a walk without his urging. Howie was encrusted with snow, from the top of his head down his frozen jeans to his sneakers. If he had a carrot instead of a nose, he could have passed for Frosty the Snowman.

"You all right?" he called back to D.T.

"That was the craziest thing I ever saw, Moon Deer."

"Come on, I rescued you!"

"Did you?"

Howie saw her point: Night was coming quickly, turning the whiteout into a blackout as the snow continued to fall. They were lost in a blizzard. He had no sense of which direction they were traveling, or even if they were heading up or going down. For all he knew, they might be riding in a circle back to Lewis and Carl. Meanwhile, Black Mare plodded forward, her hooves sinking into the deepening snow. Howie gave the horse her head, hoping her instincts were better than his. He held the reins loosely in first one numb hand and then another, keeping his free hand beneath his turtleneck sweater for warmth. His face stung with the cold.

"Good going, Moon Deer! My hero!" D.T. scolded. "We're going to die out here. You know, if you had only managed to get away, Lewis would have taken me down to jail and that would have been the end of it—my grandfather would have had me out in half an hour. Lewis wouldn't have dared to shoot me with you loose to talk about it."

It was the same thing Carl had said. Howie was too discouraged to answer, that it had not been possible to get by without Lewis spotting them. He debated telling D.T. that he had always heard hypothermia was a fairly pleasant way to die: toward the end, people had been known to take off their clothes, believing themselves in some tropical paradise. But he said nothing.

They kept riding blindly into the storm. An hour later, the last gray light faded into night.

"Let's talk," Howie said after a long time. In the darkness, he felt as though he and Donna Theresa were floating through a velvety ether, disconnected from everything, her arms around his waist.

"I don't want to talk."

"I do. I want to know what was in Charlie's little white box."

"What difference does it make now?"

"I'm curious. If I'm going to die up here, at least I'd like to know what I'm dying for."

"You're not dying *for* anything. You're dying because you got us lost in a snowstorm, that's all."

Howie's body was numb, but his mind was curiously alert, possibly the first effects of hypothermia. In fact, he felt almost wonderful, godlike; he was burning with thoughts and imagery. He presumed D.T. wasn't going to say anything more on the subject of Charlie's box, but a few minutes later, she came back to it. Perhaps her brain was burning, too.

"Cannibalism," she said unexpectedly.

"What, you hungry? Maybe you'd like to stop for a little Donner dinner party for two."

"Shut up, Moon Deer, and try to think for a change. What do you think you'd need in order to prove the existence of Anasazi cannibalism?"

It was madness riding through a blizzard, pondering the culinary customs of yesteryear. Nevertheless, Howie eagerly grappled with D.T.'s question. It was good to have an intellectual challenge while you died.

"The thing is, I don't think you *can* prove it," he told her wisely. "Not with an event that happened in prehistoric times, no written record, no eyewitnesses. Look, I've been remembering what I've read about this—about the bones that were found in Chaco Canyon, and how the skulls were smashed in the front and had char marks on the backs, like they'd been put on a bed of coals. But that still doesn't mean the folks were eaten."

"What else could it mean?"

"It could mean the Anasazi had exotic mortuary practices, like the ancient Egyptians," he fired back, happy to find his own brain functioning so well. *I think therefore I am*: Howie couldn't remember at the moment if this was said by Descartes or Isaac Newton, but it obviously came from a guy lost in a snowstorm. *And as long as you kept thinking, you still were.*

"Mortuary practices!" D.T. scoffed.

"Sure. A little sawing, boiling, roasting, and removing of organs could have been part of their religion. Just a way to get shipshape for the afterlife."

"Yeah, but the bones we're talking about in Chaco were found in a garbage dump, Moon Deer. And when I saw Ford on Saturday night, he told me the same thing—the skeletons he found in the cave were in a garbage mound along with corn husks, broken pottery shards, and building rubble. So the idea of mortuary practices doesn't wash. Why go to so much trouble just to throw the bones in the trash?"

"Garbage," Howie said thoughtfully, peering into the swirling snow. "That's very interesting, seeing as how I found Ford's head in a trash Dumpster. One senses a certain reoccurring motif here, D.T. But why toss a dead person into the garbage?"

"Simple. It's a way to dishonor the dead. You bury your loved ones, but with your enemies, you do the opposite. You scalp 'em, take a few body parts for souvenirs, dismember them, even pee on them, if you want. It's a way of gloating, of saying, I won, you lost. Indians used to do this to each other all the time."

"White people did it, too. The Seventh Cavalry had a particular penchant for the vaginas of dead Sioux women—they'd cut them off and turn 'em into purses. Good Christian boys. Manifest Destiny, and all that."

"Well, there you are. Now answer my question, Moon Deer. Even mainstream archeologists agree that there is *one* thing that would prove the existence of Anasazi cannibalism, and one thing only. You pretend to be some smart-ass college educated Indian, so tell me—what would that one thing have to be?"

They rode through the thick darkness while Howie thought. He thought so hard that he didn't even notice at first that the snow had turned to rain and the clouds had lifted enough so that he could see they were traveling on a muddy, snow speckled track through a forest. Black Mare kept plodding forward.

"Give me a hint," he suggested.

"No hints."

The temperature was warmer and Howie sensed from the dense wet air that they had descended several thousand feet in elevation. This was promising, but his brain had gone sloppy on him, and he felt a wave of exhaustion and hunger.

"I don't know. Tell me."

"I'm *not* going to tell you. Either you're smart, or you're a loser . . . there's n-n-no middle g-g-ground for people like us, Moon Deer."

Howie was very sorry to hear her stutter return. They were both coming down from some strange hypothermic high.

"Where are we?" he asked.

"We're on the old logging road I told you about. Saze found the back way off Pueblo land . . . give up?"

"No, I *don't* give up. Let me get this straight—you're saying this thing that's going to prove Anasazi cannibalism was what Charlie was carrying in that little white box?"

D.T. didn't answer.

"Holy shit!" Howie cried.

"That's right," she agreed. "I was starting to worry about you, Moon Deer, that maybe you were a moron or something."

He had gotten it, finally. Now that it was clear, he couldn't imagine how he hadn't seen it earlier, for he had studied things like this in college anthropology courses.

"That petrified twig isn't a twig at all. And Charlie wasn't saying *cop* when he was handing me that box—he was trying to say *coprolite*!"

"Yes."

Howie felt giddy. A coprolite was fossilized human excrement, a little grotty, admittedly, but a rare and incredible find. Howie's brain scanned over the scientific possibilities.

"My God, you'll be able to study the DNA of an Anasazi!"

"We can do more than that. This is the shit test, and it was put forward by a Hopi archeologist. The Hopi are dead set against their ancestors being cannibals, of course, they find it extremely offensive. So what they said was this, trying to set an impossibly high standard of proof: Anasazi cannibalism could not be proved unless you actually found human remains in prehistoric human excrement. There's a lab in Minnesota that can do the testing—it's complicated, but it's possible. Basically, if the lab finds traces of human myoglobin in the stool, the only explanation is cannibalism."

"But who found the thing? Ford?"

"No, it was Charlie. Remember, I told you he'd been hanging around up at the cave, helping out a little, trying to get Ford to talk to him? Charlie found the coprolite in an old fire pit. Try to picture this, Moon Deer: Eight hundred years ago, a group of warriors—thugs, really—somehow get up into that mountain perch where a small clan of people are hiding in ter-

ror. They kill all the people—men, women, and children—
then butcher them and have themselves a feast. Afterward,
they throw the remaining body parts in the garbage mound
rather than bury them, as a mark of disrespect. Then, just as
they're leaving, one of the warriors stops to take a dump in the
embers of the dying fire. He could have gone anywhere, of
course, but this is a final mark of disrespect, to crap in the
family hearth. It's a gesture of utter contempt. The fire had to
have died down to just the right temperature for the turd to be
desiccated, drying without burning. Then it was buried by centuries of dirt and rubble in a kind of time vault in the cave."

"And *Charlie* found it? Isn't that kind of amazing for someone who wasn't an archeologist?"

"Beginner's luck. Actually, he was about to throw it away
when Ford came over and saw what Charlie had in his hand.
He took it from Charlie and wouldn't say what it was, but
Charlie could tell that Ford was excited. When I got back to
San Geronimo, the night Charlie and I went out for burritos,
he told me about this, what he'd found in the fire pit, because
he was curious why Ford seemed so thrilled about a little
twiglike thing."

"And you knew what it was?"

"Well, sure. From the way Charlie described it, along with
Ford's reaction, I figured it had to be a coprolite."

"Then you asked Charlie to steal it for you, didn't you?"

"*Steal*? Come on, it didn't belong to Ford in the first place!
He shouldn't have ever been allowed in that cave, Moon
Deer."

"Right. It was *your* cave, and you thought the coprolite belonged to you. How did Charlie get it?"

"I don't know exactly." D.T. had been speaking freely up to
now, enthusiastically, in fact. But Howie heard a new note of
caution come into her voice. "We talked about trying to get it
back, but he had no idea where Ford had hidden the thing. The
way we left it, Charlie planned to go up there and look around,
but it seemed pretty damn hopeless, really."

They fell silent for some time after that, having used up
their store of goodwill and energy. Black Mare kept going on

and on, apparently with some destination in mind. The rain stopped and the clouds were starting to break up, showing patches of stars overhead, just as they were leaving Indian land by way of an old wooden gate that was half fallen over on its side. From here they came out onto a dirt road, passing occasional cabins that were spaced at great distances from one another, empty of life.

"You know this road?" he asked.

"What's the difference?"

"I'm wondering if we're lost."

"We're not lost. It's called Lhasa Road. There was a hippie commune back here in the sixties. Believe it or not, they wanted to live just like Indians. When they got bored with that, they went away and the land was subdivided into vacation parcels. If we keep on going, we'll come to a road that'll take us into town."

"A long ride?"

"Three or four hours."

Howie was half asleep in the saddle, listening to the rhythmic sucking sound of Black Mare's hoofbeats against the muddy road, when he heard distant gunfire coming from the road ahead, dreamy and abstract. There were two different guns involved, a deep bass gun and a smaller weapon that made a high popping sound.

"God, I've been stupid!" he said suddenly. Listening to the gunfire down the road, the final piece of the puzzle fell into place. It was absurdly simple. This entire case had been like a magic trick, a sleight of hand where the trickster made you look the wrong way, giving the illusion of truth to a lie. Meanwhile, D.T. was urging him on.

"What are you waiting for? Let's go!" she cried.

"D.T., I think we should scope this out a little first . . . *for chrissake!*"

Donna Theresa had just kicked Black Mare in the flank with her heels, sending them off into a sudden gallop down the road. Apparently, she believed this was the time for action, not thought.

16

Emma Wilder was terrified at finding herself locked in a bathroom with a tub full of human bones. She sat huddled near the sink on a scatter rug on the linoleum floor, leaning against the wall and hugging her legs for comfort. At first, she kept expecting something to happen, the door to fling open, some new danger. But nothing happened, and this soon became a new source of misery. As she listened, the storm outside the cabin on Lhasa Road gradually subsided, until she could hear only the drip of the faucet near her head. *Plink . . . plink . . . plink.* It was a maddening sound.

Emma's terror gradually faded. People get used to anything, she supposed, even being locked in a bathroom full of skeletons. Finally, she dared herself to get a better look at the horror in the tub. The bones were obviously old, not fresh, and this was reassuring. She had just picked up a legbone that looked like a giant drumstick when she unexpectedly heard something: movement from the other side of the locked door. Her anxiety and boredom turned quickly into anger.

"Let me out of here!" she shouted, gripping hold of the legbone as a possible weapon. "I'm a librarian! I'm here for your goddamn overdue book!"

The door opened abruptly to reveal a man standing in partial silhouette, his back to a glowing overhead bulb. He was one of the oddest figures Emma had ever seen, not particularly tall or large—five-foot-eight or -nine—but he seemed to take up a lot of space nevertheless. His hair was white and very long, hanging in an untamed mane. He looked to be in his late fifties, handsome in a gaunt, poetic way that distinguished older men sometimes had. Age suited him. He could have been an elder statesman or a famous novelist; physically, a cross between Andrew Wyeth and the English actor Richard Harris in his later roles. His left arm appeared to be hurt, hanging in a makeshift sling that had been fashioned from an old T-shirt. His light blue eyes glowered at her with a hard intelligence.

He smiled with childlike candor. "Dear lady, I beg your forgiveness for locking you in my bathroom. To be honest, I can't stand librarians, though I have always adored libraries. Petty minds and officious bureaucrats do not appeal to my rebellious nature. Still I've been rude, and I regret this. Could I offer you a cup of tea with perhaps a good stiff wallop of brandy?"

Emma stared at him, speechless. "Rutherford Hughes, I presume," she managed finally.

His smile didn't falter, but there was something maniacal in the man's cold blue eyes that gave Emma a chill.

"Earl Grey or Lemon Zinger?" he insisted.

"I don't think so . . ."

"Oh, come, come, come! Let's not be silly! We English have always found that tea is just the thing for life's trying moments. And, incidentally, I'd be grateful if you'd put that bone back in the tub where it belongs. It's even older than I am, which is a frightful thought."

Emma had to admit, Dr. Rutherford Hughes had a wonderful British accent. The words rolled off his tongue like a Shakespearean actor in heat, a rich tapestry of sound that no American could begin to duplicate. It was hard to resist such a voice. She put the leg bone back into the bathtub with the other skeletons.

"I'll have some Earl Grey," she agreed.

His smile took on a sad quality, not so childlike. "You know, dear lady, you broke my bloody window!"

"I knocked on the door first, but there was no answer. It was the only way I could think of getting in."

"Perhaps you weren't *supposed* to get in, because it wasn't your house. But never mind, we'll let bygones be bygones."

He turned his back and crossed the small living room to a

two-burner propane stove not far from the broken window. A cold wind was blowing in, flapping the thin yellow curtains. The cabin was sparse and utilitarian, a few simple tables and chairs. The only luxuries were the books piled everywhere. Warily, Emma followed him out of the bathroom and watched as he lit the stove with a kitchen match and put on a kettle of water, using his injured arm in the sling almost as freely as his good arm.

"So you know who *I* am," he said. "But if you'll pardon my curiosity, who are *you*?"

"I'm Emma Wilder." She did her best to pretend she wasn't intimidated, and threw out her name proudly, like a gauntlet.

"Wilder? I seem to recall a detective agency by the name of Wilder and Moon Deer. Could we have a connection here?"

The actual name was Wilder & Associate, but Emma was surprised he knew anything about Jack and Howie at all. "Jack Wilder's my husband. He was a very important police official in San Francisco before we retired here. And he knows I'm here, by the way."

Dr. Hughes shrugged. "Yes, but *why* are you here? That's the question, isn't it? What in the world would make an old busybody attempt this godforsaken road in a storm like we've had today? And please spare me the nonsense about my overdue library book."

Emma narrowed her eyes, not much liking the label "old busybody." "Overdue library books are *not* nonsense," she told him, becoming angry again. "You know, you're a very arrogant person, Dr. Hughes. I really despise the way you treated Donna Theresa, using her like you did. You've managed to cause a great deal of suffering and mischief just so you could have your egotistical way."

The Englishman stared at Emma in astonishment. Then he bent over with a great booming laugh. "Oh, wonderful! I deserve that. And you're absolutely right, of course—I'm a beast, I truly am . . . and look, I'm sorry about D.T. She was simply far too young for me, and rather boring—a natural victim, I'm afraid. Have you ever actually met the child?"

"No," Emma admitted.

"A pretty girl. But my God, there are so *many* pretty girls, Mrs. Wilder. I'm too old for that nonsense. I've played house, and I've told all the romantic lies I ever intend to. And now, with only limited time at my disposal, I've had to narrow my energies to achieving my goals. The fact is, one needs to be ruthless if one wants to do anything serious in this world. It's necessary to shut out interruptions and distractions—"

"Donna Theresa wasn't an interruption," Emma said sharply. "She's your wife."

Dr. Hughes sighed. "Yes, indeed. Unfortunately, that was necessary for me to remain in your wonderfully disunited states. I thought she understood that . . . all right, I admit it, I am not a nice man."

Emma gave him a hard stare. "You killed that person, the head Howie found in the garbage."

He shrugged elaborately. "It was self-defense, dear lady. I had no choice."

"I am *not* your dear lady. You put your earring on the head to make people think it was you, didn't you? And you cooked him because you wanted people to think it was some bizarre return of Anasazi cannibalism, but in reality it was only a way to disguise the identifying features."

"I hope you don't mind tea bags," he said, emphasizing the last word distastefully and pulling down two mugs from a shelf above the sink. "They're barbarous, but one must rough it here in New Mexico . . . you *will* have some brandy in your tea? You're not going to be ridiculous and refuse, are you?"

"I'll have just a small shot."

"Good. And, of course, you're absolutely right, Mrs. Wilder. I wanted people to think the head was me. But you mustn't think of me as some deranged killer. I was sitting at my campfire, about to enjoy a simple dinner, when a very unpleasant young man by the name of Anthony Lucero arrived with the rather bleak intention of killing me. It was only sheer luck that I survived. He had his rifle turned around as a sort of club and apparently intended to bash my brains in—no doubt that would have been more satisfying for him than simply shooting me, but it proved to be a serious error on his part . . . Simplic-

ity, Mrs. Wilder, that's the ticket! The luck for me was that I
had my revolver cocked. I turned to defend myself and when
he knocked the gun out of my hand, it hit a rock and fired—
the bullet struck him in the thigh, not a fatal wound, but it
gave me the upper hand. I was somewhat hurt myself from his
initial blow, as you'll have noticed from this ratty old T-shirt
I've been forced to string together as a sling. Oh, it was high
drama there for a while, I can tell you! We struggled and
grunted and kicked and screamed unpleasant things at each
other. But eventually I prevailed, despite my age. Unfortunately, Anthony wasn't my real problem—his father, Lewis,
was. I knew he would send someone else to kill me if I didn't
do something to prevent it. Thus the small deceit, which you
have very cleverly noted. I couldn't resist turning it into a little
joke, I suppose—I arranged the evidence so that the experts
would find themselves faced with a somewhat contentious
archeological theory, and hopefully wring their hands in confusion."

"You really thought you could fool everybody?"

"Oh, not for long. I assumed your clever forensic scientists
would realize eventually that the head belonged to a Native
American man in his early thirties, rather than an old Limey
such as myself. And of course, when Anthony failed to show
up, his father, Lewis, would catch on as well, sooner or later. I
was simply buying time, that's all. I needed a week to ten days
to finish up my work in New Mexico and then I could skedad-
dle happily home. I knew about your husband's associate,
Howard Moon Deer, from Donna Theresa. She was trying to
make me jealous one night, telling me all about this wonderful
private eye with whom she was supposedly having a hot romance. I was disparaging, and when I asked about what sort of
cases a private eye might get in a small town in San Geronimo, she told me about Moon Deer's stakeout behind the
Shanghai Café. It didn't seem much like high adventure, but it
gave me an idea of where to put the head so that with a little
luck it would be found. I knew that Lewis would be confused,
wondering why Anthony had done such a bloody strange
thing. But confusion worked in my favor, not his. Frankly,

there was a small element of revenge in my plan—this individual had sent his son to kill me, after all. I wanted him to wonder and worry, and then find out eventually that it was his son's head in the trash bin, and be fully aware of what I had done to him for crossing me."

"Why did Lewis want to kill you?"

Dr. Hughes blinked with mock innocence, enjoying himself. "Well, he had a rather good reason, actually. I didn't quite play cricket when it came to convincing him to allow me to explore a site on Indian land. He had already turned down poor D.T., so I realized I would need to be a bit more persuasive . . . Sugar?"

Emma declined. The water had boiled and Dr. Hughes was preparing their Earl Grey, pouring a good shot of brandy into the mugs. When the tea was ready, they sat down at a small yellow formica table on two kitchen chairs.

"And now I have a problem, Mrs. Wilder," he said with his candid smile. "I'm wondering if you can help me with this— I'd certainly be very grateful. Obviously, you know a great deal about this business from your husband, I assume."

"Yes."

"Well, good. If you are able to help me, then perhaps I will be able to help you. Are you catching my meaning?"

"I'm not sure."

"Then let me put it more plainly. If you can tell me what I want to know, I will let you walk out of this cabin alive. It would please me to do that, Mrs. Wilder, for I am not a violent man. I am a realist, yes, but I have been forced to use violence only as a last resort, to protect myself."

Emma sipped her tea. There were no weapons in sight and the conversation so far had been extremely civilized. But she was not fooled; she sensed his maniacal ruthlessness, that he was capable of anything.

"I'll tell you what I can," Emma said, deciding she was no hero. "But I'm not sure I know that much."

"Let me be the judge of that. About two months ago, a young Indian by the name of Charlie Concha began visiting me at the cave I was excavating. He made an effort to befriend me, offering to help out in various ways, and frankly this was useful to me. In the beginning, Lewis had assigned various tribal cops to look after me, and sometimes they gave a helping hand out of boredom, but in the last month they rarely appeared. I suppose they were busy with other things, or merely lazy. Charlie started showing up a couple of days of week, and I was glad to allow him to do various chores. It soon became obvious that his friendship had a purpose: He wanted to know what I knew about Lewis Lucero, what sort of leverage I had on the man that allowed me permission to do my little dig on reservation land."

"You were blackmailing the War Chief?"

He flashed his most charming bad-boy smile. "Well, yes. I told you I am not what the world considers to be a nice person. The young Indian, Charlie, seemed to be waging his own vendetta against the Lucero family, and that was fine with me. I fed him little tidbits of information, but not too much. I wanted to keep him as a helper, after all, and not have him go off against Lewis in some half-baked fashion before I'd finished my own project. Charlie was actually quite helpful. He found one particularly valuable artifact by accident in an old fire pit, and he was also kind enough to dispose of Anthony's head for me—it was Charlie who put the head into the Dumpster and smashed up Moon Deer's car, I'm afraid."

"That's a lot of risk he took for a few tidbits of information," Emma mentioned.

"Well, I promised him the moon, so to speak. What I said was, yes, indeed, I *was* blackmailing Lewis Lucero. I had the goods on the conniving bastard War Chief, and I would give Charlie everything in a week or two, just before I was ready to leave New Mexico. We shook hands on it, and that's when Charlie agreed to deliver the remains of Anthony Lucero in the Anasazi Grill truck—the truck was my idea, by the way, part of my little joke."

"A very nasty joke!" Emma told him.

"Well, yes. But clever, you have to admit. Unfortunately, Charlie didn't trust me—I can't say why. He decided he needed a little leverage himself so I wouldn't skip town without telling all. So he came here to my cabin one night when I was sleeping at my mountain camp near the cave. He stole the extremely valuable artifact that I mentioned earlier, the one he had found accidentally in a fire pit. I guess I had shown too much excitement over the thing and he thought he would hold it hostage, just to make sure I'd keep my word. Anyway, I won't bore you with my woes, Mrs. Wilder but this happened to be a *very* important object—perhaps the most single important Anasazi find since Lieutenant James Simpson stumbled into Chaco Canyon in 1849. I had to have my artifact back, no matter what. So I went down to Charlie's house in the Pueblo on Friday night, found him home . . . and, well, not to put too fine a point on it, we had ourselves a rather serious argument. With the advantage of youth, he was able to escape with the object. But not with impunity. No one takes advantage of me, Mrs. Wilder. I wounded him, but he got away on his horse . . . does this perhaps ring a bell for you, Mrs. Wilder?"

Emma thought back to Howie's Saturday-morning phone call, and realized she had a card to play. She nodded vaguely, not certain yet how or when to play it.

Dr. Hughes's cold blue eyes were studying her intently. "I am a simple man, Mrs. Wilder. I am homesick for London, and eager to say good-bye to New Mexico. But I can't leave without this artifact."

"What is it exactly?"

He shrugged. "It's better you don't know. It's not any golden treasure, I'll tell you that—it has absolutely no value whatsoever except a scientific one. Nevertheless, I will gladly exchange your life for any useful information you can give me of its whereabouts."

Rutherford Hughes stood up from the kitchen table and crossed the room to a cabinet drawer. He drew out a huge revolver with a pearl handle and returned to his chair at the table, holding the gun loosely in his good hand.

"I don't want to alarm you, Mrs. Wilder, but time is running out."

"I know where your artifact is," she told him.

"Do you? Of course, you could be lying."

"It's in a small white cardboard box, the sort you might get from a jeweler when buying a bracelet or earrings. Does that sound like I'm lying?"

His eyes sparkled as he watched her. He nodded slowly. "All right, I believe you. Tell me and I'll let you go."

Emma laughed. "The problem is, I don't believe *you*. How do I know if after I tell you, that you won't kill me anyway?"

With shocking speed, Ford leapt at her from the far side of the table, pressing the gun against her head with one hand, and squeezing her throat with the other, choking her horribly— using his bad hand in the sling, which was strong enough.

"*I want that box!*" he screamed. "I won't tolerate any obstruction from a stupid old lady! Do you hear me?"

Emma nodded, unable to breathe or speak with his hand on her throat. He smiled and let her go, and returned to his chair, once again the charming, eccentric Englishman. But Emma had seen the monster beneath the mask. She rubbed her throat where he had hurt her and knew she was dead if she didn't handle this properly.

"I'll tell you what you want to know," she said carefully. "In fact, I *want* to tell you. However, I may be old, but I'm not stupid, Dr. Hughes. I need some guarantee that if I tell you, you'll let me go. Otherwise, why bother?"

"Yes, I see your point," he agreed with a sigh, making an obvious effort for patience. "Let's think this over. I'm sure we can come to some arrangement that'll be suitable to us both. What do you suggest?"

"Let me call my husband. He can bring the box, and also work out some kind of exchange. Jack's good at that sort of thing."

"I'm sure he must be, Mrs. Wilder, if he was an important policeman. But, no, that won't do. You see, a copper would make this more dangerous for me."

"He's an *ex*-cop. And he's blind."

Hughes winked merrily, regaining his good humor. "Then he wouldn't be able to bring the artifact here on his own, would he? He'd need someone to drive him, and that would put me at a definite disadvantage, don't you think?"

"Perhaps," Emma agreed.

"There's no perhaps about it. We need to think some more. Would you care for another cup of tea?"

Emma didn't want more tea. They had reached an apparent stalemate and she wasn't certain how to proceed. They had fallen into a troubled silence when Emma was surprised to hear footsteps on the path outside. Ford reached quickly to yank the string dangling from the bare overhead light bulb, plunging the room into darkness. The footsteps on the path halted.

"Come here!" he whispered angrily, grabbing her wrist and pulling her away from the window. "Who did you bring here, dear lady?"

"Nobody," Emma told him. "I came on my own."

"Well, it seems that someone has followed you."

A voice called loudly from outside. "Hello in there! This is the state police. Is Emma Wilder inside?"

Hughes pressed the barrel of his revolver against the side of Emma's head.

"Tell him to go away."

Emma had recognized the voice: It was Ed Gomez. Her initial relief turned into new worry as she realized that Ed's appearance put her in new jeopardy.

"Ed, I'm here," she called out in an unsteady voice. "Dr. Rutherford Hughes is pointing a gun at my head. He wants you to go away."

"Ford, listen to me," a second voice called. "This is Jack Wilder—we'll do whatever you want, absolutely anything, as long as Emma is safe. So let's all of us just stay calm here and work this out reasonably."

"Jack!" Emma cried, nearly weeping for joy, going soft all over at the sound of his familiar voice.

"Shut up!" Ford hissed in her ear. "You don't speak unless I tell you to speak, is that clear?"

She nodded.

"My requirements are very simple, Mr. Wilder," Ford called to the outside. "I want to get safely to my car that's parked outside. I'm going to take Mrs. Wilder with me as a hostage, and if you try to stop me or radio for a roadblock, I'll shoot her—do you understand me?"

"Right. No one's going to stop you. Ed, tell him."

"All we care about is Emma's safety," Ed agreed.

"Then back away from the front door. In a few minutes, I'm going to come out with the little lady in front of me, and I don't want to see either of you."

"We're backing away. We're doing everything you want, Hughes, so just relax," Ed told him.

Emma listened to Jack's and Ed's footsteps moving away on the path. She was too tense to breathe properly.

"Well, I'm very sorry to have our tea party interrupted," Ford said, without relaxing his grip on her. "I'm also rather sorry I won't be able to take the skeletons I have in the bath-tub—I removed them from the cave the other night at rather some trouble and pain, what with my bad arm. But the little white box will have to do, I suppose. So where is it, Mrs. Wilder?"

"I'll tell you after you—"

"No, you'll tell me *right* now," he said, cocking the hammer of the pistol and pressing the barrel hard against her left temple. "Let's not have any nonsense. You're my ticket out of here, Mrs. Wilder, so I'd be loathe to kill you. But I must know where we're going in order to plan an efficient escape route. You see my point?"

With the hammer cocked and the gun against her head, Emma found herself with an overwhelming urge to talk. She told him everything, how Charlie had ridden to Howie's cabin, as well as exact directions to where cabin was located. Howie wasn't there, and a mysterious white box didn't seem worth dying for.

"Good girl, Mrs. Wilder," he said when she was finished. "I'm just going to cut the phone line—if your friends have cell phones, they won't reach anybody from *this* black hole, be-lieve me. Then we'll go to the car, I think, and make our es-cape."

Emma felt anger building as he pulled her about the dark cabin with him while making his preparations to leave, as though she were nothing but a bag of old clothes. The last few hours, she had been called "dear lady" and "the little woman," but "good girl" was the last straw. She *wasn't* going to be a good girl, not if she could help it.

"Ready?" he asked. "Then let's give this a try, shall we?"

Rutherford Hughes kicked open the front door and guided Emma outside, holding her in front and keeping the barrel of his huge gun against her head. Emma felt light-headed with anger and fear. She wanted to do something, anything to resist this humiliation, but she couldn't see what. Meanwhile, there was no sign of Jack or Ed, or Ed's car. It was possible, she supposed, that they had to park behind where she got stuck earlier in the mud, blocking the road. If this was true, Hughes might not escape so easily after all.

"Easy, old girl," he said, walking her carefully up the path.

"I am *not* an old girl, nor am I a *good* girl—I am a woman, Dr. Hughes, and you are an conceited, sexist creep."

"Just keep walking, please."

"You know, you're not nearly as wonderful as you think you are."

"I'm sure you're right."

His voice was distracted. Emma realized he was hardly paying attention to her; his focus was entirely on the darkness beyond the path, wondering where Jack and Ed were. This gave her a glimmer of hope. About halfway to the Land Cruiser, he moved the barrel of the gun from her temple toward a clump of trees just ahead, obviously concerned that Jack and Ed might be hidden there. Emma realized this was her moment, now or never. She had taken a women's self-defense class and rummaged through what she could remember. Abruptly, she kicked backward with all her might, getting Ford in the shin— a vulnerable place, she remembered her teacher saying. Not as good as kicking a guy in the balls, but still not bad. Hughes howled in pain, and loosened his grip on her arm.

Emma was about to shake free and run when Ed called out from the trees: *"Flat on the ground!"* She obeyed without question, throwing herself onto the ground as gunfire blasted all around her, a big bass gun and an answering treble gun.

She was terrified and confused, her brief anger spent, overwhelmed by the noise. Expecting to die any second, she scurried away through the mud on her hands and knees as fast as she could crawl toward a line of bushes a dozen feet away. She hid, crouching, holding her hands over ears to shut out the gunfire, shaking her head and saying, "No, no, no . . ."

17

Howie wished fervently that Donna Theresa had not kicked Black Mare in the flanks with her heels, setting the horse off into a wild run, but D.T. had her own agenda and certainly wasn't going to consulate a mere Moon Deer as to what she planned to do.

The road sloped downward through a tunnel of trees, a darkness in which Howie could not see the horse beneath them, or the hard ground, or anything at all. It felt as if they were flying. Or falling. Scary as hell, frankly, with the rhythmic sound of hooves pounding against the earth, hooves in which a wayward native could get himself trampled to death if his balance faltered for an instant. Howie did his best to pull back on the reins and slow the horse to a trot, but Black Mare was homeward bound, unstoppable. Between the galloping mare, D.T., and the gunfire up ahead, Howie had a sense of no longer being the master of his destiny. It would be a miracle just to stay in the saddle.

Howie had allowed D.T. the use of the single set of stirrups they shared, riding double, so that his own legs flapped free. They careened around a bend where they were confronted by what seemed to Howie an improbable sight: Jack and Emma Wilder standing side by side in front of a small cabin, bathed in the yellow light spilling from an open door behind them. Black Mare stopped abruptly near the front door, sending Howie sailing over her head onto the ground.

"Damn!" he cried, landing on a prickly bush of rambling wild rose.

"Howie! . . . Jack, my God, Howie's here!" he heard Emma

say as he staggered to his feet. His ears roared with a kind of ocean sound, though there was no ocean anywhere that he could see. It took a moment to piece everything together. Captain Ed Gomez was lying on his side near Emma's feet, squirming in pain, and Jack had just kneeled to be next to him. Howie couldn't imagine how they had all come to be here. In the distance, he heard a car driving away.

Emma was speaking, trying to explain what was going on. Only none of it made sense.

"You see, he had an overdue library book and I was mad at Jack so I came here but the road was so bad I got stuck."

Howie listened in astonishment as she rambled nonsensically about getting locked in a bathroom with a tub full of human bones, all because of a pound of ground round. While she was speaking, Howie glanced up at Donna Theresa who had managed to remain on the horse. D.T. was scowling, listening intently to Emma's account.

Jack rose to his feet, leaving Ed momentarily alone on the ground. "Take a deep breath, Emma," he said to Emma, for she seemed on the edge of hysteria. "We're all right now. Howie, are you hurt?"

"Just wet and cold and sore."

"Good, because we need help. Now pay attention. Ed's been shot. Not seriously, but he's losing a lot of blood."

"Then Ford—"

"Listen to me, Howie. Ford got away. He drove off in his Land Cruiser. There's a phone here, but Ford cut the line. We're in some goddamn black hole so my cell phone won't work, either. Do you have a gun?"

"I did, but I lost it on the scree. It's a long story."

"There's no time for stories. I'll give you Ed's gun and my cell phone—get back on your horse and see if you can stop Ford. He has a few minutes' head start but Emma's Subaru is blocking the road about a mile down, and that should slow him up. As soon as you're clear of the mountains, call an ambulance for Ed—Emma, give Howie Ed's car keys. Ed's cruiser is just on the other side of the Subaru. You getting the picture here, Howie?"

Howie got the picture. Unfortunately, D.T. got the picture first. In one fluid motion, she gave the horse a kick, and took off down the road after Ford. It happened so fast, Howie couldn't do anything to stop her.

"That's Donna Theresa, I presume," Jack said skeptically.

"It was."

"Well, stop her."

This was easier said than done. It was discouraging, really, how D.T. kept getting the better of him in every instance. Nevertheless, he took Ed's gun, Jack's cell phone, and he ran down the road after her. It seemed as futile as anything he had done in several hours.

Howie splashed through puddles, slipped in the mud, and came out onto hard ground with his arms flailing. He ran until his sides hurt and each breath sliced like a knife. He kept going beyond reason and strength, afraid something terrible was going to happen when Donna Theresa caught up with her unfortunate husband: a collision of two opposing natural forces.

He came out upon a straight away. Up ahead, he saw Emma's Subaru blocking the road with Ed's state police cruiser parked behind it, the rack lights broadcasting a psychedelic pattern of red and blue into the surrounding trees. Ford was trying to drive his Land Cruiser around the two stalled vehicles, but the road was a mess. The Land Cruiser had a higher clearance and a lot more power than either Emma's Subaru or Ed's police cruiser, but just as Ford was about to pull around the Subaru he appeared to get stuck in the thick mud. He was racing his engine, rocking back and forth to get free, when D.T. caught up with him, riding alongside his window shouting in Tiwa.

Howie himself was still several hundred yards back, running as fast as his weary legs would carry him. What happened next was horrible and sudden: Ford rolled down the window, raised a huge long-barreled pistol in D.T.'s direction, and fired. The barrel flashed a beam of orange fire, and Black Mare collapsed instantly, like a broken toy, rolling with Donna

Theresa into the mud. Ford didn't wait to see what damage he'd done. He accelerated out of the mud, engine screaming, and disappeared down the road.

Howie ran panting to where D.T. lay on the edge of the muddy road. At first, he thought she was dead. But then she groaned and moved. She was alive; it was the horse that was dead, shot point-blank in the head, blood still drooling out of her mouth. *Ford had shot his own horse!* Howie felt dizzy with rage and sorrow.

"Bastard!" he screamed down the road.

"He tried to *kill* me!" D.T. was saying in an amazed whisper. "It was *me* he was aiming at, but I pulled back on the reins just before he fired, and Saze raised her head . . ."

Howie watched as D.T. slowly separated herself from the corpse of the animal. He found it unbearable to look at the dead horse, so he turned away. The rage he felt had left him feeling curiously calm. He refused to be helpless any longer. He remembered Jack's tiny cell phone that was in the front pocket of his jeans. Methodically, he punched in 911 and found he was no longer in a black hole, electronically speaking. The 911 operator was a man with a pleasantly calm voice. Howie told him there was a state policeman, Captain Ed Gomez, who was down on Lhasa Road, and that an ambulance should be dispatched immediately. The 911 man wanted Howie's name and some other personal information, but he disconnected, not in a chatty mood.

He slipped into Ed's big black state police cruiser, started the engine, and backed up carefully from the muddy bog. It took a few minutes to turn the car around on the narrow road, two inches at a time, cutting the wheel again and again. He was just getting straight on the road when the passenger door opened and D.T. slid inside.

"You're not coming," he told her.

"Bullshit, Moon Deer. Just try to get rid of me."

She looked crazed, nearly rigid with shock and anger. Her face was streaked with mud, and her hands and clothes were smeared with horse blood. Howie sensed it would be a major

struggle to dislodge her from the passenger seat, and he didn't
want to take the time.

"Okay," he said. "But I am in a seriously bad mood, so
watch yourself. See if you can find the goddamn heater in this
thing."

"I'll find the heater. Just drive."

He bounced the hell out of the chassis getting down off
Lhasa Road, but the violent motion agreed with his mood.
When he hit the pavement, he accelerated as fast as he dared.
Ford had nearly a ten-minute head start, but Howie knew
where he was headed.

"You have a key for this?" D.T. asked, pointing to the rifle
that was locked against the dashboard.

"Forget the rifle. Goddamn you, D.T.—you knew all the
time, didn't you?"

"That Ford was alive? Not really, not at first, anyway."

"So when did you know?"

"When I hiked up to the cave last night and found the bones
were gone. There was only one possible explanation."

"Well, thanks for being so wonderfully helpful and coopera-
tive."

"Screw you. It was my problem, not yours."

They didn't talk again. Twenty minutes down the road, just
as he was leaving the foothills, an ambulance and two cop cars
sailed by in the opposite direction, their sirens howling. Howie
reached the bypass that cut from the south to the north of the
county, avoiding town. Once he was on the open road, he
found his own siren, feeling around on the dashboard where he
had seen Ed fiddle before. It was very satisfying to be able to
make such an angry noise and have the other cars on the road
pull over for him to pass.

Howie didn't know exactly what he was going to do. He'd
never killed anyone before, but deep in his gut, he knew he
wanted to kill Rutherford Hughes. How satisfying that would
be! A bitter joy. The butt of Ed's 9mm automatic was sticking
up from his waistband like a kind of deadly erection. Ford had
killed three people: Anthony Lucero, Charlie Concha, and a
tribal cop named Daryl whose last name Howie didn't even re-

member. But it was shooting Black Mare that made him so angry. The mare was the only one of them all who was completely innocent, and that somehow made the sorrow unbearable.

A few miles down the bypass he overtook a black sedan that turned out to be another New Mexico State Police cruiser. Howie glanced in his rearview mirror and saw the cruiser had turned on its rack lights and sirens and was coming after him. Ed's radio was off, which was probably a good thing, or he would have to listen to someone telling him to stop. Howie pushed his foot down on the gas and kept going.

"Faster," D.T. told him.

"We're going ninety, for chrissake."

"That's not fast enough."

Howie pressed his foot down harder on the accelerator. By the time he arrived at the intersection to the main road, Howie had a convoy of three cop cars tailing him a quarter of a mile back. The road here was straight and wide, pointing like an arrow north to the Colorado border less than half an hour away. Howie let the speedometer needle drift to 110 mph; the speed soothed his anger and he was glad to see that he was gaining ground ahead of the convoy of red and blue lights in his rearview mirror. Hate, he understood for the first time, was fun. Hate felt good. Hate was something warm and cozy and reassuring that you could slip into, like a drawn bath.

The highway near the turnoff to his cabin undulated in a series of hills. As soon as Howie came over the crest of the final hill, he switched off the siren, roof lights, and headlights. In the sudden darkness, he rushed down toward the private road to his cabin, braking fast, making the turn in an effortless four-wheel drift. He pulled to a complete stop where the road dipped down into a low arroyo, hidden from the highway. He watched as the three cop cars sped past on the main road, unaware that the prey had bolted.

"You did that pretty good," D.T. mentioned as they waited in the motionless car in the dark arroyo. It was the first thing she had said in a while.

Howie stared at her. "You think so? Personally, I don't think I've done much good in any of this, start to finish."

She shook her head. "Howie, you're a good guy. This has just been a bad situation, that's all. Look, I'm sorry about a lot of things. Like lying to you. I wish I had met you in a different time and place. I think something might have happened between us."

"Right," he said. "On Pluto. We would have had quite the romantic interlude."

She smiled, a soft, slow, sad smile that reminded Howie of all the things that were lovely about Donna Theresa. "You know, on the meadow, you really turned me on," she said. "Maybe when this is all over, we can get together. As sort of a consolation prize, don't you think?"

"No," he told her. "I don't think that would be a very good idea."

"Maybe I'll just have to s-s-seduce you, then."

To his surprise, she put her hand on the upper part of his leg and stroked upward another inch to the bulge in his jeans. Howie was so startled he was momentarily paralyzed. It wasn't entirely unpleasant to have a girl's hand at just that spot, but this didn't seem like quite the right time for romance. Unfortunately, by the time he figured out that romance was not what was on her mind, it was too late. She made her move quickly, reaching for the 9mm pistol stuffed down into his waistband. Howie groaned at his own stupidity. Here he was, tricked again by the facts of life.

She pointed the gun at him.

"Drive," she said. "Keep your lights off."

"You know, you're something, D.T., you really are. Someone should give you medal."

"I'm sorry, but this is my drama, not yours, Moon Deer. Now drive. I mean it. I'll shoot you if I have to."

Howie let out his breath, and, mysteriously, he felt his own killer rage seep out of him. For a complicated person, rage was much too simple; in a complicated world, farce and heartbreaking laughter were more the appropriate thing.

He grinned unexpectedly at Donna Theresa. "Come on, let's

leave the shit alone. Who cares? You gotta learn to laugh more, D.T."

She narrowed her eyes and there was something mean in the set of her pretty mouth. "I mean it, I'll shoot you if I have to," she told him.

Sadly, Howie believed her. Donna Theresa took herself too seriously; she did not have a taste for farce and heartbreaking laughter. Because he believed her, he waited until the convoy of cop cars on the main highway disappeared over the next rise, then continued without his headlights toward his cabin. Ford's battered Land Cruiser was parked in his driveway, as he had expected. Howie left Ed's police car a little ways down the road, turned off the engine, and followed D.T. out into the quiet of the night. She stood in his driveway with the pistol in hand, listening hard. A horse snorted from around the back of the cabin and there was a sound of men's voices speaking angrily in Tiwa. Ford was not alone.

D.T. walked quietly around the side of Howie's cabin, holding the gun ready. He followed, not knowing what else to do with himself and not sure he really wanted to stop her. As they got closer, he could tell that one of the Tiwa speakers had an English accent. D.T. crouched behind the low adobe wall that sheltered the west side of Howie's back terrace. Howie crawled next to her until he could see over the wall. Big Carl was mounted on a horse pointing a rifle at the sliding glass door where Howie had seen D.T. peering in at him what seemed a lifetime ago. Lewis Lucero was standing on the sagebrush near Carl alongside his own horse, pointing a pistol in the same direction. Most likely, they had ridden from the northern edge of the reservation, the same journey that Charlie Concha had taken on Friday night.

From where Howie was crouched, he could just see Ford. The British archeologist was standing a few inches outside the sliding glass door with a small white box in one hand and his long-barrelled revolver in the other. This was Howie's first look at the man who had caused so much trouble. In the moonlight, Rutherford Hughes could have been a mad Old Testament prophet with his long white hair. He was shorter than

Howie had expected, and older, too, his face deeply weathered by years in the field. Howie didn't know what he had expected to see, but Ford looked only like an eccentric little Englishman, not anyone worth killing.

"Just give us that box, white man, and we will let you go," Lewis said, switching unexpectedly to English. "That belongs to the Pueblo and I will not allow you to steal it."

"You're ignorant, Lewis," Ford told him. "Don't you want to know who your ancestors really were? Or does the idea of finding out the truth scare you too much?"

Howie had heard both sides of this argument before and he didn't believe it was going to be resolved on his back terrace by three armed men and one angry woman with a pistol. He was trying to think of something clever to do when the night exploded in gunfire. He wasn't sure who shot first: It might have been any one of them, though when he thought about it later, he was pretty sure it was D.T. There were loud cracks and softer pops, shouts, and ricochets, and the sound of breaking glass—his sliding door, unfortunately. Howie ducked down behind the adobe wall and didn't see any of it. Realistically, there were only five or six shots fired, but to him it sounded like a small war. Then there was profound silence, and in the silence he heard the wail of police sirens coming back his way from the highway. The sirens changed pitch as the convoy of cars slowed to turn onto his dirt road.

Howie peeked cautiously above the garden wall. Ford was sitting on the flagstone clutching his stomach, his legs spread out in front of him, shards of glass everywhere, sparkling prettily in the moonlight. The small white box lay near him on the ground. At the other edge of the terrace, Carl had climbed down off his horse and was wrapping his shirt around Lewis's gun hand to make a tourniquet. Lewis had been shot in the wrist and was grunting in pain. D.T. was standing behind the low adobe wall, pointing the smoking barrel of her gun at Ford.

Howie decided he needed to do something; there were times when even men of heartbreaking laughter needed to get involved. He stood from where he was hiding and turned to Lewis and Carl. Carl turned away, refusing to meet his eye.

"I suggest you guys leave before the cops get here."

Lewis glared at him. "Christ, Moon Deer, aren't you dead yet?"

Howie walked over to D.T., who was standing next to where Ford sat wounded on the terrace. She looked dazed and lost and she allowed Howie to take the gun from her hand without any comment.

"Get the box," Lewis was telling Carl from the other side of the terrace. "We'll take what belongs to us and leave."

"No you won't. That box belongs to me now," Howie said, extending his gun arm. In fact, he wasn't certain that the pistol had any more bullets left. Nevertheless, he did his best to look scary. "You'd better get Lewis to a doctor," he told Carl. "Now get out of here while you can."

Carl looked over Howie's shoulder to the three cop cars that were racing closer, only minutes away, and said something in Tiwa to Lewis. Lewis nodded reluctantly and allowed Carl to help him onto his horse.

"You're going to be sorry for this, Moon Deer," Lewis said, gritting his teeth in pain.

"I'm already sorry. Now go."

He watched their horses gallop off across the sagebrush toward the mountains, disappearing fast into the blue night mist. Howie felt suddenly old and very tired. He turned back to where Rutherford Hughes sat, gut-shot, obviously in serious pain, his mouth open, like he was trying to say something to D.T. Hopefully it was an apology, but Howie didn't wait to find out. He stooped to pick up the white box on the flagstone as he made his way through the broken glass into his cabin.

Maybe human beings will evolve eventually, he was thinking as he reached for his telephone to dial 911. Right now we're only rapacious monkeys, not too far along the evolutionary path. Would another ten thousand years do the trick? Would people get along with each other then and work together for noble goals?

Howie spoke with the same operator with the soothing

voice that he had spoken to before. He gave his address and asked for another ambulance. The operator was even more anxious than before to keep him on the phone, but Howie hung up. Outside on the terrace, Ford wasn't sitting up any longer. He had fallen over in a jackknife position. Apparently he was dead, for D.T. was kneeling next to him, sobbing loudly. Howie wasn't sure why she was crying, if it was for herself, or for Ford, or just the fact that now she wouldn't have anybody to hate. He was thinking he'd probably never understand Donna Theresa, when he heard the first cop car pull up outside, the cruiser's tires crunching the gravel.

Time had run out. Howard Moon Deer walked into his bathroom, opened the box, and flushed the 800-year-old turd down the toilet. It felt right somehow to put things in their proper place.

EPILOGUE

Curiosity and the Cat

"*Oooh-my-gaaawwd!*" she screamed.

She put her fist in her mouth to muffle her own cry. The entire bed shuddered and thumped, rocked and rolled. Claire Knightsbridge had the noisiest orgasms of any woman Howard Moon Deer had ever known. It was one of the many things he liked about her; she had never learned the art of indifference.

Howie rolled off Claire with an exhausted moan, leaving behind a few of his own dark guy hairs on her stomach. She was lanky and blond and very nice to look at, dressed or undressed.

"Was I too loud?" she asked, embarrassed, when she could speak again. Claire came from Iowa, of dour Scandinavian ancestry, where women were trained to keep orgasms to themselves.

"You probably woke a few ghosts," Howie told her. "But don't let it worry you."

"Howie, *don't* talk about ghosts! You know how freaked out I am!"

Howie had made their reservation for a sunny second-floor room at the Stanley Hotel in Estes Park, Colorado, without informing Claire that this happened to be the old-fashioned Victorian palace in the mountains that Stanley Kubrick had used to film *The Shining*. Driving up to the entrance two days ago, Claire's brow had wrinkled with concern.

"You know, this hotel looks familiar," she had mused. "It's almost like . . . Howie! It *is*! Oh my God, Howie, how could you? That movie scared me to death! We're not going to *stay* here, are we?"

Howie only chuckled and told her she'd be safe as long as she remained very, very close to him. And that's what she did, wrapped up in his arms in bed. It was mid-October, a golden time in the Rocky Mountains, and they were hungry for each other after a long absence. In fact, the Stanley Hotel was as romantic a spot to screw one's brains out as you could wish for, except for the fact you expected to see Jack Nicholson with an ax when you wandered down into the lobby—a good reason to forget the lobby and remain in bed.

Claire was a classical musician, a cello player, and Howie had lived with her and her two children for more than a year in San Geronimo before she left him to pursue her career, joining an all-woman string quartet in Chicago that was making quite a splash. Howie had picked up Claire in Denver where her group had given a concert of late Beethoven, Opus 127 and 131. Claire was exhausted after touring American cities all summer long, and she missed her children, who were spending the school year with her ex-husband due to her demanding concert schedule. She had ten days off and then the quartet was headed to Europe for a grueling three-month tour. Claire had often urged Howie to come live with her in Chicago and travel together on tour. But he couldn't quite see himself carrying her cello case through distant airports, trailing after her.

Claire was wound up and for two days now she had done a great deal of talking. A string quartet composed of attractive young women had proved to be a good idea, commercially speaking, bringing in a younger audience than classical music was prone to do. The group was on the verge of major success. Sony Classical was offering a juicy recording contract with a quarter-million-dollar bonus on signing, and in the spring they were set to do a series of concerts in the Far East, then return to Europe for the summer, and New York in the fall. Their future was guaranteed; all they had to do was get along with one other. But that was easier said than done. After a year of traveling and working intensely together, the four women had begun to quarrel seriously among themselves, splitting up into two opposing camps: an Eastman School of Music contingent (Claire and her old classmate, Erin Yaeger, the first violinist),

versus Jill Blumenthal, the second violinist, and Sharon Little-
ton, the viola player, who had both gone to Juilliard and considered themselves the elite.

Howie listened in astonishment. Here it was again: the Cannibalism Factor, as he had begun to think of it. It seemed to be
a defect in human construction, how tribes of people who had
everything to gain if they could only cooperate, ended up de-
vouring one another in petty feuds. Republicans and Democrats, Whigs and Tories, and now a Juilliard faction and an
Eastman School of Music faction in a classical string quartet.
Ridiculous, but meanwhile the four women were falling out
over nearly everything: the tempo of various pieces as well the
repertoire itself, whether to stick with Beethoven, Mozart,
Brahms and company (as Claire and Erin preferred), or get
avant-garde with late-twentieth-century music and beyond (as
Jill and Sharon wanted to do).

It was discouraging—here they were with all their dreams
about to come true, but it appeared likely that the group would
split up before that happened. Claire was confused and exhausted and she wanted Howie's advice. He answered by
telling her about his own adventures with the Summer People
and Winter People, and how a pussycat stakeout behind the
Shanghai Café had led him to an Anasazi cave, and the knowledge of a great prehistoric culture that perhaps had eaten itself
up. As Howie was finishing his story, Claire lay with one long
leg draped over his midsection, idly holding a glass of
Chardonnay on his stomach. It was nearly dawn; they had
talked and made love alternately, all night long.

"Well, that's quite a tale," she said finally. "It makes my
music problems seem sort of petty by comparison."

"Not really," he told her. "It's still the same old story. A
fight for love and glory."

She propped up her chin on his chest. "A case of do or die?"

"Exactly." One thing about Claire, she *never* missed a musi-
cal allusion. "What do you say we play it again, Sam?"

"Howie, no . . . wait a second!" she cried, giggling, because
he had moved her over onto her back and was starting to kiss
his way in a southerly direction from her bellybutton down.

"You still haven't told me everything. What about Ed, for instance? Is he going to be okay?"

"Ed's going to be fine. He met a nurse in the hospital, a Texas divorcée named Rita, who seems to think he's some kind of wounded hero. They're dating cautiously at the moment, in a kind of shy middle-aged way.

"I think that's very sweet. What about Lewis Lucero? What's going to happen to him?"

"Well, that's still ongoing. The BIA and FBI are each conducting separate investigations that'll probably be finished in about five or ten years, so it's hard to know how it'll come out. Meanwhile, no one's talking much at the Pueblo. Indians prefer to keep these in-house quarrels among themselves, you know. But Raymond told me the other day that Lewis has been given a quiet sabbatical from his job as War Chief. Big Carl is going to take over the post, at least until elections next spring, and he's promising Raymond that his first priority will be to make peace between the two main clans. The Anasazi Grill is up for sale, by the way, and the money will go back into a scholarship fund that will be administered by a newly appointed oversight committee. I'm not sure what'll happen to Lewis's other investments—there's a motel, a convenience store, and God only knows what else, and under what name. Probably he'll get away with some of the loot, but so the world turns. And that's pretty much the story, Claire."

"Aren't you leaving out a rather major part of all this?" she asked, peering at him with a skeptical eye.

Howie sighed.

"Come on, tell me about the beautiful Donna Theresa," Claire insisted. "I'm not jealous, honest. Even though you were a little bit in love with her, weren't you, Howie?"

"Well, maybe a little at first, just a tingle. She's beautiful, and that has a certain pull on a single guy. But when I finally got a fix on her, she just made me feel sad."

"Why sad?"

"Well, it was a lot of things," he answered reluctantly. Thinking about D.T. put him into a conflicting stew of angst and irritation. "She was such a victim, I guess. Knocked around by a stepfather when she was little, then used by Ford. It seems such a waste somehow, that she couldn't rise above all the negative forces that were pulling her down."

"She used you, Howie. You know that, don't you?" Claire pointed out, not with total disinterest.

"Yes," he agreed. "And she lied to me, too, and probably in her own way she's as self-absorbed and ruthless as Ford was. But still . . . I don't know, Claire, but when I think about her, I just feel like crying. It's not strictly rational. Maybe it's her stutter. It's hard to stay angry at someone who's been wounded so terribly by life."

Claire didn't speak for a moment, taking this in. "Have you seen her?"

"No, I've stayed away. It was a bullet from Ed's gun, the gun she was using that night, that killed Ford. She was arrested, but she's out on bail. The DA wants to charge her with second-degree murder, but her lawyer is saying it's self-defense, that Ford started shooting first. I think she may end up getting a year or two, or possibly a suspended sentence. You know how it is in New Mexico—people generally get longer prison terms for drug possession than homicide."

"That's crazy!"

"That's politics. Meanwhile, she's down in Albuquerque, I hear, working on her PhD dissertation until her trial comes up in December—I guess she'll be writing about Anasazi irrigation techniques in Chaco Canyon after all, because the tribal council has decided to return the old skeletons to the cave and close it up again tighter than a tomb. Whatever happened in that place eight hundred years ago is going to remain forever a mystery."

Claire studied Howie with her intense green-blue eyes. "You know, I still can't believe you flushed that coprolite down the toilet. Don't you have any second thoughts about that?"

Howie shrugged. "In this case, it just seemed best to let sleeping cats lie."

"Dogs, Howie."

"You say dogs, I say cats. *Vive la difference*."

"Hmm . . . and what about Mrs. Eudora Harrington? Were they eating pussy at the Shanghai Café, or weren't they? *Stop* that, Howie. That was *not* a hint."

"The FBI lab examined the sample foods I sent them, the mystery meat. It was just chicken, pork, and beef, as advertised."

"So it's safe to eat Chinese food again in San Geronimo?"

"Well, I wouldn't say that. There was no pussycat in the meat, but they *did* find traces of rat droppings, cleanser, and some things I think I won't even mention."

"We'll avoid the Shanghai Café, I think."

"It would be the safest strategy. As for Miao-Miao, Floozie, and Mr. Stud, I'm afraid their fate remains unknown. Maybe they're in pussycat heaven. Maybe they went to England to see the queen. As a detective, I have learned to accept a certain amount of mystery as the basis of a successful life."

Claire snuggled closer and lay her check against his chest. "This is all my fault for leaving you on your own," she said after a while. "If I were here with you, you'd be safe from dangerous women who try to lure you to their caves."

"It's not anybody's fault, Claire. You were bored in a small New Mexico town making eight dollars an hour at a job you hated," he reminded. "You had to go out into the world and play music, that's all."

"Do you still love me?" she asked urgently.

"I'll always love you, Claire. I'll be your Mr. Stud forever, if you'll be my Floozie . . ."

She laughed, her clear, free laugh that always made Howie feel like everything was all right everywhere. In a lithe second, she was on top, straddling him, and with a single warm thrust he was inside of her. She gasped with the sheer deliciousness of it.

"You know, I'm going to marry you one day, Howard Moon Deer," she whispered, rising and falling upon him. "Maybe not now, but when we're old . . . and decrepit . . . and ready to . . . settle down."

"I'll look forward to it," he assured her.